# THE LEAVES
# OF A
# NECRONOMICON

# THE LEAVES OF A NECRONOMICON

## EDITED BY
## JOSEPH S. PULVER, SR.

CHAOSIUM
INC.

Cover and graphic designer: Inkspiral Design.
Proofreader: Steven E Schend.
Copyeditor: Carrie Bebris.
Assistant fiction editors: Nick Nacario, Susan O'Brien.
Executive editor: James Lowder.

Address questions and comments by mail to:

Chaosium Inc.
3450 Wooddale Court
Ann Arbor, MI 48104

chaosium.com

Chaosium publication 6059

ISBN-13: 978-1-56882-408-6

First Edition, October 2022
10 9 8 7 6 5 4 3 2 1

Printed in the United States.

# PERMISSIONS

# TABLE OF CONTENTS

# FROM HAND TO HAND ... TO HAND—

## JOSEPH S. PULVER, SR.

**F**OR THREE-PLUS DECADES I had the one-eyed "Teddy" that was given to a two-year-old Joey to quiet me while I was in the hospital with a fractured skull. Then, one day, it was gone. (Where? How?) I still own the cigarette pack-sized Motorola "Six Transistors" AM radio, and the leather case it came in, I was given when I was eleven. I have the first novel I bought when I was the same age, *Time for the Stars*, and some of my Aurora monster models. I, like you, have my cherished mementos, from my teens and twenties and thirties and forties. . . ; they sit here with me, wrapped in *if* and *why*. Old treasures, they bring tears and joy through the memories and baggage they contain, and carry me away, as yours do you.

Possessions. *Rosebud*. We own them, and they own us. Like friends we lost along the way, ex-lovers and -partners, places we visited long ago, they are part of us, parts that can shape and/or change us. Possessions and memories (of *them* and *there* and *that moment*) that can bring the faraway near. Some move with us through the years, some come into our lives and go. Lost or broken or sold or stolen or tossed out. Gone, but not forgotten . . .

Never forgotten.

That red plastic fire truck you so adored, the only toy you received for Christmas when you were six. How often do you wonder where it went? Remember the comics your mother tossed out (or gave away) when you went off to college, or in some cases, to war? Remember the baseball your best friend gave you for safekeeping before he left for his tour in 'Nam? He did not return, and you held on to it for two decades. Then, suddenly, one day it was gone. Remember the doll you were told you were too old for? Where is your Slinky? What happened to the high school yearbook your best friend signed, the best friend who died from AIDS? Where are these objects now? Did they find their way to the dump or to other hands? Did a roommate throw a party while you were out of town on business and when you arrived home that cherished book your aunt gave you for your sixteenth birthday and the bag of records you had bought, but hadn't had the chance to play yet, both came up missing?

Where is your G.I. Joe?

Where is your first Barbie?

How did your skateboard, the blue one with the tiger and the snake, the last birthday gift from Dad before cancer took him, go missing?

Why did Mom toss out your Kenner Alien?

What beloved childhood treasure, preserved as if it were a museum piece, did you have to sell to keep the wolf from your door?

What is your Rosebud?

In the mid-'90s I had the idea that it might be fun to look at what could happen if a Lovecraftian object—in this case, a copy of the *Necronomicon*—entered and exited the lives of various owners over approximately one hundred years. I felt it needed to be a novel-length work, but I didn't want to write it. In my mind, the work needed to be told by truly *different voices*, in different styles, to reflect the distinctly different owners. It needed to be a novel-length round-robin, a form I've always enjoyed. I also thought the book's various owners (at least some of them) would not know anything about the history of the article they now possessed. I put together my rough outline and notes about the tome's owners and the time periods in which they possessed it (and in some cases, what the book did to, or for, them). All I needed were the authors and a publisher. Fifteen years later, I finally found a publisher who said, "Let's do it." The list of authors I wanted to invite came quickly; a few had been on my wish list since the day the idea for this story came to me.

You are about to see the creation of a John Dee translation of Lovecraft's famous volume and follow it hand to hand, through lives. It will change owners; it will be sold and lost.

Where?

How?

2

What of history? What of betrayal?

You've seen François Girard's *The Red Violin*, read Annie Proulx's *Accordion Crimes* (two works I love). You know the trope, how fertile it is. It's an age-old structure I still adore.

This is the account of victims and survivors, of dreamers and the passions that consume them. Of hate, and what love (or greed, or expectation) can do—and the depths of what it cannot. Perhaps the journey from Then to Now will not be smooth. It is, after all, a Lovecraftian trip (in some fashion). Perhaps it will contain knots and holes, ladders and *tar-black shadows*. What changes along the way? Anything? Everything? What will you discover when you meet this gallery of fools and villains and dreamers? What will be left unexplained?

It is now time for you to begin your . . . *journey*. Travel well, and stay safe.

# CHAPTER ONE

# THE BOOKMAKER

## NATE PEDERSEN

H<small>E COULD FEEL</small> its presence in the corner of the room, its long birth now complete, an assemblage of dark intent. The folio binding, freshly finished, rested on the workbench beneath the east window, the early moon trying, failing, to illuminate its simple black leather. Gilt tooling at the top of the spine read plainly *Necronomicon*, in the late medieval style. At the bottom, smaller letters, also in gold: *Complete John Dee edition. 1564.*

Minutes before, the bookmaker had slowly peeled away the excess leaf from those words he had tooled into the spine.

It was, at last, finished.

He contemplated his work by the feeble light, wanly resisting the encroaching darkness.

The book was, undoubtedly, a masterpiece. A simple masterpiece; not ostentatious, not elaborate. But every detail, every single detail, was correct, completed with the precision and skill and mastery of a craft that he had painstakingly honed over the long years of his life.

Mr. Calhoun would be pleased.

T<small>HOMAS</small> C<small>ALHOUN.</small> T<small>HE</small> shipping man, the book collector, the man who made a fortune running ivory out of the Congo. It was Calhoun who'd sent him across the Atlantic to London six months ago, to this dirty loft above a ropeworks in Rotherhithe.

A first, and only, meeting, an elaborate office tucked away in a discreet corner of Boston, the scent of new leather and expensive tobacco and aged bourbon lingering in the air.

Straight to business.

"I understand you are a master bookmaker."

"You'll see some of my books behind you, sir," a touch, perhaps more than a touch, of pride in his voice.

Calhoun already knew that, of course.

Rows upon rows of books in his office, a massive collection, beautifully displayed.

All the right titles, for a certain kind of person, with certain kinds of interests.

The *Book of Thoth* in full maroon calf with silver gilt.

A profane edition of *Las Reglas de Ruina*.

A third edition of *Liber Damnatus*.

A Jarrow & Marshall edition of *The Pnakotic Manuscripts*.

The 1804 edition of *The King in Yellow* in decorated cloth.

The bookmaker's own American edition of *The Revelations of Glaaki*, nine volumes bound in black, fine-grained Morocco.

"The Starry Wisdom sale?" asked the bookmaker as he glanced through the collection. "Did it actually happen?" For almost twenty years rumours had occasionally surfaced of a secret auction in Arkham, where the notorious, almost legendary occult book collection of the Church of Starry Wisdom had been sold.

Mr. Calhoun merely smiled.

"I have a commission for you."

A pause.

"You'll be assembling the rarest book in the world."

A slight smirk, and a raised eyebrow at the bookmaker's expressionless face.

"Are you not intrigued? It's a . . . singular opportunity."

Calhoun maintained a smile as he watched realization slowly set into the bookmaker, the creeping but sure arrival of awareness.

Now they both knew exactly which particular book was being discussed.

"You have a manuscript, sir?"

Mr. Calhoun nodded, slowly.

"So it does exist," the bookmaker said, in a half-whisper to himself.

"I assure you that it does. An associate of mine in London has it right now in her possession. You'll be transforming that manuscript into a printed book, a single copy, perfect in all of its details, the provenance of each of its components parts . . . exactingly arranged."

Mr. Calhoun reached into a desk drawer and withdrew a manuscript letter and a variety of pages of illustrations.

"This here," said Mr. Calhoun, as he pointed at the letter, "was written by John Dee himself. In it you'll find his account of acquiring the manuscript copy of the *Necronomicon* from which he made his translation."

A smirk from Mr. Calhoun. "I'm sure you'll find it engaging reading on the journey over. Include it in the book. Bind it directly after the endpapers."

"And those?" asked the bookmaker, his eyes drawn to the strange and unsettling scattering of woodcuts and illustrations laid out on Mr. Calhoun's desk.

"Yes, these," said Mr. Calhoun, briefly lost in his own thoughts. "Yes, these too should be included."

Mr. Calhoun withdrew another letter from his desk drawer, this one in his own hand.

A drink poured, the fine aged bourbon glowing in a crystal tumbler.

"The particular details are in this letter here. Judging from your previous work, I trust you understand the extraordinary significance of this journey you're about to embark upon on my behalf. Of course, money is of no concern to me. You'll be well-rewarded. Extremely well-rewarded."

But no one in that room that day cared particularly about the money.

A pause again, and then Mr. Calhoun asked, "Have you been to London?"

"No, but my wife was from there, sir."

"Was?"

"She died. In childbirth."

"And the child?"

A BARGAIN THEN shortly struck, money exchanged for the promise of a book, the surrender of six months of his life, a course set, a destination chosen. Passage paid on a ship across the ocean, a business contact arranged in London, a workshop at a ropeworks in Rotherhithe, access to supplies, tools, lines of credit. The bookmaker wondered if Calhoun even arranged the grey sea that he stared at for long hours each day on the long Atlantic crossing; he'd arranged everything else.

The bookmaker kept to himself on the passage, avoiding conversation with the other travelers, avoiding the crew, instead pacing the deck over and over again, reading and rereading Calhoun's letter with all of the strange and curious details for the manufacture of the book.

He'd never read anything like it.

APRIL OF 1895, London harbor. Blue Anchor Road to the Halfpenny Hatch, to Deptford Lower Road. Pass the market gardens of Rotherhithe. "Buy some fresh spring lettuce, eh love?" she asks, all breasts and a missing tooth. There, the pub sign for The Kraken, cracked on the side, a faded illustration of a dark and monstrous sea serpent rising from a restless sea. Into the tavern's shadows, to the booth in the western corner, waiting, waiting, as the afternoon drips slowly by in pints of brown ale delivered by a bearded barkeep, tobacco smoke low and heavy and so strong it stings the eyes.

Mr. Wakersfield finally arrived, Calhoun's London contact, dressed in black, bald head, curiously white teeth, all smiles, all promises and subservient obedience.

"Your voyage over was smooth, I daresay, sir? You've found London to your liking? You'll want for nothing while you're here, sir; if you need anything, anything at all, why you simply have to ask. Yes, I've just the place for your work, sir, Mr. Calhoun provided all the necessary arrangements, all the necessary tools for your work. He did say, sir, that you would find the supplies for your efforts yourself. The press, the paper, the leather binding, and so on. Mr. Calhoun was particular there, he was indeed. Though of course, sir, I'm more than happy to be of assistance; why, you simply have to ask."

They walked together in the premature dark of a foggy early evening, the gaslights indistinct in the gloom. A ropeworks shop, closed for the night, brick walls and a rickety staircase around back. They walked up to a black door, locked, but Wakersfield had the key of course. Creaked open to a large space covered in dust, abandoned ropes in the corners, faint smell of mice, but a prominent workbench against one of the walls and large windows to let in the moon and starlight once the fog lifted.

"Will this work for you, sir?"

The bookmaker looked about the loft, slowly, slowly. It had enough space. Enough light. The workbench would be stocked with all the right tools. He didn't even need to check. He knew Calhoun would have seen to it. What else did he need? It was enough.

"Yes, this will work fine."

"Very good, sir. You'll let me know if you need anything, of course? You can always find me at the Stelios Shipyards offices on Blue Anchor Road.

Extensions to your line of credit or any shipping and receiving needs will be handled there on your behalf. No questions asked, sir. Mr. Calhoun was particular on that point, very particular indeed."

THE SKIN FOR the leather he acquired from Wales, having followed rumours of the birth of a two-headed goat deep into Snowdonia. There he found a local farmer drunk on cheap ale and cheap celebrity. "Two pence, sir," to see the goat, tethered in the dark of a stone barn, the light from the farmer's torch casting shadows on the monstrosity. It bleated wanly from two black heads. The bookmaker was silent. He stayed an evening at the local inn.

The next morning, he paid the farmer enough silver to keep him drunk for a year.

Then he paid the local butcher to slit two throats.

Four weeks later, a single, large piece of leather was delivered to Rotherhithe.

THE GOLD FOR lettering the spine he acquired from a disgraced jeweler scraping together a living as a smelter in a dark alley off the Old Jewry. He would melt your gold, no questions asked, "but I keep twenty-five percent. . . ." The bookmaker always knew where to find men like him, living off the work of bolder souls, counting gold coins in hidden corners lit by fires with too little coal. He'd handed over Calhoun's gold rings, given to him for that purpose, carried across the sea on his long voyage, the rings carved with strange symbols the bookmaker didn't recognize and didn't care to, as they blurred and melted in the smelter's fire.

Now HE NEEDED the guts, the brains, the blood. The paper, the type, the ink.

The bookmaker traveled to a two-story shop in Canterbury, a visit to the well-heeled Joseph Bachelor, paper supplier to William Morris.

"Of course, sir, my particular fascination is also with the sixteenth-century-style paper, the finest there is; finest there ever was."

The bookmaker saw a small girl, blonde, peek out from behind the shop door. He heard the soft slush of water in the workroom, smelled the wood fibres dissolving in vats.

The bookmaker nodded. Cut to folio size; three hundred pages ordered, each with Thomas Calhoun's insignia as its watermark, visible only when held up to the light.

Beautiful.

Meanwhile, an order sent to Prussia, to Hannover, and the Gebrüder Jänecke firm on the River Leine, still making ink in the old way. Bottles of black liquid shipped to London posthaste, quietly rattling against their cloth wrappings in the letter carrier's leather satchel on his Rotherhithe rounds.

But the type was the hard part. Calhoun was particular, had strange wants, curious desires. Sent the bookmaker on a wild goose chase around the back corners of Europe for two months stalking rumours. It had to be genuine sixteenth-century type, it had to be original, it had to be complete, not a single letter could be substituted from another set. Paris, Salamanca, Mainz, Venice, then, finally, Prague in July, and an old man in the ancient quarter living in an attic the size of a closet, no windows, a heavy Romani accent rattling through ancient, yellowed teeth. Yes, a lifetime of roaming, a lifetime of scraping by, and this was what he was left with, abandoned by his family, forced into settlement, a few meagre possessions, and a three-hundred-year-old set of type he'd acquired from a journeyman printer in the Black Forest sometime around the middle of the century. The old man loved the way it felt, the cold, metal type, impossible to warm by the light of a campfire or a noonday sun. He had never parted with it.

And yet he couldn't have spelled his own name for all the gold in Prague.

The bookmaker overpaid. Enough gold to buy a small caravan and leave the city for good, enough coin, even, to provide a small amount of comfort in the few years—or was it months?—weeks?—that he had left in this life.

The bookmaker watched the old man in a new caravan, pulled by fresh horse, as he meandered through Prague's crooked streets, heading for the Carpathian foothills, and whatever friends or relations still remained. The bookmaker thought he saw tears streaming down the old man's wrinkled face.

No one should have to die alone in a foreign place.

Back to London, back to the loft in Rotherhithe.

THE PRESS HE found in August, after months of searching. In Faversham an old printer died, left behind his wooden handpress, lovingly kept in operation these past eighty years "because he wouldn't have nothing to do with Stanhope and those fancy new machines," said his son of an invention already sixty years old. The Faversham printer kept to the old ways, had bought the press as a journeyman, found it somewhere deep in the Midland fells, in some woody corner of oak and yew. You could see the wood worn thin and pale on the press bar where the printer had rested his hand for all those years. But the son had found a new career in explosives, hoping to be rid of the handpress ("takes up most of me attic"), priced to sell.

So the bookmaker bought.

He paid Hallingford & Sons to make the delivery to Rotherhithe, at twice the usual speed, for twice the usual money.

"Why Rotherhithe, sir, if you don't mind me asking? T'ain't nothin' there but docks."

"Shut yer mouth, young Clancy," said the elder Hallingford. "Don't ask the gentleman questions."

It didn't matter. The bookmaker wouldn't have answered anyway.

The press arrived in parts, and the bookmaker spent a glorious afternoon in reassembly, sun streaming into the gloom of the Rotherhithe loft, sending the dark to scurry with the mice in the corners. The press slowly came together, slowly back to a creaky life. The feet and the forestay, the rounce with its coffin, the girth on the edge. The ballrack, the cheeks, and the cap secured by the head. The platen and the bar.

The bookmaker drank a bottle of claret while the sun set outside the western window, the rising and falling swirl of a nightjar's evening song disturbing the heavy August air.

The next morning, a telegram sent to Boston:

*All is ready.*

A SIMPLE REPLY:

*Understood. Meet F— F— on the grounds of the British Museum, afternoon, 1st of September. She will find you. Wear henbane in your lapel. —T. C., Esq.*

September 1 arrived and the bookmaker carefully plucked a single henbane flower from an abandoned medicinal garden. The sticky flower is white, freckled, draws the bookmaker's eye deep into its black heart. He lingers a moment, breathes in the heady odor, a slight euphoria creeping along his skin, his neck, the back of his throat.

He walked to the museum, four miles along the bustling, thriving Thames. A fine summer's afternoon in London, a long wait on a bench in the sun, watching the shadow of the museum creep closer and closer as the minutes marched on. Then she arrived, dressed in black, dyed red curls spilling in ringlets down to the gentle curve of her white throat. A quick glance at his lapel—the henbane flower drooping slowly downward—a quicker motion with her hand, and the bookmaker follows deep into the gardens.

An old, yellowed manuscript and a letter exchanged in the shade of rhododendrons and azaleas. The woman whispered once, "*Sapientia Sapienti Dona Data,*" the only words she spoke, then made a strange symbol with her hand and pressed it against her lips. A sign of silence. The bookmaker nodded and the woman retreated, back into the light, quickly disappearing into the late afternoon crowd. The bookmaker thumbed through the crackling pages:

handwritten, sixteenth-century, Early Modern English—a surprise. But he did not care about the content.

Didn't think about it.

Didn't need to.

Didn't want to.

ALL INGREDIENTS ACQUIRED, laid out on the workman's table. He could start now; it was ready for him, ready for his touch, the gentle arrival of his mastery, his practiced hands moving with the efficiency and care honed by years of experience. But he didn't start. He waited. He watched the sunlight slowly sink beneath the edge of his windowsill, again accompanied by the whirring song of the nightjar. There seemed to be more of them now, more nightjars, the crescendos and decrescendos of their songs building in volume. He drank a bottle of claret, slowly. He imagined each step of the bookmaking process in exacting precision. In his mind, he assembled the book, step by step, piece by piece, until it was a precise vision of something distantly beautiful, like a far off melody, perfectly composed but just beyond reach.

He thought.

He waited.

He watched.

Until the full moon rose out the eastern window.

Then it began, the dark assembly, illuminated by smoky candles and moonbeams pushing their white light across the blackness of the floor.

The bookmaker set the type for each page, carefully referring to the strange woman's manuscript, ensuring each letter was set in its proper place.

*Necronomicon.*

*Complete John Dee edition.*

*1564.*

He inked the platen, set down the bar.

The first page complete.

Slowly the bookmaker slid into his rhythm. He felt it already, a premonition, the certainty that this would be his finest work, the best he's ever produced, a book for the ages, to pass down through generations. Each step was perfect, every detail in its place: the acidic smell of ink, the worn handle of the press bar in his hand, the coolness of the metal type, the slight graininess to the paper, each step expanding upon the previous step, a constant building, a constant strengthening, a crescendo of tactile feeling and response.

It would be a book to be remembered by.

A book worth being remembered by.

And then it was finished. The bookmaker hadn't counted the hours, hadn't counted the days, hadn't counted the nights. He slumped exhausted in the corner, a half-drunk bottle of claret from Mr. Wakersfield on the table, bold mice eating the crumbs of stale bread from a meal he seemed to remember eating yesterday or maybe the day before.

*Necronomicon.*

The rarest book in the world.

It was finished.

Calhoun had one final instruction:

"Burn everything."

THE BOOKMAKER STARED at his creation on the table, the dark thing he'd birthed from the press. His clarity had dissolved. The haunting melody he'd tried to capture was gone now. Disappeared as soon as the work was finished. His thoughts were stray dogs wandering about his mind, thin and starved and aimless.

He tried to focus. Couldn't. Hadn't been able to since finishing the book. He picked up the book, strange notions overwhelming him. Were those . . . *screams* he heard in the distance? The disturbing whirring of the nightjars outside the window kept distracting him, their uncanny songs building in intensity. Why were there so many of them? He placed the book in his satchel, summoning up his reserves, determined to see these last steps through. His mind fuzzy, unfocused. Why couldn't he think? Why wouldn't the nightjars just . . . *stop*? A compulsion creeping through him. He just wanted to lay down and listen closely to those distant screams.

Forcing himself to refocus, the bookmaker picked up the lamp oil canisters he had been saving for this moment. He doused the press, doused the type he'd smashed repeatedly with a hammer, the workman's table, the slumping bed he'd slept in for months. He poured oil on the wooden floorboards, on the rotting ropes in the corners, on the stairs as he walked down them and outside into the crisp night air of mid-September.

He paused again, cocked his head, tried to listen for those screams.

Then he saw Mr. Wakersfield on the docks. That was him, wasn't it? Why was he nodding? Then he wasn't there anymore, just the black night and the blacker water and the yellow spots illuminated by the gas lamps on the street's edge and the whirring songs of the nightjars louder and louder around him.

The bookmaker turned back to the ropeworks. He poured lamp oil all over the entrance.

He tried to light a match, failed. Tried again, failed. He couldn't focus anymore, his thoughts dancing and clawing around his head, wild and frightened and just out of reach. The bookmaker grasped in vain at their shadows.

Suddenly Mr. Wakersfield next to him, his tone now cold and direct.

"Looking for a light, sir?"

Mr. Wakersfield lit a match, smiled wanly in its pale light, then tossed it on the entryway of the shop. The spilled oil went up in flame, crackling and smoking in the eerie calm of the night, spreading quickly across the ropeworks.

The bookmaker, cold, confused, welcomed the heat, and then was surprised by the arrival of three more men—tall, strong, dressed in black. They held back his arms, removed his satchel. He couldn't focus, couldn't fight, couldn't resist. Watched limply as Mr. Wakersfield opened the satchel and nodded at its expected contents.

"You'll recall that Mr. Calhoun said to burn everything," said Mr. Wakersfield as he motioned to the three men. A mild look of curiosity crossed the bookmaker's face as they shoved him into the entryway for the ropeworks, into the roaring fire, into the welcoming flames.

His last coherent thoughts, pushing with sudden force through the fog of his mind as the fire hit his body, were of his long-passed wife and daughter. Maybe he'd join them at last. And if not, at least it would be over now. He let the relief wash over him along with the flames.

The fire raged on.

Then Mr. Wakersfield turned his back and walked off into the black London night, the leather satchel heavy with its dark contents thumping against his thigh as the nightjars scattered to the wind.

# CHAPTER TWO

# THE COLLECTOR OF RARE EDITIONS

## DONALD TYSON

**G**ENTLEMEN, WHAT YOU are looking at is the rarest and most valuable book in the world."

This audacious pronouncement roused grunts of disbelief from several of the men gathered in the private library of Thomas H. Calhoun. They had just finished an excellent roast of beef and were in a mood to indulge the extravagant whims of their host, but such a wild claim invited cynicism.

They stood together on the Persian carpet before a glass display case, resplendent in their immaculate black dinner jackets, holding brandy snifters in one hand and cigars in the other. Each man was middle-aged, successful in his own field, and wealthy in his way, though none were as rich as Calhoun, who by dint of enterprise and ruthlessness had risen through the ranks to become the most successful shipping magnate in Boston society.

The single thread that bound these men together was their shared passion for books. They were collectors, and had gathered this night to view the most recent acquisition of Calhoun, whose private library was generally conceded to be the best on the East Coast.

"What is it, old man? Another Gutenberg Bible?"

Calhoun smiled thinly at Samuel Beeman, who was not only a book collector but a dealer who traded around the world in only the rarest editions.

"Something infinitely more precious."

He stood with his arm resting on the corner of the glass display case. Inside it, on an angled platform covered in red velvet, rested a book of folio dimensions with a beautifully tooled black leather binding. It did not appear to be old. Just the opposite, the leather gleamed in the light from the gas jets. But these men were aware that ancient books were sometimes rebound between new covers. Usually rebinding lowered the value of a book, but some editions were so rare that a new cover had little effect on their price.

Calhoun opened the hinged glass top of the case and took out the book, holding it reverently before him on the flats of his hands. Like a priest conveying the Host, he carried it to a reading table in the center of the floor and laid it down.

"Gather around, gentlemen, gather around and gaze in wonder on a book that is unique, for there is not and never will be another."

He opened the front cover and leafed with care to the title page. The other men clustered behind him and peered eagerly over his shoulders, jostling for position.

"My God," one man said. "It's the *Necronomicon*."

There was a hush of silence in the room as they took in this information.

"That is a rare book to be sure," Beeman said. "But it is scarcely unique. There is a copy in Arkham, and Harvard is rumoured to have another. I have heard tales of half a dozen Latin copies in different places around the world."

Calhoun laughed derisively.

"Do you think I would waste your time with some Latin edition? Look at the name at the bottom of the title page."

An elderly, bearded collector named Brewer from New York leaned forward.

"John Dee," he read. "Can this be the English translation made by the Elizabethan magician Dr. John Dee?"

"That's impossible," Beeman scoffed. "Dee's translation exists only in a few surviving manuscript fragments. There is no complete specimen, and it has never been printed."

"A few months ago, you would have been correct," Calhoun said. "I commissioned the private printing of the Dee translation."

"But the fragments of the Dee translation are incomplete," Beeman protested. "Even if you gathered all the faulty manuscripts together, there would still be gaps in the text."

Calhoun drew himself up and faced the portly dealer.

"I assure you, Beeman, the text is complete. Not only that, but bound into the front of the work is a previously unknown letter by Dee that describes how he came to acquire the manuscript from which he made his translation."

"How many copies did you print?" Brewer asked, unable to control the eagerness in his voice.

"This is the only copy. When it was printed and bound, I ordered the printer's plates to be destroyed. There will never be another complete Dee edition."

The other men looked at him with awe.

"Then you truly do possess the rarest book in the world," Beeman said.

"Should we even be looking at it?" one man said nervously. "I mean, I'm not superstitious, but this book has an evil reputation. They say it drives insane anyone who reads it."

The others laughed nervously, but none of them tried to touch the book, or turn its pristine leaves. All of them were recalling stories they had heard whispered in book marts and auctions on two continents, about collectors who acquired a copy of the book, only to meet with tragic and horrifying misfortunes of an inexplicable kind.

A slender white hand reached between them and flipped the pages. The book fell open to a woodcut illustration depicting the glass vessels of some alchemical operation.

"Eleanor, what are you doing out of bed?" Calhoun demanded.

The men parted to reveal a blushing girl of twelve in a nightdress and bedroom slippers, her dark hair hanging down at the back in a ponytail.

"I couldn't sleep, Father," she said in a small voice. "I wanted to see your new book."

"Get back to bed, at once," he snapped in irritation.

Tears sprang to her brown eyes. She trembled like a leaf, then dashed out the library doors into the tiled entrance hall and up the staircase.

"I apologize for that," Calhoun said. "My daughter knows this room is forbidden for her to enter."

"Children are like that," Beeman said in a placating tone. "They like to explore new things."

"She knows better," Calhoun said gruffly. "It's her mother's fault. That woman indulged her fancies while she was alive. The child needs discipline, and by God, I'm going to see that she gets it."

He closed the heavy cover of the book with a dull boom that reverberated from the bottom of the table, and picked it up to return it to the display case.

"Have you read the book yet?" Beeman asked, his small eyes unable to leave it even when he spoke.

"Not yet," Calhoun admitted. "I haven't had time. Business affairs, you know. But I mean to do so."

"Take my advice, and do not read it." Brewer's voice trembled slightly.

He cleared his throat. "Nothing good can come from opening the mind to such abominations of unreason. I knew a man in Frankfurt. He acquired a Latin copy of the work for trade and decided to make a translation of a few excerpts into German, for listing in his catalogue."

He stopped speaking, and his bearded face paled at the memory.

"What happened to him?" Calhoun asked with a crooked grin. "Did a demon fly off with his soul?"

A few of the men chuckled, but it lacked conviction.

"No, nothing like that." Brewer leaned forward and met Calhoun's grey gaze. "He killed his wife and three children with a straight razor, and then made a rope from their intestines and used it to hang himself from the steeple of a church."

WHEN THE LAST of his guests departed from his house, Calhoun had his butler, McCready, bring him whisky and soda, then sat down in solitude at the library table with the book before him. He had not felt any strong impulse to read the book prior to this night, but Brewer's story aroused his defiant nature. To tell him not to do a thing was as good as insurance that he would do it.

He opened the cover and allowed his eyes to gloat over the title page. Had Dee's manuscript been complete, he would have preferred to own the original, but because it was in scattered pieces, this book was as close as he could come to having a John Dee edition of the *Necronomicon*. He wondered what the book would fetch on the open market. Not that he ever intended to sell it. No eyes but his should read it, no hand but his should caress its pages.

He read over the brief description Dee gave of his acquisition of the Latin copy, and how much gold he had paid for it. Dee had been a collector of books also, but whereas Dee valued only their contents, Calhoun took pleasure in their physical possession. To him, books were like talismans. Each contained a portion of a man's life experience, distilled down to the text on its pages. By some subtle alchemy impossible to explain, reading the book transferred that life experience to the reader. If there was true magic anywhere in the world, then surely the power of the book was its highest and most perfect expression.

Toward the end of his letter, which bore no name to indicate the person for whom it had been written, Dee became philosophical.

*I have read this wicked Booke entire, which fewe men before me have done and remained sane to tell it, yet I believe it has left its*

*Cloven foot-printe on my very soule, for the thinges it impartes are too dreadfull for the mynde of frail and mortal Man to digest with equanimitie. Nay, I say more strong, it caryes a Taint that is beyond blasphemie, though it has that in abundaunce, but is an outrage against the natural World it-selfe and its orderly Laws by which we have continuance. Having fynished my worke, I was at warre with my selfe whether to preserve it or put it to the Furnace. Upon long and laboured reflection I determyned to keep it safe for future referrings, on the consideration that all Knowledge can be put to use in its proper context, but I fynde myself sorely vexed by the effort of encompassing such Abominations as have flowed thru my pen, and I am in much doubt that my Soule will ever be cleansed of their taint in this life. May the God who is perfect in his mercy purge me with Hyssop and wash me white as snow in Eternitie, for I shall never more be clean in this charnel house of flesh.*

Calhoun turned to the text of Alhazred's book and began to read the introductory part, in which the Arabian poet of Yemen warns of the revelations he is about to make that will overthrow all scholarly authority and even the very infallibility of divine scripture itself. His madness was evident in the wildness of his expressions and the disconnect between one thought and another. It was like listening to a clashing dissonance of sound that was both music and yet at the same moment discord.

Motion at the corner of his eye drew Calhoun's attention to the library entrance. His daughter stood peeking around the edge of one of the doors.

"Why aren't you in bed?"

"I want to see your new book."

The impulse to bark at her died in his breast as he looked at her wide eyes.

"Come over here, then. I'll show it to you."

She smiled and ran across the carpet to his chair.

He tilted the book up on its spine and opened it to the title page.

"This is part of your inheritance, Eleanor. It is the rarest and most valuable book in the entire world. When I am dead, you will probably want to sell it along with the rest of my library."

"Oh, no, Father," she said. "I will never sell your library. I love your books."

He put his arm around her shoulders and hugged her.

"Good girl. Now go to bed, and mind me—you are not to come in here unless I am present, and you are never to touch this book. Is that understood?"

"Yes, Father."

19

"Get to bed. Scoot."

He heard the slap of her slippers on the marble staircase in the hall as she ran upstairs, so quiet was the house at this late hour. He returned his attention to the text and resumed his reading.

> *These things, once glimpsed, can never more be set asyde. Like rotted fish that are carried in a Basket, and are thrown onto the dung heape, yet the Stench of rot continues in the basket from that day forward, so do they cling to the corridors of the Mynde and haunt its secret chambers, loving the darke of our baser urges and conceits, and fleeing from the Light of ratiocination . . .*

Something moved at the edge of his field of vision. He looked up from the page with annoyance.

"Eleanor, I told you—"

He stopped speaking. The doors to the library were closed, and the library was empty.

He returned his gaze to the page, but his mind was distracted, and he found he could no longer concentrate on the obscure arguments made by the mad Arab. The words jangled in his head like a dissonance of tapping drums and brass cymbals.

"To hell with it," he said to himself in disgust. "There's nothing in this book that I need."

He snapped it shut with finality and put it into its case, then left the library and locked the doors behind him. The library was his sanctum. No one else entered it without his express permission, not even the servants.

THE ROUTINE OF the Calhoun household settled back into its familiar pattern. In the mornings, Calhoun took his carriage into the financial district, where he worked until late afternoon, then came home to his mansion on Beacon Hill and worked another two hours in his private office. In the late evenings he indulged himself by relaxing in his library, studying the book lists of auction houses and dealers that were mailed to him from around the world, or oiling and polishing the leather covers of his treasures.

He seldom read while in the library. Fiction held no interest for him, and his reading during the day was taken up with legal and financial documents. From time to time his eyes would wander to the book in the glass case, and he felt a tickling urge to remove it and continue reading its contents, but he rejected the urge with impatience. He had already satisfied himself that the book held no information of value to a businessman living near the dawn of the twentieth century. This was an age of steam, of steel, of electricity, and of oil, not an age of mumbo-jumbo.

Now and then, while puttering with his collection, he caught a glimpse of a dark shape at the corner of his eye. When he looked, there was never anything there. These shapes were undefined. Some seemed human in outline, but others gave a sort of animal impression. They seemed to crouch and lope or hop to the side when he turned to look at them.

The persistent repetition of this optical illusion began to irritate him. He wondered if he needed eyeglasses. He was no longer a young man, but his eyesight had always been excellent. He resolved to make an appointment with an optometrist sometime during the next few weeks, and promptly forgot about it.

An amusing incident occurred early on a Sunday morning as Calhoun came downstairs in his dressing gown to get a glass of milk from the kitchen. A self-made man, it was his custom to do for himself around his house, an eccentricity with which his servants had grown familiar, if not reconciled.

"I know what I saw, Mr. McCready, don't tell me what I saw. It were some kind of little animal thing, and it ran right between my legs when I opened the pantry door."

Something in the tone of the woman's voice caused Calhoun to pause outside the kitchen.

"Calm down, Mrs. Keel, I don't doubt that is what you thought you saw. What I am telling you is that we do not have rats or mice in this house. I examine the traps regularly myself. They are all unsprung."

"It be bigger than a rat," another female said. Calhoun recognized the voice of a scullery maid he had recently hired, Aida Thompson, a wan-faced girl of some eighteen years.

A whimsical smile played over his face as he listened. The cook, Mrs. Keel, was talking.

"She's right, Mr. McCready, it were bigger than a rat. More like a dog, or some sort of monkey-like creature."

"It looked like a little man to me," Aida asserted.

"A little man?" The butler, McCready, laughed. "How could a little man be hiding in the house with all of us moving about and cleaning it every day? It's not possible, Aida."

"I know what I seed," the girl maintained. "It were like a little hunchback, and he were all dressed in black, and he slid along the wall and right through the door when I turned to yell at him. Scared me proper, he did. I don't know how he got in. I ran after him to give him a piece of my mind but he were gone when I got to the door."

"You don't suppose young Eleanor has been playing tricks on us?" the cook said.

"Oh, I doubt that, Mrs. Keel. That's not her way, is it? I've never known her to play tricks. Maybe while her mother was alive, but since the lady's death she's been meek and quiet as a mouse. All drawn in upon herself, like, if you know what I'm saying."

"I don't say it were Eleanor," Aida said. "It weren't Eleanor and I knowed it. It were like a little man all bent over."

"Well, next time you see your little hunchback, you tell him he doesn't belong in this house. Mr. Calhoun wouldn't like him sneaking about behind our backs this way. You tell him from me to get out and not to come back."

"I will, Mr. McCready, don't you doubt that I will."

Calhoun took that as his cue and entered the kitchen. The butler was standing, but the two women were seated at the kitchen table. They jumped up and curtsied, and Aida blushed a bright red.

Calhoun went to the ice box and got out the milk pitcher. He took down a glass and filled it, then replaced the pitcher.

"Is there anything I should be aware of, McCready?" he asked, sipping the milk.

"No, sir, nothing but a bit of foolishness, as I was saying when you entered, sir."

"What kind of foolishness?"

"I hardly like to speak about it, because it is so silly. Not something you would need to bother about, sir."

"Well, what is it?"

"These two here, sir, think there's something moving about inside the house."

"It ain't just us, Mr. Calhoun. All the servants have seen it," the cook said, glaring at the butler.

"What have you seen?"

She frowned, and her fat face drew together in lines of concentration.

"It's like a shadow, sir. We see it from the corner of our eyes, when we're looking at something else, if you know what I'm saying."

"And when you turn to look right at it, there's nothing there," Aida added in a small voice.

"Well, well, well, that is a puzzler," Calhoun said, finishing his glass of milk. He set the empty glass on the kitchen counter.

"It were like a little man when I seed it," Aida added. "He were all bent over and he had a big black head, like maybe he were wearing a top hat."

"Aida, for pity's sake, don't trouble the master with such tomfoolery," McCready snapped.

"'Tis what I seed," she answered hotly.

"It sounds like quite a mystery," Calhoun said, taking care not to let his emotions show on his face. "If you do find anything amiss, you will let me know, Mr. McCready?"

"That I will, sir. But it's only foolishness, I'm sure of it, sir."

Calhoun left the kitchen a good deal more troubled in mind than when he had entered it.

ONE EVENING, AS he entered his library and turned up the gas lights, he glanced as he usually did at the glass case to experience that gratifying sense of possession that only a true collector can enjoy to its fullest degree.

The book was not in its case.

He looked wildly around the room, heart hammering against his ribs, before noticing the book on the table, as though someone had been reading it and had forgotten to replace it in the case. But that was not possible, he thought. No one else could enter the library. He possessed the only key to the doors.

He went quickly to the window and drew aside the drapes to assure himself that none of the panes were broken. They were all intact. Then he examined the book with care to see if it was damaged in any way, but there was no sign of damage. He returned the book to its case, anger mounting within him. He felt abused, desecrated, defiled.

He summoned McCready and told him to assemble all of the household staff in the library immediately. This was an unprecedented order, but within five minutes they stood on the Persian carpet in a row, the men smoothing down their hair and the women adjusting their skirts self-consciously.

"Someone has been in this library without my permission," Calhoun said coldly, eyeing them each in turn. "The individual moved that book—" he pointed at the glass case "—and left it on the table. I want to know who it is."

The servants looked at each other uneasily and shifted from foot to foot.

"Come on, speak up. It will go easier on you if you make a clean breast of it."

"Sir, I don't see how any of the staff could come into the library, what with the doors being locked and you having the only key, sir."

Calhoun glared at the butler. McCready wilted visibly beneath that blistering scrutiny.

"I am telling you that it happened. Did any of you see or hear anything unusual last night, or while I was in the city earlier today?"

One of the footmen, a youth named Thomas Bibbs, cleared his throat.

"Last night, sir, I had occasion to come downstairs looking for something to settle my upset stomach, and I heard someone moving inside the library. I thought nothing about it, sir, because I naturally assumed it were you."

"What time was this, Thomas?" Calhoun demanded.

"I don't know, sir, but it were after midnight."

"Why would I be in the library after midnight?"

Thomas looked uncomfortable.

"I don't rightly know, sir."

"Did you try the doors?"

"No, sir."

None of the other servants had anything illuminating to add, and none of them would confess to moving the book. Calhoun's anger had not diminished. He told then to return to their duties and ordered McCready to call his daughter downstairs. The butler left them together and closed the doors behind him. It was early enough that the girl still wore her formal white dinner dress, through a maid had been brushing her hair, which hung loose below her shoulders.

"Eleanor, I want you to answer me truthfully. Did you come into the library late last night, when everyone was asleep?"

Her brown eyes widened and she shook her head. Calhoun realized that his anger was frightening the girl. He attempted to calm himself and forced a smile.

"You don't need to be afraid to tell the truth. The truth is always better than a lie, isn't it?"

"Yes, Father."

"Did you come into the library last night and remove the book from its case?"

She glanced across at the glass case, trembling as she stood before him.

"No, Father. How could I? The doors are always locked."

"So they are, so they are. But you know where Father keeps his key, don't you?"

She shook her head.

He took a long breath and tried to dismiss the last of the anger from his heart.

"Very well, Eleanor, we'll speak no more about it."

He approached her and laid his hand on the top of her head. He felt her flinch at the touch.

"Your father loves you very much. You know that, don't you?"

"Yes, Father."

"Run along, now."

She fled the library as though pursued by ghosts.

SEVERAL NIGHTS FOLLOWING the incident with the servants, Calhoun was awakened in his bed by a noise. He lay blinking in the darkness, alert to the silence. Just as he was about to assume he had imagined it, the noise came again. It was the murmur of a voice from downstairs. When it was late at night, sounds carried through the old mansion like echoes in a church. The servant quarters were on the floor above, in the attic level of the house. It was unlikely any of them would hear it.

He was never a man to hesitate where physical action was required. He slid out of bed, put on slippers and a robe, and felt around on the top of his bureau until he found the box of matches he kept there. Striking one, he used it to light the wick of his bedside oil lamp. A glow filled the bedroom. Entering his walk-in closet, he took a wooden case from a shelf and opened it to get a revolver, which he loaded in the shadows by touch.

The murmur was louder as he descended the staircase. A sliver of yellow light shone into the entrance hall from beneath the library doors. He approached the doors cautiously, lamp in one hand and gun in the other. It was a male voice, and it seemed to be chanting in some foreign language with which he was unfamiliar. He realized the intruder must be reading aloud from the *Necronomicon*. Dee had not translated all of the text into English. Calhoun knew from his background research on the book that some passages were ritual incantations written in no known tongue, and that Dr. Dee had left them untranslated.

Cautiously, he reached to open the doors, and found them locked. He nearly cursed out loud. He had forgotten his key. He wanted to catch the culprit in the act. Backing away, he hurried up the stairs and took the library key from its usual place in a keepsake chest on top of his bureau.

When he returned to the front hall, the chanting murmur had ceased. Light no longer showed from the crack beneath the doors. He started to insert the key into the lock, then impulsively tried the handles. The doors opened. He entered with his gun levelled to fire. The glow from the lamp lit up only a fraction of the big room, most of which was in shadow. Movement by the windows made him turn and crouch, but there was nothing there. He listened with his breath held and heard only silence.

Cautiously, he advanced into the room, his finger twitching on the trigger of the revolver. The gun was a Smith & Wesson double-action. All he had to do was pull, and it would fire.

The feeble yellow glow of the lamp bathed the library table. Lying open on its surface was the *Necronomicon*. He noticed that the book was opened to a place near the end, as though whoever had been reading it had nearly finished.

He stood in the darkness, debating with himself whether he should rouse the household and institute a search for the intruder, who must have slipped out of the library while he was upstairs, getting the key. He decided against it. This was no burglar or rare-book thief; this was a member of his household staff. Or his daughter. It could not be anyone else.

THE FOLLOWING NIGHT, Calhoun did not undress or go to bed. He sat in a chair in his bedroom with the revolver in one hand and the library key in the other. Someone in the house had borrowed the key and had made a duplicate—that was the only answer to the puzzle. It would not have been difficult. He had exercised no particular caution when putting the key away. Any member of the household staff could have found it and taken it during the day while he was at his office in the financial district, then replaced it after having a second key made, and he would have been none the wiser.

It bespoke a cunning mind and a deep deceit. Calhoun was vexed that he had such a deceiver in his employ. He prided himself on his judgement of a man's honesty, and would have sworn that everyone who worked for him was truthful and of good character. What troubled him the most was the possibility that the intruder might be his own daughter. But how could that be? The voice he had heard last night had been the voice of a man, he was almost sure of it. Could the girl be working with someone else? That was a disquieting thought. It would mean some kind of household conspiracy against him. How was he to know whom to trust, if his own daughter was in league with a servant to deceive him?

Twice already he had crept down the darkened hall to his daughter's room, to verify that she lay sleeping in her bed. Both times he had found her there, as expected, breathing lightly with her dark hair spread across her pillow, looking much like her departed mother in the dim glow from the turned-down lamp. It was almost impossible to believe that such innocence could be bent on defying him. He prayed silently that he would discover it was McCready or one of the footmen. Then the matter could be solved quite easily by dismissing the man from his employ. He was well accustomed to hiring and firing men and found no difficulty in it.

When the murmuring voice began, within moments he was on his feet and moving. He descended the staircase with care. He wanted to catch the intruder in the act so that there could be no possible explanation or excuse. The chanting male voice sounded different as he listened to it on the still night air. It was more rapid, more intense in some way, as though reaching a culmination. He wondered why the voice seemed to chant only those parts of the book that were not in English. Did he read the English text silently to himself? Why chant the alien language aloud?

As on the previous night, a yellow strip showed under the library doors. Of course, the man needed light by which to read. Naturally he would turn up the gas. Calhoun set his oil lamp upright on the tile floor of the hall and transferred the revolver to his other hand as he readied the key. But first, he tried the handles. The doors were not locked. He put the key away in his pocket and passed the gun back to his right hand. As silently as he could manage it, he opened the doors and stepped into the library.

The intruder sat with his back to the entrance, his head bent over the book that lay open on the table in front of him. Calhoun glanced at the glass case and saw that it was empty. No one else was in the library.

The man ceased to chant. He closed the book and rose from his chair, then crossed to the glass case with the book in his hands and replaced it into the case.

"Stay where you are," Calhoun said in a firm voice. "I have a gun and I'm willing to use it."

The intruder stood with his back to Calhoun, not moving.

"Turn around, damn you."

Slowly, the man turned around. In one hand he held a revolver.

Calhoun's eyes narrowed in confusion. The man had his face. He also wore the same clothes that Calhoun was wearing. It had to be some kind of disguise. But it was too realistic for a mask. It was like looking into a mirror.

"Put down your gun or I'll shoot," Calhoun said, his voice not quite so steady as before.

"*Ph'nglui mglw'nafh*," chanted the man who looked like him.

He raised the revolver to his temple and pulled the trigger.

THE NOISE OF the shot roused the household. They found Calhoun sprawled face down on the library carpet, blood and brains oozing from the hole in the side of his head. The gun was still in his right hand. One bullet had been fired.

Her governess kept Eleanor on the upper level of the house until the Boston police had come and gone, and the body had been removed. It was judged a suicide by the police on the scene. There was nothing to suggest otherwise. The maids tried to scrub the fresh blood out of the thick pile of the Persian carpet, but after all their efforts an irregular patch of darker red remained against the red dye of the carpet, like a shadow. No one thought to lock the library doors when they finished.

That afternoon, when the excitement had died away, Eleanor entered the library. She looked around in wonder at the high walls of books, their leather spines gleaming where they caught the light from the windows. They were all hers now, even the black book in the glass case that she had been ordered by her father never to touch. Everything belonged to her.

She turned to look at an empty spot not far from the stain in the carpet.

"Now we can read it together, Mr. Pharaoh."

She cocked her head and seemed to listen, then opened the glass case and took out the book. It was heavier than she expected. She carried it to the library table. Drawing up a chair, she opened the cover and began to read. A shadow gathered from the air around her shoulders and head. She smiled and scratched behind her ear.

"No tickling," she said.

# CHAPTER THREE

# DOWN TO A SUNLESS SEA

## ALLYSON BIRD

**H**AD THERE BEEN years of preparation? Well there hadn't been many. Just the nocturnal visits she attributed to the dream within a dream. The play within the play.

Helen stared at the William Morris bedroom curtains, mostly red with the strawberry thief upon them—well, the strawberry thieves—the birds— one on each side of the flower. There was a crack of sunlight shining through a gap that she would have to close later, and then she fell into sleep.

She had that nightmare again. Her mouth frozen open in a scream. A scream that perhaps only The Elders could hear. She had been studying the book until she was so tired she could barely lift her head. Helen had turned twenty-one the previous year, in 1904. Now she was old enough to look after herself and do anything she wanted. Anything. And rich indeed. Old enough to travel but she in fact just journeyed many nights into dreamland. As a child she had read Coleridge's poem—but her dreamland, although similar, was definitely not man-made. Her land of ice and snow was underground and the latter part of the setting appeared in her dreams, night after night.

> In Xanadu did Kubla Khan
> A stately pleasure-dome decree:
> Where Alph, the sacred river, ran
> Through caverns measureless to man
> Down to a sunless sea.

"Down to a sunless sea."

*The* sacred river—green—olivine to be precise. In *the* same dream. When she could sleep, that is, which was very little—the same lines of poetry and images going around in her head for weeks on end. How little sleep could she exist on before she slipped over the edge? The edge of what? An abyss? Into madness? With no return? Once she thought she had drifted close *that* time when she thought something dark and strange lived alongside her in her father's house. But whatever had happened then was deliberately long forgotten and THE book had been locked away for years, until recently.

The book—bound in leather, and in gold letters: *Necronomicon*. Nightmares and dreams. She inhabited these as opposed to real life, which she was quickly leaving behind. Then one morning she woke up abruptly and decided she would do one particular thing the dream had been telling her to do. It involved the book.

"Everything does."

Helen left for Iceland in June. She decided to travel the first part of her journey alone and departed from Hull on a trawler. Under fishery law a British trawler could not dock in Iceland, so she was rowed ashore in a small boat by a rugged Icelander who wore a confounded expression most of the time, and kept staring at her. She avoided his eyes and her own tried to penetrate the inky sea that surrounded her. Aboard the trawler she had imagined great cities beneath the sea—she liked to think Atlantis was here somewhere. And the "sunless sea."

Iceland. Made of basalt and layers of lava. In her dreamlands, which she freely, wildly, quickly roamed through, there were ice cliffs the colour of emerald.

Snæfellsjökull would be her destination. Her guide was named Finnr Helgason. He had been paid in advance—just in case—and paid well. Recommended to Helen by a friend in Reykjavik. They had both got on from the first—he liked the look of her. Her long brown hair. A hint of copper in each strand. And she very much liked the look of him.

First they travelled by horse and cart to Finnr's farm in the Mossfellssveit parish. Here they were met by his wife, Sigga. A small boy stood by her side. When he saw his father he smiled and reached up to him.

The boy would grow up and adopt the name Halldor Laxness. He would become a writer—and would win the Nobel Prize for Literature in 1955. There was a hint of something other in his glittery green eyes. Jules Verne had it, too. In the Laxness novel the protagonist was sent on a "simple" visit on behalf of the bishop to find out what was going on in a small town.

Nothing is ever that simple. Nothing is ever just going on. And "everything" is set down somewhere. In a diary. In a story. In a dream.

The boy was playing with a piece of obsidian.

Finnr had a diary in which was written all he knew of Snæfellsjökull. Notes on how the area had changed over the years. Glacial movement. Lava fields covered with moss. The tiny pink flowers of moss campion—all beautifully drawn. Kittiwakes, the terns, ptarmigan—the one land mammal, the arctic fox. Finnr documented in detail many of the tiny Icelandic flowers which grew there. A diary that his son would read one day.

They loaded the horses with supplies. Helen wondered why they would not be taking a boat across to the peninsula and had asked Finnr. His English was not great but he had told her that his horses hated boats. That was what she had thought. And as they needed the horses packed to the gills with the essentials, that line of thought was discontinued. The satchel containing the book that once belonged to her father was never far from her side, and so they set out for Grundarfjörður. It would take a few days, but Helen wasn't in any hurry. Iceland had captivated her.

The journey. Although Iceland was renowned for the weather changing quickly, Helen thanked the furies that they had little rain at that time. But the wind—that was another matter. Where they could, they stayed at small farms along the way. Finnr seemed to know everyone and everyone seemed to like him. He was blonde, as many Icelanders were, and had that look about him that he was comfortable on his own even though married. She imagined he probably went off with a tent and his diary quite a lot, dwelled on what he saw and what he did when alone under the stars. She wondered if the handsome, tall man dwelled on her.

One farmhouse was crowded with children, seven of varying ages. Helen was mortified to find her satchel had been taken from near her chair, and one grubby child about five years of age had managed to get it open, and had started heaving the book out. His mother stopped him, but as she did so she stared at the book and then suspiciously at Helen. Helen dashed over, grabbed it and the satchel—muttering something that she hoped the woman would not understand. The woman was taken aback a little and she indicated to her husband that she wanted to speak to him alone. She left one of the older children in charge of the others and went outside with him.

It dawned on Helen that due to the ominous appearance of the book the woman might just be a little afraid of her. Every Icelander was superstitious. Around the fire at night they told each other stories of trolls, elves, and witches. Monsters which appeared out of the low-hanging mist and of other things they had seen. Spirits of their dead—tied to the homesteads by grief and devotion.

Helen knew some strange tales also, had carried them with her since a child, but she did not share them. Not with this woman who watched her with serious eyes.

Finnr had seen what had just taken place and he knew the signs. "Helen, pack your bags. I'll get the horses."

From mid-May to mid-August the sun set for only a few hours a day, so they had plenty of daylight left. It was almost the twenty-first of June—the solstice—when it would be dark for only a few hours after midnight. By the time the woman got back with her husband, Helen and Finnr had gone. Helen had left more money than was necessary for the short time they were there, and the woman considered after all that Helen was perhaps more of a blessing than a curse. Yes—as she spun the coins on the wooden table for the amusement of the children, she thought that. A blessing. She could be counted upon to remain silent. Who knows—the foreigner might call again one day. All memories of the strange nature of the book and how the young woman had held it close to her disappeared.

At the next farmhouse, Helen ensured that the book was always next to her and buried deep in her satchel. The atmosphere of the abode was different than the last. Eir kept a good house. It was clean and consisted of a central hearth with two raised platforms at each side of the room. A small child—a girl of about three—was asleep on one. The owner was happy to give Helen and Finnr the barn for the night, but before they retired she insisted that they eat with them. She served to them herring and a dark rye bread. That was followed by vinarterta, which was some sort of layered prune cake, with cream.

Finnr explained that the coastal people traded fish for rye with the Danish. Anything that could be grown in the summer months had to last the rest of the year. The Icelandic people were experts at preserving food. Helen had expected to eat more lamb in Iceland, but it had also been explained to her that the sheep were far more valuable for their milk and wool. As a consequence of that, she had been eating much dried fish on her journey and something quite new to her—seal meat—which tasted like beef to her.

After supper they all sat up into the evening and Eir told a story about Hildur, queen of the elves, which Finnr translated for Helen. At one point Eir took a torch, beckoned to Helen, led her out to her garden, and showed her the tiny elf house she had asked her husband to make for them. It was a miniature of her own turf house but great care had been taken to build a much more detailed garden surrounding it—the tiniest of flowers bloomed there—and she had placed some cake on a little plate in front of the door.

*Ritual, devotion and fear . . . All of us are tainted by it. Drawn to it.*

And then a story of the Old Gods and of the other ones, The Elders, who had been forgotten and now had no names. Helen was keen to know more of these, but Finnr shrugged and said he was having trouble understanding who Eir was talking about. She did make it clear that she was not talking about Odin, Thor, or Freya. He tried to find the words to explain "something other" and how they were "*outside* the solid realm of men," but struggled to understand and describe it. He did glean the fact that somewhere in Iceland there was supposed to be a gateway to the "hidden world" of these gods. And just before they slept there was one more story—of a *great* creature like a colossal Komodo dragon that walked out of the sea—upright—like a man—covered in armoured scales that resembled chainmail.

The journey was tiring but not too difficult. When they did get to the impressive Mount Kirkjufell, it was bathed in sunshine and dominated the skyline above the fishing village. *Hyperborean,* thought Helen. Then the clouds gathered above and it was cold again. She had been mesmerized by the beauty of Iceland. She wished that she could stay forever, told Finnr she would love to stay here, told him this land felt like home. The black guillemots welcomed them with a high whistling sound and Finnr indicated that the soup he heated up for them over a fire was made from them. She already knew a bit about the bird and that the down and feathers were used in pillows and mattresses. Not that she slept much the night before they left to cross the glacier. She found it hard to concentrate on anything—she had but one obsession. Helen knew now what she was about and it had nothing to do with fiction.

The horses seemed skittish and Finnr held them tightly by their reins as they approached the high drying racks. You could smell the fish from a long way away. The horses backed up a little but Finnr led them on. The drying racks. They looked like rickety funeral pyres for old Vikings set against grey sky and a flint sea. She has seen fish preserved before but in a different way—the curing of flounder and dab. Cod in salt for export. Helen and Finnr pressed onwards and eventually they could breathe the crystal clear air once more.

As they neared their destination Helen suddenly stopped and Finnr calmed the horses again. She felt herself slipping in and out of place. Not fixed. It was here she could hear THEM calling to her. Telling her to move forward—and when she closed her eyes her head was filled with the shimmering of stars that then dimmed and glowed, in turn. She became exhausted and stumbled over a rock.

Finnr made a grab for her so she would not fall. Shy at first but with ever increasing forwardness, he placed his arm around her waist and helped her along. He knew she was tired. He knew she was putting on a brave face. He had no idea why he was helping her to where she needed to be. He just had to. When they got to a small stream she indicated that she had to rest.

No ice in Iceland? Not true—some caves in summer had a little but the time most people visited was in winter for ice cavern tours. Finnr found the entrance to the cavern easily but it wasn't as obvious to Helen that quickly. Once she was inside, the turquoise and blue ice was simply beautiful. A labyrinthine cavern that led to a giant duomo. Images of a large honeycomb flickered through her mind. Could it be all those things that had been in her dreams? There was also the knowledge that they were on a volcano, an active volcano—although it hadn't erupted for seventeen hundred years. Perhaps it was due.

It was cold in the cavern—strangely airless. She could not breathe. She faced the ice wall. Helen wasted no time—she had the book with her. Nothing surprised Finnr—he was used to people doing strange things. She took the book out of the leather satchel—it felt cold. She placed it on a rock, opened it, and found the page she wanted.

Helen looked over her shoulder and smiled at Finnr. Sometimes she had grey eyes but this time they shone like gold. Finnr did not smile in return, just looked at her with a puzzled expression on his face. He saw the book shake slightly. There was fear in his eyes as he stepped back. The ground also shook beneath their feet and he jumped when he heard a noise—something crashing to the stony ground. Ice?

Helen started to read from the book, slowly, precisely at first. Her voice faltered for a second but she was determined to go on. At one point it was almost as if a hand tried to cover her mouth. Finnr was now some distance away. It could not be him. She carried on. Whatever was trying to hinder her seemed to lack power, and so she continued. With each word the book shook less until it stopped completely.

The clarity of her voice—the echoing in the enormous cavern. Finnr understood nothing but when she stood aside he saw a green mist rise from the book—saw the mist *dance*. She repeated the words and it spiralled up to the cavern ceiling and along as if feeling for a way out or in. It found a part of the ice wall that shimmered green in response.

They heard a sharp crack and the wall broke into hundreds of pieces, revealing yet another ice wall, this time a deeper shade of green. The mist drifted towards it and stopped. Briefly it tried to take shape but failed, and then it slowly seemed to seep through the wall.

Helen walked over to the ice. She saw what looked to be larger shape-

34

shifters surrounding the smaller one from the book. She pressed her hands into the wall. It let her. She closed her eyes and could see only white marble with silver green threads.

Then Helen was gone.

Finnr tried to understand what he had just seen. He could not. He stood silent for a long time and wondered upon it all. He would return without her—how could he explain her disappearance?

Finnr took the book away with him. His journey home took quite some time. He wanted to make sure he took the "earthiness" of his Iceland into him—the tiny pink flowers of moss campion, the roar of a waterfall that hurt his ears. The green. The grey. The blue. In certain places the mountains towered above him—in others, the desolation almost crippled him. At night he built a fire and looked up at the stars. *So many places unvisited*, he thought. He heard them call to him but each day he looked down and made sure he did not fall, and returned home. What had he witnessed? What had he seen?

Had a god been trapped in the book—and now returned to join The Elders? Helen. Soft. Girl and woman. Bewitching. Who was she? What was she? He'd ask himself whilst holding her book—a book he never once opened. Remembering her—remembering her stepping away from the fire one night and talking to the stars—laughing quietly at a reply she seemed to understand, but one he could not hear.

He held the book close to his chest and closed his eyes. There were stars and fields, and her eyes—

"Helen."

The book had been left with Finnr and she had gone to start her new life as Aylith—the Many-Mother—the Widow in the Woods. She had followed the thing through the ice wall. And what would become of their union? Whatever would be spawned—undoubtedly it would have an ice-kissed heart.

# CHAPTER FOUR

# DAWN WATCH

## DANIEL MILLS

**T**HE SUN IS down, the summer light fading.

Josiah Clarke sits in his study, the book open in his lap. He does not read but listens to the clock behind him, the spring unwinding. He hears the pause that marks the changing minute, followed by the groan of the mechanism as the bell sounds the half-hour.

Nine-thirty. He must put Aaron to bed.

He rises out of the armchair and shuffles in slippers down the corridor with its rows of white squares free of dust where once their pictures hung. He trails his finger along the wall, calling to mind the images that were displayed there.

There is an old ambrotype depicting his father, also Josiah, a Union army captain and later a bookseller from whom Josiah inherited both his name and livelihood. There is a framed tintype from Block Island, where Josiah was sent in the spring of '98 and where he met Emily, his wife. An image of their wedding day with Emily in pale blue with a sheaf of long-stemmed flowers at her breast, the irises she cut from her own garden.

Finally he sees Aaron in his uniform with his fiancée, Annie, beside him and his gloved hands folded over his belt buckle. This was two years ago, the spring of '18, before the Meuse–Argonne and the Spanish Influenza and Aaron's broken engagement.

His son's bedroom is on the ground floor near the kitchen, a converted pantry. For fifty years this room belonged to Mr. Tarbuck, the butler, who was his father's manservant and who helped to raise the "young masters" Josiah and Aaron in turn. Then Aaron's condition had worsened, so that a bath-chair was sometimes needed, and Tarbuck had given his notice with the rest of the house staff. "It's all too much for me," Tarbuck said. "It hurts too much, seeing what's become of the young master." And Josiah was unsure of which young master he meant.

The door to Aaron's room is ajar, yellow light spilling through the crack. Inside, the boy lies on the cot with his face to the ceiling. His supper is on a tray beside him, uneaten, while his eyes are turned to the electric light. The glass dome has been removed: the bolts loosened, the dome itself placed on the nightstand. The exposed bulb rocks gently in its fixture, quivering in place. The tungsten filament flickers and sparks and still the boy does not look away.

"The flare is up," he murmurs. "Still dark."

Josiah empties the bedpan and unbuttons the boy's shirt. He bundles the sweat-soaked garment away into a hamper then does the same with Aaron's trousers and undergarments.

Finally he draws up the sheet as to cover Aaron's nakedness, the body with its unmarred skin, shockingly white. Then pauses in the doorway, his hand at the switch when he hears his son's voice a second time, the terror in it: a whisper robbed of breath, insubstantial as smoke.

"Dawn's coming. Won't be long now."

Josiah turns out the light.

HE RETURNS TO his study, where lately he has taken to sleeping, and resumes his place in the armchair with a blanket draped round his shoulders. He reaches down to his feet and takes up the book, black leather smooth at his fingertips.

The volume came to him by chance as part of a library acquired at auction. This was in the weeks that followed Emily's death when Aaron was still in the hospital. He had been reported missing in the early days of the Meuse–Argonne offensive and later discovered in a collapsed forward trench where he had apparently taken shelter, though no one could explain how he became separated from his battalion. He was unharmed but suffering from shell shock and would not be released from care for several weeks—and it was around this time that Josiah received a letter from Aaron's fiancée which severed their engagement, thereby ensuring there would be neither wife nor mother waiting when the boy came home.

Josiah had burned Annie's letter and wandered downtown. He was dazed and sickened and could not bring himself to open the shop. Somehow he found himself at an auction (habit, he supposes) and lingered near the back like a man sleepwalking. He did not bid—he had not brought any money—but when the auction ended, and the hall was closed up, he noticed a crate of unsold books placed carelessly outside with a snowfall threatening, and this book among them.

He opens it now, holds it to his face. His eyesight is failing but he inhales its scent, the crisp odor of good paper. The book is a religious work, a prayer book of a sort translated from the Arabic by John Dee. Josiah doubts this attribution very much but he cannot deny the hold the book has on him. It is a queer work, yes, probably blasphemous, but in the months since the auction, it has given him distraction and solace and something like understanding.

And so he reads. He unfolds his glasses and the page swims into view: white lines and black arranged into roads or rivers that twist and double back upon each other.

He reads: *Great holes secretly are digged in the earth.*

He reads: *Out of corruption a horrid life springs.*

He sleeps.

FIRST THERE IS a sensation of heat, then a kind of awakening. His eyes open on blackness, the air dank and sour in his lungs. He becomes aware of his heartbeat, his hands, the fingers curled but holding nothing.

He is lying in a crevasse, a deep gouge in the earth with the sky overhead: an oval closed with naked bedrock like the opening of a well. The distance to the opening is eight or nine feet, no more, but he cannot move to stand. His legs are numb save for a slight tingling like the sensation that precedes a storm. The clouds flicker and illuminate, dropping pearls of violet light, and soon the storm is breaking but without lightning, only thunder. Only a series of dull concussions that shower down dirt and cause the earth to quake and rumble, driving the shards of its trembling through him, his bones and organs.

Sparks. He blinks and the sky is awash in color: purple on red though it is not the dawn. The gleaming creeps down the walls, edging nearer, revealing rubble and mud and bits of broken stone before striking his forehead at last. It is a cool light, utterly without warmth but enough for him to see by, to realize he is not alone.

There is someone beside him, a pile of gray rags marred with dark stains. The man has been dead some time. His hand is visible where it thrusts from a tattered cuff and the fingers are swollen, gorged with fluid: dark and spongy about the nails and circled with blue veins. The wrist has been shredded, eaten away, muscle and fat stripped to expose the bone.

The rags twitch and stir, begin to squirm. The movement begins near the figure's head and spreads to the chest and limbs. The ruined clothes ripple in one direction then another, bowing outward, upward—and still Josiah cannot move. He closes his eyes but sees through the lids and watches the clothes heave and breach and burst apart.

Shapes pour out of the rag-pile, furred and slick, eyes and teeth gleaming with the purple light behind them. Rats. They pass by him like the waters round a rock before turning with one body to vanish into the ground.

The earth opens up all around him and he hears himself screaming over the thunder while the clouds continue to crack and separate and the lights fall out of the sky.

THE SCREAM JERKS him awake. He shakes off the blanket and is through the door and halfway down the hall before he realizes that all is quiet. He stops himself near Aaron's door and rests his head against the wall, shaking as the dream returns to him in pieces, and with it, the memory of the scream: not a man's voice, but a boy's. Aaron's.

Aaron was nine when he fell out of the tree. Josiah had quarreled with him over the breakfast table (he forgets the reason why) and threatened the boy with a beating for impertinence. The child, frightened, had fled through the back door to Emily's garden, meaning to hide there, as was his way. Josiah did not go after him and forbid his wife from doing the same so they were both seated, sipping coffee, when they heard the scream.

Emily flew out through the hallway and the back door, faster than Josiah for all of her skirts and petticoats. She took the boy into her arms and held him to her chest and that was how he found them, mother and son together in a bed of trampled flowers.

The child's leg was broken, Josiah saw, while his face was pinched and bloodless. Emily would not look at Josiah but inclined her mouth to Aaron's head and spoke some words beneath her breath in the language of mother and child to which Josiah was not party and could not be any more than he could gather the boy into his arms and hold him safe.

Later he learned that Aaron had climbed the apple tree but was startled by a wasp and lost his balance. The next morning Josiah went out to the garden with Tarbuck and, working together, they felled the tree. The wood they burned that winter but the stump is still there, he knows, hidden by weeds and grasses and overgrown perennials.

40

This morning he paces the ruins of Emily's garden until he finds the stump, thrusting up from the muddy ground and beginning to list to one side as the roots become displaced. The wood is soft and rotten, the rings of its years hidden by dark moss.

He kicks at the earth with his slippers. Root matter flies up, clumps of yellowed grass. His toe strikes something hard, sharp, and he leaps back, swearing, the sweat running down his forehead. The sun is rising over the southern wall, promising another day of heat.

He bends over the stump and digs with his fingers in the mud until he spies a glint of metal. He fishes it out, wipes the mud away.

A tin soldier.

THE NEXT DAY is Thursday and Aaron's constitutional. The doctor insists on it, though most weeks the boy is too exhausted to walk more than a few hundred yards and afterward must be wheeled home in the bath-chair.

Only once did Josiah neglect to bring the chair. On that day they had walked nearly half a mile when Aaron sat down on the curb and refused to move. Josiah could not leave him alone and so had no recourse but to walk from house to house until someone answered, a deacon, who agreed to help him. Together they carried Aaron back to the house with the deacon murmuring soft encouragements all the while and Josiah conscious only of strangers' faces at the windows, their white hands twitching the curtains.

The memory stings, the humiliation, and he remembers another morning, in '98, when war with Spain had become inevitable. Josiah had risen early and shaved. He ironed his jacket and starched his collar and walked downstairs to the breakfast room where he announced his intention to enlist. His father the captain glanced up from his mail but said nothing, not then, and not even when Josiah slunk home in shame with the recruiter's judgment hanging over him. *Unfit.* His father merely nodded upon hearing the news as though it confirmed for him what he had long believed, and swiftly changed the subject. The captain addressed himself to his wife to ask after some matter of household business, and Josiah, routed, withdrew to his bedroom.

That was a Friday. War was declared on Monday and on Tuesday his father sent Josiah to stay with cousins on Block Island. "For the good of your health, you understand." Those were his words, though Josiah was quite well, and besides, they both knew the truth: that Josiah's weakness was a shame to his father as it was to himself and always would be, following him into marriage and later into grief and today it stalks him down Main Street, passing through bars of hot sunlight with his shadow trailing out behind.

Aaron enlisted in May of '17, weeks after war was declared, but he was strong and healthy and it was clear he would be taken, that he would see combat where Josiah never did.

Now the boy walks beside him, shuffling forward with head down, face hidden by the brim of his army-issued cap. His son is taller than Josiah by a foot or more but moves slowly enough that it's easy for Josiah to keep pace, though he pushes the chair before him, the wheels groaning and turning back on themselves with each crack in the paving.

They reach the shop, the familiar signboard advertising rare and antique books. The narrow storefront had belonged to Josiah's father before his death, at which time it passed to his only son. Since then the shop's fortunes have declined significantly. The closed sign is in the window, as it has been these past two weeks, while the books on display—just visible beyond his own reflection—are gathering cobwebs and dust.

He pushes the chair over a rut in the pavement, then pauses when he realizes that Aaron is not beside him. He looks back toward the shop and spies his son at the window with his hat removed and face turned to the glass, paralyzed by a memory or perhaps by the sight of his reflection.

No, Josiah thinks. There is someone else, a woman on the sidewalk opposite. It is Annie Duncan, the boy's erstwhile fiancée. She, too, has frozen upon seeing Aaron, though her husband, smartly dressed in hat and gloves, continues on his way, quite oblivious.

Aaron stares into the window—he will not avert his gaze—and Annie, reddening, is first to look away. She lifts her skirts to her ankles and runs to catch up with her husband. He takes her arm in his and they proceed together, the strains of their laughter drifting in the heat.

Aaron watches them go. His expression does not waver and indeed the boy makes no sound at all but merely collapses, falling backward into the chair that waits for him.

Aaron's head rolls on his shoulders. His eyes are wide and staring, his lips trembling as the wires overhead crackle and start to hum. A trolley. Josiah turns to see it approaching at speed, clicking down the track pursued by a crowd of young boys in scouting uniforms, all of them yelping and shouting: a shrill chorus. It is clear they wish to board but the car must be full for the driver merely rings the bell and continues round the bend and the scouts follow after in staggering formation.

They are gone. He can no longer hear them. He hears nothing but a faint dripping, which is the sound of urine pooling, trickling down the chair-legs. Aaron's hands are wet where they clasp the chair-arms, his clothes sodden with it. His white gaze quivers in the window.

HOME AGAIN, HE helps Aaron up and out of his clothes, then carries the sopping garments to the kitchen and drapes them over the basin so they can dry.

He returns to Aaron's room. The boy has not moved but lies naked across the bedclothes, his skin the same white of Emily's pearls, which were sold last year. His mouth is open and he appears to be asleep, exhausted from the morning's ordeal.

Josiah draws the sheets over him and closes the curtains. The sunlight blinks and vanishes, but the room remains bright: the electric lamp on, the bulb bared and flickering. The dome sits on the nightstand, as it has these past two days, turned upside down like a fish-bowl and with a dusting of insect matter visible inside.

He empties the dome into the chamber-pot and screws the glass back into place over the bulb. He retreats toward the doorway, turns the switch.

Aaron murmurs from slumber:

"The flare is down. The guns. Ours, I think. Look out beyond the German lines, the colors there. Morning coming soon."

Josiah leaves him and returns to the study. An hour or more remains until luncheon so he takes the book from the desk and retires to his armchair.

He reads. His vision blurs, worsening, and the text rises from the page to circle him where he sits.

*Not in the spaces we know but between them . . . The wind gibbers with Their voices and the earth mutters with Their consciousness . . . As a foulness shall ye know Them. Their hand is at your throats, yet ye see Them not . . .*

The author writes of a coming judgment, his phrases recalling the Revelation of John. A certain yearning suffuses the text, coupled with despair and the knowledge that he will not live to witness the coming Day of Wrath. The author thinks of himself as "one untimely born," much like Josiah, for whom the Day has come and gone, devouring all certainty, and before him lies a future without promise or comfort, where nothing can be known.

Minutes or hours drift past and Aaron enters the room. The boy crosses the rug and stands naked behind the chair, reeking of sweat and urine. The window is behind him, the curtains drawn so that Aaron appears in silhouette. He shakes and sways, fingers kneading the chair-back. He does not speak and Josiah is grateful for this, as he is for the curtains, which hide his shame from others, from himself.

"You must be hungry," he says. "I'll fix us something to eat."

AND LATER WHEN the lights are out and he has put Aaron to bed, he dons his nightshirt and wanders out amidst the wreckage of Emily's garden. The night is cool and pleasant: the moon waxing, near to full, the weeds teeming with insects. The stump shows silver in that light with the black moss visible in patches, a clouded mirror.

He walks to the end of the garden, reaching the brick wall with its spreading cracks and an inset gate that opens onto a back alleyway. The stone bench is here, adjacent to the gate, as it has been for decades. Here his father would smoke his pipe while cleaning his revolver and it's here that Josiah collapses with his nightshirt wrapped around him and opens his eyes on a world of falling stars.

The violet light is there again, brighter, and this time he is in motion. In the dream he runs through the twilight with the earth heaving beneath him. The blood surges to his temples and he throws himself to left and right, avoiding the trees that flash out of the dusk.

He is in a forest, or what remains of one, the tree trunks splintered and jagged with their leaves all torn away. The wind is behind him, a roaring he cannot outrun, making words where it howls out of the shattered earth: foxholes, shell-craters.

"Gas!" a voice says.

And still he runs—not toward the battle but away from it while around him the dead trees bud and flower. Foulness blooms from the broken branches, forming clouds that follow him like leaves: drifting on the ground, rising on the wind.

The cries grow louder, closer though he sees no one, the men like boys gone shrill in their panic and Aaron's voice among them. Then the planet rocks upon its axis, casting him into the air so he's floating, weightless. He glimpses a landscape wreathed in a boiling cloud, crisscrossed by black gouges.

Then the ground hurtles toward him. The earth itself opens to receive him and he falls in a rain of flares like starlight.

HE WAKES AND returns to the house, to the armchair in his study where he passes the rest of the night and the morning and does not stir until he hears the bell. It rings once, the sound spreading in ripples through the silence of the house.

The telephone, he thinks, lurching out of the chair. But the sound comes again and he recognizes it as the chime of the front doorbell. He goes to answer. It is noon and he is not dressed but still he withdraws the bolt and pulls it open.

"Miss Duncan," he says, stupidly.

The girl flushes. She is married now, of course—no longer a Miss or a Duncan—but she does not correct him.

"I hope you can forgive me," she says, plainly nervous. "This intrusion, I mean. But I understand if you cannot."

His rage sudden surprises him: bitter as gall in his mouth. His hands tremble, make fists at his sides.

He says: "He saw you. Yesterday."

"I know," she says. "And I saw him."

There is no answer to this.

Josiah glances down the street to the waiting car that has brought her. Inside, the driver unfolds a newspaper and holds it open against the steering wheel as though expecting a long wait.

He exhales. "You had better come in."

He waves her inside and shows her into the front parlor, adjacent to his study, where he thinks they won't be overheard. He closes the door behind them. He is dizzy, light-headed—he has not eaten since yesterday's luncheon—but remains standing, leant up against the mantelpiece.

Annie will not sit either. She closes her eyes and cinches her hands together at her waist as though to steady herself when the words come pouring from her.

She says: "He used to write to me. Every day from the front he would send a letter. They were vague, of course—the censors made sure of it—but he told me what it was like, waiting for the attack when they all knew the orders were imminent. None of the men slept. They used to watch for flares, cheering each one. A flare meant the night patrols were out, the dawn still far off. Morning scared them so much they came to prefer the dark."

The damp wells up from his scalp, dribbles down his face.

Josiah asks: "Why are you telling me this?"

"Because of what he wrote. He had a—presentiment, he called it. He said he wasn't coming back. He knew it somehow."

"We had letters too," Josiah says. "He never spoke of any such premonition. 'Every confidence of our success.' Those were his words."

"Perhaps . . ." she trails off.

The light glimmers through the curtains, doubling the pulse of the blood in his ears and temples, a constant throbbing.

"Yes?"

"Perhaps he thought you would not understand."

"And you would?" he spits the words. The rage returns, incandescent, burning all the hotter because he knows she is correct.

"No," she says. "And I didn't. But I tried."

"You tried."

"Please," she says. "I did not mean to cause offense. I wanted only to explain."

"There is nothing to explain."

"You don't understand. The letter I sent, the end of our engagement—it was Aaron's doing, all of it. He said he knew what would happen. The thing that was coming for him. He was terrified, I think. For months he wrote and begged me to release him from our engagement and always I begged him to reconsider. It wasn't enough, though. In the end he—made it impossible—for us to continue as we were."

"Impossible," Josiah says, flatly.

"Another woman." Her face reddens, her voice failing. "A French girl, a prostitute. He wrote to me. He told me about it, the things she did . . . There could be no reconciling after that."

Josiah listens, saying nothing. He averts his gaze, tracing the patterns on the parlor rug.

She continues: "I told my father what happened. He was furious and I was soon engaged a second time. Father made it clear I was to have nothing to do with you. But when I heard of Mrs. Clarke's passing—and with Aaron in the hospital—I knew I needed to write. That is why I sent the letter. I felt I owed you that much at least."

Josiah clears his throat. "You owe us nothing," he says. "Nothing at all."

They do not speak. Annie lingers in the doorway, perhaps expecting something more from him, and he thinks she means to address him a final time. But she does not, and he will not look at her, and if the moment was there then it's long past and he has nothing left to say.

HOURS LATER AND with the boy in bed, Josiah finds the letter where she left it on the end table. It is addressed to Aaron. Josiah considers reading it but decides against it. The morning's anger is gone, evaporating with the heat of the day. But he recalls an image of Aaron's face, pinched and shivering in the shop window, and he takes the letter into the parlor.

The stove has not been lit in months, the inside mounded with spring ashes. He slides the letter inside and, striking a match, sets fire to the edges. He returns the matchbox to his pocket and watches the letter burn, the paper curling up on itself so words and phrases show.

*Promises made. Anguish. That hell. I remember.*

He closes the stove and returns to his armchair. He sits and takes up the book from the side table though he does not open it but simply holds the cover to his cheek, cradling it against his skin. He savors its coolness, inhaling the familiar smells of paper and leather and something else—a sweetness like decay. Perfume.

It is from the letter, he realizes, the girl's scent lingering on the paper and on his hands. Since Emily's death the smell has become as remote to him as the battlefields of France and equally beyond his comprehension.

*Perhaps he thought you would not understand,* Annie had said, and of course he could not—any more than he might understand his son's premonition or the broken engagement or the reasons he waited up and watched the naked light-bulb flicker.

*The flare is up,* he said. *The guns.*

The fear in his voice. *Dawn's coming. Won't be long now.*

*I didn't,* Annie said. *But I tried.*

And he thinks of the book and the dreams it has given him: how little they have signified, how vast the gulfs that separate him from Aaron.

He closes his eyes, willing sleep to return. In the dark he feels his father's gaze upon him, the shame cinched round his throat and squeezing.

He comes awake gasping. He scrabbles at his collar, loosening it, and looks down at his feet where the book has fallen: face-down but open with the pages spilling from it, a white fan in the last of the moonlight.

"AARON," HE SAYS.

Josiah produces the matchbox from his pocket and strikes a light.

The boy is in bed. He lies on his back with his face turned upward, the chin jutting, not sleeping. In that faint illumination he notes the damp on Aaron's face. His son's eyes and nose are streaming and the pillow is wet.

Aaron whimpers. "She was here," he says. "I heard her."

Josiah freezes. The match goes out in his hand.

Aaron says: "I lied. The things I wrote. It never happened."

"Please," Josiah says quickly, striking a second match.

The boy continues: "I was too much of a coward. Even for that."

"No."

"The shells came down round us and I ran. The gas—"

"I know," Josiah whispers. "I know."

The match gutters, burns down to his fingertips. He shakes it out and retreats to the doorway. The window is dark, the moon long set. Josiah looks up toward the electric light fixture. Again the dome is absent, the bulb exposed. He turns the switch.

A surge of electricity fills the bulb. The filament burns white and hot and overflowing itself, blinding Josiah where he stands—until the tungsten snaps and fizzles and Aaron, rising, leaps from bed.

His footsteps pound down the hall toward the back door. Josiah staggers after him, catching the door as it swings shut. Then they are outside in the garden with the weeds spread blackly round and a cold wind gusting, rattling the hedgerows.

Aaron is running, as he did from the gas, making for the stump or the tree that once grew there. He loses his footing and falls, vanishing into the high grass.

Josiah, sprinting, skids to a halt before him and stands over him, panting. The lightheadedness returns and with it a sensation of weightlessness as in the dream.

He sways but does not fall and he cannot look at the boy where he writhes on the ground, silent and shaking as on that long-ago morning and with only Josiah to kneel beside him—to hold him safe in that darkness and watch for the sun over the garden wall.

The sky is lighter, blue verging on purple.

One car passes, then another.

Won't be long now.

# CHAPTER FIVE

# LIQUOR CITY

## NICK MAMATAS

WO WEEKS SINCE the end of Prohibition and there were already
112 liquor licenses in this square-mile dump, down from 237 in
1917, when the war was on and the slogan was "Heaven, Hell, or
Hoboken by Christmas." So you gotta suppose that "meet me at that bar"
is what a college boy would call "a suboptimal directive." But college boys
were smart, and this particular college boy was smart enough to flatter you
by deciding that you're smart enough to know the establishment he meant.
Or he thought he was, anyway. It had better be Dillenger & Jeffson's on
Washington and Tenth. The oldest bar in town, located just a few blocks
from the piers. That just means we got the tipsy trade, rather than the fresh-
faced fellas right off their boats. Back in December, the joint was serving ice
cream and phosphates, and if you were lucky, or knew the soda jerk, you
could get a little ting in your tang.

I know. I was the jerk. I seen the college boy in here, every day, though
I never served him till after Prohibition ended, when it was elbow to elbow
against the bar and snowy outside. Given our usual clientele—longshoremen,
sailors on shore leave, Pinkertons, and ferry-riders from Manhattan, where
the City Fathers demand that the bars close for five hours a day—he stood
out like a weed among the canned hams. The college boy ordered his usual: a
vanilla Coke, and a scoop of ice cream. I thought it was a prank.

"You can order a beer now," I told him. "The G-men have been called off. It's one hundred percent Constitutional! We got a twenty-one-cent special for an all-night growler. It's almost Christmas!"

The college boy leaned in, like we were pals, and tried to whisper something to me. After I shouted "What?" in his face a couple of times, he got the picture and yelled back, "Is there any sort of quiet place to meet a man in this city?"

"Meet a man?" I laughed at him.

"About a book! An important book."

"You want a quiet place to meet a man and talk about a book? Get outta here, you queer! I don't want to have to hit a man, or a girl, with glasses." College boy didn't say another word, but he didn't leave either. He just gobbled up his ice cream in three huge bites and then he skedaddled out into the winter. Musta had one heck of a headache after that stunt.

I remembered his face because I never forget a queer, and because he left a fin on the table. Not so often you get a 1,328 percent tip, not even when an entire shift of stevedores show up swimming in booze and want one more round . . . just in case the Supreme Court decided to put the kibosh on the Twenty-First Amendment. And I seen his face again, six months later, when a dark-complexioned woman came in, holding a big book. It was the Stevens freshman face book and she had the fag's face circled in a thick ring of ink, like she'd traced the circle a hundred times.

"I'm to meet a man in this bar," she told me, and I was about to give her the boss's standard hoor speech—don't use the alley, don't come back more than twice a night, and Jesus, Mary, and Joseph, wear some panties if you're going to sit on our stools—but then she lifted the book from her enormous foreign-looking satchel and opened it to the page with college boy's picture.

"This bar, eh? You sure it ain't some other bar?"

She didn't answer at first. I got a good look at her, and saw that she was dark, but not a Negro. Some sort of real African, from Ethiopia or thereabouts, with wide eyes and a sandy brown skin tone. Like a queen out of pulp fiction, she sat straight up on the stool, and then I realized that she wasn't my audience, I was hers. Her clothing, too, wasn't the usual department-store frock, but a long and flowing number that could have fit a whole other lady in it had this dame been in the mail-order bride business.

"I am not sure at all. There are so many places like . . ." she looked around, those wide brown eyes just brimming with disgust, "this, in town. I've been seeking him for some time."

I'm a soda man turned suds puller, but I have a head for figures and a pretty good memory and I don't mind flaunting it a bit, especially when some darkie is looking down her nose—regal as it is—at me and my jewel of Jersey, Hoboken. "I seen your fella around, sister," I told her. "Months ago. But he was looking for a man, not a girl, if you catch my drift."

She laughed at me, like I was a little runt or something. "Girl!" she cried. Suddenly, there was a knife in her hand. Suddenly, there was a knife right under my Adam's apple. I had a grip on a bottle under the bar, but I wasn't gonna be fast enough, not even fast enough for revenge.

"My name is Mahlet," she said. The guys on either side of her turned from her to the very interesting bottoms of their mugs. "You may not call me by my name, but if knowing it keeps you from calling me *girl,* consider it a gift."

"How about we make it a deuce and you put down the knife," I said. "Next round's on the house." There wasn't no percentage in mouthing off to her, or in telling her that the second she put down the knife I'd have her out in the alleyway, getting her ribs kicked in. Who knows if she'd manage to de-ball a bouncer before we put her down anyway? She did put down the knife, and I told her, "Anyhow, you got the right establishment, but you're the wrong sex—ah, young miss."

"Maybe I am here for him, but he is not expecting me," she said.

"'Zat explain the apple-corer, then?" I put the bottle I'd been holding on the bar top. It was about as clean as it gets, and now I would have been pleased to muss it again. "We're a place of business. Why don't you wait for him outside? It's a nice summer evening."

"Your town smells like an abattoir," she said.

"You think I don't know any *français*? That's just the river and what's being unloaded on Pier 13. Stick around. In the morning, Hoboken will smell like Tootsie Rolls, I guarantees yuh."

"What is being unloaded on Pier 13?" Mahlet asked, suddenly interested. I laughed and told her it was New Yorkers. Then I finally got out of striking distance of that crazy dame.

I kept an eye on her though. The other barback took her order—a coffee, black, which she didn't like because it wasn't strong enough—and she nursed it all evening. She pulled another thick book from her satchel and flipped through it, carefully arranging her drink, and her elbows, to keep everything and everyone away from it. There wasn't much trade otherwise. Friggin' Tuesdays.

We get all types at Dillenger & Jeffson's . . . no—strike that, we get one type. Hefty guys, like my mother would say; proletarians, the CP would call them. Not Nubian ladies reading a moth-eaten volume of the *World Book Encyclopedia* and sipping black coffee without even the common decency to come in drunk. She had to be waiting for the college boy, but why had he shown up in December, to meet some "man"?

And then *he* came in. Another skinny kid, too young to drink had he been in Newark or even dirty Jersey City. He looked like the college boy, but only from a distance. Where college boy was girlish, this kid had big wop features and blue eyes that belonged on a movie poster. He had a nervous jitter about him, but the type to lash out with a one-two combo rather than cut and run. By then the lady had been given a wide berth, but he plopped down on the stool right next to her and smiled and called her ma'am like she was white. And then he whispered something in her ear. I seen it before from this fella—every bartender in Hoboken had—but he still surprised me, because his little rap worked even on Mahlet. He smiled a slick seducer's smile, and Mahlet, I swear, batted her eyelashes. If she had her knife to his balls, they were both too good to let on. She brought out the face book and pointed, and he nodded and hiked his chin back toward the front door.

Was it a special night? A full moon, or did a mysterious star shine in the East? Had a great tidal wave delayed a ship coming from the Port of Djibouti for six months? The door opened, the bell jingled, and there was college boy, in shirtsleeves and short of breath. He ran up to the couple and announced, "I came as soon as I heard you were . . ." Then, nothing. Hoboken was still a small town. Some strange lady shows up, everyone hears about it five minutes later. Call it a fringe benefit of living in the Mile Square City.

I poured myself a drink and had to watch what was gonna happen next. No bartender wishes for fisticuffs, especially not over a dame, but like I said, I have a head for numbers and the odds were this was gonna be some kind of big to-do.

"You," said college boy.

"Seymour," said little greaseball Romeo.

College boy's eyes went to the book, then he frowned. It was his own school's face book. Under it though, was the book he wanted. The *World Book Encyclopedia*. I still call it that.

"Where did you get that, and who is this woman?" Seymour demanded. It was like a radio drama. If only the bar had an organ in the corner instead of three tired stevedores.

"Don't you know who I am?" Mahlet said. Then she said her name again. I could hear it more clearly this time, because there wasn't a knife to my neck clogging up my ears. I have to say, when I heard it I thought to myself . . .

"That's a man's name," Seymour said. He was as confused as I was. "Isn't it?"

"It is not. Not where I am from. Not in Ethiopia."

"Seymour . . ." said the other guy, an edge in his voice.

"Francis . . ." Seymour said to him, his voice cracking.

"Now Francis, isn't that a woman's name?" Mahlet said.

Francis didn't like that, but he didn't backhand Mahlet like I thought he might. The knife was on her lap again. Somehow. She had quick hands.

"I want the book. You were supposed to be here months ago."

I figured I'd better butt in before the heads started butting any more.

"The ocean is treacherous," Mahlet said. "People are treacherous. I was delayed, and found myself in a city with a bar on every street corner. I've spent weeks looking for you. Do they teach you nothing at that little mansion on the hill?"

"What, Stevens Institute?" Francis said. "Those eggheads don't know nuthin', not practical knowledge anyhow. Ol' Seymour was a pal when we were playing stickball together, but now he's a—what, a mechanic?"

"Mechanical engineer."

"—ing student," Francis said.

"Would anyone here like a drink?" I said. "If not here, maybe at one of the other fine establishments in town. Maybe down at the police precinct; you can all partake of Captain Schmidt's famous bottomless growler."

Francis turned to me and tried to stare me down. I had my tumbler in hand, ready to screw it into his pretty-boy face. He said, "Do you know who I am?"

Yeah, and that's the story of how Frank Sinatra introduced himself to me, before he became big. When his mother was still getting him gigs here and there, around town. Before he was even a goddamned singing waiter. How you like that? You're getting two stories for the price of one. But yeah, I knew who he was. He was Dolly's little prince, and Dolly spent a lot of her time down at the local Democratic Club, on her knees. Yeah, she had some pull in the city and the county, but I wasn't going to let her teeny-bopper Lothario push me around.

I also wasn't going to let him get stabbed through the ribs by some foreign fanatic lady. I liked my job. Hell, I liked my legs. The real issue was Seymour, the college boy. He was the one brewing the trouble, so I told Frank Sinatra, "Yeah, I know who you are," and then looked over his shoulder at Seymour and said, "If you're not ordering a drink, you get the hell out of here."

I have to say, I wasn't expecting the pistol, and I wasn't expecting he'd get it cocked against the woman's temple before she could stab him, or Frank Sinatra deck him, or me heave my tumbler at his nose.

"I want the book. Give it to me. I've been going from bar to bar, sure I'd missed my appointment, for months," he said.

Here's a tip: when a man has a gun in his hand and he's talking instead of shooting, make conversation. "You went to ninety different bars, looking for a man with a book, and it turned out to be a lady with a book who was talking to another man. Why'd you even keep looking? How did you know you weren't just stood up?" I asked him. "Is that right?"

"I knew that nobody else had the book, because when I look up at night, I can still see the stars," Seymour said.

"Ain't you the poet," Frank Sinatra said. He was staring daggers at Seymour. Me, too. I think we were both hoping that the lady was slowly easing her hand to her knife. Then Frank sang:

When I look up at night.
I can still see the stars.
I met a dark woman.
In a Hoboken bar.
When the stars are right.
In my lonely room
I'll hold her in my heart.

The bar stopped when he opened his mouth. Maybe you just saw the man on TV, or when he was too famous to be good, or when he was just a fat old man, but let me tell you, Frank Sinatra could sing. Everyone looked up from their drinks, or their conversations, or their friggin' peanuts, to take a look. He could croon so well, Seymour didn't even notice the knife going in. And no, there were no witnesses. Yeah, I know what I said about everyone looking up to watch the scene too. Welcome to New Jersey, son. Welcome to Hoboken.

Seymour grabbed for the book, almost tripping over his own guts to get to them. He knocked the face book off the bartop and ate a straight right from Frank Sinatra. His ol' man had been a boxer and a firefighter, so skinny little bantamweight Frank knew how to throw a punch.

The other book fell open in front of me and I looked down at the open pages.

What can I tell you about what I saw? What do you want to hear? I've got a head for numbers. I got a good memory; I never forget a face or a regular's order. I never seen a thing in my life, not before or since, like the two pages, that big open spread, of what was in that book. This'll sound crazy, but here it is: it was like Sinatra singing, but different. Like Frank Sinatra's voice, and the smell of gunpowder, and the feeling of guts in my hand as I tried to shove them back inside poor stupid Seymour, and it was also like when I finally settled down and married Stella and we spent two years living in a cramped efficiency apartment and then she lost the baby because it only had a single Y chromosome somehow, and it was like when the doctor bent me over and fingered me good and told me that just to be safe he'd have to run some more tests on my prostate and it was like the chemo running in my veins, those pages. That poison ink, doing a number on my brain and an entirely different one on my body. Don't think I ain't educated; there's more than one way to come to some book smarts. I know what the scientists say, what the philosophers say—there is no difference between the mind and the body. It's not a *dooooality*. But it was then. Somewhere north of my forehead, I caught a glimpse of the heavens opening up and angels as big as stars smiling down at me. It was too much. And my body, it was like someone had unscrewed the fuse and stuck a penny in the slot to keep the juice flowing because it was three o'clock in the morning and the hardware store was closed. There was nothing to shut me down, so it just started burning, from the inside out.

I could feel myself dying. It was glorious. But I didn't die, you see. I lived. I lived for you to come down to Washington and Tenth so I could tell you this story, because I knew someone would come and ask, eventually. I got friends all over town. You didn't know what bar to poke your head into either, because Frank Sinatra's mother had leverage with the cops, and with every newspaper in Hudson County. So you asked around, at 111 bars before someone recommended Dillenger & Jeffson's. But I don't work there no more. I'm an old, old man. Even my friggin' kids, the two that lived, are dead now.

The lady reached over the bar, snapped the book shut—I took a faceful of dust and have never stopped smelling the desert since—and ran out of the bar. Headed right back to the pier, I guess. Who knows what Seymour had promised, or what she had promised him? Both came ready to kill, that's for sure. Maybe she made it back to Ethiopia. Maybe the wops killed her when Mussolini invaded. Damn, maybe that's why the wops invaded. That just came to me. It smells right. You know they all hang together, the Eye-talians. *La Cosa Nostra*, and all that. How do you think Frank Sinatra got so famous? He could sing like an angel, but so could lots of skinny boys from New Jersey.

Frank Sinatra? Yeah, go ask Frank Sinatra what happened. He got a look at the pages, too, when Mahlet reached over and grabbed the book. The *World Book*. Yeah, I'm sure Frank Sinatra will *tell all*. Good luck with that, son. You're no smarter than a college boy. I'd spit in your goddamn drink if I were still a jerk, working behind the bar.

# IN WAVES

## S.P. MISKOWSKI

**F**OAM AND FROTH and the tug of the sea. Mr. M's children riding the ocean swells. Night broken by their ecstatic cries. Thrown headlong, arms and legs splayed, underwater and then onto the shore.

High above, in his studio, the Master turns his back to them, reluctantly. The model is waiting. She won't move until he gives the word.

"Thighs gently yet firmly clasping the broomstick, darling. Remember, you're flying. Like this." He takes her sublime flesh in his hands like a sculptor, and makes the adjustment. Not for himself, he explains, but for the photograph. He studies the S-shaped curve of her body. Calibrates. Adjusts a lamp, checks a meter. Steps behind the camera once more. Master of the studio, both Titan and Man in the eyes of his models.

The missus of the season brings tea on a silver tray. Slips into the room in a gossamer robe and out with a whisper of orange blossom. The Master calls her "Mrs. M," though her mother refused to sign papers, and slapped the girl's face and threatened with a leather strap. "Mrs. M" then did what children have done for centuries. She ran away. With a desire to live, to be seen and heard and loved, beating a manic rhythm in her heart. It's what girls of ample cheek and bosom do in droves, now, in waves. They run from wicked parents into the arms of gentle masters, men like Mr. M.

Hollywood is built on their bones. There are no markers on their graves. Only the tide and the ages.

*Chateau.* He calls this bleached white miniature castle on the side of the hill facing the ocean a "chateau." Laguna Beach he can well afford, not the Palisades. He doesn't say it out loud, but this is as far as he can bear to live from the City of Angels. Middle-aged and still burning with ambition! He's half mad. Hoping the gods of celluloid may yet call him home. He withers in the sun.

"Arch your back a bit more, darling."

She obeys. All of his children obey. Not because they're afraid. Because he loves them.

Insidious, isn't it? The longing for love. It's what they all crave. Love is Mr. M's siren call, and mine.

Among the books and pamphlets lining the shelves of every room—*Shadows of the Occult*; *Las Reglas de Ruina*; *Ritual and Sacrifice*; the *Cthäat Aquadingen*; *The Prehistoric Pacific in Light of the "Ponape Scripture"*—my pages are barely noticeable. My influence incalculable. When the doyens of his art decide to label and ruin him, when the petty realists denounce pictorialism and ridicule Mr. M's optical theories, when they call him a pornographer, Satanist, voluptuary, sadist, the only name he denies is the last.

"I've never harmed a soul. They pour themselves into me, my children. I don't take them from their homes by night and spirit them away."

He's right. He doesn't even advertise. The golden youths appear on his doorstep by magic. The salt air and white sand call them here, to dreams of fame or glory. To my purpose. To their destiny.

He merely opens the door.

CHAPTER SIX

# EYES ON FIRE

## CODY GOODFELLOW

I WAS RELAXING in the solarium after my morning bath when the orderly brought the telephone. I remember thinking that someone must have been very resourceful to find me here, and very forceful to make them put the call through.

"Willis Kester?" Her voice was low, with an undertone like silk ripping. The faintest ash-trace of a foreign accent. "The Willis Kester, the scenarist of *A Lady's Revenge* and *Voyage to Kalimantan*? Director of *Face of Satan*?"

I was.

"I want to produce *To Slay the Sun*," she said.

I didn't ask who she was. I just sat there and let the phone buzz in my ear like hair growing. "Is this somebody's notion of a joke? Who put you up to this?"

"I assure you, I am quite sincere, and eminently capable. I am unaffiliated with any studio, but I have been looking for exactly such a property for some time, as a demonstration of certain aesthetic and philosophical principles."

For the first time in nearly ten years, I caught my breath. "How'd you find it? I only showed it to a few producers, and they didn't bite."

"You gravely offended and frightened half the studio heads in town with it, and then you assaulted one." She made a sound like fangs going into a neck. "Don't you even know why?"

I rolled my eyes, looking up at the high yellow orderly holding the receiver against my face. I told her I'd always had problems with my best work.

"This is your best work here . . . or it would be, if you took it where it belongs. If you actually understood what you're playing with."

I said nothing.

She cleared her throat, or maybe she lit a cigarette with her breath. "I'd like to meet you. A car should arrive to pick you up within the hour. See that they have you ready."

This was passing strange to me, as Lake Arrowhead was more than an hour from anywhere, and I was hardly here on my own recognizance.

"The car is already on its way, Mr. Kester. Do be ready?"

She hung up, and the orderly took the phone. I asked him to loosen the straps on my straitjacket so I could get ready for my big date.

A CREAMY WHITE Packard limousine, a custom job, floated behind the hedges like the ghost of a battleship. My favorite orderly wheeled me out in the same shiny gabardine suit I'd been wearing when I got committed.

A dog-eyed brute in silver livery got out to conduct me to the open doors. A face peeked out that darkened doorway that made the sun hide its face behind a cloud. "Why, Mr. Kester, what have they been doing to you in this terrible place?"

I told her it was better than I deserved, and brushed off the driver's arm. The orderly spit out his gum and said something under his breath.

I climbed into the car with some chagrin, feeling weak as tea, hiding my eyes from the brightness of that face. White gold ringlets made a blinding corona round a heart-shaped face that was eyes and bee-stung lips that whispered, "You talk funny."

"You should hear me sing."

"Why, you've got no teeth! Are you *really* so old?"

"Probably older than your father."

"*Nobody's* older than my father," she said, "and he's got all his teeth."

I tried to explain how the clinic had perfectly good reasons to confiscate my dentures, but she wasn't having my excuses. "Tip him, Ulrich," she said. The driver caught the orderly halfway across the lawn by his collar, then knocked his teeth out his ass.

I sank into the leather seat opposite that face, still shading my eyes. The stylish white tennis dress and skirt offered no respite. The legs, in nylon socks up past her knees, were bowstring taut but never did an honest day's walking in their lives.

"You're Mr. Kester," she said, like she'd won Twenty Questions. "Ms. Hawthorne says I must put myself completely in your hands."

"To what end?"

The way she looked at me shelled and roasted me. The blood rushed to my face so hard I feared it'd soak her dress. "Why, Mr. Kester! You're going to make me a star!" If she was seventeen, I was seventy. She wasn't the dry, haughty voice on the phone. Hers was cotton candy. Her accent was from everywhere.

I showed my trembling hands and all fifty fingers. "You might want to find a steadier rock upon which to build your legend, Miss . . ."

"Gift," she said, "Sybil Gift. My agent said I should change it because it's German, but Ms. Hawthorn wouldn't hear of it." She busied herself uncorking a bottle of champagne in a silver bucket and pouring me a glass over my forceful refusals. "Fie on your condition! Ms. Hawthorn said when she read your script, that you had clearly studied the book and penetrated closer to the heart of the secret than any of the others."

We toasted the Secret, whatever it was. I needed more than one glass. I still couldn't remember as much as I pretended to, but the more I thought about it, the more I thought about jumping out at the next railroad crossing. Instead, I tried to play catch-up with this train steaming away with my future. "So, this Hawthorne party is producing the film, and you're starring . . . What studio is picking it up? Who's attached to direct?"

The Packard hit something in the road that threw her off her seat and into mine. I smelled vanilla and wolverines in rut. "There's no studio, silly. And you know who the director is."

The car hit that thing again. She slid onto and around me, giggling. I steadied myself against her hand and ripped it back before something could slap me, or worse. This girl was a lollipop, a fuzzy Easter bunny, easier to skin than an orange, but something hovered over her like the jaws of a beartrap. In my prime, I wouldn't have batted an eye, but for most of my prime, I didn't even exist.

"I suppose you could read for, uh . . ." I chased thoughts around my head like a blind cat at a mouse party, and caught nothing.

"My, you are pretty scatterbrained," she said, giggling again. She said something else, but I slept through it.

When I woke up, the Packard was parked on Wilcox, out front of my bungalow, except it wasn't there. The whole two-story crackerbox had burned and scattered to the four winds, taking most of the adjacent units and leaving the rest uninhabitable. I went up the buckled brick walk to stand in the courtyard.

Margaret had thrown me out a week before I cracked up and took a swing at some chiseling shit-heel at Paramount. I figured I'd patch it up and get back on top and we'd move into a nicer place than that shack on stilts, up in the hills above the maddening searchlights.

Sibyl came up behind me, her voice offering anything but help. "Mr. Kester, I'm sorry, I thought you knew. Those bad men at the clinic must've kept it from you, I can tell from your face . . ."

I asked what happened to my wife.

"Ms. Hawthorne said there was a fire. She didn't get out, and . . . she wasn't alone. I'm real sorry . . . Were you still real fond of her?"

I wanted to go back to the clinic, but the producer I attacked paid for it because they told him it'd be worse than jail, and they were right. I'd been staying at the Starshine Motor Lodge on Western when I got committed. Everything I had was in a trunk in a room with a week paid on it. That was three months ago.

She smiled, leading me back to the limo like leading a balloon. "Ms. Hawthorne, she went to that fleabag motel and made them turn over your things. I hope this helps a little." She put something small and cool in my hand. I looked away for a moment as I slid them into my mouth, then turned back and grinned at her.

I HAD NOWHERE else to go.

I should've jumped in the ocean.

Throwing in with some rich widow who fancied herself a wildcat movie mogul would help propel me to hitherto undiscovered depths of career suicide.

I'd been around long enough to know better, but nothing I'd done right had ever gotten me anywhere. After following the business out from New York in '17, I was a supporting player at Sennett and Reliant and going nowhere. Then in '24, I got my big break.

I was in the passenger seat of a Bugatti driven by a studio head who shall remain nameless, when he lost a race with a freight train. I lost most of my teeth, full function of my right leg and my face took a ferocious pounding, but not so bad I couldn't switch seats with the driver before the Highway Patrol found us.

The two extras and a wardrobe girl who were passed out in the back died instantly. When I recovered, I was writing four dozen two-reelers a year. My looks scared kids and animals, so I got only crime yarns and thrillers. After a few modest hits, they even let me try my hand at directing. It only took me three hobbled, castrated features to undo all the good will that lucky accident had bought me.

It wasn't the jump to sound but the damned Code that killed me. Everything I did had a Puritan chorus shouting it down. Three scenes from *A Lady's Revenge* were cut, but the Decency League assaulted us several times in public after a tabloid ran stills of the infamous castration scene. *Face of Satan* was released in a neutered form with a new title, but the League still picketed it out of theaters sight unseen.

While I did penance in cowboy serials, I ransacked libraries and morgues and police blotters looking for real horror. They wanted me to terrify them, but not with anything remotely frightening. They wanted something they'd never seen before for no money at all. Gothic thrillers were played out; this new Wolf Man with Chaney's soused, oafish sequel was a sideshow. They wanted something new and fantastic to take people's minds off the troubles in Europe and their empty pocketbooks. They wanted to see Frankenstein get pantsed by Abbott and Costello.

I wanted to give them real fear. If they wouldn't let me show them a monster, I would make them shit their plush seats with something they couldn't see at all, and make them beg me for a happy ending.

*To Slay the Sun* was supposed to do for witches what *Dracula* did for vampires. It had taken three months of intensive electroshock to make me forget all about it.

The story had come from outside of everything I knew, and had gone right back into the black. It stirred me up inside until I lost control. I'd always been fighting for my life, and never laid a hand on another man or woman in anger. I don't know what I was fighting for when I attacked that man.

I had no reason to expect laurel leaves and cocaine from any of the studios, but the rejections I'd come to depend on had always been polite, amicable affairs, sometimes over a Liberty Loaf luncheon at the commissary. But this script that'd come out like a two-headed calf from a narrow-hipped kid, that had smelled to me like no mere success, but a conquest, was a stillbirth that poisoned every well in this desert, and I had no idea why.

We went west until it turned into north, and then east and up into the tortured canyons and eucalyptus groves above Malibu's bohemian Eloi colonies. After the road went unpaved and the ruts began to rock me to sleep, I asked if she lived up here.

"Oh, no," Sibyl said, chuckling. "Ms. Hawthorne has a sizable estate in Pasadena. This—if you look out that window, you'll see it—is our location."

I both did and didn't believe it. Out of the coastal scrub and brushfire-blackened live oak arose a curtain wall and towers of rough-hewn stones, battlements and buttresses, and even a moat with a drawbridge.

"That's Declan Edmonds, our knight in shining armor." The rider who met us at the raised portcullis was dressed for a foxhunt rather than a tournament. A dashing young martinet I recognized from something I'd walked out on.

"I found him! Tell everyone!" Sibyl cried out the window as we crossed the bridge. The moat was choked with rusted auto wrecks and horse skeletons.

The castle was a dazzling travesty. An extraordinary set constructed with plaster, canvas, telephone poles and railroad ties, it at least smelled authentic. Everything not freshly marbled with paint was flossy with Old World mold. Everything falling apart in spite of the small army of carpenters engaged in cosmetic repairs as the chauffeur unloaded my luggage. I was stunned to see my trunk, seized by a twitching sense that I was overdue for my afternoon shock treatment.

"I'll take you to your room so you can freshen up," Sibyl said. She led me across a courtyard crowded with lighting stands, sandbags and flats, and up a rickety spiral staircase.

The railing swung away under my hand and fell to the dining hall floor, twenty feet below. "How old is this set?"

"It was built for *Prisoner of Zenda*, the silent one." She turned and grinned. "They said it was cursed. . . ."

My room was a garret in a tower where you could see the ocean, if you brought a picture of it. It stank of guano and cat piss and the corner of the room by the arrow-slit-window was rotted through by rain.

I sat down and shook. I suppose I tried to cry for a while.

When I could manage, I emptied out my trunk. On top of the books and notepads and stolen stationery and the dingy linen suit and the worsted wool one that were all the clothes I had left, someone had inserted a raw silk blouse and a pair of maroon jodhpurs, wool socks, underwear and a beret, and a freshly typed copy of the shooting script for *To Slay the Sun*, albeit with a new title. I dumped it all out on the floor and ripped the liner out of the suitcase. Inside the crevice between the inner and outer shell, I found it.

*To Slay the Sun* was a Medieval bodice-ripper about a young French knight smitten by Bianca, a beautiful child of the forest, though he is promised to another. When his forbidden lover follows him to the castle, she is seized and accused of witchcraft, and an unseen horror strikes down her accusers one by one.

As Sir Robert struggles to save Bianca from the stake, his enemies begin dying as well, rended limb from limb by an invisible thing that leaves no trace, but points unmistakably back to Bianca. When the monster seeks to murder his betrothed, Sir Robert must choose to save his lady fair, thereby himself falling into the clutches of the Inquisition.

Not much to it, aside from the calculated tilt towards the ladies waiting for their men fighting overseas, but the depiction of magic in it was where I had excelled myself. It all came from the damned book.

I bought it off a sheriff's deputy named Wiederhorn. Wiederhorn had a bit part as a minor devil in *Face of Satan*. Long ago, when movies were seen and not heard, I'd made the cast and crew watch *Häxan*, and let slip that I'd pay anything to see real witchcraft. Assuming he'd return to the screen if he fed me good dirt, he occasionally put me onto something too gruesome for the papers. Usually it was kid stuff—chicken blood and broken tequila bottles, chalk pentagrams around gutted black cats.

He said it was found at a possible murder scene that never strung together—copious human blood all over, and a copper bowl with a badly decayed human placenta in it. A body never turned up, but the cops always nursed theories we could never touch in the movies.

Hollywood was rife with bright young things who got knocked up instead of discovered, and some creeps out there took advantage by offering to get them scraped. Satanists liked to eat babies, occult expert Deputy Wiederhorn told me.

They staked out the spot for a week but got nowhere, and come the day when the property room got cleared out, Wiederhorn had a moment of weakness, and thought of me.

I had taken my lighter out and touched it to one of those grubby, slightly yellowing pages—but they seemed to blacken without burning at all—when Ulrich came to get me.

In a big, drafty grotto that used to be a chapel, they'd parked a bed like a Rose Parade float over the altar, sheathed in gauzy veils and musty brocade curtains from an opera house. A real stained glass rose window submerged the room and the bed's occupant in a bruise-colored murk. A nurse in a surgical mask and gloves sat beside her, reading a magazine.

She looked like a little silver doll propped against a palisade of pillows. The chauffeur crushed my arm when I moved any closer than the bedchamber doorway. Beside an intercom speaker opposite the door, a massive portrait of the great woman in her prime hung like a vengeful revenant. Wild red hair and skin creamy enough to drink, dreamy emerald eyes with the slightest, sleepy almond shape, and a Mannerist neck long enough for six hands to strangle it. Hard to reconcile with the papery crackle of a faintly foreign voice that seeped out of the speaker. "Mr. Kester, I have all the money in the world, but not much time. How quickly can we get under way?"

I told her how long it normally took to develop, prepare, cast, rehearse and shoot a five-reel feature.

"Then it's a good thing we've done most of that already. Tomorrow, you can begin shooting, but tonight, you simply must make adjustments to your script. I hate to tell you your job, but your research is shoddy. From your writing, I took you to be a devotee, but you have much to learn. . . ."

"About what, pray tell?"

"About history, dear boy. And magic."

What I knew about witchcraft you could drop in an ant's eye without bothering it. My feet started to carry me forward. I'd forgotten about the chauffeur, but he grabbed my arm again. "I can't work like this. This isn't how it's done, don't you understand?"

She struggled to rise up on an elbow. "I know how things are done down there, Mr. Kester. I know how roles are cast, and how films are pitched and deals sealed. I know what kinds of feasts are served to consecrate those bargains, and I know what they do with the scraps, when they've stuffed themselves sick.

"I've seen that if one wishes to make a motion picture and not a monument to one's own ego, then one only needs an army of artists and technicians, a mountain of gold and the will to step over blood. I have all those things in abundance. I would now like them to make me a motion picture. *Your* motion picture, by your hand, through your eyes, but the heart of it . . . you must find that in the book."

How did she know about the book? Of course, she'd had them go through my things, and she must have picked out something in the mumbo jumbo I threw into the witches' orgy scenes in the script.

"I have taken pains to choose a proper cast and a crew familiar to you. Have you met them yet?"

"The only one I've met is your ingénue Sibyl, and she doesn't add up. What role did you have in mind for her?"

"I see her in both leading lady roles. She is an accomplished natural actress, and will readily hold any shape into which you bend her."

"I don't doubt it, but . . ."

"She is wise beyond her years, unlike most of the idiots of her generation."

"You wouldn't hate their youth so much if you could buy it."

"I'd have no use for youth, but I would happily purchase their stupidity. Now, about Ms. Gift. . . ."

I scoffed. "Bianca is much too mature for her. We need Rita Hayworth, not Shirley Temple. I'm not going to fight the Hays Code on two fronts."

"Never mind the Hays Code," she said. "This film will not be savaged by censors for a pedestrian audience. I want you to be true to your own vision, and go where the material takes you."

I told her what I thought of the new title. The intercom yawned. "So these . . . changes . . . you want me to make?"

"Just as I said . . . You'll know what to do, when you've seen what real magic is for."

Once, I could have argued all night, but lock a man up for ninety days and drug or beat or shock any resistant impulses out of him, and he'll find it hard to frame any reply but silence.

"I suppose you're hungry," she interjected at last. "Dinner will be sent to your room, just tell Ulrich what you'd like. And be prepared to join us at midnight."

"For what?"

"For your education in witchcraft, Mr. Kester. High time you learned how the nonsense in that book of yours actually works."

I WAS DRUNK enough to see two of each of them sitting around the Arthurian round table when Ulrich poured me into my seat. I slowly came to recognize them all through the clouds of cloying incense and syrupy light from a Moroccan lantern.

Taking my left hand, Herman Bialecki, a brilliant cameraman whose private blue films got him hounded out of Weimar, Germany; Dabney Thiessen, once a silent-era leading man, drummed out for his piping voice and raging dipsomania; Cleon Hamilton, the brilliant stage actor and operatic tenor, exiled to France after his youthful minstrel show career was cut short upon revelation he was a natural Negro with a host of mulatto bastards on his heels; across from me, Hildy Patrice, a costumer and protégée of Erté, narrowly acquitted of poisoning a director who was "beastly" to him; R. L. Askew, my trusty second-unit man and a great auteur in his own right, of cross-burnings, lynchings, and Klan parades; holding my right hand, my old art director, Lionel Sharrock, opium fiend and rapist. Well, if they could spring one dangerous lunatic, why not two?

I said something glib about attempting to contact the world of the living, and was hushed like a child in church. This wasn't my first séance, but this one went off the script pretty quickly. A medium in a hooded linen robe circled behind us, reciting a litany that felt dimly familiar. "Colpriziana, Offina, Alta, Nestera, Fuaro, Menuet . . ." Something from that damned book, no doubt. She left us enclosed within a circle of salt.

The mumbled mantra devolved into animal grunts, then twisted off abruptly in a growling shriek from a cut throat. The medium climbed onto the table and paced around its circumference, pouring another circle of salt, then a triangle within it. As she passed, I recognized the coltish legs, at least. Ms. Hawthorne hadn't lied about her range.

The others took up the corrupted chant, "Agla, Tulu, Alim, Toxodo, Adon, Schadai, Iog Sotot Tetragrammaton." My lips moved, making the words I'd thought scrubbed out of my head. The medium turned in tighter circles, breathlessly intoning, *"the obedience of the living, the wisdom of the dead, the favor of those Outside—"*

It was pathetic. It was absurd.

For the first time in living memory, I was awake.

"I abjure and command thee to appear in the similitude of fire . . ."

If they could have seen us huddled down there in our phony dungeon, praying for glory and revenge, what would the principalities, thrones and powers of Hollywood do? Would they quake in fear of our occult potency? Or would they choke themselves laughing?

That's what I did. I laughed from the belly until I shook free of the hands of my condemned fellows, until I'd crushed every other voice in the room, until I began to vomit.

The incense and the alcohol and the unforgivable wrongness of it all came surging up out of me and I sicked up all over the table. I clung to the edge of it like a lifesaver in a hurricane, only dimly aware that no one was saving me because all the others were worse off than myself.

Through smoke and tears, I saw a white form floating motionless above the table. I saw a face made of twisted light. I heard a voice, speaking only to me, and a wind swept over me, brushing away incense and sickness. The wind carried the smell of her hair and the sound of her saying my name.

*Margaret*—

I smelled her hair, breath, sweat, blood. *So sorry I never believed in you,* I heard her say. *But you have real power now, the power to make a world where we can be together forever*—

I remember weeping and crying out her name and feeling ashamed of myself, but when I looked around, I was the only one in the room.

THE NEXT DAY, we began shooting.

What I remember of it was not so different from any other film shoot. It was war: a war upon reality. Sets were dressed, scenes were rehearsed, shots were blocked and lit and printed. We worked furiously and with a giddy joy to find ourselves working at all, together, with other damned souls who could never judge us.

The cast were almost fanatically dedicated, the crew as quick and quiet as the shoemaker's elves. The caterers set out banquets, with chalices of cocaine and Benzedrine beside the coffee before dawn, bales of marijuana, ziggurats of opium beside the champagne and caviar when we wrapped sometime around three every morning. My unit and Askew's ran concurrent on shifts Von Stroheim would've balked at. Some bulbs were inevitably burnt out and had to be quickly replaced, but otherwise, no one left the set.

From the first scene, I had trouble with Sybil. She made the wardrobe changes handily enough, but her Bianca was no different from her Lady Eleanor. The young peasant girl is innocent at the outset, but wounded, haunted by some past trauma, or insight into her tragic fate. Well she knows the unspoken currencies of nature, and the price to pay for taking what she desires. Lady Eleanor is chaste and loyal, an ideal of courtly love that leaves Sir Robert cold and unfulfilled.

After dinner, I rewrote the schedule. I opted to shoot her downfall first.

Originally, I had called for the appearance of Satan amid the cavorting witches—every prostitute and unemployed taxi dancer from Hollywood to Boyle Heights—to be a moment of supreme shock, to hint at, if never to blatantly depict, a bestial monstrosity plowing through the mounds of undulating flesh like a shark through a sea of meat, to imply such enormity and ferocity that Bianca's surrender to it renders her a pitiful thing, a broken blossom.

But the *Necronomicon* had a better idea. When the Devil emerges to defile her and grant her domain over her unrequited love, he is a handsome, worldly Negro who gently renders her untouchable, for all her wild beauty. Even a few of our professionals rebelled at the prospect of being seen in such a scene.

When Hamilton emerges from the orgy—glistening onyx majesty, clinging white limbs—the hooded acolytes hold her down and she utters the Egyptian gibberish of his true name, as taken from the Book, as he claims her. The camera drifts away, dazed, taking in the lascivious, bestial and imbecilic stares of the coven, the inscrutable leering of the moon and stars, and then something passes in front of the moon, plunging the scene into merciful shadow.

I tried to get away from her after we wrapped for the night, but Sybil followed me, asking in her highest, breathiest voice if we should go again. I pleaded a headache and retreated to my room, but she only cornered me there.

"You don't think I can do it," she pouted. Her tousled black wig hung down to touch her nipples against the sheet wrapped around her body.

"Never mind what I think. I'm just another hired hand. Go ask your Ms. Hawthorne where to find your motivation."

She came closer and I backed away unto the window. The floor buckled under my foot. I closed my eyes and wished her away.

"You'll just have to teach me."

I could smell the smoke from the torches and the incense and hairspray and a dozen kinds of sweat, but when I closed my eyes and took a breath, all I could smell was my dead wife's breath.

I opened my eyes.

"Teach me to be bad."

"No." I pushed her away.

"Punish me, then. What do bad girls get, Mr. Kester?"

I shoved her towards the door.

She slapped me, nails raking my skin. "You don't *know*. You write all those nasty, tantalizing things, but when it's real, you don't know what any dog in the street knows about how to take what you desire."

She went to slap me again and I trapped the hand, twisted her towards the door. She pivoted and slapped me with her other hand, raking my cheek. When I caught them both, she reeled me in and bit my chin, then my lip, until I bit her back. "Is that what you want?"

"Who cares what I want? I've been bad. Punish me."

I punished us both.

GOING FORWARD, THINGS went swimmingly. That must be why I remember almost none of it.

The second night, Dabney Thiessen, sleepwalking through the role of the inquisitor Brother Maurice, attempts to torture Bianca, but the whips, screws and hot irons only give her the giggles. I'd cut Thiessen off since breakfast for this, his most demanding scene. In an ecstasy of misplaced fervor, he was to torture her until an invisible party cut and defenestrated him. As Bialecki's camera drooled over Sybil's helpless form on the rack, a slender white tongue trapped between black teeth, Thiessen sweated and fretted until I tossed him to Askew to shoot his death scene, and stepped into the role myself.

I ordered Bialecki to tilt up from the torturer's ministrations to frame the moon and drooping wild roses peering through the barred window of the dungeon, but he lingers upon our elongated torchlight shadows on the slimy undressed stones. The hooded form works over the writhing body like a physician, expunging peals of corrupt laughter until the screams flow like clean, pure blood.

The next morning, she was still moody. Her Lady Eleanor smoldered, leering at her handmaidens like a scissor-kissing dyke. We wasted three takes before she took me aside.

"I can't find her," she says, in that low, smoky voice ravaged by hours of screaming.

I studied the book when the others slept, but there was no ritual for unscarring a soul.

"Did they," she asks, "at the clinic, did they give you . . . shock treatment?"

Lots of times.

"What was it like?"

Like dying in the electric chair, except they leave just enough to do it again tomorrow.

"Do you . . . know how to do it?"

I have the doctor give her a small dose of sodium pentothal and summon the electrician.

The film used us to make itself. Ms. Hawthorne issued her edicts via the intercom network that riddled the castle, and we scurried to obey until we collapsed, but her orders were wrung from her by an invisible mainspring. When it was done with us, we crawled into holes and drank each other dry. Rejected by coffins of our native earth, we emerged at the Magic Hour to feed ourselves to the ravenous camera.

And in the small hours when both shifts slept or toiled, entranced, I let the book read me.

This plane of being was a bubble being gnawed at on all sides by the vengeful dead and the insatiable unborn. The world was Swiss cheese, and the holes were filled with mindless gods and holy monsters. The universe was a shoddy clock mangling worlds, stars and galaxies in its blind idiot gears, and against all of it, we were not even dust.

But we could speak the Names and shed the Blood and the gods would heed us. At our command, the gears would race or grind to a halt. And as I came to know the Names and relish the taste of ionized blood in the air, I came to see how much more powerful a magus any director could be, if he only knew the Names of his true audience.

Draw a circle on the ground and evoke a miniature world, impervious to the hell summoned without. Within the circle of this set, within this relentless death-march orgy of a shoot, every glassy, bloodshot eye gleamed with the stardust promise that if we built it perfect, something great and

71

final would come, and we would go on forever inside the world we made, impervious to time, death, law and love.

What will they say when they dig us up? When the ones who come next find all those temples with skeletons in rows before all those tattered screens? They'll say we made humans into gods, we made a perfect afterlife and sacrificed our best and brightest to it on the wings of the worship of an unbearable world. They'll say we were the demiurges who got it right! We built heaven and hell and let anyone in for the price of a ticket. To rule the world, to know wealth, beauty, courage, love and death. We *should* become dust. The movies alone deserve to survive.

But there was still a hole in our cast. We required a stuntman. For the closing of the second act, Sir Robert proclaims himself Bianca's champion and demands a trial by combat. Wounded by this seemingly diabolically influenced betrayal, Lady Eleanor's father, Guy d'Averoigne, steps in to defend her honor and prove the witch's guilt.

Askew had already shot a boatload of footage of Declan Edmonds and Farley Wilberforce, the swashbuckling silent-era heavy.

Wilberforce's stand-in is wheeled out into the courtyard in Patrice's gaudy chainmail costume, and the hood is ripped off his face.

He stumbles, limping into the lights. He's older, fatter than Wilberforce, a lot older and fatter than the last time I saw him. Crooked nose, gold-framed spectacles, thick impeccably manicured silver hair surgically transplanted from a handsome cadaver.

I step into the light, letting him see my own limp, my smile like a mouthful of hobnails. And my smile is unfeigned, pure surprise and joy.

"What's the big idea? I've always paid what you asked? Why the rough stuff?"

He doesn't recognize me. "You haven't been here in seventeen years. I don't blame you for not recognizing me. The last time you saw me was the last time you were here . . . seventeen years ago."

"Good lord," he says, gasping, "Kester, isn't it? I always figured it was you, but my people could never connect you to it. Ten thousand or more every year, and you couldn't even get decent teeth. It didn't add up. Was this what you were saving it all for?"

"I've never squeezed you . . . not for money. I was just a face in the crowd in *Prisoner of Zenda*, but I was at the wrap party. I was soused and I needed a ride home, and the president of the studio gave me a ride, me and a bunch of in-the-bag nobodies . . . And you wrecked the car and killed three of us— nearly killed me too—and you weren't even drunk."

He looked around. "What kind of shakedown racket is this?" He couldn't see anything but black silhouettes behind the walls of lights and cameras. "Who put this together? Just *you*?"

"Maybe you know her better than me," I said. "Lorna Hawthorne."

"Lorna? You mean Lena?" He went white and tossed around like he was going to bolt. "Are out of your mind? What do you want from me? I gave you a career and you threw it away!"

I send Edmonds in with his sword drawn. His own tabard torn and bloodied, he staggers into the frame and drives the portly duke back against the wall. Here, Sir Robert proves his superiority in arms and turns away, but I order Edmonds to cut the stand-in's throat unless he talks.

"How did you know her?"

"It has to be her, but it can't! Her name was Lena Hathaway then. How did *you* know that *verrückte* whore? How'd she get her claws into you?"

"She's upstairs," I said.

It wasn't the right thing to say. He practically tried to cut his own head off on Edmonds' sword. "No, you're all insane! She can't be here! She was in the car, you moron!"

I was close enough now to make the jump. "Was she already dead from the abortion, or just dying? Were you trying to make some kind of deal with her baby?"

"It was *her* goddam idea, damn you! Lena was a grifter and a hophead. Goddam twist told me she could bring me power no money could buy, but she just got herself knocked up and tried to blackmail me. She said if I did what she wanted, if we gave it up, then we'd both be free. She wanted to have the Devil's baby, can you buy that?

"So I put her in the picture, and when we finished shooting, we go up on the hill and we chant some gibberish, and she lay down in the circle and made like she was fucking the sky and the moon went away like something in the sky just blew it out.

"Then she said it was hurting her, to cut it out. When we wouldn't, she cut herself, so help me. She set it down in the circle, and some others came and got it, I never saw their faces. She was bleeding out, but she was going on and on about these plans she had. I was trying to save her, you've got to believe me, but we got stuck on the tracks . . ."

He was openly weeping. "I'm sorry, Kester. We can work something out, you know we can, but whatever that *shiksa* told you about me, it's not true. She used me, and someone, I don't know who, used her . . ."

I told him I believed him completely, and summoned the second unit.

In the script, Sir Robert walks away from the defeated Guy d'Averoigne, when suddenly, the duke is lifted off his feet and rent asunder in midair by the bodiless abomination conjured by Bianca's unholy union with the Black Man.

I didn't stick around to watch. The stand-in's shrieking assured me that everything was going in the can.

I ran into Ulrich outside Ms. Hawthorne's boudoir. I thought he'd block me, but he shoved me into the chapel and shut the door.

"I'm so sorry to have put you off before," said the mummy over the intercom, "but I think you're ready to see the rushes."

I wasn't ready for anything that was happening. I ripped through seven veils to find the bed empty, the clammy eiderdown thrown aside as if Ms. Hawthorne was overcome by a miracle.

I shook the nurse. "Where is she?" The nurse arched her eyebrows at me over her mask, reached over to the intercom console on the nightstand and hit a switch.

Half a dozen projectors lit up and painted the walls with black and white blood.

It wasn't the film I'd been making, and it was. There must have been cameras as well as intercoms throughout the castle, because all my best work was on the screen: here, torturing Sybil with alligator clips and a car battery; there, attacking Dabney Thiessen with a hatchet, cleaving his splayed hand down to the wrist, down into the cavity between radius and ulna before giving it up and going for his eyes with my thumbs; and over there, I'm rolling on the floor in my own sickness before a column of smoke and fabric with my dead wife's face projected on it.

The invisible monster, revealed.

"I didn't do any of this," I said.

"Of course you did, darling, don't sell yourself short. Pictures don't lie, but they will. It'll be time-consuming to remove you from the frames, but I'm told there are remarkably talented artists going cheap since Disney's animators went on strike."

"You can't . . . use this . . ."

"Our audience is most discriminating. They understand the true costs and rewards of Art. A shame to erase such a performance, though. Your gifts as an actor quite eclipse your other talents."

"I'm not half the actor you are," I said, "Sybil."

I finally got to hear what her real laugh sounded like. "It took no particular talent to become my mother." She let the age and apathy fall away from her voice in layers, until she was a seventeen year-old succubus again. "I simply let her out. But you . . ."

I told her I didn't kill ———. I never touched him.

"He took your teeth, Will, like the studios took your teeth and killed your art."

I told her I couldn't go through with it.

"It's already done. See it through, and everything is yours. Everything you had, if that's all you can imagine. Everything, Will.

"Those nobodies out there, those worms, beg to be ground under our heels because we're the nearest to gods on this earth. We can be the ones, you and I, to step through that door, to be the first ones to ascend. A god is just a worm that feeds on worship. We can be gods, Will."

I ripped out the console and smashed the projectors. I threw myself on the bed and smelled the sheets and cried. The nurse didn't have to say anything when I demanded to know where they'd taken her, she only had to point.

The hill overlooking the castle had a pair of telephone poles set up atop it, and a crowd of men held torches.

I run up the hill, stumbling, crawling on all fours through scrub and thorns, and into the circle of cold white spotlights, through the mute mob of the crew, the cameras, the lights—

Bound atop the same pyre as the witch who stole his heart, our hero must stop her from uttering the words that will stop the dawn from coming by plunging the world into blackness in the only way he can—by inciting Lady Eleanor to set fire to the pyre and destroy them both before the hideous living darkness can engulf the sky and stop the world turning.

Edmonds is tied to a stake atop a pyre of pitch-soaked railroad ties. In a burlap shroud soaked in paraffin, he botches his lines until he vanishes inside a cone of orange-white fire when the kneeling Lady Eleanor touches his pyre with the torch.

Sybil turns and curtsies, then throws her torch at the witch's feet. "Everything you wished for," she says.

I run and leap into the fire.

I call her name, but she is still too sedated to recognize me. Under the burlap, she is bound to the telephone pole with iron chains. The smoke enfolds us in a perfect eclipse. The flames roar and feast on our clothes and hair. I scream and scream, but I pry at the red-hot chains until the flesh falls off my fingers in crisp black gobbets. "Margeret!"

She tries to say my name and inhales fire. I try to push the stake over, I try to break the links of burning chain with my teeth. I try until someone says *Cut.*

# CHAPTER SEVEN

# HORRORS WORSE THAN HELL

## ROBERT M. PRICE

**M**Y TEXT THIS morning is a familiar one, Mark 8:35: "He that seeketh to save his life, the same shall lose it." It is a ringing call to discipleship, to give all for the Lord Jesus Christ. We know it well, and we try our best to live up to it. And we live in a time when that call to self-sacrifice is no cliché, if it ever was. For everyone is well aware of the challenges the world faces today. The clouds of war, invasion, and devastation are looming like thunderheads on the horizon. Chancellor Hitler rants and raves and rattles his saber in Germany. Mr. Mussolini would revive the Roman Empire in unwitting fulfillment of biblical prophecy. In Japan we see the rise of Imperial Japan's so-called Greater East Asia Co-Prosperity Sphere. Isn't that what they call it? Many Bible students see in these developments the unfolding of the End Times. And I must confess it looks more and more that way.

In such a time, you have to ask, "Can things possibly get any worse?" Beloved, I believe they can. And that they will. We face very serious risks and must consider serious decisions. Remember the parable of the unjust steward. Caught embezzling, he knew he would be put out on the street with no livelihood. So what did he do, this rogue? He got busy cooking the books, forging bills for his master's debtors, cutting their debts in half. He figured they'd feel they owed him something and would take care of him after his sudden "retirement." And they did. Now, our Lord wasn't endorsing such shenanigans. What he was endorsing was the man's decisive action. And such decisiveness, my friends, is now required of us.

I am something of a wide reader, as many of you have remarked. I have always believed that wide reading is an important part of the Christian life. True, it is faith that saves the soul, not learning. Even the simple may be saved, and that is the glory of the gospel message; it is open to all. It is true that "knowledge puffs up, but love builds up." Amen and amen. But I have always supposed that, tempered with humility, knowledge gives us a better grasp of God's creation and our place in it. Ignorance is not holiness. It is not even an advantage.

But lately I have had cause to reevaluate that stance. A book came into my hands, a book from the Middle Ages. I could not resist its pages, though it was rather slow going. It was a strange and disturbing book. It was full of many weird and terrible things. I suppose that to most readers it would seem a compendium of the merest gibberish. There was no single subject. The book collected superstitions and legends. It was a religious volume, but whatever religion its writer belonged to, I had never heard of it. Strange names and stranger ideas. It was a curiosity shop of a book. At first I was amused. But not for long. The old book soon revealed itself as most unwholesome. I found myself wishing that I had not opened its covers.

I thought of Adam and Eve in the Garden of Eden. There was a tree of knowledge from which their Maker had commanded them not to eat. That passage had always puzzled me. How could there be knowledge that we would be better off not knowing? Did not our Lord Jesus declare that "the truth shall set you free"? But isn't that precisely what the wily old Serpent told Adam and Eve? And you know the result. That particular piece of knowledge, so sweet and tasty to the curious mind, proved to be a deadly poison that has infected the whole human race ever since. Look to Mr. Hitler and Mr. Mussolini if you want evidence of that. Or can't you see that far? Are you a little near-sighted? Then look into your own heart. Look at your own desires and your real motives under the microscope of your conscience.

When I put down that book, I felt like I had taken a bite out of that apple. And it was just like the little scroll in chapter ten of the Book of Revelation: it was sweet as honey in my mouth, to my curious mind, but it turned exceedingly bitter once I had swallowed it down. There was knowledge here, but knowledge I immediately wished I didn't know. Have you ever had a friend or a loved one reveal some dark secret about their past that you wish they had kept buried? Because of it, you can never look at them the same way, or feel the same way about them, again. It was the truth, all right, but you felt you could have gotten along perfectly well without knowing it. A fool's paradise? Maybe so. But any paradise lost to us is something to regret.

Childhood is like that, isn't it? Sometimes, don't we wish we could return to that small and simple world of easy choices and delights? Don't we occasionally wish we had never learned the things that make us adults? That neglected book Ecclesiastes puts it well: "With much wisdom comes much sorrow." Perhaps this is what the Lord Jesus means when he invites us to turn and become as children again if we would enter his kingdom.

But is that possible? Is it possible to unlearn the knowledge that has burdened us? I fear it is not. Saint Paul speaks of our much-vaunted "knowledge" as so many childish baubles. He says we will lose interest in them and never think of them again once we reach the maturity of full realization, "when the perfect comes." The perfection, he says, of "knowing even as we are known." What will we know on that day? He does not say, for the simple reason that the day had not yet come, so he didn't know.

But it is about to arrive.

Indeed, it is close enough that once-certain truths are starting to look like those childish trinkets. All the dogmas we have always been so sure of, sure enough to debate and dispute about, to hurl anathemas and divide over. They have begun to seem to me a pile of threadbare rag dolls and broken toy soldiers. The unnamed man in John, chapter 9, said, "This I know: I once was blind, but now I see." Amen. But the eyes of Adam and Eve "were opened," too. And there may be things we never saw, never knew, that we were better off being blind to. The Book of Revelation calls them "the deep things of Satan."

And, God help me, I know them now. And very soon you, too, will know them, like it or not. The world will know them. And they will make the atrocities of the Germans and the Japanese of which we are now hearing seem like a child's toys, too. They even make the fires of hell and judgment about which we preach look paltry by comparison.

The Revelation of Saint John says something else, too. It says that the Son of God whose eyes are as a flame of fire, whose voice is as a crashing cataract, would spare his children "the tribulation that is about to come upon the whole earth." How would he do that? What form would that deliverance take, do you suppose?

When I dropped that old book I was telling you about and picked up God's book, I paged through it, looking for some clue. And with the Holy Spirit's guidance, I found it. Suddenly I saw our text from Mark's gospel in a new light: "He that seeketh to save his life, the same shall lose it." I had always imagined that our Lord was warning us here not to be cowards, not to make compromises in order to save our skins.

But now I see what he must have really meant. He was telling us what to do if we wanted to save ourselves from the impending hour of trial: we must take definite action. We must be as decisive as that crafty steward who recognized the severity of the crisis that had come upon him. And I thought of what the Apostle Paul told the Corinthians about "the impending distress." He said, "I would spare you that." And, brethren, so would I.

*Attached note in police file: "Survivors report that at this point the Reverend Hoadley reached behind the pulpit and took out a rifle. He took aim and began firing at the fleeing congregation, finally turning the gun on himself. Police afterward found the bodies of his wife, his mother, and his three young children in their blood-soaked beds at the parsonage."*

# CHAPTER EIGHT

# LAYING THE WORDS

## DON WEBB

S URVIVORS REPORT THAT at this point the Reverend Hoadley reached behind the pulpit and took out a rifle. He took aim and began firing at the fleeing congregation, finally turning the gun on himself. Police afterward found the bodies of his wife, his mother, and his three young children in their blood-soaked beds at the parsonage."

Sheriff Wade gave me a copy of the police file the day before the Japs bombed Pearl Harbor. I had a first cousin on the *Arizona*, Joshua Lloyd Walton. We grew up together in Flapjack, Texas. His folks had moved away to Vernon, Texas, and I wound up in Mayflower, Arkansas, on account of blonde-haired Maggie Sue. I met her when her car broke down in Flapjack. Well, Reverend Hoadley put the period at the end of Maggie Sue's life sentence at the conclusion of his last sermon and made it pretty damn unlikely (if you'll pardon my French) that the Little Hope Baptist Church will ever have an organist again.

I wanted to enlist. I had tried before but my club foot had kept me out of the service. That's what they call irony, having a club-footed deacon working for the bedeviled minister at Little Hope Church. The world (as the Rev liked to say those last few months) is a funny place, and mankind is the butt of the joke.

Of course, they passed me by again.

So I threw myself into visiting the sick, feeding the poor and fixing the roof of the church. It might be awhile before we got a new minister, but the Southern Baptist Convention is pretty understanding and the church board began paying me a full salary so I didn't have to fix cars at Red's no more. I took to reading the Good Book and some literature of a wholesome sort that the SBC provided me with, and after a while I started services up again. We'd washed—that is to say, I'd washed—the blood from the church and parsonage, and I put in a hell of a Victory Garden with the help of the Sunday School. We started having special Wednesday night services for the boys in the war—and we always said prayers for Maggie Sue and Mrs. Hoadley and the little Hoadleys and Dr. Christensen and his wife and Abel Deering, who had been our mail man. And life went on, which is its habit.

Round about Groundhog Day I got a package from Hawaii. It seems that Cousin Josh had had a locker on base even though he was on the *Arizona* on the day that will live in infamy. It seems he had given my name instead of Aunt Betty's if stuff ever needed to be returned somewhere. I actually broke down and cried. I was at the parsonage and nobody was around. Dad had always taught me men can cry as long as no one is around and they don't have access to whiskey or guns. Mainly, I cried for my own fool self. I wasn't in church the morning Reverend Hoadley decided to clean up the world from the cosmic disease of man. I wasn't even in Mayflower much less at the little white painted church on Lollie Road. That Sunday I was at a convention of the Royal Order of Memphis-Misraim in Little Rock. I had told my family that I would be at a prayer breakfast that morning—after all, belief in a Supreme Being is the first pillar of the Order. In reality I was plowing a five-dollar high yellow whore named Gwendolyn. Three times a year I would step out on Maggie Sue, and when the Rev got out his big gun, I had my little one out. It has never occurred to me that I had anywhere other than hell to go to after that morning, and it has never occurred to me that this destination would in any way be an unjust one.

So I looked at the cardboard box and I cried. I cried for not being in the navy like Josh, so he didn't have to die. I cried for not being in church—I'm sure I could have made Hoadley hesitate; I cried for not burning that damn book that sent him over the deep end. I cried at being lonely. I cried for being weak. I cried for being here in Mayflower, Arkansas, instead of at home when Daddy couldn't face the Depression anymore and killed himself with Granddad's pistol. I cried that my brothers were at home taking care of Momma and I was here being a sham minister to good people who needed a real man of God instead of a whoremonger that lusts after darkie flesh. I cried because of the war. I cried for my sins of commission and my sins of omission. I cried for the atrocities in China and Poland and Russia. I cried for looking the other way when the KKK lynched Claude Bishop for "making eyes" at Lucy Downing. I cried for cheating at the pie-eating contest. I cried for the killing of the Indians. I cried for stealing watermelons from my uncle's farm. I cried for teaching those teenage girls how to French kiss last year. I cried for crying so much.

I heaved, I sobbed. I cried until I couldn't cry no more and my shirt was wet. Then I cleaned myself off and life went on, which is its habit.

I didn't open the box until the next day. Inside were a harmonica, a Bible, a Baptist hymnal, two shirts, a tie with a Hula girl painted on it, a nice pair of dress shoes (perhaps never worn), an eight-page dirty comic that featured Popeye screwing a French whore, a carving of an octopus made from a coconut shell, a small bottle of something called *sake*, a corncob pipe, three pieces of white coral, a tin whistle, and a photo of some light-skinned Negro woman dressed like Betty Boop. There was a tiny figurine carved from a greasy-feeling dark green stone that looked like a cross between King Kong, a gargoyle, and a squid.

I had seen the figure once before. It was in a woodcut in the Book that Reverend Hoadley had obsessed about.

I had truly meant to burn the Book. When I drove back to Mayflower that Sunday night and Sheriff Wade had told me about it, I knew which Book. Hoadley had taken to poring over its contents. He suggested I might be interested because of my interest in "esoteric Masonry." I didn't clarify that my interest was in the conventions. He told me the Book had different texts if you read it by moonlight, or that it explained the reasons for human cultic practices like "Corpse eating." Took me a long time to figure out that he meant Holy Communion. I was pretty disgusted at him when I figured out what he meant. He was going to write an article showing that Jesus's "hidden years" were in someplace called Leng.

Anyway, I had planned to burn the Book, but Sheriff Wade said to hold up on that as it might be evidence. He wasn't sure if he should take it as evidence—books having never been evidence in our little city. The little pocket demon from Josh returned that impulse to me. I had put Hoadley's stuff in a couple of boxes. I had made no attempt to send them on. I figured any family he was like to have, would not want to remember their connection with him. He owned a lot of books, but the One was old. I decided that I would look through it for the woodcut just so I would know what the little figure was, and then I was going to douse it with coal oil. After it had been reduced to ashes, I was going to piss in the ashes and drop them in the old privy behind the church. Then I was going to take a dump on top of that, throw the figurine in the shit and be done with it. I would say the Lord's Prayer, I would go to Maggie Sue's grave out back and tell her my true confession, and then I would spend the last of my days getting right with the Lord.

On page 239 there He was. My little figurine could have been the model. Except, of course, the book had been typeset shortly before the turn of the century and what looked like an original letter at the front from Dr. Dee in Mortlake was dated 1586. Some of the illustrations scattered throughout the pages looked newer than the letter, but others could have been even older. My cousin had bought this little good luck charm in Hawaii in 1940. I felt it right then.

The Pull.

The Pull to figure it out. Mystery is a Pull. But I decided that Mystery hadn't served Maggie Sue or even Reverend Hoadley very well. So I went and got my biggest bucket. Since I had new shirts from Cousin Joshua I decided to burn the shirt I had cried on so much as well. I wrapped my still damp shirt around the Book and put that figurine in the wrapping as well and put them in the bucket. Then I went for the kerosene and found I was out. I tried lighting my tear-damp shirt with matches, but no dice. I got frustrated—I thought about just throwing it all in the privy, but decided to wait until next month when I would have some ration points for fuel. I added the coconut octopus and the sake and the dirty comic and just stuck the whole bucket of shit in the attic over my bed. I would burn it all later.

And life went on, which is its habit.

In 1942 I became a "for real" minister. The church board asked for a council of pastors from churches hereabouts to ask me questions, especially about my theological positions and qualifications as outlined in 1 Timothy 3:1–7 and Titus 1:7–9. They held a little ceremony of Ordination, and I was both proud and humble. I quit the Rite of Memphis-Misraim. My little church had grown quite a bit. I got my own deacon, Richard Becker. I now had two services on Sunday morning, Sunday evening prayers, my war service each Wednesday, and a prayer breakfast the first of each month. We shared ration coupons, and I put in big bins for aluminum and paper and scrap iron. I began to pray every night in the church about midnight. It was my personal prayer for forgiveness. I was beginning to be at peace. Then come September, a strange man dropped by the church. He was an older fellow, in a long black coat and heavy glasses. I didn't hear him drive up, he just knocked on the door of the parsonage one Tuesday night. I was washing my dishes, planning my next sermon and laughing at the broken English of Little Beaver on the *Red Ryder* radio program. So I know it was Tuesday just after 7:30.

The man introduced himself as Austin Emme and said he was a friend—no, a *colleague*—of Reverend Hoadley. He was here because of the war effort.

"The Little Hope Baptist Church of Mayflower, Arkansas, is very serious about helping the war effort. We gather metal and paper and we even buy war bonds every month. We have weekly prayers, and we have a special Mother's Day service for our silver and gold star mothers. How can we help you, Mr. Emme?"

"I am interested in the security of the world. I know that Mr. Hoadley possessed a dangerous book, and that it gave him dangerous ideas."

"I believe that that piece of news did make the Little Rock *Democrat-Gazette*, but I long ago sent the book into the flames that no doubt welcomed its author, Dr. Dee."

"You are confused, Reverend Walton. Dr. Dee was not the author, merely a translator of the text. You are also lying, sir. I can smell the book."

Now, in fact, before this man had spoken, I thought I had burned the Book. That's odd—I am generally thought of as a man with a good memory. But the sin of Pride took hold of me at once. I was not to be called a liar on the porch of my own home. Even (if in fact) I were one.

"Sir, that Book cost me my wife's life. Who are you to be asking for this? What would that have to do with the war effort?"

"The Book is a weapon, and there are times, such as face the world now, that such weapons are more dangerous. I am sorry that I was blunt about the lying. But I think you could be in danger. Besides I would make a hefty contribution to your church for the Book."

"But I already told you I have burned it."

With the irony that marks the world, Little Beaver said rather distinctly on the radio, "White man speaks with forked tongue." Mr. Emme smiled. He said, "No, you didn't burn it. Are you a man of science, Reverend Walton?"

I shrugged—I don't know what I was conveying.

"Science tells us that there's a force called gravity," he began.

I said, "Yes, we've even heard of it here in Faulkner County."

"Gravity captures planets, asteroids, moons and comets. It makes things run in an orbit. Some words, some symbols have a force like gravity. Hitler's swastika, for example, is making a lot of otherwise good people orbit it. The Book you have has a sinister gravity. It affects you all the time just because you own it. It affects you strongly because of your wife's death. If you tried to hide it, it will affect you even more. Secrets have an effect on the manifest world.

It may affect your dreams or it may affect you by outlandish coincidences, or it may make you do rituals you don't understand. But it will affect you."

"So, aren't you afraid it will affect you? If I still had it, I mean."

"Of course, it will. Gravity isn't a bad thing; ask any boy bouncing a ball. It isn't a good thing, either—remember how you felt when you broke your mother's rose vase? I am like the playful boy; you are still the clumsy boy."

"How did you know about my mother's vase?"

"Reverend Walton, every boy breaks his mother's vase. Just think about it. I have business in White Castle, Louisiana. I am going to see my old friend Amos Carter there. I may swing back to get the Book. I can give you money for it. Even happiness, if you've decided that you're ready for that. If I don't come, it may seem to you that something else will. The Book picks its owners."

He walked into the September night. I was so stunned I closed the door and just stood there for ten minutes—almost holding my breath. I held on to my pocketknife in my left hand.

The next day I did something that had never been done for the parsonage in Mayflower. I bought locks for the doors. I locked both front and back doors. The church board asked me about the expense (normally the board pays for every change in the parsonage). I lied (again). I said that a hobo had come to my door—a common occurrence, but not like it had been during the Depression—and that I had a sense that he had meant me harm. Like all effective lies, this did have an element of truth involved. They paid for the locks, and people made jokes around town about Reverend Walton going "Little Rock."

I thought about buying a gun. Dad used to take me to shoot coons and possums back in Flapjack. But in the end, I relied on the only weapon (other than the Word of the Lord) that I had, Grandpa's old Barlow pocketknife. I had never been without it since he gave it to me when I was fourteen.

Lastly, I went up in the attic and got my bucket. The sake was gone from the bottle; had the little demon drunk it? I smiled. My shirt had mildewed, but oddly did not stink. The eight-page dirty comic was still dirty. The coconut sculpture had broken.

I took the stuff out of the bucket and moved it (except for the broken coco-pus and the empty booze bottle) under my bed. Mr. Emme never came back. He did mail his address from White Castle—Mr. Austin O. Emme, 1616 Leary Street, Salem, Massachusetts—and told me he would make a two-thousand-dollar contribution to my church, and another fifteen hundred for me, for the Book. His business card simply read *Rare Books and Enchanting Antiquities.*

This money would repair or replace everything the church needed fixed, buy new Bibles, even build a small library. I could get a car, all-new clothes, and even have a small bank account. Part of me saw this as rational and desired; I tried to tell myself that I was holding back because the man and/or the Book were "evil." But frankly I couldn't understand the parts of the Book I tried to read—and whatever it was about, Hitler and Tojo seemed much more dangerous than "Azathoth." How could adults fear dreams when real men were shooting real bullets at each other?

But then why not sell it?

I couldn't find words to answer that, or I was perhaps too frightened to find such words.

I grew obsessed with checking the Book and figurine every night before bed. I would pull it out from under my bed. I would put the figurine on the nightstand. I jokingly would tell it to watch for me. After a few weeks, I stopped saying my midnight prayers in the church. After all, it was just me: did God care where I said my prayers? I kept thinking about Emme's threat to send "something." Well, actually he said the Book would choose the right owner. But by the second or so weekend in October with no visitors—human or otherwise—I began to relax. I still checked on the Book every night. In fact, I sometimes put it under my pillow, but I stopped expecting a strange man to step out of the shadows.

And life went on, which is its habit.

I did notice that there was a lot about idolatry in the Book. There was even a ritual called the "Manifestation of Images" that actually caused an idol to fall from the sky. This Book stood against the teaching of God's Book—in this case directly against Exodus 20:4. Well, I decided to take a stance against the Book. So I preached four sermons against idolatry: one against Hollywood/movie idols, one against "keeping up with the Joneses," and the last two against Halloween. My congregation was surprised. The younger folk love Halloween for its mischief making—surely there was no harm in carving pumpkins? These ideas were just games and sports. But I countered with the Song of Solomon 2:15: "Take us the foxes, the little foxes, that spoil the vines, for our vines have tender grapes." I pointed out that little games let the Devil in. In my heart, I knew I was a hypocrite. If I truly wanted to fight the Book, I had coal oil now. Some of the older folk in the church liked my attack on the raw paganism of the jack-o'-lantern and the taffy-pull. So I proposed that we would have a Harvest Festival at church on October 31.

Many teenage members did not come. But I had made my stand against the idols of Halloween. Now I could burn the Book.

At midnight I made the short walk across the field to the parsonage. We had some baked goods (made with molasses, which unlike sugar is not rationed) and coffee, and sang the wilder hymns. But as I crossed to my door I could see, by the light of the silvery moon, the door was kicked in. I ran in. Someone had painted:

*Trick or treat*
*fail or pass*
*scary Halloween*
*the foxes have kicked your crippled ass.*

My kitchen chairs were knocked over, my Hills Brothers coffee was spilled on the floor, my books pulled from my bookcase. But the shocking thing was in the bedroom.

There was a female mannequin (with a cheap yellow wig) wearing Maggie Sue's wedding dress lying on the bed. I'd kept the dress in my closet for years. I had intended to give it to some poor parishioner, who might need it someday. On the wall, painted in red, "I Do!" with an arrow pointing to the mannequin's face. Pinned next to it was the Betty Boop photo and several pages from the dirty comic. Under some of the dirty drawings were the words *Oh la la, Reverend W!* and *Exodus 20:4 from the Tijuana Bible!!*

The rest of the treasures of my sin were on the bed. The figurine lay on my pillow, the Book lay opened to a strange angular diagram, the mildewed shirt was laid next to my mannequin bride—as though it were me, with the little figurine being (I guess) my head.

I collapsed with tears, the second time I had cried after Maggie Sue's death. I literally went on my hands and knees before the bed, as though it were a pagan altar and I an ardent devil-worshipper.

After half an hour, I knew I would weep no more in this life. I went to the storage shed, got some white paint, and painted over the graffiti. I burned the photo and the comics. I examined the mannequin—it came from J. C. Penney in Little Rock. It could be opened in its midsection, I guess so its legs and torso could be stored separately. I put the Book inside her; I figured this was a safe place because I wasn't letting my new "wife" out of my sight until I had shamed and punished the boys. I wasn't 100 percent sure as to which boys (and maybe girls), but they had to be the ones who'd skipped the Harvest Festival. I was going to dramatically confront them with the evidence. Until then, I would be as cool as a cucumber.

And life went on, which is its habit.

I didn't tell the church board. I didn't say squat or diddley in my first two sermons. I planned and waited for a sign. On November 13 the USS *Enterprise* sank the *Hiei* off Guadalcanal. If the *Enterprise* could take on the best ship in the world, I could take on Arkansas teenagers. God bless Captain Oby Hardison!

The next Sunday, I put my "wife" at the organ, and noticed that there was still some blood on the keys. Tiny brown drops of her. I had combed the wig and put on some of her perfume. I wore the mildewed shirt and the Hula tie. I paused for Maggie to play. I preached on the respect due to men of God and their families, and I told of the little surprise waiting for me two weeks before. Some folks left, others came up later and expressed their sorrow and shock. I preached the same sermon for the mid-morning service and then I kept her at the organ for evening prayer, but didn't tell the story again.

The church board visited me during the week. They would catch and punish the kids. They didn't like the parallels I drew between our troops kicking Jap butt and my actions against the heathens. They were less thrilled when Maggie remained at the organ for the Wednesday service. Next Sunday about half of my parishioners weren't in attendance. I noticed that Aleister Smith was—with his bright red hair and his smirk. He had just turned eighteen and the rumor was that his rich daddy had arranged for him to be classified 4F. He smiled through the whole service. Almost no one came to evening prayers except for the Ladies Auxiliary. These old bags told me that they were very worried about me. They told me that my heart was in pain and that Jesus would help. A priest of the corpse-eating cult, help me? I told them I hoped Jesus would help the children that did this to me. I hinted to Velma Smith it had been her grandson. I could see that she understood my hints, but what could she say? Her family was already suspect. They had had a Jap gardener before the war. If Tojo ever came to Arkansas I think we would know who to thank. She did tell me that the way they had dressed Maggie was a disgrace. I agreed.

On Monday, I drove to Little Rock. I left Maggie at home, but I had her measurements. I bought her a lovely (but modest) dress. And shoes—no wife of mine was going to be barefoot like the hicks here. And perfume, women should smell pretty, unlike the corpse of this world. As I walked to my car, a young darkie woman smiled at me and waved. At first I could not imagine that any Negro would address me familiarly. I could not recall having met her. Then I remembered that she was Gwendolyn Washington. I told her loudly and in no uncertain terms that I had no truck with whores and that I was a happily married man. She fled the streets with the eyes of righteous whites and Negros judging her. No doubt she fled to an opium den to plot the destruction of other marriages.

When I got home, red-headed Al Smith was sitting on my porch. If I were a gun-carrying man, I would have ended his freckled face. With all the acting ability his eighteen years had gained for him, he told me how sorry he was that my wife had been killed. But I didn't have the right to get him in Dutch with his grandmother. Yeah, he and his friends had had their own holiday party—but they hadn't been within a mile of the parsonage. He told me that he came from an important family and I had better watch myself.

I replied, "Oh yes, Colonel Smith, I know your family is an important family. Important to Emperor Hirohito."

"You son of a bitch. If you weren't a man of the cloth, I'd tan your crippled Texan hide."

"I thought Smiths were too chicken to fight. Surely a crippled man isn't too much for your skills."

I reached into my pants pocket; I was going to grab Grandpa's pocketknife. Not much good in a fight, but something. To my surprise I drew forth the little figurine. How long had I been carrying It? I held it my left hand and tried to menace Al with it.

"You are completely bug-fucking nuts is what you are Reverend Walton. You ain't even a real reverend. I know because my dad is on the board. They just gave you the job because they were sorry that Hoadley killed your wife. You ain't shit. What's that, some kind of voodoo?"

I swung my left arm down, but missed his worthy skull. He just laughed at me.

"Red said you were no good at fixing cars neither. He hired you because Maggie was his cousin. The cousin he diddled on the side, but you were too stupid to know that. Hell, you're probably too stupid to know that ain't your wife, just a dummy."

I stepped toward him, but he leaped off the porch. With my clubfoot, I knew I couldn't catch him if he ran. A fact that had made my childhood hell.

He continued his taunts, "Your wife was pregnant with Red's baby, that's why she came to Texas looking for a husband. She was going to find a college boy in Austin, but her car broke down in that place you're from—Pancake, Hot Dog, whatever the hell it's called. She knew a guy with your condition would be an easy catch. Y'all married but she lost the kid. What did you think, that she was just a little fat? She had to get away from here because everyone here knew about Red and her."

I jumped off the porch. I nearly dropped the figurine.

"You know they don't pay you as much as Reverend Hoadley. They pay folks based on brains."

He ran toward the cornfield. Mayflower is a cotton town, but they've always grown corn on Lollie Road. When he hit the stalks he yelled, "A dummy fucking a dummy! Don't get splinters in your pecker, cripple, don't get splinters in your pecker."

I went in and asked Maggie, but she had nothing to say.

I had her in her new dress for the Wednesday meeting. Only the church board came. Robert Smith just glared hatred at me the whole service. Afterward they told me enough was enough. If I needed to take off a few months they could let Deacon Becker take over. I could stay in the parsonage; maybe I could return, maybe I wasn't the right fit for Little Hope.

"So you'll just ordain a new deacon, like you did me. I suppose in your eyes he won't be a real pastor either—'cause he's not well-read like Hoadley. Because like me, he has got no degree."

"We're not here to replace you. We realize that you are under huge strain. We should have never made you preach in the same church your wife was killed in," said Mr. Smith.

"Or the same church where she and her cousin broke the Law of Moses. Oh, I have forgiven her, but I'm not about to forgive you bastards for laughing at me. What did you call it? The CCC? Crippled Cuckold for Christ?"

"Reverend Walton. Go to your home. You will not give the services this Sunday. Next week we can talk. And take that *thing*—you should return it to Penney's," said Mr. Smith.

"How did you know she came from Penney's? How did you know? Your son told you, didn't he? You've probably shared many a laugh at the club-footed cuckold. You'll be sorry. I've got friends in low places."

"Reverend Walton, go home. Pray. If you're drunk, sober up. Tell me, Walton, you did burn that book, didn't you?" asked Mr. Smith.

"Of course I burned it."

"Because my boy said you were carrying around a Negro voodoo fetish. We don't want you to go the way Hoadley did."

"You don't pay me enough to go that far," I said. "So, did Emme pay you for this? Is that what you want?"

They admitted nothing. They left. I took Maggie and we went home.

On Thursday (with very little sleep), I called all of the church board. I apologized. I told them I would leave Saturday night. I said the strain of preaching in a building that had seen such tragedy had simply been too much. I was going to go back home to Texas. The Foursquare Baptist Church of Doublesign had a job opening for a second minister. That much was true; one of my brothers had written me a note back in October. I asked if they could give me some privacy as I put my affairs in order.

Of course, they were relieved.

I raided the ration bank and got as many gasoline stamps as I could. I visited three different stations so that no one would see it coming. Then I bought whiskey. I'd never been a drinking man, but I figured that Maggie and I deserved a little party. Friday night I played dance music on the radio and I had a few drinks. It took Maggie awhile to open up, but then she had a few drinks. She did a little striptease for me. I had to use Grandpa's Barlow, but with surprisingly little effort she was a very serviceable wife. She was a little dry, but then she always had been. In a literal sense I was able to do to the Book what it had done to me.

On Saturday I packed up. I wanted to see the fire reaching into the night sky. I wanted to remember that forever. After making sure my car was full, I poured half the gas over the pews and pulpit. I lit her up and ran as fast as I could manage over to the parsonage. I threw gas on the bed, the closet, the kitchen table. I splashed it on the walls. I emptied out my kerosene and I threw candles (from the Christmas service) all over the floor. I lit my matches. I "ran" to my car.

Maggie looked beautiful. I told her we were heading to our new life. She asked about her wedding dress.

"Honey, I left it. You don't need it anymore. I'll get you plenty of new dresses in Texas."

She wanted it. For our daughter, someday.

I am a good husband. Oh, the Devil has misled me in the past. But the past is the past. It just lies there dead and dreaming as the Good Book says. I ran into the burning parsonage and pulled the dress from the closet. Through the open door I could see Maggie Sue Walton in the car.

She had just begun to drive away when the beams of the attic fell, trapping me in the front room with the burning rocking chair and the useless burning Bibles.

And life ended, which is its *other* habit.

# MYSTERIES DON'T SLEEP

## ANNA TAMBOUR

**S**OMEONE DID IT. Half a Bath Oliver lies on the carpet just behind the desk chair, the other half, a trod of sodden rubble on the way to the door. The unstepped-upon broken biscuit perches rakishly over a thick layer of clotted cream and a glint of something else. On the desk, on the book itself: goldly glistening, an archipelagic curve of amber cabochons, though they're no amber to a nose. Stronger than the smell of tuberose. Wattleflower honey.

If the house were in a cartoon, it would be a rocking box, bulging all the straight lines out. Visitors aplenty could be guilty parties, from the "I've been paleo for five years" to the low-metabolismed who only eat zucchini spaghetti. There are five children amongst the guests, so it can't be them. Not for Bath Olivers—as appealing to a child as a length of silence. And not in *this* room, the library (in the archaic sense: nothing with keys except the ring of them in the back of the top desk drawer, no pads except legal; and no screens except the folding silk beauty with the scene, privacising a generously cosy corner of the room).

There are no curtains on the windows, so anyone could have witnessed. But the time is now 3:30 A.M., and unless someone were some hovering ghost, the likelihood is low.

From the height of each medieval-blingy honeyjewel still proud on the leather cover of the book, the act could have taken place within the past few moments.

But from the thin black line snaking down from the tin ceiling, down the clapper boards of the wall, across the Kauri-pine board floor, then the carpet from Qum, up the sidemost claw of the wooden lion's foot, up the skinnypants-straight unadorned leg, traversing the overhang upside-down in a way only inhumanly possible (no cameras, no selfies, no high-fives— and what an amazing number of high-fives could be achieved amongst this mob), then up and over the lip—and then that short sprint to the summit, that butte—book's cover.

The Shinings. Not just those ephemeral jewels, but each glossy *Ochetellus glaber*—those tiny little (they are *that* small) house ants. Their mandibles are hard at work, each set of jaws taking as much as it can of the golden manna as a burden, not a meal. The scene looks so old-fashioned, so unconsumeristic, as archaic as this room which looks in the daytime like a tomb for the dead— but the house ants' thin black line is positively post-modern, going both ways at the same time.

As each *Ochetellus* is smaller than a linseed (a comparison carefully chosen for you who know linseeds, with our condolences), the population of the nest up there under the roof must be as linseeds in a five-kilo bag. But as the *Ochetellus* have no honeydrop-fall alarm, so the ants must have had to be alerted by their roving hunters—searching for silent screams of scent.

So the act must have taken place a half-hour or more before now (now being 3:46), but not before 1:15, when the last of the guests was out and day-shoed about in the uncarpeted halls of the hundred-year-old house.

We pause to contemplate, first leaning on the edge of the desk, then draping over the chair, but not wanting to step in the mess on the rug; this is no place to sit, so we turn around and get curious about that folding screen, or rather, what's behind it. Not really curious, you know, but we've come here phoneless so there's nothing to do and we're so bored already, we've forgotten why we even "entered the library" (an act of irony?). But now that we've taken the three steps necessary to reach the screen, we're too bored to leave, so we walk around the screen and find . . . wow! Weird! What a hideout—a right-angled dell of smelly old Grove Press, and a shelf of netsukes.

5:00 A.M. already!!!!!!!!!!!!!!!!!!!!!!!!!!!!!!!!!!!!!!!!!!!!!!!!!!!!!!!!!!!!!!!!!!!!!!!!!!!!!!!!!!!!

We freshen up at the sink nestled in shelves (not that we know which came first), and slip back to the room proper.

So much light now shines into the room that everything on the desk, except for a clean matte line, glows gold from dust.

The honey drops are our collective memory. The ants have vanished.

But what is that buzz?

The fallen trumpet of a Formosa lily of a certain age rests on the book cover now, its yellow pollen smeared onto its slightly wrinkled yet still sensuously curved white lap. Not that the mud dauber wasp is attracted to flowers as such. But on that curve, the dauber's black and signal-yellow abdomen pumps, pinning a flower-spider under its corsetly curve, stinging the spider senseless. The mud dauber mother-to-be (burdened not a bit by her cumbersome proper name) seizes the spider and carries it in her undercarriage, up and out the cracked-open window to one of her brood chambers in the eave. *Sceliphronina* (not named by a salesman, let alone someone with an ear) is quite a developer—she builds neat lines of adobe chambers. Now, in the newest one, she places the inadequately disguised flower spider, all white and pretty as a bride's bouquet—packs it in to be fresh and ready, paralysed-pure food for the dauber's grub.

And whilst we can't hear it, and she doesn't seem to—in the corner of our collective eye, see that little flash of emerald? It's another she—another mother-to-be. The tiny, gorgeous, mellifluous *Chrysidida*, the size of a dieting-guest's dinner—that cuckoo wasp has just seen the dauber wasp lay an egg in the chamber.

The dauber hums as she works, but the cuckoo springs silently.

# CHAPTER NINE

# THE SUN SAW

## MIKE ALLEN

**A**GAINST HIS BETTER judgment, John Hairston did these things:

Parked his Plymouth across from Pollard's book shop, in the shadow of an ash tree, the same tree where a mob strung up another black man just seven months ago, set him on fire as he begged for mercy.

Stepped out of the car into the shade of the tree, the dead man's howls still breathing in its leaves.

Popped the trunk, as a red-haired boy on a shiny blue bike rounded the corner and stopped to stare.

Picked up the cloth-wrapped parcel inside the trunk, big as two cinderblocks bound together, tucked it under his arm, ignoring the gawking boy.

Crossed the street to the shop's front door, keeping his cool, acting as if he weren't a brown-skinned man out alone in a town full of racist whites who would savor putting him in his place, whooping and hooting at every cry of pain.

Pollard, Lord be praised, wasn't like that. He was white as a painted picket fence, but Hairston was alive to make this nerve-wracking drive to Grandy Springs because Pollard had killed for him as their squads fled Kunu-ri, felled a Chinese sniper with a bead on Hairston's back. Not three days later, Hairston saved Pollard from a lonely death in a wind-swept rice paddy.

This was no matter of trading favors. Their debts to each other could never be repaid and didn't need to be.

Only because he knew Pollard's goodness in his bones did he dare bring his uncle's book to Grandy Springs.

Pollard's last letter had been dire: "I never wish to witness such an awful thing again . . . Come in the morning, before ten. I'll assess your uncle's treasure and have you out by noon. Again, I apologize that I can't instead come to you."

This bowel-knotting fear discombobulated Hairston worse than that awful quiet before the Chinese bullets came slicing over the dam in Kunuri. It shouldn't be this way, he shouldn't have to live every moment on the blessed ground of his home country like a sniper might sight between his shoulder blades, like that boy on his fucking bike was an enemy scout. He so admired the bravery of the boycotters in Montgomery, that woman in Oklahoma leading the lunch counter sit-ins.

Their bravery could not save him if a mob came.

*Not gonna take me alive*, he thought, and knocked.

"Come in," Pollard called, his voice sounding oddly close, as if no door stood between them. Hairston stepped into his friend's bookshop, the "appointments only" sign clacking as he swung the door closed. Hardbound books in muted golds, reds and browns filled tight shelves in a room too small to house a proper business. The pleasing must of aged paper summoned thoughts of how easily it all might combust if the townsfolk chose to teach Pollard a lesson over his choice of friends.

*Get the business done, get back to Baltimore.* "Bill, where you hiding, brother?" Hairston called, advancing between the tall, narrow shelves. Pollard had to have spoken from just inside the entrance, but the shop was empty. Hairston paused, listened, pictured how many moves it would take to drop the book, pull the switchblade from his inside jacket pocket, spring it open. Its weight where he normally kept his cigarettes reminded him that he wasn't helpless.

Uncle Mansfeld was convinced a fortune could be had, that this hidebound, sparsely illustrated tome recovered from the Franklin property didn't belong in the estate auction, instead should be offered to people who'd recognize its real worth. Convenient that his nephew made a white friend in the war who happened to be an antiquarian book expert, because maybe, just maybe, the Big Apple fat cats would give credence to a white man's appraisal.

"I'm in the back," Pollard said. Sheer reflex kept Hairston from smashing into a bookcase, because it sounded like his friend spoke right in his ear. At the same time he thought he heard a pained shout, the kind made by a man bleeding out in an empty rice field.

Maybe the high shelves were distorting the acoustics. He stepped into Pollard's back office, its desk crowded close by more books in stacks upon stacks. Something huge and white wrapped an arm around his neck and pressed a cloth to his face. A searing stench of fruit-sweet gasoline.

POLLARD SHOOK HIS shoulder, rousted him to the icy wind, the rocks beneath like molars.

"It's really me this time, John," Pollard hissed. "My owner's fed good tonight, so he's sleeping. But he's gonna send the overseer for you when he wakes up. You gotta wake up first, you gotta. You can free us both."

Hairston had slept with helmet on, though it failed to mute Pollard's jabbering. "What are you talking about?" When he opened his eyes, the sun saw them both over the Korean hills and chose the moment to meet his gaze and blind him. "Damn." When his focus returned Pollard was leaning down to whisper in his ear. Blood sheeted his face.

"What got you?" Hairston started up; Pollard shoved him back down.

From the other side of the hill, thunder, and the eerie whistle of a mortar round.

Deep corrugated slits regular as ladder steps marred both sides of Pollard's face from temple to jawline. "You gotta wake up for real, John. NOW!"

Flames licked out from his wounds.

*Wake up, John!*

Cold soil under his back became cold concrete against his cheek. He lay face down with arms and legs twisted at painful angles. His head throbbed with hangover agony. The coarse mesh of a blindfold blotted his vision.

His new accommodations stank of singed meat and sawdust. He coughed involuntary, almost split his chin on the concrete, tried to move again, deduced he was hog-tied, tight cords pinning his wrists and ankles behind his back.

That cough could have given him away. He listened, heard nothing but his own breath. The wise bellow of his non-com in his head, *Let your guard down, you're dead.*

He relaxed, took inventory. His hands and feet were not touching, there had to be a length of cord between them. He was still dressed. The lumps of his wallet, keys and matchbook still weighted his trouser pockets. The switchblade pressed against his ribs.

John Hairston did these things next:

Rolled awkwardly onto his side.

99

Bent his arms as far left as he could, gathered the fabric of his coat in swollen fingers, shook it to drop the knife out.

Suppressed a gasp of relief as it clattered loose.

Carefully rolled over so his back was to the knife, wincing at the strain on his shoulders.

No one watched him. A guard would have acted by now. Who had taken him? Couldn't be the Klan. They'd have beaten him awake, made sure he was alert for every minute of his drawn-out death.

His fingers found the handle's smooth wood, circled it with a solid grip. Despite his caution, he nicked his forearm when he opened the blade.

Didn't scream at Kunu-ri when the sniper notched his ear with a bullet. Wasn't going to now.

Were someone observing him, sadistically biding their time, their moment to intervene had arrived. No one did.

The cords—butcher's twine, it seemed—wrapped his wrists in layers: still, he praised the Lord that he didn't have to cut rope or wire. Careful as he was, severing strand after strand with each stroke, he cut his wrists over and over, the blade slicked with his own blood.

He heard a moan and stopped. He counted to ten, holding his breath. Quiet.

He resumed worrying at the twine.

Abruptly the cords went slack. He stretched his arms apart, sat up and pulled off his blindfold.

His first sight, a wall hung with saws, drills, miters, hammers, pristine as a catalogue spread. A thick, fresh-planed board supported by four sawhorses dominated the chamber like the posh mahogany table in Uncle Mansfeld's meeting room, where he sat down with grieving families and their lawyers to talk business. A single lighted bulb hung from a chain above the workbench, and past it squatted a gas-powered generator the size of an icebox, with an equally cumbersome device hooked up to it by steel belts, some kind of bandsaw.

The wall behind him held two exits, one at each end of the long chamber, a single plaque mounted equidistant between them. If someone stood at the workbench with their back to the tools, they'd be looking up to that plaque as they worked, just like a chapel cross.

Hairston had never seen letters like those on the plaque. Not Arabic, Russian, Greek, Hebrew or Chinese.

Both doors were open. Whoever had intended to hold him here lacked military discipline. Maybe it was the Klan, out celebrating their big catch, too stupid to properly secure him.

After five years spent grateful that his rifle no longer burdened his shoulder, he sorely missed it now.

"You have to kill us all," Pollard whispered.

Right in his ear again. Ingrained survival instinct kept him from screaming.

He finished freeing his ankles. When the pins and needles sufficiently subsided, he stood. He picked a toothy backsaw from the shrines on the wall. It had a symbol scratched on its gleaming blade, like one etched on the plaque, vaguely recalling a seven-pointed sun.

Another moan.

Weapon in each hand, Hairston stole to the door closest to the source of the noise, peered into a dim cinderblock hallway. One end opened into light. At the other end, behind a shut door, a man bleated in pain.

No one in sight. The man moaned again. At the same time Pollard's voice whispered, "John, get the gasoline."

Hairston whispered back, "You a ghost?"

"You'll see soon enough. Please buddy. You gotta hurry." He had never heard Pollard's voice so high-pitched with fright. "When my owner wakes I won't be free to talk. I'll say what he makes me say."

"What do you mean, owner?" No answer.

Pollard's constant use of slavery terms amplified the nightmarish disconnect that threatened to make Hairston's head swim. Though he damn well knew he was wide awake.

Two big metal gas cans stood sentry by the generator. He stuffed knife and saw into his outer coat pockets, picked up both cans. Hall still clear, he hurried to the shut door, pressed his ear to the wood. This time, when the man moaned, he detected other sounds, a dog-like whimper, someone else softly blubbering. He set the cans down, re-armed, eased the door open. He did not at first comprehend what awaited in the shadows.

Seven figures crouched naked, sealed in a circular stockade, their filthy bodies down on all fours outside the wooden cylinder, their heads and hands trapped inside, facing one another, their faces practically mashed together. Except that couldn't be because their shoulders weren't touching. Their heads were inflated somehow, misshapen.

He groped, found a light switch, flipped it.

The gray, fly-swarmed corpses of Korea lay five years behind him, but sometimes, at night, as he fought for sleep, their maggoty skins stirred. Those memories fortified him against the overwhelming urge to scream.

Whatever demons did this had burned and sliced these captives beyond

101

recognition, their faces scabbed together in one raw, continuous wound. Hairston spotted stitches in the crusted flesh, regular as zipper teeth, binding each face to its neighbor, but that didn't explain how the skin stretched and fused. No chemical agent Hairston knew about could do that.

"John, help me." Pollard in his ear.

"Where are you?" Hairston whispered.

"Find my eyes. Find the book."

The poor saps trapped in the stockade moaned with one voice. He paced around their shaking, atrophied bodies—men or women, he couldn't tell, it was as if their very bones had twisted, their bellies bloated red, pale spines jutting like fins. He spotted Pollard's eyes staring straight at him from a ruined face within the circle.

"Shit," he said, no longer whispering. "I'm gonna get you out of there."

"There's only one way to help me."

"Yeah, spring you loose, my brother." He crouched beside Pollard's rib-jutting, skin-sagging, excrement-reeking form. The hollow cylinder of the stockade seemed to be carved from a single tree trunk. He found no seam, no way to pry it open. "How the hell they got you in there?"

"Kill us, John. Before it wakes up."

Worse than finding no seam, he found no separation between the oddly-smooth wood and Pollard's neck.

Panicked, he groped the other bodies. They too were melded in seamless. All shuddered and flinched at his touch but one, whose skin was like ice-packed meat.

"That one . . . the overseer means to replace him with you," Pollard said. "You have to get the book out of there, and end us."

Hairston blinked at his friend's mangled face. "The book?"

"The *Necronomicon* your uncle acquired. My owner recognized it from the description in your letters." Pollard's gaze flicked down.

The book lay open on the floor inside the cylinder, beneath the circle of heads. It rested on a complex pattern of runnels, its leathery cover soaking up the blood that filled them. It was open in the exact center, an inhuman eye with a star-shaped pupil staring up, a drawing that spanned both leaves, surrounded by indecipherable symbols. Hairston could not stop a second's heart-skip of dismay at the damage done to his uncle's hoped-for fortune.

"Tell me how to get you out!"

"You can't. My owner's awake now. End this, *please*."

Hairston couldn't explain the sensation that crawled across his skin, as if the air filled with invisible insects.

"Please, John!"

Instinct came to a boil in Hairston's gut, telling him Pollard spoke truth. He considered the problem. Bill wanted him to burn the place. Was there another way? He could stab them all, but given their bizarre half-alive states, such wounds might not be fatal.

He put the knife hilt in his mouth, double-checked his back pocket for his matchbook. Still there.

He dashed out to grab the gas cans. The largest man he'd ever seen filled the opening at the other end of the hall, draped in a white robe but no pointed hood. A huge smile puffed the cheeks of his fat, hairless head. He loped forward.

Pollard wailed. "The overseer!"

Hairston transferred his switchblade from mouth to hand and brandished it. He could take one man.

The son of a bitch had speed. He seized Hairston's coat collar with a massive hand before Hairston could block. He lifted Hairston off the floor by that single arm, unleashing a moist giggle as his free hand closed on Hairston's throat. Hairston stabbed the giant's left eye, and when that didn't loosen his grip, stabbed out the other. Then he buried the blade in the brute's throat.

The overseer hurled Hairston against the wall, then clutched oddly at his face, not even trying to remove the knife from his neck.

Head ringing, back bruised, Hairston snatched the backsaw from where it had fallen. He scrabbled across the floor to draw the full length of the saw's teeth across the Achilles tendon of his opponent's right ankle.

The overseer toppled. Hairston scurried back on all fours into the torture room, pushing the gas cans before him. Pollard said, in his ear—in his *mind*, Hairston comprehended now—"Hurry, he ain't down."

Hairston stood, poised to pour the first can of gas into the stockade.

"No! Get the book! Without it you'll never get out!"

"Damn, Bill, make up your mind." He reached between those mutilated faces, the hair on his arms standing on end with the strangeness of the air down there. He peeled the book off the floor, took in that the runnels formed a star shape, each of its seven points terminating beneath one of the heads.

When he looked up, the room was full of people, naked, most of them brown-skinned, flesh sagging from their bones, bandages stretched over their faces. He knew their still forms stared at him, though he couldn't see their eyes. He *could* see the symbols etched on the walls through their translucent bodies.

"John, finish it."

He stood, lifting the book out of the circle. The crowd vanished.

He tossed the heavy tome toward the exit, dumped the first can all over the heads and the strange stockade. Gasoline-thinned blood swirled and splashed. The prisoners opened their mouths to scream, exposing the charred stumps of their tongues.

With the second can he soaked the seven bodies, efficient and methodical, using the last dregs of gasoline to draw a trail to the door. Scooping up the book, he hopped outside.

The overseer had vanished from the hall. No trail of blood gave away his whereabouts.

No time to wonder. The match blazed on first strike. He set it to the damp floor and jumped back as flames leaped jubilant.

No mistaking Pollard's real in-the-flesh scream. The same as he had sounded under cover of rice stalks halfway around the world, when Hairston wound a tourniquet above the blood-spurting hole in his arm.

"Sorry, brother," he whispered to his old friend.

An inhuman keening scorched the air, though what direction it came from, Hairston couldn't sense.

The torture room combusted, flames cascading up the walls. Hairston backed away but didn't run. Lord knew what he'd be running toward.

The book was like a stack of bricks under his arm, cover sticky with blood. Maybe he needed it, like Pollard insisted, but it wouldn't do for a weapon. He spied the backsaw, reacquired it. The teeth had scraps of the overseer's flesh lodged between them. How the fuck could there be no blood? Was he fighting a vampire?

Under the rumble of the flames, a series of thuds from the tool room.

The overseer, so tall he could prop a bare leg on the workbench, was using the twine from Hairston's escape to brace three short slats around his gimp ankle in an improvised splint. Slime drooled from the pits of his punctured eyes.

The overseer completed a knot, swung his splinted leg off the table and turned his eyeless gaze toward Hairston. The switchblade still protruded from his neck.

Hairston immediately forgot whatever plans he'd formed for what came next.

Attention fixed on Hairston, the overseer casually lifted a three-foot hacksaw from the workbench. Gripping its handle with both hands, he dragged the blade across his chest, shredding the robe. Smiling, he drew it next across his forehead, meat and bone spraying like sawdust from the wound. Then he slashed his own throat, twice, carving a bloodless X, grinning all the while. Hairston's knife fluttered loose to clack on the floor.

The huge man's mouth moved. No sound came out, but Hairston distinctly heard, "Your turn."

Hairston sprinted out the hallway's open end. He banged out onto a steel mesh balcony that overlooked an assembly hall full of people. That inhuman keening returned like a bat shrieking past his ear. He actually ducked before he registered that nothing was physically attacking him.

Behind him the overseer emerged into the corridor, silhouetted by flames, for which he showed no concern at all.

Hairston pounded down the spiral stairs, until the horrendous stench rising from below, worse than a corpse-stacked battlefield, stopped him cold. He took in the white-robed mob waiting for him, seated around rectangular tables like you'd see at a church potluck. The only light came from a bulb on a chain, suspended from a ladder straddling the opposite side of the room.

The overseer clanged onto the balcony.

The forty-some people at the tables weren't wearing hoods, like he had first thought. Bandages wrapped their heads, like the ghosts he'd seen upstairs. Only their mouths were uncovered, and they were using forks and knives to shovel their faces full of the reeking meat piled in sloppy gray mounds on the tabletops. Eating and chewing without pause, the soft slobbering and smacking like a thousand tiny creatures hopping through mud.

Those closest to him sat splayed in metal chairs, their legs missing below the knees.

"Christ Almighty, soldier, run!"

Pollard's words, the same shout from across the hills that saved him in Kunu-ri, shocked him into bolting just like it had then. Yet he drew up short because he saw no way out.

"They won't touch you!" Pollard barked. "They eat for our owner, that's all they do. Keep going!"

He charged through the middle of the feast, gaining speed as the overseer clang-clunked down the stairs.

The inverted V of the ladder hid an archway in its shadows. Just inside it stood bins of silverware beside a rack holding stacks of large porcelain trays, the same ones from which the eaters were slurping their mounds of meat.

While Hairston delayed in the doorway, the overseer again fixed on him, advancing with a grin. Whatever his powers, he was blind for sure, or else he'd have seen Hairston fling the tray, or at least have tried to duck as it spun toward him. Will of the Lord or sheer dumb luck, the tray smashed the brute edge-on in the forehead, shattering at the same time bone cracked. The overseer dropped.

Rather than plunge into the pitch black with its rotten flesh smell congealed thick as fog, Hairston groped for and found another light switch.

Anchored in the ceiling of this long, low room, rows of hooks suspended skinless corpses. Pigs, cattle, people. The red ichor that coated them wasn't blood: too bright, too rose-hued, as were the wisps of steam wafting from its surfaces.

Behind, the clunk-clomp renewed.

Hairston sprinted, eyes fixed on the open area beyond the flayed sacks, desperately wanting to cover his face against that reddish vapor. But he dropped neither book nor saw, though he couldn't fathom how either would do him good.

The overseer's footsteps changed timbre as he thudded into the slaughterhouse, the same moment Hairston emerged from the rows of corpses. Before him loomed three more workbenches like the one upstairs, their boards blood-drenched, piled with hides, skins, entrails. Here, clearly, was where the bodies were cleaned before hanging.

*What the hell is this place?*

He forced himself to think, even though the overseer had almost reached him. His success with the tray provided hope. He tiptoed quickly to the furthest of the benches, out of the overseer's immediate path. Holding his breath, he set down book and backsaw as the white-robed man bulled out of the hanging corpses and kept running.

Hairston carefully pulled himself onto the bench and crouched down beside a mound of what looked like pig's guts. He squatted right in plain sight, but his opponent had no eyes. If demon's magic gave him sight, there was no hiding anyway.

The overseer stopped. Turned. Sniffed the air. Amidst the overwhelming stink, it had to be damn near impossible to pick out one frightened human.

The overseer mouthed words. Hairston continued to hold his breath. His lungs started to burn.

Slowly—but not looking at him—the overseer ambled in his direction, still snuffling. He rounded the end of the next bench over, came up the aisle that would lead right to Hairston.

Moving as if underwater, Hairston gently lifted and tossed the book so that it plopped on the floor between the benches. The overseer lunged at the noise. As he bent to grab at the object, Hairtson leapt onto his broad back, executing the maneuver he'd spent the past four seconds rehearsing in his head. He clamped one arm around the giant's neck, used the other to press the teeth of the backsaw against his spine, put all his strength into a stroke that tore meat and grazed vertebrae.

Strong as the overseer was, Hairston's leap knocked him prone. He heard Pollard's voice, repeating syllables he didn't understand.

The star symbol on the saw blade glowed.

The overseer rose beneath him, grabbed his arm to throw him off. Hairston stuffed his hand into the wound in the man's throat, seized cold tubes of flesh with adrenaline-jazzed fingers, and kept sawing.

The overseer flipped onto his back, squashing Hairston under his bulk, crushing his testicles, squeezing the breath from his lungs. He gripped Hairston's arm with such pressure that skin and muscle parted. Hairston screamed and used the agony as fuel for his own attack, ripping the blade against bone. Its teeth tore far enough through to bite his own fingers as they clutched inside the overseer's neck.

The head came free like a cork jerked from a bottleneck. No wine poured from the wound.

That horrible keening returned a thousand times louder, dynamite inside Hairston's skull.

The overseer's headless body sat up, arms outstretched like Frankenstein's monster. Then it slumped and sprawled.

Hairston clutched his ears in a useless attempt to block the keening. A desperate call swelled within the noise, a baby's squall, something that could be quieted only if you gave it what it wanted.

He had to give in to its wants. It wanted him. Its need flooded his veins.

Whispers. "I can protect you but you need the book. I can help you read it, John. John!"

Hairston crawled to where the book lay, pages open to that same staring eye. Every motion brought stabbing pain. The overseer's head had come to rest against a sawhorse leg. Its mouth twitched.

"Just what that ape deserved," Pollard growled. "Was him hauled the rope that pulled Beddows up into that tree. He was the sacrifice that got all this started. If that hell-bound mob knew it would come to this, I still don't think they would have cared."

With a snarl of disgust Hairston kicked the head away.

"Those pages," Pollard said. "I can read them through your eyes. Repeat what I say."

Insanity. Hairston cradled the *Necronomicon*, staring into that star-pupiled eye, repeating the sounds Pollard made. Of its own accord his gaze moved in circles, following the symbols that surrounded the eye.

The keening dampened to bearable volume. When it did, Hairston perceived his own name, wrapped repeatedly inside that endless wail.

"My owner wants you to take that gorilla's place. If you hadn't freed me from his yoke, you'd have no choice but to obey. But you gotta keep reading. There's no getting out for either of us till we end this, buddy."

Hairston nodded. *Let's do it, then.*

SOMETIMES THE LORD'S work and the Devil's are the same. Korea was like that, and what Hairston did in that pit deep underground was like that, too.

Pollard's ghost talked as they descended the bunker tunnels under Grover MacCutcheon's plantation, where Pollard said they'd both been brought as prisoners. "That wasn't me who answered your letters," he whispered. "He's had me since they killed Beddows. I learned how it all works, trapped inside his disease."

The old man who lived here had made pacts with things worse with the Devil. It had been easy for him to whip up the townsfolk, to carry out the things he needed to open himself to the fallen angels, strange creatures with stranger names that lived outside human time. When Pollard whispered those names it was as if his spirit spoke in tongues.

Hairston understood only a fraction of what Pollard struggled to explain, but when he found the plantation owner one thing became plain. Pollard's assertion that "He got what he wanted and it overwhelmed him" was one hell of an understatement.

What had once been a man lay on a pallet, frame shriveled to bones draped in flesh gone the texture and color of pus. Purplish mold had sprouted from the remains of its skin and spread across all the surfaces of the cellar.

Hairston took in these details only through peripheral vision, his gaze still tracking the symbols inked around the center pages, the vocalizations coming out of his own mouth turning his throat raw. The creature continued its keening and calling, though the energy—it wasn't truly a sound—radiated from its swollen yellow eyes, protruding tumors with pinhole pupils. The chant Pollard led him through kept it from digging claws into his mind, but he felt those claws probing, like bayonets stabbing the underbrush.

He didn't dare set the book down, so against his better judgment he waded into the sprouts of bruise-colored mold. A red vapor rose as his shoes broke the stalks. Still reading, he stepped onto the pallet, shouting Pollard's syllables against the rising shriek.

He set a foot in the creature's putrescent belly. It burst like a puffball, more of the vapor clouding below him. In the corners of his eyes, figures in white robes with faces suffocated by bandages rose from the floor, vapors themselves, watching.

He stepped on the creature's chest. His legs started to go numb as more dust billowed. The creature's shriek at last became true sound as he took another step and his shoe descended on its face. The head crunched flat, no stronger than an eggshell. The horrible keening didn't stop. Rather, it slowly faded, as if it were a water ripple, dissipating in all directions at once.

Hairston lost all feeling in his legs. He toppled off the pallet, the book splayed in front of him.

The white figures faded away.

"What now?" Hairston asked, but Pollard's ghost no longer answered. And though he screamed Pollard's name, again and again, some part of him knew all along this was how it would end.

The horrors in the cosmos that Pollard had yammered on about with such tremulous fear held no candle to the fate he'd abandoned Hairston to face.

He was on his own, not knowing how far underground he was, or where to go if he even made it to the surface with no legs to carry him, in a place where anyone he called to for help might just decide to string him up and burn him alive.

The earth above and below longed to swallow him whole.

# CHAPTER TEN

# AMERICAN GHOST

## JOHN CLAUDE SMITH

**I**FIRST HEARD about the book psychotropically during an acid trip at Venice Beach. Amid the sand dunes and egotistical, muscle-bound goons, my two colleagues in the quest to turn on, tune in, and drop out, Hans and Sally, started in about a book that either was "dark and evil, with accounts of the Old Ones, whose ultimate goals align with the apocalypse," or "opens doors to the purest distillation of self, enhancing the essence," or some combination of both, which made no sense to me. I had no idea who the Old Ones were. Geriatric occult explorers? Aged members of the Golden Dawn, post relevance . . . as if they ever were relevant? I tuned out and listened in . . .

"Why do you think Morrison's dead anyway? He dipped in and it shattered his soul," Hans said. "Evil shit, man."

"Not evil. He just couldn't handle it," Sally said.

"Too intense? You saying the concentrated expression of his talent was too intense?"

"I say he was a mediocre poet and performer who will probably be forgotten in the annals of history. But for those few years, he was godlike . . . and so beautiful. Until he got hold of the book."

Sally's smile filled the landscape. Flowers bloomed in her hair and eyes.

Hans smiled, too, but I saw something black flood out of his face as it melted, waxlike and disturbing. I turned away and woke up hours later under a star-littered sky. A seagull stared at me under the blind eye of a winking crescent moon. Its beak moved as lips, mouthing something I could not make out. It launched into the black heavens, sweeping up a tornado of sand that reflected the colors of a rainbow in the swirling shards of broken soda bottles.

I woke into this reality with the translation of the seagull's mute words floating as neon dressed in a skirt of fog before my eyes: *The book is the key to your destiny.*

In what manner, I did not know. I knew nothing of the book until the acid trip. Was there even a book? Was this simply psychedelic mindplay while two tabs of Black Sunshine socked it to my imagination? It did not matter. I needed to know more. I felt Sally's interpretation—enhancing the essence— was meant for me, a poet deserving of a wider audience. Of accolades and fame nonpareil.

My destiny.

That was a year ago, 1973, me still living off the dregs of the long dead '60s. The Morrison in question was Jim Morrison, the lead singer for the band The Doors. He'd been dead a couple years at that time, passing under suspicious circumstances in a hotel room in Paris in 1971. Though much to Sally's disdain, proving her prognosticating abilities less than those of Nostradamus, Morrison's legend has only strengthened since his passing.

But because of the words of the seagull or simply a drug-enhanced tolling of the subconscious bell, I knew it was time to stop drifting.

I needed to find the book.

Tracking it through heresy and whim and the wily machinations of the occult underground, I made my way to San Francisco, to talk to minor poet Samael Plotkin. He had known Morrison. He allegedly knew of the book. I'd heard he had fallen on hard times, lost his mojo, and was living off the good graces and worn sofas of fellow poets when not sharing time with shadows on the streets. My muse had been on hiatus for well over four years at this point. I knew finding the book would bring magic back to my words.

When I hit North Beach, I asked around and was given the phone number of the latest acquaintance he was staying with in a small hotel off of Columbus Street. When I called it, a woman answered the phone.

"May I speak to Samael Plotkin?"

"You gotta make it quick. I'm expectin' a call on this line. Quick, 'kay?" She sounded agitated. Quick or not, I needed to talk to him.

"Is he there?"

"Quick, 'kay? Lie to me, at least." Gum popping with real urgency.

"Of course I'll be quick," I said. Giving her what she needed.

"Groovy." I heard her call out Samael's name. Muffled sounds and a car honking somewhere within the telephone receiver's reception.

"Yes?"

"Samael Plotkin?"

He audibly sighed.

"I need to talk to you about Jim Morrison and the whereabouts of a book by the name of the *Necronomicon*."

Silence. So silent, I thought he'd hung up.

"Samael?"

"Why? The past is dead. Let it sleep forever."

No matter his reluctance, I could not accept no as a response. I didn't need to give him reasons. I needed the book. I'd heard part of his downfall was a love of liquor. Anything to inebriate and dance off into the shadows of a mind gone to rot.

"We can meet at Vesuvio. Talk. Drink. My treat." Vesuvio was a famous bar frequented by the Beats, next door to City Lights Bookstore. I let the suggestion hang loose on the line. Giving him room to allow his addiction to answer for him.

"Fine. But if you want to talk about . . ." He paused; seconds crawled by, perhaps a minute or more. I remained stalwart and let the addiction take the reins. Patience loomed as a vulture awaiting scraps. "If you want to talk about this, you'll want to be sober. I'll want to be sober. Meet me at Caffe Trieste. Noon, tomorrow."

His willpower surprised me. The tone of his voice suggested it was a struggle to divert his addiction from what it really wanted. As if it mattered to me.

"Fine," I said into the dead line. He had already hung up.

I could smell coffee done black and bitter. My nostrils flared, leading my way to Vallejo Street, and Caffe Trieste, a staple here since the 1950s. Clear glass reflected bodies in motion, those who passed by me without glancing up, slightly warped by a curvature in the glass or their corroded auras. I visually pushed them away and stared inside, where gaunt figures scribbling in notepads occupied a few tables, scattered about, distancing themselves from each other. Work of such personal importance, yet most people would never read any of it. Desperation whittled hope to the bone, sucked on the marrow.

I did not need any of this. My words carried weight. I just needed—

A figure more gaunt than most waved at me from the far right corner of a large wooden table in the back. Greasy hair to his shoulders, a hippie by any other name, but his damaged countenance suggested otherwise. Plotkin was about my age, early thirties, but even from the entrance, I could register the weariness in his large, haunted eyes. One would guess him much older. He raised a mug to his lips as I wound my way around the pastry display and sat across from him at the table.

Discarding the niceties and small talk that hindered most conversations, I said, "What can you tell me about Morrison and the book? Did he own it? By what means did the book . . . enhance his career?"

Plotkin pulled the mug from his lips and laughed.

"What do you know of the book?"

"Enough," I said, whether truthful or not. My interest exceeded my knowledge.

"You think this is about his career, as if the book had anything to do with his success?"

"Well . . ."

"Well? That's your response?" His hands were shaking. His nose was running and he sniffled as he laughed again.

"My motivation is not the issue here. I was told you had info on Morrison and the book." I reached into my pants pocket and pulled out a few bills, pressing a ten to the table.

He stopped laughing, his eyes narrowing to the cash on hand. He reached for the ten. I slapped my hand over it, pulling it to my side of the table.

He turned away, glancing toward the front door, where a young woman with long blonde hair was walking around, handing out pamphlets. I could not hear what she was saying. I did not care. Though my peripheral vision gauged her presence, my focus stayed firm on Plotkin.

"I knew Jimmy. Went to UCLA with him. He was kind of a prick, but he had obvious talent. Well, to most. Charisma. We met in Jack Hirschman's class on Antonin Artaud. Artaud was part of the inspiration for Jimmy's stage theatrics, but this was well before the Doors had even formed. We got to really know each other in a poetry class taught by Albert Jasper." I'd heard of Hirschman, a radical poet and professor, though never heard of Jasper. "We hung out, got high, got laid. A head start on the late '60s free love agenda."

"Get to the point," I said, not needing to waste time with his roundabout recollections.

"Point being, I knew him. Hung out. Heard through the grapevine he was interested in an occult book of some curious merit. This was early in '65. He thought it would be fab to get a hold of this book."

"The *Necronomicon*."

114

"No shit." He leaned back, then forward. Antsy. Pupils dropping to the money again. Purpose.

"At a poetry reading in February at Cinematheque 16—Jimmy wasn't reading, his interests veered more toward film at that time, having made some short films, even one I worked with him on, *First Love*, which was released to the public—his niggling interest that bordered on obsession about the book peaked. He was to meet a mysterious woman who allegedly had knowledge as to its whereabouts." Plotkin's eyes glistened, as if he was visualizing events from the past as they unfolded before him now. "Jasper was there and started hounding Jimmy to no end about the book. Apparently, he also wanted it, was quite vocal about this, eyes manic and voice lifting to interrupt the proceedings. He ranted at Morrison to the point where he was dragged out of the club and tossed on the street. A couple days later, he committed suicide."

The young woman with the pamphlets interrupted Plotkin's flow. "Peace, brothers. We're having a rally tomorrow at noon. You're welcome to join us," she said, handing us both copies of the pamphlet. *Stop This Senseless War Now!* While Plotkin smiled dimly, a mask of understanding, perhaps allegiance, I crushed the pamphlet in my palm and glared at her. A dark cloud spread across her complexion. Peace was so '60s. We were well beyond that pipedream notion. No matter illusions otherwise, Vietnam was a way of life.

"Continue," I said to Plotkin.

"All for naught. The woman never showed up."

"What really *is* the point, then?"

"Your desperation reeks," Plotkin said, sniffing the air. "The Doors were off and running soon thereafter . . . and I kept in touch with Jimmy only sporadically. Anytime I saw him around, he'd ask if I ever saw that woman, ever heard anything more about the book. I'd respond in the negative and he'd be off to somebody else, with similar questions. Rather irritating. I moved on, pursuing my own poetic inclinations. Moved to Soul Francisco in early 1970. Received a correspondence via the post from a mutual friend toward the end of the year. Apparently, that woman had finally shown up out of the blue. Morrison got the book."

"He finally got hold of the book . . . only months before he died?" This timeline threw a wrench in my initial thinking about the book. Morrison was already famous when he got it? What good was it then, enhancing the essence or . . . or perhaps he was simply weak and whatever more it could do for him was never utilized. I wasn't wired that way. I wasn't *weak* that way. Juggling thoughts on the book's true purpose . . . perhaps simply having it in his possession for a few months was enough to set up his legend. Imagine what it could do for a poetic force like me.

Plotkin snapped his fingers in my face, pulling me back from my wayward thoughts. He leaned toward me, conspiratorially. "Look, dreamy eyes, do you even know what you're dealing with? This thing . . . this book, the John Dee's translation, as if you even know this much—even know who he was—is potent. Its origins are sketchy and you don't want to fill in the gaps. You've hinted it will help you attain some sort of fame. Who told you as much?"

*I heard it all while tripping, man. I heard of its origins while tripping. But it's real, the book is real, so why not the whole picture?*

"Fine. Don't answer me, but know this. The essence of the *Necronomicon*, though perhaps wildly fantastical and quite implausible, is inherently apocalyptic by nature. End of the world stuff, at the hands of the Old Ones." Mention of the Old Ones again, as if these fellas were the substance between the lines. "Morrison was already into opening the doors of perception." Plotkin snickered. "But he did not need the book to help him leave some sort of legacy. From what I've heard, though, the broader apocalyptic aspects can also be stripped to the core of an individual. Just one person."

"What's that supposed to mean?"

"The book can lead to a meddling individual's personal apocalypse. That's why Morrison has been in hiding since . . ." He stopped abruptly: terra incognita. He'd crossed into unknown territory . . .

"In hiding? He's dead. Can't get any more hidden than death."

He twitched, rubbing the wrists of each arm once, twice.

I pulled out the few bills, tossed another ten on the table. Temptation was lethal, digging talons into his fevered addiction.

"Listen. Just listen." He leaned in even closer, the words for my ears only. The curdled stench of alcohol seeped from his pores. I would have flinched and backed off under different circumstances. "As I've said, and you should heed my warnings, the book is potent. There are those who are meant to know its secrets. True researchers of the black arts. There are those who are not meant to know or, as in Morrison's case, his interest was frivolous, mostly harmless. Yet, even at that, the potency of the book ignited his personal apocalypse."

Gibberish. Plotkin was spewing gibberish. Spouting horror stories as fact. Insubstantial. I gathered my cash and stood to leave.

He grabbed my wrist.

"You don't have to believe me. I know how it sounds and know how I look and expect you think me mad. Fine. But it's true."

Against my better instincts, I sat back down, though left my hand on the cash. But there was one angle his fantasy inspired me to tackle.

"If Morrison is still alive, do you know if he still has the book?"

"I've heard nothing to suggest otherwise." His eyes were glossy, his focus again on the money. He wiped his nose on the already snot-crusted sleeve of his denim jacket.

"If he is still alive, do you know where he is?"

He licked his lips and turned to stare at the black and white photos on the wall. The poets we both aspired to accompany. Ferlinghetti, Ginsberg, even Hirschman. Only I would succeed.

He reached inside his jacket, into a pocket that held a notepad and set it in front of him. Dug in some more and pulled out the nub of a pencil no longer than the first joint of my thumb. Wrote on the paper and tore it out. Set it next to the two tens.

I read the note: *Chateau Marmont 33.*

"You heard of Cassandra Christ? She's a poet down south. Los Angeles. Does stuff to her body while reading her poems. Performance art." I shook my head. I had no inkling of where he was going with this. "She allegedly confirmed Morrison's whereabouts a few months ago. Tagged along when groceries were delivered. Seems Morrison won't be leaving since his condition has . . . spread." Plotkin's fingers nervously tapped on the wood table, right above where some forgotten poet had carved into the wood, *No Future Here, Not Yours Or Mine.*

"His condition?"

"I am the lizard king," Plotkin said. I'm sure my brow curled upward, though it had probably been stuck in that position for much of the conversation. "Just go here"—he stopped his chaotic tapping, the drum solo now a one-finger affair as he tapped it atop the piece of paper, the address—"you'll see. Or not. No guarantees. Cassandra Christ reported this to those in the know, then disappeared." His eyes wavered, as if looking through me. Knowing more, but I didn't need to know more. I picked up the piece of paper.

"Morrison doesn't take kindly to intrusions," he continued. "Guests are null and void. Just like your aspirations." His smile was a sprung switchblade ready to slice.

"Fuck you," I said, as Plotkin slid the cash from beneath my fingers. A fair exchange, exit stage left.

He pocketed the cash and said, "I saw you read once, maybe five years ago. A small hole-in-the-wall club in Los Angeles. Maybe Santa Monica."

I stood up. "What of it?"

"Your words were all surface level. Pretty on the outside, but no depth. But that isn't the point, is it? I heard you talking to a few people afterwards. All ego. All about you."

"This from a failed poet no more substantial than a shadow." I shoved the chair toward the table a little harder than necessary.

"One of the biggest failures in the realm of words, perhaps. I know this. But I'm still better than you. I got heart. All you got is ego."

"I didn't come here to get preached at by a loser." Plotkin feigned being shot in the heart. "My whole future is ahead of me. Getting my hands on the book will seal my fame—"

"You believe that shit?"

We paused, a stare-down without resolution. Guns forever holstered.

"You're like a balloon filled with helium, raising yourself to the highest levels in your own insipid mind, but all it takes is a tiny prick to bring you down."

I slammed my open palm against the wooden tabletop. *Just shut the fuck up.*

"See what I mean? You're chasing a book you don't even understand, with the idea the book is going to somehow prop you up to standards you would never achieve otherwise. You hone skills, perhaps you have a chance at something, but I clearly don't see skills worth honing. At least Morrison had talent, a justifiable foundation upon which to flaunt that ego. You flaunt artifice. Nothing more."

I turned to leave as the weasel continued his misguided verbal taunts. Taunts shaped by jealousy, I was sure.

"Give up the ghost of your so-called career as a wordsmith and get a real job, poet. Flip burgers, poet. Mop the floor, *poet.*"

I seethed, though there was no real basis for my reaction. He was beyond help. Twenty dollars later, he would be drunk and sleeping in an alley, for sure. Not worth my anger, yet it burned inside

The jaunt up north to San Francisco stretched the limits of my old Ford Fairlane, bought on the cheap a year ago because it had many problems; problems I'd yet to deal with. Back to Venice Beach, I had only one item I needed to pick up: my never-used gun. The good Boy Scout, prepared for anything . . .

Los Angeles proper always smelled like car exhaust, or perhaps that's hope being incinerated in the hearth of dying dreams. Nectar to the City of Angels.

As expected, the Ford Fairlane died in a belch of metallic groans and coughing fumes just outside of my destination in West Hollywood. As I walked afterward, I passed by the Troubadour, where just a week ago John

Lennon and Harry Nilsson were kicked out of the club for heckling the Smothers Brothers.

Circling up La Cienega Boulevard, I spotted the Alta Cienega Motel, the most popular of Morrison's home fronts in Los Angeles. So popular his admirers (groupies . . .) have corrupted "the green hotel" with their devotion, scribbling graffiti on the walls of room 32, where Morrison had scribbled lines as well. Poetry buried amid affections bland and pathetic, giving vicarious meaning to lives never lived. Sideshow entertainment.

I was close to my destination.

Back to Sunset Boulevard, I took out the scribbled note only to confirm proximity. I knew the location, knew where I was. To my left, one of the other hotels Morrison frequented loomed large: Chateau Marmont. I strolled into the lobby and immediately upstairs toward number 33. Perhaps it was the Hollywood bungalow made famous in the Doors song "L. A. Woman." Perhaps not.

It did not matter. I knocked on the door and immediately slipped my hand back in my jacket pocket. Cold steel was strange comfort.

I'd spent the summer of my eighteenth year loafing about Los Angeles with a gang of misfits like myself, disabling security systems and picking locks of the houses of mid-level celebrities and wannabe celebrities on vacation. Couldn't go for the big shots—they had guards as well as alarms—but those in the middle and waiting for fame or attempting to hitch a ride with fame were less inclined to do anything but set up security systems, if that. The skill I learned back then came in handy now as I picked the lock and furtively entered Morrison's hotel room.

The light of dusk as it faded into evening dimly splashed across a table near the open window, thin teal curtains rippling at the insistence of a light breeze. I had a momentary impression of swimming underwater. A chair was set askew to the left of the table, while a notepad, pencil, and lamp sat on top. Further to my left, I could barely make out a bed and a small end table next to the bed. That was it for amenities. Though I suspected other rooms had more furniture, it seemed this one was gutted to bare minimum. There was lots of empty space.

I glanced all around. The door to the bathroom was closed, but there was no light peeking out from below. If Morrison lived here, he was not presently here. So much for tales of his hermit existence.

Still, I padded softly toward the table and the notepad and read the top page.

American Ghost

I.

After Paris, endless night
I kissed the anus of America
& death shadowed my every step

In the womb of Times Square, fevers & desire
The South sways large hips to voodoo fire
Stigmata palm of the golden plains bleeds
Los Angeles, the mouth, bringer of disease
moon rises in the palace of nightmares
snakes kiss as an Ouroboros halo
& hiss as the gods define myths
Blood smeared black on white sheets
Naked beaches
Home
Rattlesnakes tremble, radiators rattle
A leather satchel adorned with strange symbols
(burnt through from the inside)
A dark companion
A prison cell of words
The scaly prison of self
Fame
Famine of the soul

The Old Ones watch from halls of mirrors
Smile like crocodiles in blue cars
And wonder at my wandering
(Quiet!)

Skin pale, translucent
Transformative
I see the truth beneath the lie
& lie in wait
A passive beast
I am the jeweled lizard
King of the glitzy wasteland

A ghost shedding skins
A man no longer human
Finally free . . .

II.

I lifted the loose page to continue, but the page beneath bore nothing but fingerprints smeared in what looked like blood. I reread the unfinished poem, "American Ghost," and wondered as to the meaning of Morrison's meanderings. Rumor had it, fame was not his friend. Rock stardom a hindrance to his true poetic ambitions. Perhaps he faked his death and has been holed up here since . . . and when would he be back?

I noticed some scribbling on the wall, just like in "the green hotel." Noticed again a line I'd read only recently: No Future Here, Not Yours Or Mine. I leaned forward, placing my hand on the tabletop to get a closer look at other lines, phrases, random words. Immediately I jerked it away, my fingers filthy with something sticky.

The meager light from outside was not enough to reveal what it was, so I reached toward the lamp and clicked it on. The bulb brought only feeble brightness, but it was enough to distinguish a two-foot wide smudge of indecipherable gel leading out the window. As I leaned in for a closer inspection, a meaty stench nipped at my nostrils, pushing me back.

I turned around, taking in the room, lamp still in my hand. Something was discarded on the floor, behind the chair. Perhaps a shirt, a jacket. I stepped forward to get a better look when the cord for the lamp reached its limits, so I set the lamp on the seat of the wooden chair.

Crouching down, I scooped up the item, taken by the unexpected texture. I rubbed the fingers of my left hand over . . . whatever it was, and then pulled at the corners to take it in. Pulled at the shoulders, to be more precise . . . and was shocked at what my eyes beheld. It was a weird sort of skin, the memory of scales inlaid throughout, yet in the shape of a man!

*A ghost shedding skins . . .*

I gasped at the implication, when I saw through the weird skin, on the table next to the bed—a leather satchel.

*A leather satchel adorned with strange symbols . . .*

I dropped the skin, no matter allusions bizarre, preposterous, and moved toward the table . . . when the shadows spoke.

"This is not for you."

I hastily pulled the gun from my jacket pocket.

"Morrison?"

A gurgling suggestion of laughter.

"Only a chosen few are allowed to experience its gifts. A few others are allowed to dabble, such as Mr. Morrison. Though dabbling promises nothing of a positive nature, only harsh truths buried within and brought to the surface. Most are not even given opportunity to glimpse the book. This is not for your eyes."

I ignored the words of the one in the shadows.

"I suggest you move aside. I'll use this if I have to," I said, waving the gun, semaphoring a death warning.

Again with the gurgling suggestion of laughter. "You dare think you are worthy of the book. You dare think you can handle it. We—" the voice echoing, a ripple across a vast, empty lake "—the guardians, cannot allow the fulfillment of your misguided quest." The words ricocheted around me, causing me to hunch over, as if avoiding their invisible trajectories.

I had nothing to lose. Nothing but time. I fired once and the shadows thickened, as if swelling. I fired again and again, emptying the gun into the dark shape, yet it did not fall to the ground. Did not stop its approach. I stepped back once, twice . . . and slipped on the weird skin, a comical Keystone Kops swooping tumble, the back of my head crashing into the edge of the wooden chair with a crack, dazed. The lamp landed on the ground next to me, light tossed in every direction, unsettled.

Shooting stars and twanging guitars and piping organs, bass drum smack, 2, 3, 4—*fading* . . .

Shaking my head. A meteor shower. A heavy, ponderous sound from the direction of the window, plodding, scrabbling . . .

The shadow presence hesitated, dispersed. Black holes devoured the periphery.

Above me, behind the disintegrated shadows, a large reptile stretched out across the ceiling, pale flesh . . . unreal.

I blinked and almost passed out again. Glimpsed a man's silhouette as the large reptile turned its head toward me in a disturbingly human manner. Moaned with the ache as disorientation filled my eyes, my ears—

Shooting stars and twanging guitars and piping organs, bass drum smack, a voice; his voice! Muffled, but I heard him.

The large reptile shuffled swiftly from ceiling to floor and now hovered over me much closer than comfort would permit. A thunderclap, a jaw unhinged. I raised the gun toward it, to no avail. It opened its mouth wider and I heard the familiar voice more clearly now, familiar yet perverted under these circumstances. My vision fluttered as the wings of a dying moth.

I dropped the gun to fend for myself, battering at the scaly hide; again, to no avail. The pale reptile's mouth opened wider. I heard the voice that echoed from within one more time . . . and screamed into the cavernous maw as the singer, the poet, the avaricious creature annihilated my grasp on sanity as what must be the second section of the poem I'd read mere minutes ago bubbled up from the belly of this beast and coiled around me as a straitjacket. In Morrison's voice, I heard it all, my destiny set in stone for the eons that would follow . . .

"But free in what capacity
The only truth is what's left to experience
As the corpse of belief rots beneath a tapestry of curious darkness
Crematory heat washes over me
An eternity in the mouth of Hell awaits all who follow in my steps . . ."

# CHAPTER ELEVEN

# FLICKERING I ROAM

## E. CATHERINE TOBLER

**T**HE HAPPY ENDING to this story is: I don't have a hole in my heart—but if you ask Lisa, she will say I do, I do.

SHE RUNS ON the beach under a gray, clouded sky. Fluid, long-legged, shedding clothes, a laughing shadow. She outruns the drunken jackass chasing her, to the ocean that accepts her with a sloppy kiss. In the water, she is lit only by the rising sun beginning to stain the sky.

Then: swallowed by a thing unseen.

Her shrieks don't wake the man who has stumbled to the beach; he is lit by the vague sunrise on the inward rushing tide, asleep and maybe naked, but I don't care. My thoughts stay with her. Her, thrashing in blood-clouded water that doesn't look like blood-clouded water. Things unseen in the half dark of a morning that will never come.

No one understands what draws me to such images. I am only fifteen, I am only seventeen, I am only nineteen, they say. (I am only remembered in odd ages, never even, never steady.) My mother couldn't understand, my sister couldn't understand. Even my landlord wonders at the way I vanish into the fading Art Deco glory of the Photodrome every Sunday morning as though it were a church—and it has become such, the old screen the pulpit, the flickering camera light the glow of holy candles. A hole in my heart, I wanted to say.

But she alone upon the screen, shrieking that it hurts. She alone, drawn beneath the bloodied water as the sun rises higher. They cannot understand and I cannot explain. In the cool theater dark, I am her. She alone—me alone—silent shadow, drawn into the darkness a moment before camera lights stutter and stream onto the warped screen. Effortless and true, sinking into skins as the other people did the old chairs. I was anyone and everyone in the dark, in love with each and every single one of them. Majestic Sugar Hill, fierce Van Helsing, long-legged Frank N. Furter, fanged Carmilla, innocent Catherine, blood-drenched Carrie. Even Chrissie, swallowed by a shark. For hours after, I would exist in a haze, my steps not quite my own.

Life was easier this way, for my steps were complicated enough. The things I felt, the things I wanted. Life was easier and no one understood until she—Darlene—sank into the theater chair beside mine, the theater for once crowded because it was a premiere, a *new* horror, a thing that promised to truly terrify. Her arm jostled into mine, her cola sloshing down my pant leg in a cold rush, and she said "sorry—oh, sorry," but that it would be okay because we'd be in space soon, wouldn't we, and no one would be able to hear us scream—the posters promised. I knew then that she understood in a way no one else ever would; what happened within the theater was sacred. The silent and unseen transformation, the way a person became something else, became anyone else.

Darlene's warm arm nestled against mine in the theater dark and I knew; she would rub me black the way the old red velvet on the chairs had been rubbed black, with carelessness and age. I could not move, felt bound to stay precisely where I was, dark sweet cola soaking my sock as on the screen above us the *Nostromo* pushed itself into star systems it had no business entering. These things never ended well; ocean dark, planetary dust, a woman went in and always emerged changed (different, alien, other), if she came out at all.

Sometimes, we didn't come out.

(*lezzer* scribbled in iridescent pink lipstick on my door, smeared under the heel of my hand)

When the theater lights rose, the credits over, I sat alone in the row of worn chairs, heart pounding, sprawled. Darlene had gone and so too every other patron as if they had never existed, and the ushers swept with disinterest the popcorn that had been spilled. I walked out as if in a trance, but it was not the film that held me then. I could feel the press of her arm against mine as I walked the length of the theater to the doors. Only when I emerged into the spring night and could see the stars high above did I feel as Ripley might have, gazing across the unplundered fathoms of the universe.

(Ripley after, having woken, staring numb, because she knows.)

Every point burned utterly clear, more than they ever had—as if all of L.A.'s smog had been carried away by a giant hand. I walked to my apartment with the world humming in my ears, distant starship engines thrumming a melody that would call the aliens across the heavens.

Fany sees my ridiculous glowing face when I get home; she and her family run the restaurant beneath my apartment, and live in the apartment next door, a tangle of children and aunts and uncles. I wait tables at Pequeño's and Fany feeds me because she can't stand to see me so skinny, so deprived. She wants to know how anyone can make a meal of theater popcorn and cold soda as she shoves a plate of steaming tamales in front of me and bids me to eat. I eat and I don't explain because I can't explain and really, she doesn't want to know. No one wants to know.

*A hole in my heart and if I don't have to be me, it isn't there, it isn't there.*

"You call your sister?" she asks.

She doesn't want to know the answer to that either, because Fany turns away before I can give any, shuffling into the kitchen to finish her cleaning. I eat, and wash my dishes when done, and climb the stairs to my small room. It is not much, but it is mine. My family thinks I am going to film school, thinks that's why California and Los Angeles, and once this was so; now, it is not. My days are films and books and studying my own way; my days are writing letters to my sister Lisa, and folding them into a drawer.

Other mornings, it's not the Photodrome, but the used bookstore that occupies my interest, squatting on the corner across from Pequeño's. I think it has been there about forever, its roof beginning the slow collapse into its foundation. This morning, she's in there—Darlene—parked in the corner of my usual section, a copy of *The Howling* in her hands. Her fingers slide down the page and come away blackened, as if the ink was still fresh enough to lift, to sink into the whorls that mark her. I stare at her because she looks like Marki Bey stepped straight out of the movie screen, tall and black with her hair a great thundercloud around her face. Her mouth lifts in a questioning smile. I nod at her book.

"You read *The Shining*?" is what comes out of my mouth. Her eyes brighten.

"They both have Hallorans," we say together and I can't shake the feel of her arm against mine in the theater. I laugh and stare and she stares back and I wonder if the Hallorans in the books are connected, but it doesn't matter because she's staring at me.

They're holding a book for me at the desk, but after I pick it up and come back to the shelves to browse, she's gone. *The Howling* sits on the shelf, poking out from the rest of the row as if left to be found, and I snatch it up, clutching it against my chest as I wander the cluttered aisles. I breathe in the smell of used books, but it's her scent that lingers, spilled cola in the dark, even if I do not find her. I pay for my books and go, and when I get home these books go into a drawer, because some part of me can't bear the idea of opening them; they need to stay as they were when my path crossed hers. Until our paths cross again. Laughing shadow, accepted with a sloppy kiss.

SHE DREAMS AND is terrified. Her hair is a seaweed tangle around her face, dark strands trailing down across breasts barely concealed by a pink nightgown. There is something regal about her even in terror. The slant of lashes against pale skin, the sneer of lips.

She dreams of being enclosed into a coffin—No, a sarcophagus; it gleams in the torch light, gems from another land framing her face. I can feel the heat of Egypt within them, can hear the footsteps of Anubis approaching. The priest bends to his work, piercing my nostril to extract blood and brain, that these things may be preserved for another life.

Then: my hand taken, severed at the wrist.

I know it's coming—I have been here before—but I still jolt, mostly because I feel the warmth of fingers steal around my own wrist. I hold my breath and don't dare look away from the screen; blood spills from her wrist and why would they ever take her hand, but the hand around my own—

It quiets the hole in my heart.

It draws me away from the screen and back into my own body, where my heart runs the way it always should have—smooth, easy, calm. I close my fingers into those holding me, and float inside my own skin, trusting what it feels, what it *knows*. By the movie's end, that hand is gone, I am again alone. The hole in my heart whistles soft.

I leave the theater as always, alone and not. My step carries the pride of an Egyptian queen brought back from the dead, but then must also carry the inevitable betrayal she suffered. I reach Pequeño's during the afternoon quiet and my shoulders have slumped, Egyptian queen drained. Fany sees me and clicks her tongue.

"You call your sister."

I have always heard this as a question, but realize it is not and never has been. I settle at the bar, only two of the tables in the room taken, and Fany slides a heaping plate in front of me—she has saved carnitas with fresh corn tortillas and I am helpless before such offerings. Once I have cleaned my plate, I bus my own dishes; I have a shift today, a shift I would rather not take, but as I tie my apron around my hips, I see her. The girl with the thundercloud hair.

Fany seats her in my section—the girl slides into the booth, sets a stack of books on the table, and eyes the menu as if she means to rip it apart item by item. Fany shuffles back to the kitchen, but not before thumping my shoulder. I don't know what she means, affection or irritation, but I move toward the table. I approach with a water glass that has seen better days; its plastic is hazy and nicked on the bottom edge, but it reminds me of the buildings outside, Art Deco ladies showing their age.

She is alone in the booth. She looks up at me and the world condenses. There is only her, glowing and dark face within clouded hair. She shows her age, too, but within there is a sprinkle of barely visible freckles that splatter nose and cheeks. Thirteen, there are thirteen. She is a movie screen and I am no longer myself, but her. Sinking.

"Well, hullo," she says and I cannot find so much as a hello to say in return. "Darlene," she adds, and it sounds like *darling* and I remain lost.

(It's not iridescent pink that colors her lips, but full-bodied wine, grapes with vines tangled. It's not *lesbo* or *lezzie*, it's only *love*.)

"Can I—" Take your order, that's what I'm supposed to say, but this is not what comes out.

*Have this dance?*

*Take you to a movie?*

*Talk to you about those Hallorans, because how could they not be connected?*

"Champurrado," she says.

It takes me thirteen freckles to realize she is ordering. I slide my pen from my apron and write this word upon my notepad (last sheet, she is the last sheet in my pad of paper).

"And maybe a side of churros?"

I look at her over the edge of the notepad. "Maybe?"

"Definitely."

In the kitchen, Fany wrinkles her nose at the too-sweet combination, says to suggest horchata and no churros, but still makes the order. It is perfect, the champurrado steaming, the churros crusty and sweet. I set Darlene's food on the table and her long fingers enclose my wrist. Swallowed by a thing seen. She nods to the bench across from her and I sit.

Fany will eventually holler at me, but the restaurant is quiet, the other tables are not mine and nearly done, so I sit and I watch Darlene as she drinks, as she bites into one long churro and sugar flakes onto the plate. She laughs and wipes her mouth clean. (Warm fingers, warmer tongue.) She takes a breath and I feel it stir in my own chest.

"There is a movie this Sunday," she says. "A movie we should see."

"There is always a movie," I say, then I manage to spit my name out in an inelegant lump between us.

"Rachel." In her mouth, my name is anything but a lump; it is a thread woven back and forth across my heart and pulled tight.

Months may pass as we sit, my name on her tongue along with the champurrado she continues to swallow, but it cannot be months, because the sky outside is still, early summer sun flooding through Pequeño's painted windows to leave strange shadows on the floor, to become tangled in the myriad brown curls and puffs of her hair. I think the shadows move— Chrissie cutting through the water, sunlit—but it is only Darlene's hand, placing mine upon the stack of books she brought. They hum.

"I brought you these."

They are nothing I have seen at the used store before; one is old and bound in what looks like leather, a golden title down its spine in letters I hardly recognize. Others are battered, having seen many readings even if I know them to be new. *The Shining* is there, a book I borrowed from the library but could not afford to buy, and beneath it a stack of magazines. *Terror Tales, Ghost Stories, Whispers.* I shiver to look at them.

I want to ask her why and want to ask where she goes after the movie ends—before the movie ends?—but can only feel the hum of the books through the palm of my hand.

Then: the heat of her champurrado-warmed fingers against my wrist. She moves, standing, a laughing shadow, sunlit windows behind her. I think she will sever my wrist and I will bleed into every container she brings forward, allowing her to carry me into another life, but she goes as she has gone before, leaving me to sit alone with her stack of books, with the promise of a movie on Sunday, with the taste of her champurrado in my very own mouth.

ON THE SCREEN, everyone prone on the floor, breathing, breathing. A person might wish to retreat, but cannot escape what is coming, what arrives, but Frank doesn't arrive so much as he already exists within every person within the room. He is a heartbeat, he is the insistent stomp of a glittered white heel against a black elevator floor. He is gravity, descending. Prowling confident because he is not of this world (different, alien, other) but has made it his own. These are his people, this is his time, warped or not; he will use both as he will.

I slide into him, stride up the aisle in that lanky body, turn on the stairs, and survey the people before me, the people beyond me. I am tall in these legs, in these shoes, and through his eyes, I find Darlene, Darlene who sits beside me with the stuttering film light raining through her thundercloud hair, and I kiss her mouth, her soft wine mouth and become—I become.

I flicker *through* Darlene, seeing the Photodrome's screen through her eyes. The screen vomits stars, endless glitter running in a stream that billows upon the unused stage, but within the glitter I see coalescing star systems— the motion of a vast and unknown universe (galaxy, cradle, womb) above me, and I look for known things, I reach for Ripley, but it is only her numb and knowing stare I find in the black of space. She knows and I am about to.

Planets whirl into being, pressed inward as they press outward until they are perfect spheres hurling through the glittering black. Some planets assemble into systems, but still others pull away, spinning deeper into the black, to the edge of a galaxy where at last they tire and cling to one another as they spiral around a throbbing star. This star is not red, blue, or yellow; it is a word, I do not know, and when I press my finger (Darlene's finger, darling's finger) into the flooding glitterstream, it pulls me in, down, over.

A map imprints itself onto my skin, paths burning into me the way the first fires burned into the universe, shaping the cosmos as iron is forged with hammer and fire, and I can hear distant screams

(swallowed by a thing unseen)

but they do not register as my own even as my throat grows raw. Pathways shine outward from my skin and I know where the world is going, I know the thing that will consume us and if I—

(if I look)

(blood-clouded water that doesn't look like blood-clouded water)

I lift my head and *look* and the thing (the undoing, the unbeing) that will consume us rushes toward me, through me and *into* me the way I did Darlene, the way I did countless people over countless years if only to escape my own skin. My body no longer my own but a body that has been burned into a map for a thing to follow—A map to show It the way, the way to the end of the—

It looks at me, through me; my eyes itch with the creature behind them. It lifts my hands to study the careful char of my arms; It presses its oily hands into each and every mark until I am running with black oil, until It sets me aflame and I wake screaming, screaming in the theater dark and the ushers are there, trying to touch me, to calm me, telling me it was only a movie, it was only—Only.

Darlene is gone and I crumple alone on the sticky floor until I can finally pick myself up, until I can flee the theater, but even the night sky—did it become night, even though it was morning sunlight that caught in darling

Darlene's hair when we walked hand in shaking hand, into the theater and buried ourselves into the seats we had always occupied—had it become night, and when was the night sky naked and hard, and I cannot run fast enough to elude its gaze; I cannot escape the scrutiny, the *it* that follows me to my door, my door marked as one might mark a tomb, a plea, a warning to stay away—marked with pink lipstick insults, *lesbo, lesser, lezzie, les les les*— Then: swallowed by a thing unseen.

MORNING COMES WITH its normal speed, but the world is slowed for me, seen through eyes burned to ash. I observe things I have never before: the careless motion of dust in sunlight, the oblique tracery of shadows across a floorboard, the way paper becomes not-paper when its edge is frayed enough, as it is on Darlene's copy of *The Shining*. I reach for the book, but my hands are streaked with lipstick and my arms are burned with black patterns that make too much sense to my aching mind, so I draw back into myself where the hole in my heart wheezes.

Later (it is later than I know) I pull my long sleeves down my arms, even if there is a whorl of burned map visible at my collar still. I have a shift at the restaurant and need to hide even as I am seen. I suppose it was always there, running under my skin in secret rivers. Visible now—this pathway to the end—but never not there, infecting every part of me. It was easier to deny; admission was too hard, allowing that there were things unknown, matters uncontrolled, desires the world would refuse. Easier to let everything pass unseen and unconfessed—until the world (until I) reached a point where such denials became impossible, when my skin would burst and every hidden thing would spill like sunshine across snow, illuminating everything no one ever wanted to see—to feel.

The lipstick will not come off of my hands. Every line is stained pink and I leave blotches on the letters—the letters—to Lisa, Lisa, Lisa *someone*. The letters—

The letters are not here, not pressed into books, and drawers, not stuffed into pillow cases, not hidden in plain sight over lampshades where the writing fades under incandescent glow. The letters were mailed, the letters arrived and went unread, the letters were rejected as I have been rejected, and it's only darling—It's only Darlene who—Who.

I stagger from my apartment, tugging long sleeves down as my skin bleeds light over the walls. Another slur on my door, but I leave it, counting every downward step to the restaurant, because I'm late, late. Inside, Fany has been watching the door and she exhales when she sees me.

If I look—

I slide into her for a moment, to feel the relief that pours through her, to feel the way that breath moves in her chest. I look at myself through her eyes and want to cry—I am not me, I am become something else, something beyond explanation. I glow with the light of a very distant sun, a lamppost in a darkening forest. But she smiles at the sight of me, and I feel something inside Fany wanting out, something is ready to burst, but she turns before it can, laughing shadow, and vanishes into the kitchen.

Darlene orders champurrado when she arrives and I sit across from her, as if I have done so every night of my shift forever. Fany doesn't care, doesn't holler, and Darlene holds my hand, presses her thumb into the star that marks my wrist, and smiles.

"Oh you," she whispers.

Everything is connected then. If I am a lamppost, if I am a map, she is the one wandering. I open my mouth to ask, but my tongue is clumsy and also burned with a thousand tangled paths. She leans in, the scent of chocolate and ozone between us, and reads my tongue, and only then do I ask.

"Those Hallorans?"

"Everything is connected," she says. "These heavens are made of circles, without corner, without cease. You start where you end, Rachel. A hole is also a circle."

There is a knot in my chest and Darlene pulls the threads tighter. The hole closes, vent shaft drilling itself down to a pinprick, metal whisper in the dark. Darlene stares because she has seen and because she knows and her body ripples. She moves as if she is a storm gathering over the ocean, both things impossibly wide and I feel the sky break, water colliding with water. It would be easy, to sink into her, to let her sink into me, but her mouth—

It opens, unhinges, and my body, though burned with the map that will bring *It* to us, refuses.

I bolt from the booth, from the restaurant, but she is quick on my heels. There is a momentarily relief at the glimpsed night sky (come, my body screams, and light pours out of me, throwing stars and lines against the side of the building), but I refuse it the way I refused Darlene. I lunge for the stairs, but Darlene tackles me from behind. It is a hard, mad scramble upward, and I think *if I can reach my door, if I can reach my room, seal myself up, sleep it away*, but Darlene pulls me down, ripping at jeans and blouse until both are tattered beneath sudden, fearsome claws.

I don't stop to think because the light rushes through me, will soon burst beyond the shelter of the building and into the stars, and I am in a panic to get away, to stop this from happening even as I know I cannot, even as I crave the light, the thing that will come for the light. Everywhere Darlene touches me, the light spills free, as if my skin has been stripped to reveal the ceaseless spin of an eternally living sun beneath. Her touch liberates, decimates, and she is swallowing the light before I can stop its eruption out of me. She swallows and I scream, paddling up the stairs, to my door, my ever-distant door, but I cannot escape.

Her (my) shrieks don't wake anyone; if anyone stumbles upon this scene, they are drunk, asleep, unaware. She alone upon the stairs (me, oh darling), shrieking that it hurts; she alone, thrashing in a blood-clouded storm that doesn't look like a blood-clouded storm. Things unseen in the half dark of a morning that will never come. They cannot understand and I cannot explain. Under the water, it is calm, calm and so quiet, and I cannot hear the thing swallowing me.

She dreams and is terrified. Her hair is a seaweed tangle around her face, dark strands trailing down across hands still stained lipstick pink. If it is only a dream, it isn't there, it isn't there. She can watch from a distance as her body vanishes down the black maw and comes apart. Fingers that aren't quite fingers sift through the rubble of her, tracing the paths burned into skin, into lung and heart. But it's not a dream, and she doesn't only watch. She can see blue sky through the tears in her eyes, and she's going home.

She—

I.

I.

I reach for those not-fingers, ripping them away before they can touch the hole in my heart. Is this thing Darlene? Has It moved through her body and into my own? I do not know, for I cannot see her face in the endless dark. Only the presence of It, creeping ever closer. Chrissie was consumed, pulled under, but not Ripley and not Frank, and I plant what remains of my feet upon the stairs, saying no, no further, and the darkness shrieks.

It swarms over me, a million stinging mouths, and there is nowhere not in anguish, and for a long while (a year, a decade, the time it takes a star system to form) I hang inside that pain, unable to get a hold on anything else. Then, my fingers latch onto a mouth, holding hard to teeth that mean to rip through flesh and bone. I disregard that, hauling the mouth closer, bringing the beast within swallowing range.

Then: swallowed.

It sees me every step of the way and has wrapped Itself so completely within me that It cannot escape. I swallow and swallow, until the darkness is beaten back, until I can see the edge of the roof high above, and the gleam of distant stars (home, the thing inside me screeches). My hands come away empty, my skin splattered with blood but not ash, not oil. I never burned, was never a map, just a girl, a confused girl, until—Until.

It is Fany who finds me. Fany who crumples to her knees at the bottom of the stairs and weeps at the sight of the wreckage. *You call your sister*, she says. Blood has colored the white steps red, my body folded at the threshold of my door. I watch her, I become her yet again, and she is (we are) unable to stagger up the stairs to take a closer look. She has seen enough. The body, the blood, the slurs on my door.

It is Fany who smooths my hair down before they carry me away and Fany who later goes through my things, placing them into carefully labeled boxes. Fany who contemplates the tube of pink lipstick and wonders, because she never saw me wear it. It is Fany who tells the police about the strange girl who came to the restaurant, the girl who bothered me for weeks on my shifts. Of this girl there is no sign but for her name that decorates my books, my walls, my letters to Lisa.

Darling.

Darling.

Darling.

They cannot understand and I cannot explain as I flicker ever on— toward this girl, this woman who climbs the steps (cleaned, cold), calling my *sister* who knew and did not know. I cannot explain but for the flare of pain that will flood her (it always comes), cannot explain but for the way she stares, numb and knowing. I sink into her, the hole in my heart pulled tight, and I become—

I become.

# CHAPTER TWELVE

# SEWN INTO PIECES, STITCHED INTO PLACE

## DAMIEN ANGELICA WALTERS

**B**REATHE NORMALLY. COUNT backward from one hundred. No matter how strong you are, no matter how much you fight, you'll never reach zero.

Never.

LISA'S DRIVING TOO fast in her still-smells-new Chevette, driving too fast and not paying enough attention, but her body knows the route well enough: through the heart of Towson, past Hutzler's on York Road, down Joppa Road to Goucher Boulevard. The roads are empty—everyone home snug in their beds—and all the dark windows make the Baltimore suburb feel like a ghost town. Lisa fumbles for the radio dial. Blondie sings *Call me,* but she can't call away the chaos in Lisa's head.

Left turn here, right turn there, and then into the apartment complex; lock the car, cut across the parking lot, keys in hand, heading inside where everything is fine and right. Too much coffee has turned her body into a mess of jitters—almost thirty-six hours at the hospital this shift but she's a first year resident and she has to prove her worth and pay her dues—but she's so tired she can't untangle her thoughts.

*Count backward . . .*

The patient did, she counted backward, and Lisa said, "You'll be fine. I'll see you when you wake up."

But there was no waking up, and it wasn't Lisa's fault—she was anesthesiology, not surgery—but still, she told the woman (who reminded her so much of Rachel) she'd see her soon.

She locks the door behind her, drops her keys on the small table in the foyer, and heads for the bathroom. Paws through the medicine cabinet, tubes of lipstick and a bottle of aspirin landing in the sink, until her fingers touch the scalpel's handle.

Her scrubs are a size too big and when she unties the drawstring, they fall to her ankles. The skin of her inner thigh is marked with a line of narrow scars, and Lisa traces them with her fingertips, searching for the message they contain. *I know who you are*, they say.

The scalpel in her shaking hand makes a quick bite of pain like a rough kiss—not too deep, never too deep—a lipstick smear of red, a release, and she sits on the edge of the tub, breathing hard, her thigh warm and sticky. Her thoughts stop flying in a thousand directions, settle like birds on a telephone wire. She counts backward—start from one hundred—until her breath slows, until the wound stops bleeding.

She cleans up the mess; no stitches needed this time, only a bit of gauze and tape. Only a flesh wound, as the men from Monty Python would say. She catches her gaze in the mirror—clear now, focused—but she doesn't look too long because there's judgment and guilt hiding there, too. They can both go to hell; everyone copes in different ways, and she isn't hurting anyone but herself, and even that's negligible.

Sleep doesn't come easy, it rarely does these days, so she puts in a load of laundry instead and pours a glass of wine. Every time she blinks, the patient's face swims into view, a face so much like Rachel's: dark lashes, high cheekbones, a dimple on one cheek, wide green-grey eyes. It was the eyes more than anything, eyes holding hurt in their depths, and Rachel's were ever that way, even when they were young, as if some secret insult was tattooed on her soul. A wounded animal, bracing for another kick.

Maybe if the resemblance hadn't been so strong, the loss wouldn't sting so much. Patients died sometimes and while this patient's death wasn't her fault, Lisa knew if she practiced long enough, there was a strong chance she'd wear the stain of blame on her hands. Lead a patient into the grey of almost-death and eventually, one would remain there.

Glass in hand, she paces through her apartment, passes the spare bedroom once, twice. Inside the closet, three boxes sit. They've been sitting there for three months, waiting for Lisa to cut the tape and pull out the contents. Three boxes, all that's left of her sister. The police can't find the woman who killed her and don't seem bothered overmuch by that inability. A silent message that Rachel (*that* kind of person) isn't worth their time.

Lisa refills her empty glass, and her feet steer her into the bedroom. Hands drag the boxes out, palms skim the shipping labels. Carefully taped by Rachel's landlord, the boxes survived the trip from California to Maryland well enough, but what an ordeal that was. The woman, Fany, first insisting that Lisa come and get the boxes, eventually understanding she couldn't and agreeing to send them. Lisa sent money for shipping along with labels to make sure they arrived at the right place.

Boxes still unopened, Lisa perches on the edge of the guest bed. Funny, since she's never had a guest here, but she thought maybe one day Rachel would come back, would come home, and might need a place to stay while she found her footing.

"Your sister is dead," so Fany had said, and it took Lisa several long minutes for the words to sink in because how was that even possible? Rachel was too young to be dead, which was such a stupid thing to think, because Lisa saw the dead and the dying all the time and death didn't give a shit how many wrinkles you had.

(Damage done can't be undone.)

And then Fany said, "You never call your sister."

Who was she to judge?

Mouth pressed in a thin line, Lisa fetches the scalpel from the bathroom, picks the heaviest box and slices open the packing tape, her finger guiding the blade in a neat line. The cardboard flaps gape (there are a million kinds of wounds) and the scent of old paper emerges.

Inside the box, a pile of books. *The Howling, The Shining.* Such dreck, such a waste of anyone's time, and for supposedly creative people, their titles were anything but. One of the tags shows the price: $8.95. Who would pay that much for such crap?

So like Rachel, though. Head in the clouds, feet in the shadows, sleepwalking in a nightmare of her own making. She once said that in a book, you can be anyone you want to. Lisa doesn't remember what she said back. (This may or may not be the truth. She may have rolled her eyes and said reading that sort of shit can't make you anyone else. Go back to school, read something that matters, *do* something that matters.)

Lisa grabs *The Howling,* reads the back cover copy, flips through the pages. A word is written over and over in the margins—*darling*—the handwriting ranging from small and neat to barely legible scrawls, but still recognizably Rachel's. The next book holds the same, and the next and the next. Some pages are covered almost completely, the letters thick and torn through.

She holds the book to her forehead, eyes closed. *Rachel, what in the hell were you going through?*

"You know, you always knew, but it doesn't matter anymore," a voice whispers. "You judged her, your parents judged her, and she ran away like the gingerbread man. Ran away, found darling, found Death. And where were you?"

Another voice says, "You never call your sister."

Wedged between two books, a tube of lipstick; Lisa uncaps it, rolls out a shimmery pink tube, the top mashed flat. It's a color she can't imagine Rachel wearing at all, but her sister was always a question Lisa couldn't answer, or maybe she was an answer Lisa refused to accept.

Tucked on the side of the box, there's a stack of letters bound with a rubber band, the envelopes sealed and unstamped, Lisa's name and address carefully written. Lisa fans the letters with her thumb, sets them aside. Not now. Not yet.

At the very bottom, there's a book much larger than the others. Bound in old leather with no title on the cover, flaking gilt on the spine. When she opens it, she smells the tang of antiseptic, the hint of blood, urine, and feces beneath—the smell of the hospital, the smell of everything that makes sense. Some of the pages have handwritten notes, impossible to read. Some have strange illustrations. The others make no sense to her. She drops it back into the box with a thump. Junk and rubbish, nothing more.

LISA, WORKING; BLUE scrubs, paper shoe covers. Count backward from one hundred, she tells the patient. A middle-aged man, safe to look at because he doesn't resemble anyone she knows. Minor surgery, no complications, full recovery expected. Already beginning to stir when they wheel him into the recovery room.

Out in the hallway, she wipes sweat from her brow and contemplates another cup of coffee. Maybe a quick nap. No time, though. No time for anything but a quick breather and that's okay because that's the way it always is.

The sound of a voice drifts down the hall, and she doesn't pay it any attention at first; the hospital is always full of voices.

*Lisa?*

She whips her head around. An orderly passes, nodding as he does; a nurse heads in the opposite direction, her eyes focused elsewhere. Then the hallway is briefly empty save Lisa and—

*Lisa?*

—a strange sensation runs through her abdomen, a pushing. Gentle and feather light. She touches her belly. Nothing there. Of course nothing and—

"Doctor?" The nurse, a new one whose name Lisa can't remember, smiles. "Mr. Thompson's wife is asking to talk to you, if you don't mind."

Lisa puts on a smile of her own. "Of course not. Lead the way."

WAITING ON A cot in the doctor's lounge. The lights dimmed, the room shadowy. Lisa's stomach roils from the shitty coffee. No wonder some of the doctors pop uppers. She hasn't needed them yet, but yet is the operative term; everyone has an exhaustion point.

The door opens and another resident comes in. Tall, dark hair, circles under his eyes, too. Michael smiles. Locks the door. Pulls off his scrubs, his cock already half-erect. The cot is cramped, but they're used to it by now. They say not a word, stifling their moans against palms, each other's shoulders.

If he feels the scab on her thigh, he gives no sign. Once, he asked about the scars, but only with his eyes, and when her gaze gave no answer in reply, which was all the answer he needed to know, he said nothing more.

After, his chest to her back, he says, "Maybe dinner this week? We're both off-shift Wednesday."

She makes a sound, noncommittal.

"Come on. If I'm good enough to fuck, I should be good enough for dinner."

"It's not that."

"Then what?"

She nibbles her lower lip. "I like things this way. No complications, no declarations of love and forever."

He nuzzles the side of her neck. "Dinner doesn't mean forever. It's just dinner. Not like I'm going to ask you to fetch my slippers and call me darling."

*Darling.* A chill races down her spine.

"Are you okay?"

"I'm fine, just chilly."

He grabs the blanket, pulls it over both of them, and in minutes, he's asleep; Lisa closes her eyes, listens to him breathe. Feels herself start to slip away; *call me darling, call me darling,* flicks through her mind and—

Something shoves against her abdomen. She sits up, holding in a cry. The sensation again, softer now but still there, inside her.

He blinks. "What's wrong? Did you get paged?"

She can't find the words to describe what she felt, how to make it sound like truth instead of madness.

"Yes," she lies. She gets up, dons her scrubs, kisses his cheek.

He grabs her hand. "Think about dinner, okay?"

"Okay."

In the bathroom, she lifts her shirt, and her stomach is flat, as always. Still, she presses knuckles against it, thinks of the movie that came out last year with Sigourney Weaver, and barks a mirthless laugh. Then her name *does* crackle over the intercom.

Count backward from one hundred, darling. Count back . . .

HOME AGAIN, HOME again, jiggity-jig. Take-out Chinese, chopsticks she can't use properly so she threads them through a twist of her hair, fixing it tight against her scalp. She puts the radio on. Blondie again. *Call me,* she sings.

(You never call your sister.)

A chunk of pepper steak sticks in Lisa's throat, and she chokes it down. No, she didn't call Rachel, but Rachel didn't call her either.

(You never write to your sister.)

Lisa pushes her plate away and stalks into the spare bedroom, rummaging in the box for the stack of letters. Carries it back into the dining room. Blondie has been called away, and Pink Floyd is building their wall of brick, but when Lisa slides the rubber band from the letters, the music fades to an afterthought.

Gauging by the ink—faded to ghosts on some of the envelopes, strong on others—the letters aren't in any sort of order; Lisa picks one at random and uses her knife to slice open the envelope.

*Dear Lisa:*

She closes her eyes against the burn of tears. Blinks them away. The rest of the letter is cheery, talking about Rachel's apartment and the cheap rent, her job, her landlord, a movie she saw in a nearby theater. The phrasing, the cadence of the sentences, sounds exactly like Rachel speaking and Lisa wipes fresh tears away, thinks of what she said to Rachel when she told Lisa she was moving and why.

"Stop saying that. You're not . . . one of them. You're just confused, that's all. You need to go back to school. Or get a better job."

And the look in Rachel's eyes—the wounded animal hurt once more.

"I know who I am," Rachel said, her voice soft. "I know what I am."

Then she hung up the phone, and that was the last time they spoke.

Another letter contains much the same, but the third tells of a woman Rachel's met, no name, but that she's sure, really sure, and she's sorry if this hurts Lisa, but she can't help who she is.

With a grimace, Lisa tosses the letter aside. Opens another. The page is filled with the word *darling*. Nothing more, just the word written over and over again like in the books. Lisa lets the letter fall to the floor, presses fingertips to her temples.

*Lisa?*

The push against her belly, and there's no mistaking, it's coming from the inside and Lisa gets up fast enough to knock her chair down.

"Stop it, just stop it."

The push again. Lisa slides her hand beneath her shirt, feels the shape of another, fingers splayed, pressing against the skin below her navel. She yanks her arm away and falls to her knees, breathing through her mouth. The hand pushes; Lisa squeezes her eyes shut, moans through a clenched jaw. Refuses to look because it isn't real, this isn't a movie, especially not one of the grim movies Rachel was so fond of, and there are no monsters gestating inside her or anywhere else. There are no monsters at all.

(You never call your sister.)

"Rachel?" Her voice, a rasp of sandpaper.

But only silence replies, and the sensation of a hand ebbs. Now she looks and her skin is perfectly fine, perfectly normal, and she's crying or laughing or both, but it doesn't matter because everything is fine—

*darling*

—everything is more than fine. She runs to the bathroom, takes up the scalpel. Makes another cut next to the one still-healing; shudders in relief when the blood trickles down her leg.

"Everything's fine," she says.

LISA, IN THE morning: coffee, toothbrush and mouthwash, still not quite awake but stumbling into the shower. Hot water, shampoo, soap. Running her fingers along the scab on her thighs, but only one scab. She steps out of the spray, looks down. The new cut isn't scabbed, but it isn't bleeding either. The edges are smooth from the scalpel's blade; the cut itself gaping slightly open. She shudders, but there's no pleasure in it.

*Lisa?*

It's Rachel's voice, coming from the open wound, and it echoes off the bathroom tiles, echoes in Lisa's mind. She scrambles from the tub, mouth open and making a sound inhuman and raw. The cut opens and closes with her movements and—

*Lisa?*

—inside, she's inside, she isn't dead but lost, only lost and—

143

Lisa crouches on the bath mat and presses her hands over her ears. *No, no, no, please stop, please stop. Nothing inside me,* she thinks. Nothing but blood and veins and organs and Rachel is dead and buried and gone and damage done can't be undone and there are no darlings, not here, not anywhere.

She rocks back and forth and when she realizes the voice is gone (*was never there, never there*), she covers the wound with a thick pad of gauze.

LISA GATHERS THE letters, puts them back in their envelopes, slides the rubber band around them, drops them back in the box of books. It was a mistake to read them, because she wasn't ready. She's been working too hard and too many hours and she doesn't have time to grieve. She shed plenty of tears at the funeral; for now they'll have to suffice. Like the others, the cut will heal in time. The scalpel must've slipped and cut deeper than usual; she should've stitched it closed.

She shuts the door to the guest bedroom. Beneath the gauze, the wound throbs in concert with her heart, two beats over and over again: *Ra-chel, Ra-chel, Ra-chel.*

THE WOUND DOESN'T heal. At night, Rachel calls for her, her voice slipping from beneath the bandage like ribbons of blood drawn into a syringe and coiling. Layers atop layers of gauze, and still Lisa can feel the wound opening and closing. A mouth with Rachel's voice. A song, a plea. Call me, but—

(You never call your sister.)

—it's too late and Lisa doesn't answer. A hand presses a gentle touch, retreats, but Lisa takes a deep breath. Rachel is gone. She's gone.

Michael asks her to dinner again, and they go to a small place in Little Italy, drink red wine and twine spaghetti around their forks. Walk around the Inner Harbor, marveling at the newly opened Harborplace and the National Aquarium both, and make plans to come back and visit the latter. But when he asks her up to his apartment, she thinks of the voice buried behind its blanket of gauze and says "no."

She tells her patients to "Count backward, count backward, darling," and they do.

LISA STRETCHES AWAKE, aware, beneath her sheets; the tape holding the gauze to her thigh catches on the fabric, and the bandage pulls free.

*Lisa?*

(You never call—

The scab has fallen off the older cut, revealing a pale pink line.

—your sister.)

The edges of the new cut pulse; not a mouth, but a vulva, swollen and ready. Gaping open, preparing to give life.

*Lisa?*

Rachel's voice is louder now, and Lisa blinks back tears. Her sister is still here, lost, but still here, and the girl who died in California must have been a different girl, a *darling* girl, but not her sister, not Rachel.

Sobbing, Lisa slips her fingers into the wound, opens it wider. She reaches in with one hand, then the other. One arm, then the other. She takes a deep breath, and slips into the waiting dark, wriggling her body until she's fully inside. Once there, she's surrounded with a red glow, not a darkness at all. It's warm and the walls are slick with moisture and smell of copper and musk.

"Rachel?" she calls out and her voice echoes.

In the final syllable, Rachel responds. "I'm here. I'm here!"

"Hold tight. I'll be there soon."

Ahead, there's a circular wall with a hole in the center. She pushes her fist through, dilating the hole wide enough to crawl through, and emerges into a cave, all striations of muscle in light and dark. Lisa wipes a slick of sweat from her brow. On each side of the cave, there are tunnels, and from deep within the one on the right, a flash of movement.

"Rachel?"

"I'm here!"

Lisa follows the voice into the tunnel. The walls press against her here, leaving her skin damp and sticky, plastering her hair to her skull. The warmth of the air tightens her chest, but she pushes on. At the end of the tunnel, an ovoid shape. On her belly, she slithers inside, and there, Rachel, curled on her side, eyes closed and knees drawn to her chest, within a transparent spherical casing.

"Rachel?"

No response. No movement.

Lisa digs her fingers into the casing. It's thin and rubbery, and she peels it open like a grape, but Rachel doesn't stir.

"I'm here. I'm here now. Everything's going to be okay."

Lisa strokes her shoulder and recoils. Rachel's skin is cold and not right, this is not right. No, it's okay. It will be okay. She just has to—

*Rebirth.*

Yes. That's what this is. A rebirth, a second chance for both of them, and Lisa will make everything right.

She loops an arm under Rachel and pulls her free. Her body is heavy, so heavy, but Lisa moves back through the tunnel, pulling with her free hand and scooting with her feet, holding tight to her sister. Slowly, she makes her way out of the tunnel, back into the cave, but the walls are melting, running, and the floor is a clotted soup. Sweat runs into her eyes as she grabs Rachel with both hands, lifting her up and over one shoulder.

The ground sucks at her feet, trying to drag her in and she falls to her knees. Rachel falls boneless and limp, and begins to slip into the murk. "No, no, no," Lisa whispers. She tries to pull Rachel free, but her hands slide over her sister's slick skin. Reaching around Rachel's back, she begins to lift her close, but her fingers sink *in*, and with a cry of surprise, she lets go. Rachel falls back into the mess with a squelching plop. Lisa grabs for her again and again, trying to catch hold, trying to hold tight, but Rachel is melting into the floor, slipping through Lisa's fingers.

"Stay with me," Lisa shrieks. "You have to stay."

But Rachel's skin sloughs off in Lisa's hands—shimmer of tendon, glint of bone—and Lisa turns away, retching. Her hair hanging ragged in her face, sobs breaking from her mouth, she crawls toward the still-dilated hole, each movement liquid and heavy.

She wiggles through headfirst, and behind her, there's a sound like a waterfall crashing onto rocks, and warm liquid splashes against her lower back and legs, but she keeps moving. The last passage, she only has to make it through this part; moving with her elbows and knees, she can see the gaping wound pulse, but with each pulse, the opening becomes smaller and smaller.

She shrieks again and moves forward, fingers touching, then grabbing, gripping, the edges of the cut. A hesitation, a thought of letting go, of slipping back into the cave and letting it take her in, but she heaves her body up and out, the edges of the wound whisking along her skin like a damp veil, and she collapses on her bed, covered in blood and muck.

"I'm sorry," she gasps between sobs. "So sorry."

*Lisa?*

"Rachel?"

The voice is coming from the wound, but Lisa presses both hands over her ears. No, she will not listen, she will not, because it isn't Rachel. It's a lie and a trick and a cruelty, but it isn't her sister. She presses her palm against the cut to muffle the sound and staggers into the bathroom. Grabs a needle and thread, no time to worry about sterilization. She holds her thigh tight against the sink so she can thread the needle without hearing the voice, but her fingers are shaking and—

*Lisa?*

—finally, the thread goes in. She jabs the needle in her skin, pulls the thread through. The stitches are messy and uneven (and she won't be able to hide this from Michael, not this) and the false-Rachel is calling her name, but Lisa makes the last stitch, ties the knot, and lets the needle fall from her hand. She sees the impression of a hand against the wound and small fingers of pain strain against the stitches, but the thread holds fast. The voice falls silent, and Lisa sinks to the floor, draws her knees beneath her chin, and sobs into her palms. Damage done can't be undone, and Rachel isn't inside her. She isn't anywhere but gone.

When her tears stop falling, she washes her face and hands and heads for the guest bedroom. Moving on instinct alone, she hefts the box of books to one hip and carries it out to the curb, the wound on her inner thigh thumping with a thick and heavy warmth.

Necrosis: the death of living cells.

Michael kisses her forehead and says, "Everything's going to be okay, baby. Don't worry. Everything's going to be fine. You'll see."

Lisa nods because her voice is buried inside in the pain. She wants to wipe away his mask of guilt; it isn't his fault she let it go so long, isn't his fault she wouldn't answer his calls, isn't his fault she collapsed—lucky, so lucky he was there to catch, to hold, to keep. Why, he wanted to know, why? She couldn't explain that she had to kill the voice and then make sure it was dead and, too, this was her penance, her price, because she never called her sister, not even once.

Sorry, she's so sorry, and he needs to know, but when her voice starts to emerge in a tremulous croak, they wheel her away to bright lights and antiseptic white.

The anesthesiologist has a kindly face and a genuine smile. "You'll be right as rain in no time at all, Lisa," he says. "Doctor Harrow is one of the best."

Yes, one of the best and he's promised to do everything he can to save her leg, but his expression said, "I wish you'd come to see me sooner," and some things, once lost, can't ever be saved.

"Breathe normally," the anesthesiologist says. "Count backward from one hundred."

*Rachel, are you there?* Her thought, a thread floating in the growing dark, and then a hand takes hers and holds tight.

Count backward, darling. Count back . . .

147

# CHAPTER THIRTEEN

# TOO MANY PAGES

## SIMON STRANTZAS

**Y**OUR FIRST SIGHT of the book is indelible. Your father is yelling at your mother on a busy street for reasons you cannot grasp. She does not say anything, but you can see her wincing from his tone, and when you look to those passing by for help they seem purposely oblivious to what's happening. You feel as though you should be crying, but each raised word frightens the tears away. All you can do is listen and wish you were someplace else.

When everything is done, he buys both you and your mother an ice cream at the soda fountain, and for a few minutes everything seems okay. Your mother is still shaking, it's true, but he has his arm around her and is giving you that wink he gives you after baseball practice. It feels good, but that feeling also makes your stomach uneasy. Maybe it's the ice cream. You ask to excuse yourself, but before you go, he gives you a dime and says, "When you're done, why don't you go across the street to that bookstore? See if they got anything you like. I want to talk to your mother about grown-up stuff." You look at her, but she doesn't look at you. Still, she nods, and you don't hesitate, worried about what he'll do if you dawdle. You run over to the bookstore as fast as you can manage.

Inside looks like heaven. For a while, you forget everything that has led you there to that time, to that moment. You are among friends, even though no one is around. You walk through the stacks, trying to take it all in, but worry your eyes aren't big enough. Books pile from floor to ceiling, two rows deep. Stacks hang off random shelves or are pushed into corner piles. The air smells of moldering paper, but the man sitting behind the counter is dressed in a sharp blazer and tie. He wears thick-rimmed glasses and stares at you over them.

"Are you here alone?" he asks you.

You nod.

"Do you like books?" he asks you.

You nod again.

He stands, leans over the counter, and with a swish of his arm he says, "Then by all means, look around."

The shelves are endless to your child eyes. Stacks tower over you, multicolored totem poles of spines. Most of the books are too old for you, too dry, too boring, but you love to look at them, run your fingers along them, pretend they are strings on a great harp that only you can play. You hear the notes in your head as you walk by, but one note rings wrong. You stop and move back to it. The book, that book—there's something there that's not right.

You've never seen a book like this. Its unevenly gilted spine feels cool, its cover smooth. The book lies flat on the shelf, a stack of books about it that look dry and brittle, a few books beneath that have grown moldy. You hesitate to put your fingers on its spine to pull it free, convinced it will feel like the skin of a snake, even though you touched a snake at the zoo only a month ago and you know their skin is dry. Nevertheless, your tiny fingers find the edges of the spine and you start to pull it free. Even then, you aren't sure why you need to do so.

But before you can extract the book, the shop's door swings open, thrown aside to allow your father's entrance. By the smile on his face, he is proud of himself, and even as a child you know this is all about presentation. You pull your finger from the book, worried he will notice, and instead approach him to say hello. Your father seems inordinately pleased to see you.

"Did he cause you any trouble?" your father asks.

The store clerk shakes his head.

"As quiet as a mouse," he says, and winks in your direction. You smile weakly, shyly, in response.

"Good," your father mumbles, then kneels down to talk to you face-to-face. His breath is like a liquor truck has exploded. "Pick a book," he says. "Any book. Your mom and I will pay, but make it fast because we're leaving. Your mom isn't feeling well."

You aren't feeling well either, and you look across at that sagging shelf upon which the book, *that* book, is resting inconspicuously. You want to suggest it, but your father's eyes are strange, and the store clerk's indifferent. Instead, you settle for the first thing that comes to hand.

"Really?" your father says with a frown, looking at the book whose cover depicts a young girl sitting on a stoop, fists on her chin. Worst of all, the book is much too young for you. You shrink from embarrassment, squeaking out a nod.

"Okay," he says, resigned. "You're the boss. Just like your mother."

He smiles and winks again and your insides shrivel all the more. He takes you by the hand and leads you out of the store. You turn back for just a moment before you pass through the door and into the sunlight. The store clerk has his head down, reading something on the counter. But you aren't looking at him.

Since seeing that book, you've had nightmares about it, strange memories of being in that store, of watching that book peel itself open unattended, of watching all shapes and non-shapes of creatures crawl forth from its far too many pages—a portal from somewhere or sometime else. Amorphous, winged, indescribable, the nightmares spew forth from within your nightmare, crowding you back in your dreamtime construction of the store. When you awaken, you find yourself disoriented, sure the teeth and the tendrils are still around your throat, and on the best nights your hoarse cries call your mother forth. She holds your trembling body and strokes your hair and whispers to you until you fall back asleep. On the bad nights, though, it is your father at the door, and the only reason his punishments don't frighten you as they should is because the nightmares still linger in your memory, a comparison against which even your father's belt comes a distant second.

But the worst of those nightmares recede over time, and soon you forget they were anything but the foolish dreams of youth, an outlet for the violence that lives with you every day. Your mother still shakes whenever your father is near, regardless of how happy or angry he is, and as time passes, he grows angrier more than not, which leaves you shaking with impotent rage, unable to do anything to stop it. You sometimes imagine those nightmares from your youth made flesh, imagine them crowding overhead, plucking your screaming father from the ground, swallowing him in a pit of endless nothingness. But still your father remains. He remains until it's neither nightmare nor alien god that consumes him but instead it's his own anger that stops his heart.

Your mother, unexpectedly free, grieves, but afterward you see her happy on occasion, relaxed, and you, too, feel the clouds eventually part. You meet a woman with hair as blonde as the sun, and a smile that dispels your shadows. You find success in work, are able to buy that home you and she spoke about. You have a son, and your mother watches him grow. You miss your father, at times, but less often than you uneasily expect.

In an effort to show your boy the sights that made you, you inevitably return to that small, nondescript seaside town. It looks as though nothing has changed in the intervening years. Still, the ice cream parlor occupies a prime corner in the city square, still, the rows of boats remain tethered to the old wooden dock. You try to explain how you experienced the town as a child, but your own son is already tired of your stories, even at so few years of age. You laugh and rub your hands over his head. He squints and spits and reminds you of how much you love him.

When you see the bookshop, you hesitate, filled with that childhood discomfort. A meandering foreboding envelops you, and yet you cannot deny your curiosity is piqued. There is also something else, something that draws you there, and despite the years since you have thought of the place, made a life for yourself elsewhere, somehow still you have found yourself in that same little town, a few blocks up from that same little corner you left your parents at all those years before. You tell yourself you'll go in for only a moment this time, just to prove to yourself the fear is gone. Moments turn into hours so easily.

You walk with your son's hand in your own, and you do your best not to crush it when the bookshop clerk appears even before your eyes have adjusted to the shop's dim light. The clerk steps out from a small doorway behind the overburdened counter to look you and your son over. Your instinct is to hide the boy.

"Can I help you find something?" the clerk asks. "Our children's section is around the corner."

"No, thank you," you say. "We're just browsing."

"Certainly, certainly. But let me know if there's anything you need. I've made a career out of finding things."

You smile and nod, but inside the fear grips you. It's his smile—are there too many teeth? Are those tiny eyes hidden behind his glasses pointing the same way, or is their direction off, just a fraction, enough to give him a doll-eye appearance? Briefly, the idea that he's something else inside a person suit grips you, and you shake it off. You wonder where such an idea might come from. Around and through your legs, your son travels, desperate to amuse himself while his father scans the stacks for something he can barely remember.

The book. You remember, vaguely, the book—its thick leather covers, its yellowing paper. You remember the worn edges and creased pages, and like blood seeping from an old wound the memories of your childhood nightmares stain your thoughts. You feel sick, your hands wet, your throat dry, and you wonder if those shadows edging your sight are about to slither away and reveal some ancient secret best left buried. You're trembling, but your son is oblivious to your struggle, and it's by focusing on him that you manage to pull yourself from the gravity well and back into the world of the living.

But . . . that book.

The desire to possess it seizes you, but you do everything you can to avoid searching it out. Is delaying your anticipation intended to allow you to savor it, or avoid dealing with it? You remember exactly where that book is—you saw it in your dreams for decades—and do all you can to avoid encountering it. You simply need time to think, to understand why you are there, but your son has fallen bored, and proceeds to announce the titles of books as though calling a train. Your eyes continue to scan the spines facing you, but your thoughts are on your screaming son.

Perhaps this is why the book's sudden appearance surprises you. It's not where it should be. Your dream-self had been so certain, it jumps before you do, before you realize why. Your heart jolts and turns you cold—your brain utterly unable to process what it's experiencing. When the thoughts manage to trickle back in, the logic of what's happened—a book moving to different section of the store is not unusual over a few decades' time—is conflated with the impossible—the book has relocated itself to ensure you rediscover it. Nothing makes sense in the presence of that leather-bound volume, and as you reach out to pull it from the shelf you feel the hairs along your spine rise, the electric air intensifying. It has clearly been waiting for you.

"What is it, Dad?" your son asks, though his voice is receding.

"Have you found what you're looking for?" the clerk asks as he hobbles forward on limp legs.

*Do you know why you've sought me?* the book asks, as though you have an answer it could possibly understand.

"I told you, we have everything one could want here," the clerk continues over your son's probing. "You just have to ask. We carry—" He stops, looks at the book your frozen hand is about to light on, and you wonder if that shiver that travels down his body is real or just your imagination. His whole being wavers. "That shouldn't be there. It's not for sale."

"What's not for sale?" your son asks. You shush him.

"What do you mean?"

He doesn't answer; instead, he walks between you and the book, breaking your connection to it.

"Is there anything else I can help you with?" he asks, and the dread in his voice has gone, replaced with the cool, varnished patter of a salesman.

"I'd like to see that book," you say, somewhat sternly, despite wondering if it's really what you want at all.

"Daddy, what book?" your son asks. You do your best to ignore him. The clerk, however, is as confused.

"Which book would that be?"

"The book you're hiding from me."

"What's he hiding, Daddy?" your son asks, breaking loose from the grip you have on his hand.

"Can you step aside?" You're speaking to the clerk in voice you didn't know you had. It sounds familiar. "I'd like that book."

"Sir, I assure you I don't—"

"Here it is, Daddy!"

You see your son dragging the book from the shelf, and the world stops spinning. The vacuum of space has sucked away the air, the sound. Your son is mouthing words, but all you see is that leathery tome, and you are overcome by something you have no name for.

"Stop that!" your father bellows, and your hand goes to swat the book away but instead connects with the side of the boy's head. He drops the book, screams, and the world rushes in. You grab your son and pull him close. He's screaming, pushing away from you, but you are bigger, stronger, and he can't break free of your embrace.

The clerk seems frightened now, as though he has suddenly realized it's *you* who is not as you seem, as though it is *he* who has mistakenly come too close to something he cannot understand, and cannot withdraw without risking his life.

"I'm not sure what you want," he says, and if that quaver in his voice is more of his act, it's stage worthy. You step away from him, suddenly unsure whose reality is truest. You hold up your hands in surrender. Are they even your hands?

"I—I'm sorry," you stammer, continuing your slow withdrawal, child hugged to your side. The terror on the clerk's faces grows. "I'm sorry."

You don't stop apologizing until the bookshop has receded into the furthest reaches of your memory.

Never in the following years do you question if it was truly the book you were aiming for. Never once while everything is falling apart. That book . . .

that book . . . it's not so easily forgotten any longer, and you feel it's crawled inside of you, lowered a screen over your eyes against which it's projecting the most terrifying images you have ever seen, and no matter how you try to dispel them they continue to infect your thoughts and your life. Gradually, everything unravels. Your son . . . he is no longer your son. No one believes you, but it's true. There is something there, something inside of him, ever since he touched that book. Something malignant and ancient coiling itself behind his eyes, and no matter how many times you scream or shake him, no matter how many times he tries in subtle ways to corrupt you, forcing you to strike him, your not-son, still it doesn't go. Your wife . . . it takes your wife as well, and though you see flashes of the people you once knew, once loved, more often you see the corruptions of a million stars there, and the anger you feel cannot be contained. You don't remember when they leave for good. All you remember is that you are no longer sure if there is anything left of the people you knew. All you have left are a few scars, and even fewer photographs.

Time moves strangely afterward. The house is all you have left, but you barely recognize it. Rooms appear larger, or move their position. Sometimes they multiply, and it takes you forever to find your way from one end to the other across distance as vast as the cosmos. Other times, it's as though everything has constricted claustrophobically, and you can barely move without feeling wood and plaster pressed against you. You wonder if you've fallen asleep and now live in a nightmare dreamscape of things prodding the borders of what's real. There a great hum beneath your legs that feels like the heartbeat of the world, but you know that's impossible because the hum you feel is much too old.

When you finally open your eyes, everything looks different. You are no longer at your home but standing on a street you barely recognize. The people walking are aliens in flesh suits, driving futuristic cars and talking into strange glass slabs. There is no ice-cream parlor, no wooden boats docked in a row. You shuffle forward though it's difficult to move, and it's only when you encounter a window and see your reflection that you realize how much time has passed. Your face—your face has loosened, the flesh pulling away from your skull in a desperate attempt to flee, but instead only sagging into folds. Your hair, too, has changed, drained of all color by the transition of the world around you. It's only your eyes that remain familiar, and those twin orbs reassure you that nothing of importance has gone. As long as you can trust your eyes, everything will be fine. When those eyes bring the window you are staring at into focus, you discover they are not the only things you recognize. Beyond the glass is a display of books you have seen in life but twice, and countless times more in your dreams. You step back to find the bookshop towering over you, and you feel a strange terror creep up your back. That bookshop has not changed since you first laid eyes on it aeons ago. That bookshop that has been summoning you all your life, but you were never conscious enough to hear it.

The bookshop clerk is ancient. His every move is slowed. His shaking, imprecise fingers find the pages of the book he is reading. He is dressed in the same natty style you remember, though the clothes themselves are worn and frayed. You wonder how he can be alive after so many years, especially when you feel so close to your own end. It doesn't seem possible. And yet, there he sits as you push open the door.

He looks up with expectation, but his dropping face is confusing. Can he really not recognize you? Especially when his features are been so permanently etched in your mind? You press on. You have only one reason for being in this nondescript seaside town.

"Where is it?" you demand.

"I beg your pardon?"

"The book. Where is it now?"

"I have a store full of books," he spits back. You will not be deterred by his tests.

"You know the one I want," you say. "You've know since the first day I came in here. I think you've known since before even that. I think that book has been sitting here, waiting for me, since this store first opened. Since *before* this store first opened. I think the book has always been here, occupying this space in the world, hovering in the air until someone came and built this bookshop around it. Maybe this book simply *is*—a fact of existence; a fixed point in space and in time; a dream waiting for its dreamer to find it. I'm here now, and I'm finally prepared to take it."

The bookshop clerk seems confused by what you've said, but you can see it's an act. It's all an act.

"I think it's time you leave," he says, and reaches for a rotary telephone. You are distracted by the sound coming from the room behind him. It's only a whisper, and though your ears are not as they'd once been, you can hear well enough to know what that sound is. Chanting. There are voices, chanting some unspeakable spell into the world. You look back at the bookshop clerk and he is still slowly dialing numbers. You reach across the counter and yank the phone cord. It comes free from the wall, and also rips the telephone from his hands. The plastic shatters on the unswept floor. The look on the clerk's face is of horror, but it seems over-practiced.

"Is the book back there? Are they using my book?' You try to sound intimidating, but the words stumble out of your dry mouth.

"I don't know what—" the clerk says, but he is interrupted by a cacophony of noises from that back room. You smell something heavy and wet in the air; it's sulfurous, like seaweed in the damp.

"What's back there?" you say as you storm onward.

"You can't go back there," the clerk says, and steps between you and the door to stop your advance. But you will not be denied, and even though your arms are weak, they are still strong enough to shove the old clerk aside. His flesh gives as though boneless, and he crumples limply, collapsing into a heap. But you don't pay it attention, so intent are you on that back room, on throwing aside all obstacles between you and that chanting rhythm. When you step through the opening and see what the single spotlight illuminates you don't know if you understand it. You don't know if you possibly could, not without travelling backward in time to your own conception and rewriting every moment of your life.

You stagger from the room, the horror more than you can bear. The clerk does not move, and the odor of so many books rotting overwhelms you. The world is spinning out of control so quickly you cannot hold on. Forward you move, step following step, feet of concrete dragged forward, lagging behind your racing mind.

That book. That horrible book. That terrifying book. It's in here with you, somewhere in the moribund shop, staring at you from its perch somewhere in the stacks, its secrets whispering from the pages. You can hear them. You can still hear them. That book—it's laughing at you.

And, despite yourself, you feel your own smile begin to grow.

# CHAPTER FOURTEEN

# 11:00

## NIKKI GUERLAIN

11:00

LYLA DRAGGED HER bleeding fingertip across the black tabletop. She couldn't recall how she had cut it and had no idea why it wouldn't quit bleeding, but she wasn't really concerned either. With no real intent she drew two red lines, two red spots, two circles. It was after the completion of the second circle that she looked up from her bloody scrawls and saw the man.

Amber honey bulged from his lips. The smooth skin of his face slid over his sharp cheekbones, underneath his crown of curls, and back out in a perfect shell of an ear, drawing Lyla's gaze to his long pale neck. Her gaze flowed down his graceful spine, all the way to that perfect ball rack of a pelvis clad in leather. He wasn't really wearing leather, but in that moment, to Lyla, it sure felt that way.

Lyla watched with an unaccustomed yearning as this strangely captivating man heartily devoured his peanut butter and honey sandwich. Her eyes worked over his bobbing Adam's apple as he washed his sandwich down with a tall glass of ice-cold milk. Lyla wanted to lick the cool condensation along the glass all the way to his lips and wondered what it would feel like to have that part of him between her legs or any part of him as long as it was *there*.

She placed a hand below her table and touched herself. Moving her fingers to the rhythm of his rippling neck. She grew self-conscious for a moment, pausing mid-circle. *What would Harold say of me publicly whacking myself for all to see in a little hole-in-the-wall café on the East Side?*

Fuck Harold. He never made her feel this way. And as far as whacking went, just last week across town, some guy carrying a machete had whacked himself a path through a subway train. The whacker had made it fourteen stops before exiting and promptly shooting himself. Lyla had thought that very strange, to go all that way and not pull the gun out until the end. Perhaps there are reasons to take a gun to a knife fight—if the battle was all your own, for instance. She could hardly feel bad about her own intimate activities, after all. They were completely benign, given the current climate. *What am I going to do? Eye rape this man until I climax? What's the harm in that?* The worst she would do is write a song about it later. He seemed a bit conservative, even in his imagined leather pants, to come to one of her shows and listen to such a thing.

The mysterious man cleared his throat and looked in Lyla's direction, locking his eyes to hers in a moment palpable with queer sexual attraction. It was then that Lyla gave him his nickname, Boober—for no other reason than that it had inexplicably popped into her head during that hot and weird moment. Boober's eyes shifted colors in the low fire of the room, making Lyla feel like a wild beast tethered inside a dark barn. She stroked herself furiously beneath the table.

The moment held until a woman slipped down beside Boober, slipping her hand into his in a very familiar and intimate and annoying way. Boober broke their spell to smile at this woman. This *other woman* took a drink of his milk, licked honey from the bottom of Boober's jaw.

*What a bitch*, Lyla thought. That said, Boober was a messy eater.

Boober's response to the woman's lick was slow and reserved, but even from where Lyla sat, she could see his interest grow. It made her want to shove the jaw-licking woman off a tall building. She had never felt this way before, despite her angry punk exterior. Where other punks were full of spite, she was like a bundle of whee all cozied up in a blanket of cotton candy. Yes, she was usually very sugary and generous towards people, but there was something about this particular man that made her think and feel hot and animal, both predatory and protective. Stirred. Like some alien swarm was running roughshod through her blood. Like she wanted to fuck something up.

Guns N' Roses came through the café's speakers. Lyla pumped her hips and bobbed her head to the music, all the while staring at this other woman she completely loathed for no other reason than that her tongue was in the wrong place at the wrong time. Lyla was placing a piece of her own sandwich, peanut butter and grape jelly, into her mouth when "Paradise City" melted into "Sweet Child O' Mine." It was then that she decided that she would call this other woman, *this jaw-licker*, Renee, after an especially mean and gassy dog she once owned as a child.

That dog had died a horrible death after being hit by a Schwann truck packed to the gills with prepackaged meat and popsicles. Lyla decided that she would not give Renee the dignity of being pushed off a high building, or being hit by a frozen foods truck, so she imagined shoving her onto the third rail of a subway track to watch her snap, crackle and pop to a smoky death.

*Suck it, bitch!*

"Did I just say that?" she whispered. Somehow, through some strange magic passing between her and this man, it was like a switch had been flipped—one connected to all of her most important sensitive bits, and it made her want to have a bat in her hands.

As "Sweet Child O' Mine" melted into "Welcome to the Jungle," Lyla began working her shoulders, still staring at poor, oblivious, jaw-licker Renee. After Lyla began making too much noise with her involuntary grunting and jerking, other deli patrons stared at her, something they normally wouldn't do because of her tattoos and the fuckyou face that she, like all '80s punkers, wore in perpetuity.

*They're staring because they find it odd that I'm moved by GNR. Little do they know! I fucking adore GNR!*

Renee refused to look Lyla's way though she knew she was having holes burned into the back of her skull.

Doing her best to summon any previously latent telekinetic powers, Lyla strained to send out a message to jaw-licking Renee: *Look at me, bitch! I'm totally whacking myself while I stare at you! You fucking straight!* But the woman continued to dote on Boober as he launched into his second sandwich. Though Lyla was pretty sure Renee could not hear her words specifically, she was pretty sure she got the message.

Renee talked at Boober while he ate and paid her very little mind. Lyla was sure it was because of the intense chemistry between her and Boober. That he didn't want to break the connection and cause a scene with Renee and ruin this glorious moment for the two of them. It wasn't every day that you met your soulmate in a café while eating sammies and jilling off to GNR.

Maybe it was the overall atmosphere of optimism and opportunity that permeated the room, but she was pretty sure that Boober would be breaking up with Renee later that evening. *So sweet. So considerate. My sweet, sweet Boober! Oh, the times we will share, my sweet Booby-Wooby!* He would be hers.

Lyla climaxed to the last bite of Boober's second sandwich despite never again catching his slightest glance. The once-staring patrons had quickly become distracted by a homeless man pressing his dirty, bare ass against the deli front window while lighting a crack pipe (and this was the good part of town), so the moment had been private even if completely public. The warmth and glow of her orgasm washed through her while she took in his casual-looking yet purposeful indifference, and she thought: *Finally, this is love!*

LYLA LEFT BOOBER to work out his separation with Renee and went home to feed her cat, Ming, before her band's show. Harold was there, and not wanting to ruin that first flush of love with a bunch of domestic maneuvering and Harold's accompanying raw pussy emotions, Lyla let him pump one in her while she thought of Boober's mop of curls, his beautiful bobbing Adam's apple, his obviously enormous penis and, of course, that sweet-ass Stingray she saw in a pawn shop window down the street a few days ago. She should feel bad about thinking such things, but Harold loved the abuse. It was part of what made their arrangement work.

After Harold came, he turned to her, whining under some guise of affection, "Where are you? It's like you're not even here."

Lyla pushed him off her and snapped back, "Is it not enough that I let you inside me? Can't you just nut and leave?"

"Where should I go?" he fired back, smiling through tears.

"I don't know, Harold. Go get some civet coffee or take a midnight stroll through Central Park or something. I don't fucking care. I've got a show tonight."

Lyla turned her back and asked Harold to bring her a cold glass of milk, which of course he did. It wasn't until she could hear him locking their front door that she could summon Boober's presence in her mind and fingers. The lips, the curls, the honey, the total lack of emotional bullshit. It had been so long since she had enjoyed someone's company so thoroughly. The best kind of love is purely physical, animal, something not to be understood. While Harold leaked out of her and onto the bed, he had already been completely erased in her mind. There was only one now, and that was her precious Booby-Wooby.

Lyla relished the feeling of the cold milk filling her tummy, the cold sheets against her skin. A sharp delicious pain pierced her swollen ladybone. She arched her hips up into the cool path of air coming from the window a/c, chilling her throbbing flesh and the fluids that dripped from it. Her breath came out in a hiss. A buzzing growl filled her chest. The radio on her nightstand turned itself on. Lyla's eyes rolled to the back of her head as Peter Gabriel's "Shock the Monkey" filled the room. Like a heavy smoke, the music seemed to coil its oily tendrils around and throughout every particle of her so that in the end it was like she wasn't even there. She writhed in the darkness, mind cloaked in a fever dream of blood, smoke and honey.

HAROLD AND LYLA weren't the only ones dealing with more than a modicum of discontent and weirdness. Shortly after leaving the café, Boober and Renee went back to his place where they got into a huge row over his apparent fascination with the slut eye-banging him from the corner. Boober pointed out that Renee had been eye-banged as well, but it did nothing to help the matter. Boober pushed, "You know, you only think she's a slut because her hair is a bright color and she wears a lot of leather. What was that bit with you licking my jaw? Granted, I quite liked it, but it's so un-you. Were you trying to mark me like I'm some tree? That's so uncomely, so pathetic."

Renee didn't know what came over her, or Boober, for that matter. She had never licked his jaw and he had never berated her before, but it made her inexplicably hot and slick between her legs. She felt herself throbbing everywhere, compelled to Boober pelvis-first. She slipped out of her too-conservative clothes and writhed against him like some drunk and horny over-the-hill secretary instead of the proper young mergers and acquisitions lawyer she was trained to be. She felt all hot in the ass and ready to go.

Renee ripped Boober's pants off and immediately took his, indeed, magnificent whang in her mouth, and although she wasn't very good at it, Boober was both very pleased and disgusted with her eagerness. As Boober thrust himself into Renee's generous throat, he heard the faint sounds of "Paradise City" in his mind. He couldn't help but to move to its rhythm and think of her, the strange punk girl in the café whom he had shared a weird moment with before all the jaw-licking and loud finger-banging.

Renee kept looking up at Boober as she gobbled his pole. This disturbed him deeply as it brought him away from the café, that hot strange woman, and back to this moment, in this room, engaging in an unabashedly and uncharacteristically depraved scene with his normally proper Renee. Boober attempted to cover Renee's eyes, but this only made her stick his fingers in her mouth, too. Removing his whang from her pie-hole, she said, "I don't know what's wrong with me. I just can't get enough of you in my mouth. Let me see you, baby. Take me in the ass! Take me in the ass! I'm so horny!"

This made Boober very angry. His rage boner flopped hard against her heavily blushed cheekbone. She darted at it tongue-first, but he pushed her away. If he wanted some filth-talking tart like this he—well, he wouldn't. Besides the fact that he wanted that strange girl, besides the fact that he wasn't into assplay, besides so many goddamn things, he almost had a fit. He grabbed Renee and threw her across his lap and spanked her bottom until it was good and pink and almost wanted. Then he threw her on the floor, closed his eyes, and humming Guns N' Roses' hit song "Patience," blew his fat gooey load all over Renee's not so conservative heaving breasts.

"Ermergerd!" she screamed. "Ermergerd! *Do. It. Again.*"

But at this. *At this.* He could bear her no more. He said loads of mean things about her choice of words and her general inability to rock to Bob Seger, finally telling her to "Go take a hike in Central Park if you don't like it."

Renee was inexplicably mad for the bone and this only drove her further into sexual madness. In fact, the moment the words "Central Park" left his lips, she was seized with mad joy at the thought of the cool moist air of the park turning her hot wet panties cool against her lips—such joys were to be had to be sat like that upon a patch of grass, or perhaps fucked hard in the ass against the rough bark of a tree. Not that she ever had done that before. *Oh fuck me fuck me fuck me*, she gushed to herself, then set into action the proper sequence of events which would allow her to merge into the night and acquire what it was that she so desperately needed. Renee quickly gathered her clothes and left, hell-bent on taking that walk, but not before asking Boober to open his mouth so she could spit in it. Boober quickly obliged this odd request to get her to leave.

Once she left, Boober spat Renee's spit into his palms and crawled into bed with a mumble of good riddance. He turned on his alarm clock radio because he knew, just knew, that Bob Seger's megahit "Like a Rock" would be playing just at that moment. Boober clapped his wet hands to turn off the lights, and rolled around on his bed in a way that felt right, his thoughts spinning around that strange and beautiful moment with the mystery woman, the devil-may-care, nimble-fingered minx with the intense eyes that bore straight to his core.

Boober grew restless and hot, could feel the warm drip of honey down his jaw. Like a shadow she came to him, threading her shaded fingers through his damp curls, pressing his hungry mouth to hers, and he knew in that moment he was lost to her forever. Her skin smelled of ancient leather, her breath was the steady flip of eagerly turned pages and her heart—her heartbeat—was the stuff that slaughtered lambs and heavy smoke were made of. Or maybe that was his heart, for there was another sound so mingled with the beat in his chest that he could not tell which was what, and that sound was the pulsating buzz of some flying thing's wings. Boober felt a sharp sting in his tongue followed by warm rivulets of what he assumed was blood dripping down his chin, mixing with the heavy slick of honey. Excitement and fear spidered out from his heart and his groin. His flesh grew so heavy against her cold shadow that he seemed to fall into himself, completely cocooned by his bleating need for the cold sting of her heart, for the sweet smoke upon her lips. She reminded him of his beloved book.

He didn't know why he didn't think of it before, but it became abundantly clear then: she had his goddamn book! She was possessing him! He was sure he would've sensed if his book had been so close to him, so he doubted that she actually had brought it with her to the café. The book had left a taint on her so powerful that by merely being in the cafe she had managed not just to shift the atmosphere and ambience to total weirdness but to also leave an indelible mark on Renee and Boober. Boober let out a growl. He would let her haunt him and possess him and draw him in, and he would get back what was rightfully his.

The radio changed its channel in a loud scratch of warbled white noise and screaming, settling momentarily on silence. "Sledgehammer" weaved itself through the strange mix of blood, smoke and shadows filling the room. Animals screamed inside Boober and he could feel things moving coolly beneath his fevered skin. The thought came that it'd been forever since he'd listened to Peter Gabriel—that this dude could really give Seger a run for his money though they weren't in the same wheelhouse. The thought, like his shame over his momentary disloyalty to Seger, flitted away, brought back to his senses, he was, by her many hot mouths, her chilled kid leather skin, and the cool squirm cradling his fevered viscera. The feeling of giving up control was both delicious and disconcerting, much like her taste in music.

Lyla's eyes fluttered open to sunlight streaming onto her alarm clock radio playing "Sympathy for the Devil," a Rolling Stones favorite of hers that made her think that despite her overall wooziness from whatever it was that happened last night, today was going to be a great fucking day. The answering machine and its sixteen urgently flashing messages told her that she had missed her show. She threw on the kind of cotton slip that made her feel clean and innocent, as well as her Ray-Ban Clubmaster Classic sunglasses— one of her favorite gifts from Harold. She paused by one of those overly large, expensive mirrors leaning against the wall and took herself in. She might feel like shit but she looked good—real good. In fact, it seemed to her like she was looking a tad bit curvier than normal, but in a good way.

In the kitchen she started a pot of coffee and noticed Harold had left his briefcase on the counter. He had been especially protective about it over the last week, but she had never asked about it. He never left her alone with it. Ever. She was hardly a snoop, but given his erratic behavior over the last week and the fact that he appeared not to have come home last night, Lyla was more than a bit curious. That, and she hadn't been feeling quite herself either. Lyla thought back to last night's events, at least what she could remember, and her face grew hot, not with shame but something close to it. She shivered and shook it off. How the hell had she come up with a name like Boober? Just the thought of him sent strange sexual electricity through her pelvis. She felt her nipples stiffen, her skin grow very cold.

She whispered his name and felt a sting snap across her tender bits like the telltale sign of a urinary tract infection, only over a much wider area. Maybe she was infected. She felt both strange and sure. Maybe she should've gotten up and washed off after Harold finished. Or maybe not.

Lyla grabbed Harold's briefcase and brought it into the bathroom with her. She'd take a bath and decide what to do with it later, and if Harold came home in the interim she would claim that Ming had sprayed it. The alarm clock radio hiccupped, then started the same song over again. Over and over and over. So much "Sympathy for the Devil." She was okay with that even though there was no reasonable explanation for such a thing. Her life had been far too reasonable for too long. She could stand to have some of her good sense eroded.

She started her bath, then fumbled in the medicine cabinet for some Vicodin. While, generally speaking, Harold was fairly square, he always had Vicodin and lots of other things. He and his lawyer buddies got anything they wanted from the firm doctor. Because, like all straights rationalize, it doesn't count if it's prescribed. She riffled through the rest of the bottles and found a few more things to palm. A pill for everything and everything for a pill. Bottoms up and up the bottoms. "In your nose with a rubber hose!" she squealed.

As Lyla slid her hand down the smooth leather side of Harold's briefcase, she felt a twinge of sadness for him. Sure, he could be a dick and overly emotional, but he wasn't evil or cowardly. He was basically a good guy, for a lawyer anyways. It had all been fine until last week, when the atmosphere had suddenly shifted into one of general discontent and confusion. When Harold's skin had taken on a strange pallor, she had dismissed it as him working too much on an extremely disturbing case. He never shared any details or told her what he was working on specifically, but it was somehow related to that machete guy who went crazy on the subway. Harold wasn't per se a criminal lawyer and the guy had shot himself anyway. But people used lawyers for all sorts of things. The only reason she knew Harold was working on something related to that awful tragedy was because of an offhanded remark he had made over coffee one morning when she had asked him if he read yesterday's article about the incident.

"What do you suppose makes someone get up and do such a thing?" she'd asked Harold, while picking idly at her bagel and cream cheese.

He'd given her that look that was akin to a knowing wink and told her that he had it on good authority that the guy was some sort of cult member or Satanist freak.

"Well, I just can't imagine being part of something like that, and if I was, I can't imagine being able to stomach such a thing. He chopped the head off his baby. Can you believe that shit?"

Harold's face had grown dark. "I think the hardest part for you to fathom is the prospect of doing what someone told you to do regardless of what that was."

"People tell me to get toast or orange juice or whatever and I do it," she resisted, not entirely earnestly, since it had been quite some time since she had waited tables or worked any sort of job.

"Although, that said," he lowered his voice to a sort of woo-woo spooky tremble, "I don't think he had a choice."

"You mean, he was possessed or something? Get the fuck out!"

Harold had raised his eyebrows in response and given her a quick kiss on the forehead. Then he left, telling her that he wouldn't be home until very late. Which was fine with her; she enjoyed her time alone. It was one of the benefits of having a lawyer for a sugar daddy.

That morning something had shifted. Each day after that, Harold had become more neurotic and especially protective of his precious briefcase, even going so far as to have it by his side while he slept.

*So, is that the key to all of this weirdness?* She looked at the briefcase from a tub full of bubbles. Her pelvis still ached wildly, but it was nothing her hands couldn't control if she didn't think about Boober too much.

A heavy knock at the front door made her jump. She quickly got out of the tub, threw on a soft robe and wrapped a towel around her head before quietly padding to the door. She thought it strange; no one ever knocked on their door. Maybe Harold had lost his key? Harold's knock had always been weak and uncertain, which she had always found strange for a lawyer. This knock had been long, hard and queerly foreboding, so it was with a smidge of trepidation that she looked up into the surveillance camera display.

She saw a very intense-looking leather-panted, shirtless Boober. *Get the fuck out.* Lyla grew deliciously dizzy. Maybe it was from jumping up from the tub too quickly with a head full of pharmaceuticals, or maybe, just maybe, Boober could work his spell through a slab of steel. In any case, all of her blood and most of her head had gone distinctly south.

He knocked again.

Lyla ran her fingers slowly over the locks as she unbolted each one carefully and crisply. She opened the door. Boober wasn't wearing leather pants and he wasn't shirtless. He wore layers of clothes and a coat that was akin to a robe, and he was heavily disheveled. Lyla didn't care. She wasn't thinking about how he came to find her in a place that next no one knew about. She wasn't thinking about why he had on all of those warm clothes on a bright sunny day. She was thinking that his eyes looked like they'd seen some serious Ouija board troubles, and his hands were white-knuckled.

"Shadows rise from the sulfurous light," he said, with all the inflection of an automaton preacher.

"Only the dead live forever," she replied, completely involuntarily, in the voice of an answering machine believer.

She slinked out of her robe, let the towel fall from her hair, then stepped aside to let Boober pass. He grabbed her by her neck and roughly pulled her through the loft to the flokati rug in front of the fireplace. He pushed her down to her hands and knees, her bare ass sticking up in the air. Her lady bits were swollen, rouged, moist. He gave her bum a hard open-handed slap, but she neither winced nor resisted, but rested her head on the floor relaxed and sideways so she could look at him while he did his good work.

A hand-shaped welt rose on her ass. He smacked her harder this time, and again she did not move. Her mouth twisted in a smile and she smirked at him. A grave look of consternation came across his face. His spank hand began to tremble with rage.

"I hope you fuck harder than you spank."

Before he could help himself, before he could gain some semblance of self-control, he'd sprouted Fabio hair, an impressive set of pecs, and the pants of a pirate—no boots. His whang looked like a zucchini wrapped in leather, and it rested pert, upright, so enormous, in fact, that it appeared to push that side of his pelvis back.

"Oh, Boober. My sweet Boober!"

The nicknamed annoyed him although he still found her incredibly hot, with her pink ass so warm and sticking up in the air just waiting to get smacked. *So this is what it is like to live in a punk sugar baby's head.* Her scent was heady and thick, a mix of bubble gum, sulfur, and lightning. She felt like a living, breathing boardwalk carnival. And he was like her monkey shaking a tambourine.

He got on his knees and stroked her cheek with one hand, thinking that he might get what he wanted by being nice to her. She stroked his hand and broke out in a twisted grin, mocking, challenging him. "Such soft hands, Booby-Wooby! An academic, are we?! But not a normal one, no. Not you. Your wear your gloom like a mantle and your skin smells like incense and blood."

Boober lost it. "Listen, bitch—"

She propped herself up and sat Indian style. "Give it to me!"

He put his hand over her mouth to shush her but her eyes still said *Yes!*

"Will you just shut the fuck up for a moment? My name is not Booby-Fucking-Wooby. I'm not against playing around, and I must admit, our chemistry is undeniable, but first things first—where the fuck is my book?" He removed his hand.

"So, I take it you're an English major?" She smiled.

He slapped her across the face. She snickered.

"You think this is funny, do you?"

"I've never been slapped by a pirate before, and the whole Fabio hair thing and your absolutely ginormous leather-clad whang is pretty fucking funny. Hot, yeah. But fucking hilarious. And if there's one thing that makes me want to fuck more than anything, it's a gigantic sense of humor."

*There's no slapping the look of ho-ho-ho off that face,* Boober thought.

Boober pulled out his knife, which of course came out looking like a sword because of the whole pirate getup. He held it to her throat. "The book," he demanded, fighting back the urge to speak pirate.

"Do you want to read or do you want to fuck? I gotta whole lotta books on my shelves, but I have a feeling that Jane Austen isn't your cup of tea. . . . You know, we should get Chinese food. And RC Cola. Chinese restaurants always have RC Cola."

Before Boober could stop himself, he had agreed and even added, "And peppermint ice cream!" He removed the sword from her throat.

"How about you fuck me 666 ways to Jesus on that awesome bed of mine, and after we're done, we'll order takeout."

Boober answered with an emphatic *Gee whiz gosh golly darn.* Almost followed by the L-word. He was going to have to get away and reevaluate his approach or risk turning into her perma-boned pet gummy bear.

Boober had no idea that Lyla had yet to even hold the book, that despite her incredible controlled madness, she was merely stoned on the book's physical proximity—that it had unlocked something inside her. He had greatly underestimated her as merely being a mix of sugar and sass. Something he could use and control. Difficult to deal with, at the most. So he slumbered, oblivious.

169

Lyla slipped into the bathroom. The briefcase was locked, but it was one of those spin number-code locks. Her nimble fingers moved unhindered, resulting in a series of liberating clicks. She cracked it open slowly to savor the moment. The first thing she noticed was a general blighting of all noise around her, like she had opened a can of vacuum. From this emerged a sound alien yet reminiscent of the sea. An intense vibration followed, and finally the briefcase flew open revealing its treasure. A blacker-than-black book adorned with untarnished gold leaf that was so intense in its goldness that it appeared of otherworldly karat.

Lyla picked the book up. It felt oddly magnetic. The pages flipped of their own accord, creating the effect of a flipbook, only in real-time footage. To Lyla it had the feel of a cartoon, so simple was the image in comparison to the book's beauty and complexity. In it, her and Boober's bodies were snapping and crackling on the third rail of an abandoned subway station while the very book in her hands settled in like a song among the sodium-lit squalor of dead soldiers, blood, and gore, its pages trembling and turning of their own accord.

"Shadows rise from the sulfurous light," Boober called out tenderly in his sleep.

"Only the dead live forever, Booby-Wooby," she replied.

# CHAPTER FIFTEEN

# VOID KISS

## MICHAEL CISCO

**T**HE DROPLETS OF blood that spatter nearly all of the black subway windowpane shine like trembling, dark red loops of luminous wire. Hard and bright in outline, like wire, but with a gelatinous wobbliness nothing at all like wire, seeming to encircle nothing. The droplets of blood wriggle in place, absorb smaller specks of red. When they are fat enough, they streak down the pane, leaving a ragged trail of emptiness behind them. It's strange to think that so much of my blood should remain after all this time, and not have been washed away somehow. But then again, it's strange that I should remain at all, to think it. My face is so dim the reflection is more glass than face. I experimentally open and close my jaw a few times. The effect is grotesque. I look like a rubber facsimile. I look like a special effect. A cheap one.

The mouth movement is artificial. The eyes are lifeless. Lifeless but suffering, somehow. I am riding in the subway car that ran me down. When it struck me, I was killed. No—the train struck me, but there was no moment in which I could say I was killed. There was such an enormous length of time between being struck full on by the train, travelling at top speed, and the moment when I somehow mounted to the space between the cars, entered this one—the first—and sat down. Looking out this window, as I have done for an enormous length of time, I see that my blood sprayed nearly all the way up the right side of the silver car, fanning back from the red wheels.

Droplets cling, still uncongealed, on the window. Thinking back now on that expanse of time, I can't say that, at any point, I was aware of any marked change in myself. The tip of one of my smaller fingers is still there, too, a ragged shred of bleached white flesh with a fingernail, glued to the base of the window. Yes, the train cut me to pieces.

My death was so sudden that the subway spirits and lemures and orixás, psychopomps who lie in wait to bear off the souls of people like me when we die, must have been taken by surprise. They didn't get me. They hunt me now. The lemures are like hyenas, gibbering just beyond the platform ends. The subway spirits are like colossal sharks cruising up and down, bellowing in the dark, circling, their cold lamplike eyes watch for me, and they call me, with chattering, automated voices. The orixás are white-hot searchlights probing the gloom for me, the light haloed with a creepily insistent, numbing rhythm that wants to seduce me out of hiding and caress me until I tumble apart in a heap of dust. The train car itself is the safest place for me.

The pain has never stopped. It's with me now. Always. Never wavering. Always fully with me. You may not hear it in my voice.

Now, about that. Think about that. Think about the calm in my voice, and the agony of my being. I was run over by a train, Lyla. You pushed me, I fell on the tracks, cracking a rib—the shuddering wail of the train bore down on me with its rush and the vibrations went all through me as if you were kissing me, and then the train was on me. My left arm was pinched off at the bicep, and both my legs, my bowels were ripped out of me through my back. Somehow my head wasn't touched. It bounced in stinking water and a condom blocked my vision, bobbing against the bridge of my nose. I have the sensation of every instant of my death, from the first jolt of mere fright to the crack as my spine splintered, the putrid, custardy water in my mouth, and the last despairing bark of my nervous system, drawing a red circle with me simultaneously, and I am still able to speak calmly. Do you understand?

No one approaches me—no one does anything out of the ordinary with respect to me, except for the staring. They must all be taking me for a hallucination. I do notice, from time to time, someone turning to the passenger sitting beside him or her, talking furtively and stealing glances in my direction. It's as if they were discussing what to do with me. What more could be done to me.

For now, I am part of these tunnels. I go up and down, back and forth, never leaving the tunnels, though I long for night air down here. I long to see the orange streets slide by. The car is now very old-fashioned and the passengers dressed in the style of a hundred years ago. The doors have opened.

Passengers leave, new passengers board; they avoid me, grouping themselves toward the back, and staring. Nobody can take their eyes off me these days it seems. That also started with Lyla.

The train pulls into a station from about 1960 and stands for a moment, the doors open. A girl in rain boots has noticed me, and she slips behind her mother, who is talking to a goatee'd Puerto Rican man. The girl peers at me from behind her mother. The wind from the tunnels bells out the skein of incense that surrounds me. The train operator snaps the lock of his compartment and steps out into the car, belt jingling, stopping at once to stare down at me. He seems incredulous, and disgusted. His lips move, but there's no sound. He seems to be speaking inaudibly to himself. He crosses to the open door, breaking eye contact with me only long enough to look down the length of the train, presumably for some signal or other from the conductor. An older man in a brown suit boards the train and comes over to me. It's been a very long time since I saw that little girl. Even a knot of three or four large rats stops halfway across the platform to stare at me, wanting my soul. The man sits down beside me.

"Hey!" he says under his breath. "Hey! How're you doin'?"

"Fine," I say. "The same."

"You still in there?"

"I'm fine," I say more firmly. "I'm the same."

"Yeah?" he says. "You don't smell too good."

He pulls a red kerchief from his pocket and begins dabbing at my face, which is still wet with subway water. A grey moustache nearly conceals the man's mouth, and he casts nervous glances at the other passengers as he speaks with me. Suddenly, the train operator storms back into this compartment, glaring furiously at us both, as if he hated having to transport us around town, but couldn't refuse. The door slams behind him.

"What the hell happened to you?"

"I was standing on the platform at 149th Street Grand Concourse. A woman named Lyla pushed me onto the tracks, in front of an oncoming Woodlawn-bound 4 train. This one. I fell beneath the train and was killed. I have not been able to leave."

"And the book?"

"At the moment, she is reading the book."

The man's face hardens.

"How did she get the book?!"

I make a little gesture with my hands, which is about all I can manage in the way of movement.

". . . as I said."

The book had been ours for a time. A man named Parris had been charged with conveying it to our colleagues in Washington, but had gone mad, attacked people on the subway, then shot himself. The book had been with him at the time, but was not reported found with his body. Someone took it, tried to sell it, approached a lawyer for that purpose.

"It came into Lyla's possession through her husband. I came into Lyla's possession also, for three days. I decided then to take back the book. So, she killed me."

"Where is she?" he demands curtly.

"Gene's Motor Court on Buckeye Road, in Cleveland, Ohio. She is travelling west."

The other man stares down at the floor, which is made of some warped, tan material.

"She keeps it in a pink Japanese backpack."

The train brakes and slows into a station. His body lists forward with the deceleration. My body does not.

"She is travelling alone."

When the doors open, the man gets up to leave. Halfway to the door, he turns to me,

". . . Can I get you anything?" he asks, almost as an afterthought.

"I need an anchor on your side," I say. "I must not go on."

He's gone.

One day, Lyla, you will ride the train again, and you'll see me. I won't be looking at you, but I will see you, and you'll know it. We'll pull into the next station, the doors will open; passengers will leave. You won't. You'll come over and sit beside me, where you belong. We are like two adjacent lines in the same story. The story wants to keep going, which means moving from my line to your line. You were the first of the two of us to realize that.

You will choose to sit beside me, because you dispatched me prematurely... On the second day, you told me that I always keep something back. It was a generalization, even a smug one, but, on balance, you were right. You knew I was holding something back from you; you'll sit beside me, hoping that I will understand without requiring any explanation, and simply tell you outright what it was. You won't want to address me, even though you, being my murderer, are now more my companion than before.

I won't try to force you to speak to me, although I yearn to hear you speaking to me again. I don't want revenge. It will be, however, necessary for you to open your mouth, although not to speak. What I have to impart

174

to you has to be given in a very special way, if it is to be communicated properly. I could simply tell you, nothing prevents me, but what I have to tell you is impossible to express in any clear way, at least for me. Telling you simply would put you at risk, because the secret, even though it can be phrased briefly and in ordinary words, has, for that very reason, a virtually infinite number of possible meanings. For reasons that I believe you already understand perfectly, what you are looking for from me could only be something like that. If I don't articulate the secret just so, it will come out wrong, but it will seem perfectly right.

I have created an explanatory method for you that cannot fail when it is correctly performed, but you must open your mouth to receive my instruction. You will be reluctant to do it, and suspicious. I promise I will explain the secret to you. You killed me, that is true. Even if I were to forgive you, there would still be that to account for, but that is all in the book, *mektoub*, it is written. It was written in, backwards. That's a clue.

I need an anchor on your side. I am on the threshold, and I am not strong enough for what comes after. I have to remain on the threshold, but for that an anchor on your side is needed. You can anchor me, if only you will come see me. That's why I lied. I told him you were in Cleveland when you haven't left New York.

The work must continue. The task is bigger than we are. From the first moment our eyes met, work, above all, united us, and united us in with all those other fine people—that worthy company!—milling away at the cosmos, grinding it, sanding it down, melting space, melting time, turning them to fumes, making things run backward, writing the world backward. You wore nothing but space and time, like perfume. For no reason. Our dreams and hallucinations un-troduced us to reasons. What we did, what it was necessary for us to do, we did without hesitation or pointless reflection. The task is infinitely vast and long, the work is unrewarding, an end in itself or nothing at all. You need me for that work, and the work stills needs us both.

I tore your clothes to shreds, but it was no use, your tattoos made nakedness impossible for you. Even then that callous sadness was stubbornly wedged in me; I couldn't even look at your body without feeling my face contract, settling into its usual, irritable expression. Meanwhile, you had dropped your towels, you were parading. Watching you walk away excited me terribly. You smelled like gossamer and folded yourself like a cubist experiment. That gave you some feminine kind of gratification, a riddle suspiciously unintelligible to me, and you wanted me to fold you, late in the dully murmuring orange afternoon, stretching out toward each other, spreading ourselves like clay, looking forward to reading the pelvis a little before breaking it, pushing against the walls, exchanging bright lengths, bright angles, warming our distances and sinking, sinking the feeling, and the city surrounding us moans under its seething plumage of traffic, and the subway shakes the roots of the building inside, already threatening me. Thunder in the root, savoring heads turned pumice-white, barrel bodies of charred cork weeping exhaust pipes, mispeled emotions, reading with eyes closed in tomblike darkness, dancing with omitted gestures to forgetful music full of the best forgetting. You had no objection to my holding back then, and devoted as I was to your orgasms pure and simple, I read all of your numberless comes like a palmer saying his beads, I read words in your beautiful cries, as sweet and piercing as birdsong . . .

I see your red alarm clock reading 11:00, two red lines, two red spots, two red circles on a black pane . . . two pairs of red cherries decorate the base of your neck. Cherries give you an intense impression of violence, you said, on the first day, although come to think of it I recall it was the taste rather than the color, you said. I really didn't understand, but I don't believe now that you were warning me.

In fact, people on the street seemed offended by us, and tried to pull us apart and demanded to know what we saw in each other, who we thought we were, canoodling in the street together like that, as if people like us could have anything to do with each other. It is the secret work which unites, and death—what has it been? Not a separation. It did not separate us. It separated you from me, but not me from you. It only seems to separate you from me. Perhaps you can never rid yourself easily of a person who climaxed you. The mad red line comes back around, your circle and my line are one line, at 11:00. More and more mad, more and more intimate, more and more intimately mad, and secret. I had to be run over by a train to learn that the book wanted itself through us. I wrote your name in my mind with the pen of Mexico, and you had mine needled onto the sole of your left foot, but in the end it was all the unseen handless fingers writing bloody smoke in that stolen book. That book can only be stolen, it can't have a legitimate possessor. That's because the book possesses you, not the other way around. It stole me, then it stole you. A few courtesy tears dribble onto the pages, dry, cigarettey, and the book flutters indifferently shut again.

Now, a stiffened corpse, I am marooned on the threshold of a "door" put here especially for me that I must do everything I can not to go through, and which must inevitably open to admit me. My portrait, my legend, my semen, my dust, anything of mine can anchor me to the side I came from, of life, your side, and only that can keep me here on the threshold. A horrible place, but nowhere near as terrible as what that "door" will conduct me to, when it opens. If I have no anchor when the door opens, it would have been better for me to fall into the hands of the lemures.

Passengers come in, stamping snow off their shoes and sit down next to young women in summer dresses that leave their beautiful backs exposed. The train is filling with passengers. They cluster tightly together and fill the rear half of the car, but with each stop their tightly compressed line advances in my direction.

What if I manage to find my anchor, what then? Worm my way back, of course, by hook or by crook. I want to find you again, and warn you—we have been conning ourselves, thinking we've understood the book when at most all we've managed to do is read it—and that badly. That's the lesson, if any, they should learn from my example. That, and "dames is trouble." And if I do find you again, I will part you like a river parts a city and leave you in ruins more beautiful than new buildings.

When I died, the lemures came rushing out to get me, clamoring like a pack of frenzied hounds, and I heard the powerful voices of the orixás spread through the air like fire spreading on oil. My heart tore open, and I immediately heard them. It was like a single thrumming voice coming out of a thousand different tinny speakers. The voice was pain, and a wrenching, nightmarish anguish. It was like the voice of someone being horribly tortured, but, instead of confessing, the victim was giving orders, screaming in a voice that only gained in power and authority, as if that were what the interrogators wanted. The torture chambers reserved for the worst torments were prepared for me, I was impatiently awaited, the torturers were standing ready, eager to begin, to get past the preliminaries and hurry on to the heart of the trauma. The sound came out of the obscurity of my own damaged senses and responded to my least thought, so that even a flicker of my attention made the voice rise keenly. At the time, I could think nothing, I was in a blind panic. I only know that I tried something, actually the very first and only thing that came to mind, and it seemed to work.

The train pulls into a station backwards. Darkness pours from trays in the floor and light is chased into corners and behind objects. Shadows hurry to board the train, stepping on with their backs turned while others retreat onto the rails, the train rides the platform, the platform is a humming slab of low frequencies, glistening moistly with sound. Decomposing ribs support a ceiling of foul milk. The train rolls out into a wan landscape of iron columns which strain, encumbered under a mountainous sky. A malign gaze pours from granite boulders. A suggestion of distant figures crawling along the horizon freezes me. Granite tombs without any plan are scattered in all directions, and I can hear the muffled shouts of horror rise from them. For reasons I can't understand I am wildly terrified by those tombs, I think one of them must be set aside for me, I think I will become one—in some way, that I already am one—of those maimed, frail, far-away figures, crawling all in the same direction.

There are moments like anti-meditation when you would be caught and held in the present, unable to tear your mind away from here and now, unable to remember anything, unable to expect. You told me, on the third day, the morning of the day you killed me, that those were the most recuperative moments—listen, you're healing, you can hear yourself healing into something else. I am caught and held in the absent, unable to tear my mind away from nowhere and never, unable to forget anything, unable to be surprised at anything.

As it is, I can only just manage to sit here, the red droplets spangling the windows fall sideways, as if this subway car, filled with exhausted commuters slumped open-mouthed and dozing, with elaborately-coiffed black women and rail-skinny black men who can't sit still, up to the Bronx, and harried Dominican mothers with babies, and fashionable young men and women, and toothless bums haggard and miserable, were rocketing through space. The car is full now, and people continue to crush on. I am surrounded in stale breath, staring eyes, and body heat, pressing me up against the window. Eventually the window will give, and I will be pushed out into that boundless wilderness of torturers . . .

We've stopped between stations. Through the window, I see the older man standing in the tunnel outside. He is no longer looking in my direction. His eyes are brimming with tragic wonder. I see—they didn't get him, either. The train jolts forward an inch, then glides. I float away from the older man. The train is crossing a plateau at night under constellations that hover only a few feet off the ground, and the horizon is luminous, like the edges of a white hot length of metal.

There's nothing special about being insane. It's the void within that counts. You have it. You have the right kind, isomorphic with mine. It is the same, it produces the space needed to unite us in an ever-accelerating creation of differences between us. Incomparable. The void kiss. Like no other. The only kiss. It's a sign. The signs of chaos are perfect. You on one side, and I on the other, braiding time into a nerve membrane and making it fire, and it's all and nothing, the impulse travels and gives a void every time it returns. Come back to me! Throw me a line!

You slipped out of your no reason, and music seemed to coil its oily tendrils around no reason. Your dreams and hallucinations—in the end it was like you weren't even there. I won't be purely physical, animal, something the passengers will leave, even as Harold leaked out of your seat. The cold sheets understand, chilling your flesh, each page, and we were united in work, in the book. You write in the darkness, mind cloaked in two red dots on the red alarm clock, because you dispatched me. I need your kiss again, filling us with eyes, and our outlines will tremble and shine like hot filaments, hollow at last, finally empty, the way clear, the hollow ovum, the hollow semen.

You told me through my damp curls, pressing what once was a hungry mouth, those were the most recuperative moments—you can hear yourself healing into her forever. The pain never dims. It's with me now—the pulsating buzz of some flying thing's wings. Always. Never wavering. The pulsating buzz of some flying thing's wings. You may not hear it in my voice. I was run over by a train of honey, felt a rib crack, the shuddering heart and groin and flesh grew so heavy wail of the train bore down on me with its rush and against your cold shadow I seemed to fall into the vibrations, cold shadows reached out to seize me—I fell on the tracks, felt a rib crack, the shuddering of honey. Excitement and fear spidered out from the wail of the train as if I fell against her cold shadow that seemed to fall into kissing me.

The doors open. It's you, on the platform. The flowers in your hair I can taste from here—carnations. Their fragrance cuts through the musty odor of these passengers like a lifeline.

Lyla, I'm terrified. You have to help me. It will happen to us both, you and me, separately or together. Better together. Come sit beside me, where you belong. You knew I was holding something back. Do you see the words have appeared on my skin? Cherry words. The crowd parts, forming an aisle for you. You have to open your mouth. I'll give you what I was holding back, I will ink you. I will seize you very suddenly and press you to my new-written-word body and kiss the secret into you: you're wasting your time. You don't escape the loop by breaking the circle. You escape through the middle. Somehow I'm not adequate to that yet. *You might help me with that.* Can you hear me over the roar of the subway? We are the book. We're not real. None of us are.

The doors close between us, cutting you off from me forever. I am immobilized in total darkness, feeling the press of the passengers against me. Waves of excruciating cold emanate from the window. Cling to my agony, or succumb to that cold—that is the only choice, and I no longer have it. It's time.

The train rolls slowly forward for a few seconds—then plunges down into the abyss, wildly, the press of the people flung forward rams me against the freezing window and the window pops out slightly—cold belches onto me and I'm screaming no! . . . no!—the window slips again . . . is slipping . . . the cold has got me—the window gives way completely . . .

# LETTER FOUND SITTING ATOP A RARE OLD HANDBOUND BOOK OF DARK PORTENT

## ANNA TAMBOUR

**H**EY MR. W,

You're busy, we're busy, so let's get down to it.

We heard you're planning quite a scene. Some cockroach is supposed to walk up to some old book which is just lying around on the sidewalk like a piece of gum. And the cockroach?

Walk up to the book.

Climb up to the cover.

Walk around and leave, walking out of the picture.

(In the daytime, with people walking around; people with shoes with heels, no less)

Yeah, those are the directions. The question is: Why?

We've talked it over, and while we're not averse or contrarian in principle, this type of behaviour doesn't make sense.

Unless, of course, the backstory is, say—

X (the protagonist) has suffered brain damage from poisoning,

or (and this is what roughly 48 percent of us think you're getting at) X has been implanted with a chip by a nefarious overlord (it's not for us to say this is a stale trope, so, okay, not a bad plot but one in which you must plant the gun well ahead of time),

or (and we hope not) this is "comedy,"

or (and knowing your history, this is a distinct possibility, most of us feel, but to carry it off, you must be more disciplined than you have been with your last three oeuvres) this is the peak dramatic scene. You aren't asking for mindlessness or illogicality for no reason. No, X's soul is turbulent with angst.

If this is so, we not only applaud you, but look forward to the final rushes, and the glorious, if you edit right, success.

In the meantime, just so you know and we're all on the same page, no matter who amongst us (and you should be congratulated, Mr. Twenty-First-Century Bergman, for your perspicacity in choosing us), no matter who amongst us gets the part, whether one of our stars, a young instar, or say, someone working restaurants, the contract for this part must be commensurate with the part. Doing *Weltanschauung* is exhausting.

Of course, whichever your directions re: emotion, the cauldron remaining the same (daylight with people), the rate includes two stars extra (Danger Danger), three stars if stilettos are involved.

We look forward to working with you.

All the best,
on behalf of the members
NYC ch., GCTU (German Cockroach Theatrical Union)
*All as one*

PS: This is just an afterthought. (Hi, I'm the one who boiled down the members' arguments and hopes to write the above letter to you. You can call me "Pete." [To reach me, tap three times on the floor tiles—you know where: in the stall where you go after lunch every 2 p.m., M–F.]) Everyone else thinks you want to get across a to-ing-and-fro-ing, a nervous turbulence—merely the aforesaid *Weltanschauung* (a piece of cake to act, if you ask me, though they gave you drama about it—I had to write that stuff— "draining"! I'll give you *draining*. Sometimes I resent the collective.) But I sense something higher in you. You are really plumbing, in this scene, a richer depth of character, in despair, an almost catatonic *Weltschmerz*—all slow, dragging steps, and to show the windows of the soul, the closeup. This part fits me so well, it's like we already *know* each other.

# CHAPTER SIXTEEN

# AND I WATERED IT IN FEARS

## SUNNY MORAINE

**T**HREE DAYS AFTER receiving it, she locked the book in a drawer and didn't take it out again until the end.

How she got it is no longer important. In truth, she doesn't even exactly remember anymore, except that it felt like one of those inevitabilities, those things that crash down on you like lightning bolts. She does remember that much; she remembers holding it that first time, feeling its weight and heft, the texture of its cover, its leaves. They whispered to her when she turned them, let her fingers trace their edges. In that moment, the image of a tree had in fact come to her, and she hasn't been able to shake it since. Except in those moments it was a tree of early summer, all spreading bows and nodding leaves dappling the sun. It was something beautiful, something that promised. The return of things lost. The resurrection of a career, a muse, a life. Of something beyond all of those things.

Now it's twisted and the leaves have fallen. Something about it glowers at her. There are knotted holes in its trunk, and it feels like something is tucked inside them, staring out at her with incomprehensible focus. It's part of why the thing ended up in a drawer, but the image remains.

And the drawer makes no difference. Part of her hungers for it, wants to take it out again and caress it, beg it for some nudge in the right direction.

She knows that's irrational, it's just a goddamn book, but again, there had been that promise, and she had been in a mood to need promises.

Desperation is weakness. She knows this. Desperation is also hate, and she knows that, too. Now she stares at a blank white horror and she fights that hate back because it's choking her. That blankness used to also be a promise, an open, undiscovered land approached with appropriate fear and trembling and joy. Now it's a wall against which she throws herself again and again until she feels broken down and has to stop, have a drink, stare at her shaking hands until they stop shaking.

The tremors began a few months ago. She knows what they mean, but if she's honest she struggles to care.

And there is that drawer. In her desk, less than a foot to her right. She locked it, put the key someplace so weird and random that she expected to forget it, but she hasn't. On that same day she went to Renee and asked for her help, asked for her to take it and put it somewhere safe and not tell her no matter what she said, but Renee only looked at her with hollow eyes and shook her head, and said something about the bottles of wine without saying it in so many words. Then there was anger and stalking out of the room.

You can resent someone for dying. This is something else that she's learning. Someone's body turns on them and you feel like it's turning on you as well. You're angry at them like they failed. Like they couldn't hold something back. They were weak and now you have to suffer for it.

The key is in the freezer. The contents of the drawer burn in the dark like a little coal.

IN HER DREAMS the tree extends its boughs like a malevolent willow, curls them around her ankles and drags her across stones that become claws that rip at her flesh. She wakes up soaked in fear sweat and horribly, disgustingly aroused, and she turns her back to Renee and tries not to hear the harsh rasp of her breathing, the sound of the cancer choking the life out of her.

There's really only so much you can do.

HER TV INTERVIEWS. Her face on the cover of trade mags. She always sort of liked book tours even though she was always fighting a cold by the end. She had a column in a rather notable literary magazine whose name she won't speak anymore, nor will she read it or have it in the house, but hadn't that been impressive, because *genre fiction*—say it with your nose slightly upturned, just a bit nasal, not condescending in any explicit way but making it a point to condescend all the same.

She liked the writing, but then she liked everything that came along with the writing. It's hard to give that up. It's also hard to make mortgage payments. It's hard when the medical bills keep piling up and piling up like some kind of malevolent, Tolkien-esque tower.

This was supposed to get better. It's not. At some point it occurs to her that she might be too jaded for real panic. Instead she's numb and confused, like a deer staring down an oncoming set of headlights. She doesn't yet appreciate what this final, slow slide down into failure really means. She knows that at some point she'll understand the full of it.

SHE WROTE HER own terror. *Once upon a time.* People used to fear those words, because they meant wolves and giants and wicked witches, the devouring of flesh and souls. In the earliest fairy tales there were no happy endings, only endings, finite and dreadful. She had her fairy tales as a child, the sanitized ones written once terror as a teaching method went out of fashion, but she has always sensed the darker, older things hiding behind the cheerful facades. Those happy grins all looked, in her mind, like frozen screams. Eventually it occurred to her that she could drag the truth back out of them with her bare hands, with the *tap tap tap* of her fingers. Drums to call the elder gods.

She perhaps should have taken lessons from those ancient stories, taken them to heart and kept them well. When you call the elder gods, and they heed your call, they always exact their price.

SHE STANDS IN the doorway and stares at Renee where she lies supine under the covers, a wasted little thing of skin and flesh that's learning how to die. She was a small woman to begin with, petite and delicate—one of the things first and most appealing about her—but now she's a twig, a dry pine needle, her brown skin oddly colorless, her long braided hair poisoned to patchy stubble.

Once Renee seemed salvageable. This whole thing did. One more book, her best one, the one that brings back everything she lost when the inspiration dried up. The attention, the adulation, the money. The idea came to her so clear and complete, like a sculptor seeing the shape hiding inside the block of marble, and all that remained was to help it emerge. But that was three months and many doses of radiation ago, many drips of that poison, and the blank white horror remains. The treasure is still locked in its treasure box. Death is startlingly expensive.

Renee turns, twists weakly, moans in the grip of some dream. She hasn't slept well in weeks, but sometimes she lies so still that she already seems like a corpse, and a long time ago it became an expected thing that one might awaken to find her gone cold in her narrowing territory of mattress.

One shouldn't have to share a sickbed—a deathbed—but the couch seems like a kind of rejection.

*Teach us how to die.*

Renee has never thanked her. This probably shouldn't make her as angry as it does.

THE IDEA: PIECES of a world disappearing one by one. The protagonist is the only one who notices. Entire sections of a city, once familiar, fade into a white barrier that can't be broken through. Friends vanish and everyone acts confused—they've never known these people, never heard these names. History is gone from the books, well-known cities are no longer marked on maps, significant websites are offline and gone from search engines. Growing panic. Everyone begins to regard the protagonist as hysterical, delusional, then completely insane. A mental institution. A daring and violent escape. But the world outside is white nothing. A house of the mad is the only refuge. The doctors are gone, the orderlies, the patients. Until finally: sitting alone in a chair in an empty room, he watches his hands disappear, starting at his fingertips and moving upward, upward, until the end.

It could be done. She thinks it could be done. But she waits for it until her hands are clenched and white-knuckled, and she pounds her fists against the desk. It faces a window. The light coming through is as white and brilliant and blank as the page on the screen.

THE TREE IS a tall, pale, naked man with eyes like tar pits. He grins at her, ear to ear, easily a hundred teeth in his wide mouth. His arms are unnaturally long, and fingers as white and hard as bone brush the ground. He extends them, parts his twisted jaws, and nothingness flows out of his rotting mouth like mist.

SHE DOESN'T KNOW when she was last outside. She looks at the door for a while. The kitchen is fully stocked—someone must have gone to the store but she doesn't remember doing it and no one has come over to help. The phone hasn't rung. No texts. When was the last time someone sent her an email? She checks. Weeks ago. No pestering from her agent, no encouraging but vaguely disappointed missive from Mom. No weird fan mail—admittedly the only kind of fan mail she's ever gotten. Nothing.

*Teach us how to die.*

Once she would have almost preferred to be forgotten. Now she sits in silence on the couch, listening to Renee upstairs moaning in pain and fear—or is that the wind?—and her nails bite into her palms. They bought this house because there was so much light. It seemed like there were so many stories to tell. No one could fuck that up. How do you stop being able to do what you've always done?

You look for someone to blame. You run through a shortening list of names. Everyone is drifting away. She's actually forgotten some of their faces, but she remembers the image of their receding backs. Everyone checks out when you need them. Everyone fucks off.

This wasn't supposed to happen. Just because it's cliché doesn't mean it's not true.

The diagnosis. The first moment of realization. Revelation. Sitting together in front of a doctor's desk, holding Renee's hand, she felt like both a supplicant and an anchor, at once powerful and completely powerless. That she couldn't stop it. That she could see it, but neither of them could get out of its way. She has written stories like this, where—despite courage and virtue—her heroes and heroines are devoured in the end by whatever figurative or literal demon has decided to make a meal of them. In her stories it's not enough to be good. Being good doesn't save you. She writes these things—or she used to—because this is the greatest horror she can think of, the greatest horror of which she's ever been able to conceive: that nothing can save you.

You always die in the end. You die badly. You die ugly, terrified, in agony, and you watch everyone you love die, too. Even if only in your imagination. You know it. No one can be saved, not one.

What life is for is teaching you how to die. Be a good student. Pay attention. This will all be on the test.

It didn't just stop. The cut-off wasn't that abrupt. It was very gradual, so by the time she noticed the desert she had already been in it for over a year. It began with a certain clumsiness in the structure of her sentences, her turns of phrase. Things came out flat. Things ceased to flow. She had never been exactly known for the elegance of her prose, but once she liked to think that her work was better than workman-like. But then that became exactly what it was. Just . . . words. Words, one after the other, conveying the basics of an idea but nothing more. Brief, undescriptive description. A difficult way to frighten anyone.

And then, bit by bit, the words stopped coming at all.

Writer's block is not block-like, not in her experience. It's slow starvation, a wasting-away of a body once healthy and robust. You arrive at a diagnosis long after the disease has already become considerably advanced. And then the fear, the panic, the clawing inside yourself, not trying to dig out an invader but instead a desperate search for what's gone. What's abandoned you.

It was said that gods abandoned temples that ceased to honor them with the proper rites. For weeks after her own revelation—before that other and more lethal one—she sat up nights and hit herself, slow and despairing blows on her own arms, legs, eventually her face. Not hard enough to bruise, but something like that seemed indicated. Penance. Pleas for the gods to return. Rage, because she had clearly done something wrong.

If she was good enough, maybe it could have saved her.

SHE HASN'T GONE outside. She's sure of it. She sits at the desk and doesn't look at the white terror, and she ponders the possibility of *outside*. The door in the front hall, the lock. The silent phone. The brighter white is all gone and gray seeps in through the curtains, and the beating whisper of the rain. It's all an abstraction now. Nothing is really real but the white and, slow and creeping, swelling like an infected limb, the book in the drawer. It's whispering to her with the voice of the rain, and if she could only hear it, she could find her way through the white wall and tell her horrible stories again, and save them all.

She doesn't need outside. She picks up the bottle of whiskey and sips delicately at it until her hands stop shaking.

It was a dream. It was a dream she loved. A beautiful house, a beautiful wife. Now a treasure of leaves, a tree to cultivate, even if it's gone to bone and black blood, curling its branches around her throat. A tree with something hungry inside it. Something old.

She asked it in. She stares at the drawer. She asked it in, and this is no way to treat a guest.

AT SOME POINT—hours? days? weeks?—later, the rage truly takes her, and she spins through the house like a twister, gathering up breakable things and smashing them against walls and furniture and each other. She turns a thin, honey-colored antique chair to splinters. She falls to her knees and claws at an expensive ornamental rug, and then she has the presence of mind to find shears with which to go at it. She tears paintings off the walls. She screams and pulls at her hair. All her pretty things, all the pretty little remnants of a life, and behind her eyes the book is whispering *Yes, yes, give it all to me and I'll give you what you want.*

*I can save you.*

In the end she's crouched on the floor in tears, her hands and face bloody and scored. She has shredded first editions of her own books, the paper all around her like a colorless autumn, the leavings of a wind. The rain has turned hard and it batters at the house, but for as long as she can remember there has been no lightning.

Upstairs, she thinks she can hear Renee sobbing. Weak and soft, something bleeding slowly out of her.

AFTER A WHILE she gets up, slowly and painfully, and she finds herself staggering toward the door. The room is spinning and her head is full of wadded paper, and she's half sure that she's about to vomit, but her shaking fingers manage to work the lock and then the door is open, and she's staring out past the porch and the eaves to a gray wall of nothing, utterly opaque.

Lines are scrawled on it, lines through the rain. Words that she can't make out, that she's not even entirely sure are in a language that she knows. But they're everywhere, all around her, and the vomit becomes a scream.

She swallows it. Steps back inside. The door closes and the house goes quiet as a tomb in which the dead are lying down at last.

THERE IS NO moment of final decision. There is no choice following consideration. For a long time she stands at the bottom of the staircase, listening to the silence into which Renee has fallen. Her hands aren't shaking anymore. The tree is behind her, her tree, its branches resting on her shoulders.

It's all right. This will save them. She starts to climb.

She remembers when she met Renee. A trade conference, though she actually doesn't remember which one. Renee had been standing at a vendor's table, looking down at a copy of something that had nothing written on the spine, her long coils of beautifully braided hair all glossy and shining, that sly curve of her mouth just visible, the up-tilt that always made her look as if she was amused by something. Approaching her was equal parts curiosity—about her, and about what had her so interested. The book was inconsequential. That curve meant everything.

Great sex less than twenty-four hours after meeting her. Marriage four months later. It happened fast, and that was okay.

Everything with Renee happened so fast. Everything.

Now she's moving slowly, because this deserves careful attention, this is the big ending she's been searching for, except it's really very small, and it's also a beginning. This is where she breaks through the white and finds the words. This is where she finds the courage to break that final lock. She doesn't need a key. She just needs her bloody hands.

Renee is still and small under the sheet, her breathing so quiet that for a moment the possibility that she might already be dead once again asserts itself. But then her chest rises and falls again, hitching, struggling, rendered strange and uncertain by the streaked light from the rainy windowpane. Approaching her now is no part curiosity. There's nothing left to wonder. Everything is known: the beginning, the middle, and now the falling action sloping down toward the end.

The pillow is like air in her hands. It doesn't take much strength. There's a little more struggling, and then, after a while, there's just stillness.

And that's that.

DOWN IN THE broken hell, facing the wall. No key but a hammer. She crouches, raises it, and the whispering crescendos into a raging hiss of joy as she strikes the lock twice, three times, and it clatters to the floor. Her hands still aren't shaking as she reaches inside and lifts out her treasure, her tree, her source of salvation. There are faces in its cover, she now realizes: laughing faces, faces with their mouths twisted into screams, no clear distinction between the two.

She's not good, but she can be saved. She can.

She lifts the book to her chest and cradles it like she used to cradle Renee's sleeping body. She lowers her head and runs her lips across the edge of its cover. Moving with deeper purpose than she's ever had, she takes her seat in front of the white, holding the book against herself like a lover who is a shield, who is a face she wants to turn to the world. She stares at the white without blinking. She will mark it, she will make her lines. She will break through. She's very sure of it now. She's left everything else behind.

Very soon, it will happen.

Her tree closes its boughs around her and presses its grinning face to the back of her neck.

*Teach me.*

# CHAPTER SEVENTEEN

# MILES AND KATHRINE AT THE CRIMSON

## MICHAEL GRIFFIN

*"Suffering is permanent, obscure and dark
And shares the nature of infinity."*
—William Wordsworth

**W**E'RE ALONE IN a rising elevator.
"Don't be jealous of James." Kathrine leans, presses her lips against mine. "He's nothing, just my husband."
I haven't said I'm jealous. Probably it shows.
My fingertips trace her scar, pink threads branching cheek to jawline. It's a birthmark really, but she always refers to it as *my scar*. I've heard her say those words so many times, until now I think of it that way, too. The way she wants.
"That'll be over soon," she says. "And then, until the end of everything, it'll be just us. Miles and Kathrine."
We're going to this restaurant, a place I don't belong. Four mirrored walls make me feel scrutinized. My face reflects, multiplies. Eyes smudged dark, three-day beard, hair wild like I've just pulled a shirt up over my head. This isn't how I picture myself, but there it is. The sell-by date on my conception of self is long gone. The mirror never lies.
As if Kathrine senses my rising self-consciousness, she brushes lips

across my cheek, toward my mouth. My body reacts in a wild impulse of wanting. I know this desire will never diminish. She moves so we're front to front. I squeeze her into me, press our bodies into proximity. I want to occupy the same space. Want to feel more.

She exhales exasperation. "I know, it's been nine days."

"I can't wait like that. Never again." I reach up, under her loose sweater, where her skin hides, warm. Nerves thrill at the pleasure, more visceral than mere touch. A shivering hypersensitivity, like the pinnacle of sex. Every surface of her body and every molecule of my own, all starving for each other. Straining, vibrating with need.

Me with Kathrine, together like this at least, this is new.

"Never again," she promises.

The elevator counts 43 . . . 47. This restaurant, the Crimson, it's on 61.

Under the sweater, Kathrine's body shifts, a muscle trembling against my hand. Her torso snakes sideways, pressing. I feel desire in her skin. Her body, long and straight, so unlike Paula. Kathrine's shape still feels new, her color and smell unfamiliar. The tone of her voice, a thrill.

I reach, fumbling for her messenger bag. "Did you bring it?" I ask. "I want to see."

She pulls the bag beyond my grasp. The long strap lets it hang mid-thigh, like Peter Hook's bass. "Are you crazy, here?" Eyes dart, as if she too feels watched. "It's hidden at home. Always."

59 . . . 61. The door hums open.

The landing is vacant, cream marble and accents of polished brass bright as golden mirrors. Down the floor's center runs a carpet, dark red saturated as pomegranate fruit. Blurred movements beyond a glass door suggest our destination. No sign, just a red capital "C" in a gold square. We approach.

I whisper. "What if James finds it?"

She pulls my hand, stops me. "He wouldn't dig through my heirloom chest. To him it's just wasted closet space. He wouldn't know how to use it, anyway."

We start again toward the door.

I remain irritated, though I have no right. James is my friend. I'm fucking his wife, in love with her. More than that, this new start we're planning won't be easy on him, or Paula. I'm the one who's wrong, not James. He's just coasting along, living life. Same apartment, same bed. No clue what's coming.

Kathrine's eyes scan, as if my thoughts are audible. "It's for you and me. Not James, certainly not Paula. In case you forgot her."

I push the glass door open. Kathrine enters first.

The host greets us, wearing a black suit with thin silver pinstripes, pristine and unwrinkled, a costume in a movie. I can't understand how people afford clothes like that. Lately, everyone seems wealthy. I'm getting worn down, used up. It's excruciating. All the black is scuffed off the front of my leather jacket. Paint-scabbed boots.

Kathrine's jeans are more shredded than mine, but for women, damage like this seems intentional, fashion-driven. Skin shows pale through a hole above the knee. An opening by her back pocket flashes tiger-stripe panties.

If the host thinks we don't belong, he conceals it. Grabs two menus, thick red leather folios, and leads us into an opulent room. Red and gold tapestries hang between classical paintings, and cream marble sculptures stand draped with red capes and gowns. Maybe Kathrine can identify the artists. She's a modernist herself, but knows proper art history, all that theory I never got. That's why James gets so frustrated with her minimalist paintings, color field stuff like Rothko meets Franz Kline. She's good enough to paint commercially viable work, if she wanted. Landscapes, nudes, maybe cheeky pop-surrealism. Whatever investment bankers buy for five-million-dollar condos. Kathrine won't do it.

We get a corner booth. Three o'clock, the dead zone before dinner. Only one other occupied table, a sixty-something woman in a pink and white first-lady suit across from a swarthy younger man. Her son, maybe a gigolo. They don't notice us. The host leaves us.

Kathrine's eyes widen, seeming at once awed and disapproving. "This place!"

"We just need to stay discreet a little longer. I figure nobody who knows us would stumble in here in a million years."

"It's a good idea." She picks up a menu. "It's just, holy fucking wow. These prices."

"If things are headed the way you plan, soon bank accounts won't matter." I reach across the table for her hand.

"Fuck, aren't you utterly sick of worrying about money, and bills? Our generation owes a great big fuck you to Bukowski, guys like that. This idea that if you've made a poem or painting, it's okay getting evicted, electricity shut off, going days without food." Kathrine hugs herself with both arms, as if trying to prevent herself flying apart. Sleeves of the baggy sweater slide up to reveal tattoos. Finger and hands, wrists and arms. Colored birds flit among vines surrounding an ominous godhead visage.

Her smile returns, a shapely outline, perfect red. Those lips convince me everything's going to be okay. All our burdens left behind. A new start. I surprise myself, smiling too. Finally daring to hope.

THE WAITER APPEARS, less ostentatious than the host, at least lacking the five-thousand-dollar suit. How the hell does someone who's basically a receptionist at a restaurant afford such a suit? It's still bugging me, but this waiter seems nonjudgmental, makes eye contact, no attitude. Maybe he figures we're a couple of artist weirdos headed to a SoHo gallery, stumbled into the wrong place. He asks if we're ready to order.

Smiling, Kathrine replies without looking at the menu. "The veal Kadath. I think that sounds perfect for the day."

Her words hit me in the gut. Our secrets. What's she doing? My heart booms in my chest.

The waiter's face goes blank. "The veal . . ."

"My favorite." Kathrine raises an eyebrow.

She's kidding. Trying to get a rise out of me.

The waiter looks at her menu, as if confirming he's still in the right place. "Apologies, madam, we have no veal. Maybe you're thinking of another . . ." A circular gesture completes the thought.

Kathrine's smile broadens, all bright teeth, like she's just received wonderful news. "I'm sure the fault's mine. It's been years since I've dined here." She checks the menu cover. "Here at the Crimson." She flips pages, seeking alternates. "I'll really be eating today, like a dying woman wanting a last supper. So then, pesto and scallops fettuccine, also the prime rib sandwich. Extra horseradish please. I realize that's two lunches, both for myself. My lover, Miles, will order his own."

The waiter looks at me, unsure whether she's kidding. Really, I'm not interested in food. I'm still under Kathrine's spell, distracted by proximity to her. I barely see the menu, and order the first thing I notice.

I'm all nerves and jitters. Katherine's excited, wide-eyed, ready to devour everything in the place. Clearly the situation affects us differently. Maybe I'm feeling guilty about James, and Paula.

After the waiter departs, I'm aware of some shift between us. All new couples have moments like this, after they first cross the threshold into intimacy. It's like we both remember how it was before, the way we used to be. Our present and prior selves glimpse one another across time. The old Miles and Kathrine can't believe what we're doing now. Momentary awkwardness, a flashback to the just-friends perspective. Even touching her hand seems like crossing a line. How did we get here?

Part of me still can't believe it.

Tentatively, I reach. Her right hand flinches from my touch. I loop my index finger through hers. Fingernails of her left hand drum the table, fingers tattooed A–K–L–O. I catch her eyes, look away. She does the same. One moment, partners in a new venture, this incredible flower just curling open. Next moment, shy, stunned at all we've dared. Touching and kissing, lately fucking. I've seen her body, all her skin. Hard to believe. This final stage now, making plans. Nerves on edge.

Neither of us is backing down, losing determination. We understand where things need to go. Desire persists. It's only natural there's fear, too.

"Remember Vermont?" Kathrine asks. "Diamonds in the air. The blood?"

Of course, I remember.

She begins the story, tells every detail, as if I've never heard it before. I was there. James too, and Paula, four of us snowshoeing in the mountains near James's family cabin outside Killington.

"Approaching that high ridge, the sun breaks through clouds. Like a razor cutting the sky, that crest. We walk the edge, out to where the tip becomes a sort of platform. A viewpoint, with a locked ranger's hut. The wind gathers, spins ice crystals up the slope. They swirl at the top. This brilliant flurry, like spinning diamonds."

She exhales through pursed lips. I think maybe that's all she's going to say for now, but she continues.

"Why can't life be always like that moment? So bright, it makes your eyes burst. So much beauty."

"But then—" I lead, knowing the story will shift.

"Then we're descending, all dizzy with altitude, lack of oxygen. And freezing, but so giddy with that otherworldly beauty that's just filled us up, like. . . ." Her eyes flit away. "Like heaven. A million diamonds floating, whirling. Better than diamonds, they're weightless. Then on the way down, maybe I'm distracted."

"You stepped—"

"I lose my balance, stumble forward." Her arms pinwheel in reenactment. "It's funny. Everyone laughs, I'm laughing, maybe you think I'm clowning. But I can't stop. I fall, my leg strikes this sharp rock, sticking through snow. I don't remember any hurting. Just jumping up, thinking *how stupid*. One minute laughing, then . . ."

"We were so young, everything seemed—"

"It's just four years ago. My leg, I try to walk. James tells me I'm not hurt. I'm mad, so I keep limping on, drinking schnapps from your flask, trying to go. Mad at myself, but mostly James, his whole fucking world. How things always . . . Just, you're in your twenties—how are you supposed to know? This guy says, we'll be together, it'll be a certain way. What he promises seems better. Good enough, at least. Then you're married. Things keep breaking."

I stroke the back of her hand, feel the skin raised in the pattern of ink vines. "We've always been young. We still are."

"That's the thing, the whole fucking thing," she says. "Yes, we're young. We have always been young. But we won't always be."

I release her hand. We've discussed this problem, and agree. It's our prime motivator. The way everything changes.

"Do you remember the blood?" She's not really asking. She knows.

We all remember. Even James, who didn't believe it at the bottom, when she rolled up her pants leg. We saw the blood streaming, sticky red filling her boot, bubbling around the cuff. Even later at the hospital, when they cut off her stretch pants and boot. The doctor showed us the X-ray. James kept insisting you can't compound fracture a fibula without breaking the tibia. It's impossible, he kept saying.

"I do remember." I stand, excuse myself.

THE BATHROOM MIRROR reflects sick yellow. I splash water from the sink, trying to revive my dead-looking face.

I'm supposed to be happy. This isn't something I have to do. I can stop. Tell Kathrine *No*.

But I can't go back. My old life, such a dead end. It's a new beginning for me, for us. A chance to erase every trouble, every failure. The ultimate clean slate.

Two of us, Miles and Kathrine. Together forever.

This joint, they've got real fabric towels. Crimson, naturally. I dry my face. My guess is these two-dozen hand towels, in two neat piles, must cost five hundred dollars. There's a brass receptacle with a foot pedal so I can lift the lid, no hands. I drop in the used towel. There doesn't seem to be anywhere to put actual trash. Probably they incinerate whatever you put in there, towels, anything. Guys like me forever washing and reusing towels, clothes, keeping them until they fray apart, until you can see through them. Like Kathrine's jeans, her ass hanging out. Holes you can put your fingers through.

Places like this, also where we're going, you never need to worry about lack. Everything's abundant, luxurious. Every day stays *now*, forever. Each new tomorrow, just another today.

MUSIC STARTS PLAYING soon after our food arrives.

Kathrine pauses over the scallop fettuccine. "Your namesake. Miles." She draws out the name's vowel.

The tune's superficially similar to "So What?" by Miles Davis. What she means is, that's where my parents got my name, no doubt hoping their kid would create music, that I might one day perform onstage, be admired, receive applause. They didn't bestow this name hoping I'd write two-hundred-word music reviews at fifty bucks a pop. Not even reviews. Mini-critiques, impactless blocks of filler text, useful for balancing page layouts.

I know what she thinks she hears. "It's Coltrane's 'Blue Train.' The beginning sounds like 'So What.'"

She wrinkles her nose. "I've heard this a hundred times. It's 'So What?' from *Kind of Blue*. Miles Davis, Blue Note Jazz."

"Listen to—"

"Bzzzt! Ha, ha, Mr. Walking Music Encyclopedia. I'm right, you're wrong."

"Hold on. When the horn starts here . . ."

Notes spill, almost tripping over themselves in a flurry. Sax, not trumpet.

Kathrine's scar flares red, blood coursing hot through vessels too near the surface. "Shit! Damn." Her smile returns, but she doesn't look at me.

I worry about having corrected her. "They're playing it so quietly, you only hear the two-chord piano figure. These crappy little ceiling speakers. Sounds like Muzak."

"See, that's what's wrong." She rubs the mark, as if it pains her. "All this."

"This restaurant?"

"No. Life, everything. The volume's too low, too politely fucking quiet. It's colorless and bland." Trembling, her hand moves, covers her face. A tear falls, in anger or frustration. "Life should be vivid, you know? Sharp. Radiant. Don't you want that?"

"Of course, that's what all this is about, why I'm willing to . . ." I grab her hand. It seems inadequate, not the grand and forceful gesture required.

Kathrine composes herself, wipes away tears. Wetness glistens on her cheek, the scar red, like a smear of blood. Her mouth draws that beautiful longbow curve, and everything's good again.

Blue Train plays, the whole album. I watch Kathrine eat.

"In 1995," she says, "I would have killed myself if not for John Coltrane."

"For me it was '88, freshman year at Pratt. Other kids had The Cure, Joy Division. I rolled myself up in Trane, like a blanket. This one, and *A Love Supreme*."

"Those cool parents you had, no kid of theirs was going away to college without being fully prepped with Coltrane, Miles, and Brubeck." Her expression appears light but conveys no mirth, just hollow sadness and the burden of regret.

I try to muster some counterbalancing observation, anything positive about Kathrine's parents. Daddy's Chicago elite, major pharmaceutical money. Kathrine says he found doctors willing to keep Mother permanently in a coma. Kathrine ran off, now Daddy abuses jailbait runaways, kind of a golden handcuffs arrangement. They don't complain. Most need to be dragged out, begging to stay, once Daddy's used them up. Kathrine's talked to some. All proclaim love for the man, would go back eagerly, if he'd have them. Every one of them tall, willowy brunettes with tattoos. One even had the same letters on her fingers as Kathrine.

I halt the stream of thought. "So how does wordless music convince people not to snuff it?"

Kathrine considers. "I remember feeling it like a poem, or incantation. Anyway, *A Love Supreme* has words. Those songs promised me a future existed. A period of enlightenment to come. Something worth sticking around for." She squeezes my hand.

"I have this theory. The people who feel music most deeply never make their own." I swirl my ice water. "I should've gotten hooked on heroin, tried playing a horn."

"Painters can do smack. You should've tried."

"Remember how it shifted for you? I mean, how it became about painting?"

"The first time I came here, left Chicago. I'm fifteen, reading *Interview* magazine on the train one morning, and decide instead of going to the academy, why not New York? The fare left six dollars in my pocket. I remember Penn Station, digging french fries out of the trash. Walking all night, thinking if I'm going to sleep in the park, it's safer in daylight. Once I got hungry enough, preconceptions about what I was capable of fell away. Still had my rich girl clothes, so panhandling was easy. Twenty dollars, thirty in an hour. I didn't spend it on food, or a room, not at first. Museums. I walked endlessly, morning to night. Spinning circles in the Guggenheim. Staring into the MOMA Pollocks, so close, my nose almost touching canvas. Then zoom back, the wide view. I got to know paintings like a lover's body."

"The first thing I remember's my dad's Time-Life Library of Art, those beige slipcovers. I obsessed over those books like porn."

"You know what blew my fucking mind—art that looked so small in books, pointlessly decorative, but when I saw it panoramic, live in person, totally ripped my eyes out? The water lilies. Fucking Monet. He painted actual things he'd looked upon with real eyes. All aquamarine and cerulean, abstract shapes, crazy patterns. He made the world into this deep hallucination, better than real." She grasps my hand, clutches hard. "The water lilies made me happy for the first time. So when I finally had a room, I bought paints. I taught myself. I was eighteen, before James. I really wanted to live, for a while."

Her eyes shift focus and she notices me, seems almost startled. "What about you? Tell me why you went from sculpting to painting."

"When I first started Pratt, I remember thinking 'this is it, I want to create shapes.' Form carried almost religious power." I gesture, both hands in front of my eyes, molding a shape. This conveys nothing at all of what I'm seeing, that visceral gut-punch of dimensionality. "Painting, you can imply depth with flat color and tone. It's just easier, I guess. A trick in the perceiver's mind. Why bother building the form? It doesn't actually need to exist. You just need the implication and perceptive inference to collide, and it seems real. That's magic."

She rubs both eyes with her knuckles. "What could we have done differently, either of us? To make work that ended up meaning something?"

"It does mean—"

"No, not just work that we enjoy ourselves. Both of us have stacks of paintings nobody buys. We've got all this feeling, more than anybody. It just doesn't manifest, you know. Doesn't come out big enough. Coltrane, or a Pollock or Manet, they light fire to the world. That beauty, it's huge. We inhale that, but when we breathe it back out, it's so fucking small."

I want to argue, but it doesn't matter. That's what we keep forgetting. "That futility, it's about to change. No more small gestures."

After being apart so long, the atmosphere between us sizzles with intensity. Touching fingers, gazing at each other. The burning eagerness of shared anticipation. Partners in the ultimate intimacy, big enough to beat everything.

I'VE BARELY TOUCHED my bacon sandwich. Kathrine's making progress on her second lunch, looks capable of devouring everything.

My cell phone rings. When I pull it from my pocket, Kathrine looks, trying to see who's calling.

Another ring, I flip it open. "Hey. Got my message?"

The waiter sweeps by, takes Kathrine's empty pasta plate without pausing.

"That's what I meant. I'm not sure what you'll need to say. Just try." I watch Kathrine, wondering how she's interpreting this. "Tell her I asked you to take them all. Yeah, if you have the room."

Angles shift in Kathrine's face.

"Look, I'd better go. I'm having something to eat. No, alone."

Disconnect.

Kathrine works a mouthful of prime rib sandwich. I weigh what I might offer. She swallows, sips water. "Sounds like making plans."

"I asked a friend, someone you don't know, to stop by my place. Get my paintings out of there."

"Friend? Who?"

"From Tohza Gallery, this new intern. Don't think you've met."

"What's Paula going to say? Someone shows up, says trust me, Miles says I should carry off his life's work? A whole apartment full of paintings?"

"There aren't so many. I just don't trust what Paula might do."

"Stop worrying how things will be, after." She completes the thought with a gesture, a circular motion I've never seen her make. It's the gesture the waiter made when she tried to order Kadath veal, or whatever.

"It's just better somebody has them."

The waiter returns but hangs back, gauging whether we need anything, or prefer privacy.

Kathrine looks from him to me. "You want to go?"

"Not too hungry," I admit.

Her face brightens. "Let's order drinks. Big, posh ones."

The waiter steps up, offers suggestions. I'm glad for the change of subject. We both order the special, the *Fin de Siecle*.

"What's that mean?" I ask. "Last century, something like that?"

"End of an age," she pronounces with stilted intonation, like a foreigner speaking words meaningless to themselves by phonetic imitation.

After the first drink, I feel better. By the second, I'm eating, glad Kathrine didn't let the waiter take away my plate. I feel alive. We're ourselves again, not our original selves, predating one another, but the more recent and true Miles and Kathrine. We laugh, hold hands. Give each other looks of outsized adoration and crazy lust. Rub legs together under the table. Try to one-up each other's raunchy double entendres.

Kathrine leans in, mutters some kind of sexual offer including words, possibly Latinate, I'm not sure I understand. Her eyes make clear it's something sexual. "It's something I've never done," she says. "And I want to, with you."

"Are you kidding? Never with James, or any other guy?"

"There weren't any other guys. I mean, boyfriends, but I never had wild sexual adventures. Everyone thinks 'she has tattoos, she makes weird art, she must be some wild free spirit.'"

I'm still unsure of the mechanics of what she's suggesting. "So, what are we talking about? This first-time something you want to do?"

"I can't . . . I'll have to show you."

"But it's, you know, sexual? My parts, your parts—"

She whacks my leg under the table. "Yes, it's sexual, but more. It's an aspect of the other thing." She waits for me to catch up. "Relating to that."

I understand, some new aspect of the other possibilities she's opened up to me.

A FOURTH DRINK.

"You want to hear one thing that summarizes, one single perfect detail that tells you why James is so totally fucked?" She leans hard across the table. "When he introduces me to work friends, those magazine cocksuckers, he pronounces my name wrong, intentionally. He knows I hate it, but he can't stand people asking why's it pronounced like that. Tureen, nineteen, unforeseen, Kathrine. Oh dear, were your parents French? He wants me to be what they expect. A proper Catherine, with knee-length skirts, brown stockings. Shoes that are sensible." She pronounces this last with contempt.

"Baby, you shouldn't drink. Let's—"

"I love it, fucking love a drink." She lifts the glass, tilts it back to drains the last amber liquid from the ice. "Did you ever really like her?"

"Who?"

"Who the fuck do you think? I'm telling about James, real shit from my marriage. You know I never gave him head, not once? Maybe wanted to at some later point. By then it had become standing principle. No blowjobs. For that man. My fucking husband."

"Weird. An edgy girl like you, squeamish over something ordinary."

"No, we're talking about Paula." She raises her glass, seeking the attention of our distant waiter. "Did you. Ever love. Her."

A vision comes, so foreign and long-forgotten I think it's my mind's invention. No, memory: our second date. Paula, an elaborate dinner, pasta with wild chanterelle and porcini mushrooms in wine sauce. I remember thinking, she did this for me. So appealing then, Paula leaning, wooden spoon through rising steam, offering a taste.

My drink runs out. "I must've. I remember being into her at first. You say you never cared about James even when you married him, but Paula, I guess I . . . I used to love her, in certain aspects. Her body."

"Another thing. Want to hear one more?"

"What, you and him?"

"The man's name is James. He's cheated on me all along. You never asked why this principle, no blow jobs. That's why. I've known about the other girls since early on, right after college. Then work, he's triumphant, working at the magazine. More money than anyone expects to make before thirty, James makes by twenty-four. Starts fucking that copy editor, total nerd girl stereotype. Glasses, knee stockings, like Velma from Scooby-Doo. James fucked Velma. Funny how he never felt the need to confess those things. The women, I figured them out on my own. He never admitted anything until he went with another man."

"What? You're drunk."

"Drunk, yes. But an hour ago I was sober. If you'd asked then, has James been faithful, I would've said it's been six, maybe seven girls, going back to relationship year zero. Then, recently, he sampled cock."

I shake my head, trying to keep up. All she's telling me makes my head spin. I feel relief, decrease of guilt for being with Kathrine. "I wonder if Paula, do you think she . . ." If I'm oblivious to James's secrets, what about Paula's?

"Paula unfaithful?" She shrugs. "Who cares, really? That's one virtue of our future: it renders all that shit obsolete. Everything we leave behind becomes meaningless."

I can't help picturing Paula keeping secrets, counting days, impatient for the next chance with someone she desires. Time alone, bodies mutually craving. Like Kathrine and me.

THE LAST *FIN de Siecle*. Kathrine covers what she's been scribbling on her napkin with a fine-point Sharpie.

"Our first kiss, remember, the hallway? James on the other side of the bathroom door, Paula around the corner, in the kitchen. We look at each other, no words. This sudden agreement out of nowhere. So certain."

She flips the napkin around, shows me. I recognize the glyph, what Kathrine calls the sigil. The image from the book's interior describes the unity of all creation.

"A better secret," Kathrine says, "our first fuck."

That memory has obsessed me since. So quickly things change, barriers fall. We mixed blood, hers and mine, with very old red wine from Kathrine's keepsake chest. She drank, offered, and I drank. Back and forth, intimacy of the body, words intoned from a centuries-old volume. When I first saw the sigil, I thought it resembled a stick figure, a single cyclopian eye, horns like a crescent moon atop its head. Kathrine brought me into a circle of intimate knowledge, secrets. I learned what the image promised, the power and utility of the book in her closet.

She transformed me. We opened each other to potentialities neither of us dared consider possible. Delving into the forbidden, a gateway drug to pleasure without precedent, mouths burning with the sharp tang of blood-mixed wine.

"Don't be afraid." Her words pull me back to now, the restaurant. "You wanted to kill yourself. This is better."

I almost argue, instead nod.

"You still believe, don't you?" Under the table she strokes my leg.

I'm reassured by this intimacy. No one else could understand. No other eyes but ours are capable of seeing what lies ahead. "What would you miss?" I ask.

She flattens the drawing, looks up. "Nothing."

"I'll miss . . ." I reconsider, prevent myself making a list, all the things we've talked about, Coltrane and Miles and more, Miró and Kandinsky. I can't explain.

"What were you going to say?" Her darkened eyes fix me, determined yet sad. Her mouth a bow, almost a smile. "What would you miss? Are you certain about this, absolutely?"

"It's not that I'll miss what I have, what my life is like. I'll miss the way I used to hope. I used to think it was possible maybe I'd become the kind of person I hoped to be. I'll miss thinking that. I already miss it."

"That's not something you're going to lose." She takes my hand. "It's something you never really had."

THE ELEVATOR TAKES us down. Like before, alone together on the way up, I'm compelled toward her body. My hands seek skin, beneath her sweater, through holes worn in jeans. The lust overwhelms, this time with a promise of release. The few hours we have seems barely enough. I feel out of control, groping in desperate urgency.

She stops me. "Are you ready to choose a name? Your new name?"

"What, already?" I don't understand. "You said that was the last thing."

"And you said you couldn't wait again. You're ready, aren't you?"

Suddenly I'm afraid. "Yes." I hope she sees in my face how much I want this.

Kathrine reaches behind herself, slides her messenger bag around. I step back, give her room. Our bodies conceal the bag between us. Nobody can see. She unzips, reaches in.

"I brought it." Her eyes widen.

She pulls out the book, within an antique cloth wrapper. Of course, I recognize it, the focus of as much obsession these recent months as Kathrine herself.

"You've had it. All this time."

"James is out tonight. Let's go home, do it now. By the time he gets back, it'll be done."

She means now. I can't believe it. The elevator display counts down floors: 54 . . . 52. . . .

"Tonight, we choose our final names, then back at my place, prepare everything. Join our bodies one last time, then say the words. Our plans become real."

Descending, numbers ticking away. Down, down. Is there any possibility this goes wrong? The ceremony, an incantation for two voices. Veils, incense and candle fire. Two of us, ready to transform, to unfold.

She leans close, mouth shaping that longbow curve. "What name will you take for our next life? Who will you become?"

I lean in and whisper, for the first time sharing with her the name I've chosen. She smiles. Her scar flushes red, seems to pulse with her heartbeat. She turns, lips to my ear. Tells me her name.

Tonight, everything changes.

# CHAPTER EIGHTEEN

# PASSAGES FOR THE DYING AND THE DEAD

## S.P. MISKOWSKI

**T**HE FIRST COP on the scene was a rookie, a stupid kid, already a target at the precinct. To top it off, the guy was a new dad, running on bad coffee and about two hours of sleep. No surprise the P. O. known by his fellow officers as "Dickwad" fainted when he saw the living room.

"Sorry, sir," he sputtered from his seat on the front steps. Not even trying to stand up. Drool and tears spilling down his chin onto his uniform. "I've never seen this kind of thing. On my beat we get traffic violations, B & E, domestic disputes . . ." Sobbing from the solar plexus like a goddamn child. His partner, a capable gal who kept a thumb poised next to her holster, stood over him. Babysitting, eyes flickering with pity and disgust.

The neighborhood was posh, all right. Some of the most expensive condos in the city. Mostly gentrified former crack houses. But this one was new from the ground up. Mosaic kitchen counters, winding staircases, skylights. The kind of place that seems to clean itself because the maid's under orders to take the service elevator and not be seen. That's who called the police: the maid, the cleaning woman. We took her statement and let her go. Everything she told us checked out. Also, obvious by the way she kept shielding her eyes from the mess, it wasn't hers.

The homicide unit spread out, photographing, measuring every inch of the place. What else could we do?

Pristine kitchen knives, antique razors and bathroom scissors in plastic evidence bags. Likewise, an ornamental Japanese sword. Couple of stained-glass pictures. Collection of hand-painted snuff bottles. All clean. We bagged everything that looked plausible. Procedure. The whole time, we're staring at this roomful of blood, this lake of black paste, and my partner and I keep shaking our heads.

"What the fuck?" Ben said at least three times. "What the fucking fuck?"

"More to the point," I said. "*Where* the fuck?"

"I know, right?"

Crimson- and purple-saturated carpet. Venetian blinds scarred with wave after wave. The liquid wasn't entirely absorbed into the rugs. There was so much of it, it just pooled, about half an inch deep. The puddles vibrated whenever somebody took a step. Blood dripped from the overhead light. It smeared the windows, blocking a pricey view of the city, and ran down the walls. It oozed out of the overstuffed furniture.

But the most shocking thing was what we couldn't see, no matter where we looked. And the lab report would bear this out. No skin. No marrow. No sinew. No fibers. No hair. No fingernails. Only a fluid, vast, human eruption. Without the humans.

I use the plural because the best guess made by our best people (with degrees from half the Ivy League universities in America) was that the blood lake we discovered that day contained contributions from more than two dozen people, none of them identified by any records we could locate in any system. It was like a roomful of anonymous people decided to off themselves by exsanguination, and then somebody came and hauled their corpses away without leaving so much as a footprint or an eyelash.

Naturally we had questions for the couple who owned the place. The husband, James, arrived at around noon. Hungover and apparently freaked out. Waving his hands, screaming for his wife, Kathrine. Not even claiming he was innocent. Yeah. Nobody's innocent. Anybody's capable of anything. That's the first thing you learn. But you also learn to read individuals. Even when they don't know themselves, you get to know them by these little signals, physical reactions only a sociopath could fake. And believe me, no matter what you see on TV, sociopaths are a rare breed. Most people break down under pressure. After seventeen years at this kind of work, I had to take the husband's behavior as a slight indication that he didn't know what was going on.

Once he calmed down enough for questions and realized he was on our shortlist of suspects, James didn't hesitate to offer up an alibi. And it was a doozy. He had no idea where his wife had been during the previous twenty-four hours, or where she was now, because he'd been knocking back the champagne and caviar with an associate, one Kevin Shuster, with whom he also shared what he delicately referred to as "intimate relations" at a very expensive hotel. They were at it most of the night, ordered a room service breakfast in the morning, called a taxi around eleven.

Why I mention the case is that we never got any closer to figuring out what happened. Forensics never had a day in court. No corpse. No blood identification. No DNA match. No witness except a guy walking his dog who said maybe he saw a couple enter the building the night before, or maybe it was the building next door, or one block over. The best we could offer was a missing person's report on the wife and a friend of hers, and that only came about when the friend's wife called the police a few days later. Two and two can take a very long time to add up, in my experience.

Sure, we checked out the friend's wife. Nothing. We interviewed Kevin Shuster, who confirmed everything James told us. We interviewed both of them for hours. Checked and double-checked the hotel, where half a dozen staff members, plus computer and credit card records, supported their alibi. Released them, had them followed for a couple of weeks. Nothing.

We did a background check on the maid and the security people. Nobody saw Kathrine and her friend (or friends) enter the building. The only camera in the lobby, near the elevator, was broken. Stopped working on the night in question. No explanation for that. So, yeah, we had nothing.

The husband, James, was let go from his job about six months later. Not so much because of the scandal but because he lost his edge. Gave up. Fell on hard times, as they say. To a guy like that, hard times meant having to sell off his art collection and his summer house. Eventually auctioned off all of the stuff that wasn't held by the police, or ruined. Mostly old books, trunks full of heirlooms and artifacts from some dig he went on when he was a student. Sold the condo after spending a small fortune having it cleaned and redecorated. Not exactly desperate measures, though, right? Poor little rich guy. I wish I had his problems.

No. You know what? I wish to hell I knew what the fuck happened in that goddamn room. I do. My mind won't let it go, not completely, and some nights it just about drives me nuts.

Because all that blood doesn't come from nowhere. Something terrible happened to somebody. Only, in my game, what you can't prove doesn't count.

So, there you go. The one that got away. The biggest one, anyway. No suspect and no identifiable victims. Could've been the case of a lifetime, right? Fuck it.

You can put another shot of tequila right there on the bar, my friend. Lime, no salt.

THERE ARE DAYS in the antique oddities business, weeks, when you long for the bizarre, the truly strange, and you get nothing. Then, all of a sudden, a real gem walks through the door. You start to glow. You do a little dance inside. You take your promising item to an assessor and spend good money, only to find out it's a fraud.

Once, years ago, a former transit authority employee brought in three two-headed weasels. All fake. He'd sewn them together from dead animals he found in a subway tunnel. Worthless. Except you have to wonder about a man who would take the time to do such a thing, stitching together animal parts on his mom's Singer sewing machine.

Every now and then you get lucky. A mummified cat turns out to be two hundred years old. A whale-bone corset is embroidered with the initials of a president's wife, and it matches a wardrobe inventory kept by her lady's maid. A glass jar full of nail clippings contains DNA from a royal family.

Or you buy a suitcase of miscellaneous books left by someone's dead aunt and you discover a leather-bound edition of *Moby Dick* with the original pictorial endpapers and color illustrations. One of our best days yet. The final sale was over seven hundred dollars.

The other items in the suitcase were good. They were fun, just not as valuable. A gorgeously handcrafted medical encyclopedia from the 1920s; two volumes by Emerson; a guide to tribal art of Papua, New Guinea.

The tribal art book sold first, for a hundred dollars, to an anthropology student. The medical encyclopedia went to a young Goth couple, a wedding gift to themselves. They chose several detailed illustrations and had a tattoo artist copy them, in anatomically correct positions on their bodies. Sweet.

Emerson is on my nightstand because, well, Emerson. Nobody reads any more.

A few days after I sold the medical encyclopedia, a guy I didn't know brought in a single volume, a nicely bound and serious-looking grimoire. The guy, Dmitri Something, said he'd bought the book at a public auction. He said he was moving soon and had to unload everything, so I could name my price. I offered five dollars, half joking, and he accepted.

The grimoire sat on a display shelf for a few days. And I figured, considering what I paid for it, this would be an easy profit. Just goes to show how wrong you can be.

Granted, we were close to our slow season. But I noticed even the regulars I counted on weren't stopping by. After three weeks without a sale,

I rearranged the front of the shop. Pushed the sexier items, the handcuffs and corsets and dildos, right out there. Now and then, one of the street pervs would wander slowly past the window. But no buyers.

Over the years, I've handled my share of items believed by their former owners to be haunted or cursed. In my experience such a rumored provenance makes the object more appealing. The kind of person likely to frequent a shop full of weird and dead things is also likely to pay a bit extra for a creepy story. I've sold amulets said to have been stolen from the crypt of an angry magician. I've made a neat profit off a jar of hair supposedly shaved from the head of a witch burned at the stake. Crazy stuff. Yet no amount of salesmanship worked during those lean weeks.

By now I was in a silly kind of panic. Unable to grasp what I was doing wrong. I should have remembered the first rule of this business. No matter how bizarre or mundane, an object will find its owner. It can be a test of patience but you have to await the arrival of She Who Must Have It.

In this case, SWMHI turned out to be Betty Bradford. I hadn't seen her in so many months, honestly, I thought she might have checked out. She's been hospitalized quite a few times. Says it's the only thing her mother will pay for but I'm betting her rent's covered, too. I can't imagine Betty earning money.

You know how people who are disgustingly wealthy say they're broke and destitute, even if they live in an ancient brownstone and their groceries are delivered as if by magic every week? That's Betty. Her mother is one of the great art matrons of the city, fundraisers starting at a thousand dollars a plate, that kind of thing. Mrs. Alfred Bradford III inherited control of her husband's fortune, and her grandmother's fortune, and oversight of one of the most esteemed museums in the country, built by her family in the 1920s.

Once Betty was past the age to provide an heir, Mrs. Bradford cut her out of the family album and began to concentrate on her nephews and their children. Mean, maybe, but I can understand. Betty's a wild card, all right. According to her, she had art shows in three of the best cutting-edge galleries back in the late 1970s, but her work was too unusual, too new, to attract a steady clientele. That's her story. I heard from one of our regulars Betty used to hang out with Mapplethorpe and Jack Fritscher and their pals. Then she drifted away, and the artists and musicians she used to know forgot about her. She became one of those peripherals who shot heroin and slept with everybody until she was kicked out for a younger model.

I don't mean to be unkind. I like Betty. I even admire her spirit. She has a certain stubborn style, even if it isn't terribly original. Trashy, messy, stitched together, grounded by a pair of scarred combat boots. Leather satchel slung across her chest. I've seen her haul shrunken heads, the limbs of a porcelain doll, a dead garter snake, thirty-year-old bottles of perfume, and a thumb in a jar of formaldehyde from that satchel. Never anything I could sell, although I admit I bought a couple of poison rings from her out of pity. But don't tell anyone. I don't need all the junkies in the neighborhood waiting on my doorstep in the morning.

Betty spotted that grimoire through the front window, and it must have struck a deep chord. She walked right in, the first customer in nearly a month. She rolled her eyes and walked around the entire shop twice, acting coy, pretending not to be interested. Some invisible magnetic force kept drawing her back to the shelf, though, where she would duck her head and flick a page open, then shut, open, then shut. Humming to herself.

"Well," she said at last.

"Find what you're looking for?" I asked.

"Oh, don't know what I'm, um. Wasn't looking, but . . ." And this must have taken all her concentration. "Hate to leave without buying some little thing . . ."

"How about the book over there, on the corner shelf?" I nodded in that direction and I might as well have slapped her. The squirrelly smile fell from her lips and she stared at me like I was trying to trick her. "Or anything you like, Betty. You tell me."

"What's the deal? You want that book off your hands? Why?"

"You nailed me," I said.

Look, you can say what you want. Judge me. All I knew was that I had to make a sale that day.

"Yeah, Betty. It's true. That book's been a hard sell. It's been here for a while. I could let you have it for, say, twelve bucks."

Okay, like I said, I'm not running a charity. A gal's got to make a living.

"Oh." Her eyes went sad, and she started pulling one-dollar bills from her satchel, shuffling them between her fingers.

"Or, tell you what," I said. "Since you're a good customer. Make me an offer."

She stared at the bills in her hands. She must have calculated another five times before she spoke.

"Seven dollars?"

It was a ridiculous price. A two-dollar profit. A month earlier, I'd set my original goal at fifty. But you know what I said about the right customer? My fifty-dollar client might not walk through the door for another year. Or, considering how things had been going, never. I reminded myself, this was an ice breaker. A luck changer. I had to make a deal that day.

"Sold," I said.

I offered to wrap it up but she insisted on carrying it home in that huge satchel. I saw her head off down the sidewalk, clutching the bag to her skinny body as if it were full of Halloween candy.

Before I lost sight of Betty, another two customers entered the store and began to browse.

GOLDEN. GOLDEN AIR sparkling. Not gold roses, cut, dying, dead on Mummer's table. Particles. Dust. Shining dust. Gold clouds. Catch that! Can't even see. I can see. Yellowjackets. Fitted, tight, honeycombs. Yum.

Hear this? No. Dummies with dogs.

Hear this? No. Shoppers with bags.

Hear the yum? Gold yum.

He goes past. She goes past. They go past. He goes past. They go past. She goes past. Blank. Nothing. Stupids.

Inside invisible. Silence invisible. No sound slipping out. The yum, the buzz, on my chest, in the lungs. Invisible. Inside.

Three more steps. Two more steps. One step.

Home! Lock. Lock. Lock.

Breathe. Dark leaning back against my door. Safe. Inhale. Inside. Nobody saw me. Safe.

Red love seat. Crimson, velvet, love, sink down, down. So sleepy. Dark and sleep . . .

Smoke. Silhouette. Man of smoke. Whispering . . .

*All spirits . . . melted into air, into thin air . . .*

Man of smoke and mirrors. Give me spells! To quell. To conquer. To kill Mummer. I'll do anything. Ask. Anything!

Shutters open, shut. Open. Shut. Sleep. Wake. Sleep. Wake. Signs. Open. Shut. Messages. Moths. Moonlight.

Morning! Inventory time.

Sixteen cashmere sweaters warm the floor.

Seven broken candles. Wax to seal the door.

Five scratched records turning, conjuring.

Plates on wheels.

Twenty-five pieces of gold to steal.

Eleven words to kill the crone.

Three miles more to carry me home.

Sleep. Wake up. Sleep. Wake up.

Wednesday. Lunch day. Dress and stockings. Clean face and hands. Wait by the curb. Mummer's driver. Mummer's car. Bentley purring like a leopard. Wednesday. Driver with mirror eyes. Flint eyes. Mummer's dirty spy.

"Nice day, Miss."

Hat tip. Liar. Liar. Three little miles north.

City. Freeway. Trees. Canopies. Driveway.

Sassy Mac opens the front door. Reaches for my satchel. Devil eyes when I slap her hand.

"Upstairs, Miss."

Marble steps. Nineteen. Stop. Breathe. Twenty-one more.

Good china. Irish linen tablecloth. Chandelier. Too much light! Silver light! Thin, brittle bones and jewelry slung on chicken necks. Clack clack clack. Ambushed again! Mummer, Auntie Brigid, Auntie Claire. Mummer is Alice, also Alfred. A–B–C. Clack clack clack.

". . . something for your skin, Betty . . ."

". . . see my hairdresser . . ."

". . . send my seamstress . . ."

". . . help you, dear . . . she can work miracles . . ."

Miracles! Miracles! Just wait, clacking bitches!

". . . for your peace of mind . . ."

". . . for your liver . . ."

". . . my Pilates man . . ."

"Hallefuckinglulu!"

No. No. Too soon. No. Stone faces. They heard the word. Outside. Slipped out my lips. Shit! Shit! Not invisible! Quiet. Careful. Shh. Careful. Conversational. Slip it out like a tiny silver spoon.

"Oh, Mummer?"

All eyes. Six eyes. Hydra! Three tongues to lick. Peeling my skin off. Scratch.

"Maybe you've had enough today, Betty."

"Stop scratching your face, Betty."

"You're bleeding."

My hands in my satchel. Slick sweat, my skin against the cover. Words roll, tasting of smoke.

"Cthulhu fhtagn . . ."

"Oh, dear."

"Oh, no."

"Not today."

Clack clack clack. Cups in saucers. Pearls on dry necks. Clack!

"I'll call the driver."

"Cthulhu fhtagn!"

"Claire, would you please find the syringe in the cupboard?"

"Fhtagn!"

Light crashing down through the ceiling! Golden light! China bones breaking!

"Too late."

"Brigid, call for an ambulance."

Goldenrod light! Crashing down! Here! Here! Here they come!

"Sit down, Betty!"

They're waking! They're here!

"Betty, the ambulance will be here in a few minutes."

They're here!

Plaster and bricks falling! Mummer's face split open! Chandelier thrust against the wall! I'm flying! They're coming for Mummer! I'm flying! Gold light burning my skin! I'm flying!

MRS. ALFRED BRADFORD III surveyed the scratches across the balcony rail. There was no question about the circumstances of her daughter's death. The tread of Betty's awful boots contained a sliver of wood from the railing. Three other witnesses—Mrs. Bradford's two sisters and her housekeeper, Sassy McClain—observed the suicidal leap, heard the scream and the awful sound when she hit the marble floor below.

Betty had a long, well documented history of instability. First claiming, at age eleven, to have been "interfered with" by her father. Terrible girl, dreadful imagination. Two years in an excellent facility upstate were wasted on her. The best prep schools in the country had no effect. Everything she ever touched became soiled and damaged. More years inside than outside one institution after another.

Given the witnesses and clear physical evidence, Mrs. Bradford saw no reason to confuse the issue. Before the police arrived, she collected the hideous book her daughter was clutching when she leapt to her death, and instructed Sassy to take it outdoors, to the trash.

NIGHT BROUGHT ON bitter cold in waves. The boy, Mason, didn't mind the alternating spoiled sweet and rancid smells inside the metal dumpster. He wanted to stay warm for a while. Out of sight and warm.

In this part of town, only rich people were allowed to walk the streets in the evening. Bundled in spectacular coats and gleaming boots. Black boys didn't belong here. Unless they were the adopted pets of childless, lonely women with secrets.

Ray had died because a white woman with a poodle on a pink leash screamed at the sight of him and ran indoors to cower. The doorman, a former cop, came to the rescue. Shouting, arms pumping, leading with his broad chest, bearing down on the child.

"Eating garbage!" The white woman, Mrs. Pritchard, told her neighbors, who also cringed and crept to the glass doors of the apartment building, peering out, turning away, peering out again, pretending they were too delicate to see such things.

Garbage. Ray had discovered the discarded remains of a cocktail party, hundreds of warm croissants piled into the trash like nothing, like soiled paper. Mason had sunk down in the bread, unseen. Ray never moved. Gaunt and staring, too hungry to run. The doorman, showing his prowess to the bitches behind glass, grabbed Ray by his hair and threw him, face first, to the pavement.

Ray never lifted his head again, not once. Later, Mason heard from Jose, who sometimes paid for things the kids found, that the story was on the news. The doorman retired early with a pension, and relocated somewhere upstate. People called it a tragic accident, the way Ray's brain had hit the back and then the front of his skull.

"Haematoma," Jose said. A word. Just another word.

Ray had been so thin, so starved for so long, at first the police described him as ten or eleven. But Mason knew Ray was thirteen.

After that, Mason had to be careful, more careful than ever before. Waiting for the news and the fear to die down. Night after night he watched, hidden, hungry. Hunkered down inside dumpsters, in the discarded oysters and champagne bottles, in the diapers and feces of the aged, decrepit filthy rich.

Tonight, stomach growling, hands pinched under his armpits, balls aching and knees bumping together, shivering with the unforgiving night, Mason rummaged through the waste and found no food he could trust. Only this new reject from the careless rich, a book bound in covers that felt like skin. He wanted to disbelieve his instinct. But he was fourteen, not a boy. Living like this, he was a man, and he knew what men would do just because they could.

He shivered. His stomach kept roiling. Before dawn, before the fuck-you-up cops came around to show off, he would have to slip away and go downtown to look for Jose. Surely the book in the dumpster was worth five dollars. And that could make all the difference. With five dollars, he could survive another day.

Mason was thinking how good a mouthful of cheeseburger would taste, when he heard a dog yapping. He edged forward and pressed his forehead against the dumpster lid. In the arc of a streetlight, he spotted her.

The old woman, Pritchard, had come back. After all that time. There she was, in front of Mason, walking her poodle alone again. Because Ray was dead. She didn't have to fear the night. The criminals had learned their lesson. She could do what she wanted.

She took her time, lingered in the shadows. Letting her dog skitter and piss where homeless people used to sleep before the cops beat them and drove them away.

When at last she was close enough, and Mason saw that look on the white woman's face, the lazy smile that said, "I own this world," he sprang from the dumpster. Reeking of fish and expensive wine gone bad. He made her see him, made her freeze. Too far to run to the lobby to hide, this time. He stepped right in front of her.

This time, this time something new welled up inside him. Not fear. Not even anger. A nothingness. An absence, like hunger, spread through him. Nothing mattered. These were the terms, set by other people, not by him. This was the world given to him.

Mason reached down and scooped up the yapping dog. Without hesitation he slammed it, headfirst, onto the ground. Never taking his eyes off the woman, who was too horrified to scream. Her pale eyes full of death, her pink ears full of the sounds of the mangled and dying animal flailing with broken bones and blood. So many things her delicate mind had never encountered, things she would not forget after that night.

When Mason was certain the woman would never sleep again without hearing and seeing these things, he smiled and turned to the dumpster. He stuck his arm inside it and grabbed the book, slippery with sweat and garbage. He tucked it under his arm, turned, and ran.

WHEN HE WAS younger, Jose smoked only sativa. He liked to feel relaxed and alive at the same time, ready for the next moment. Nowadays, he had a paunch from too much Belgian ale and he preferred the sleepy caress and the body-high of a fine indica. Especially when he heard the stories. Not only runaways. Kids abandoned. Kids raped. Beaten. Killed. More of them every day, all over the city, and nothing he could do about it. Except buy the crap they hauled up to his apartment every day.

He used to do business only on Monday and Wednesday. There were no rules anymore, and fuck being professional. Kids came to him with garbage they found or stole and he paid what he could, knowing what he'd get for it would barely keep a roof over his head. He drew the line at sharing his food and his weed. And after getting ripped off twice, he drew the line at letting kids crash on the floor.

The day's merchandise was among the worst he'd seen all month. One boy, who called himself Kevin, actually tried to sell him a fucking CD player. Kevin got twenty-five cents and a slap across his stupid face.

Goddamn kids.

Aside from the CD player, which didn't even work, Jose counted a couple of phones, an iPad, an emerald brooch, for crying out loud (and the bent pin made him wonder if it wasn't torn right off some lady's coat), a skateboard, and a fucking Mr. Coffee still in the box.

He stepped around the pile of junk and leaned down to look at the book lying on his zebra-skin sofa. This one was a prize, a completely unexpected gift. Courtesy of one of his favorite kids, Mason.

The surface of the oversized volume reminded Jose of his ex, her ass to be exact, creamy and warm. Might have been a history text but he was hoping it was something else, something twisted, like the trophy book of a serial killer. Everything about it said sinister and that was very good. Because whatever this guy in the online ad, Garrett Somebody, had been scouting for, he wasn't looking to save the world with it.

Jose picked up the book, walked a circle around the dim living room. A wave of nausea ran through him. His palms were slick with sweat although he wasn't perspiring anywhere else. With a frown, he placed the book on an end table and covered it with a silk scarf. Later he would wrap it up for shipment to the new owner.

As soon as the book left his hands, Jose regained his enthusiasm. This was definitely a good catch in an otherwise dismal month. This thing was exactly what the guy online wanted. Made to order.

Jose strolled to the refrigerator for a bottle of La Chouffe, talking to himself, not usually his habit but why not congratulate himself out loud? Distantly, he heard scuffling on the stairs. Music. Not the usual in his building. Heavy metal. Junk. Loud, longhaired junk.

He tried to tune out all the noise. Concentrate on what his new girl, Holly, would say when he took her to that stuck-up place she liked downtown. All the girls she knew at work went there with their asshole married boyfriends.

The noise outside and the music grew louder. Jose picked up a pair of headphones and put them on. He walked to the window and looked down on the street, where some fight was going on. Nothing to do with him. With the heavy metal music climbing in the background, he leaned out the window and laughed.

"Five bucks out, five hundred in," he said and smiled. "Easy. What the hell could go wrong?"

# CHAPTER NINETEEN

# MÉNAGE À TROIS

## ROSS E. LOCKHART

### IV

**A**S THE WIRE tightens around his throat, cutting deeper and deeper into his flesh, Josh comes to a series of realizations. The first, and most immediate, is that he is dying, that the razor-sharp garrote has already sliced through the important veins and arteries in his neck, not to mention all sorts of other vital bits, and that his blood is ejaculating wildly from the wound, gushing onto the bed, the pillows, the girl . . . correct that, the *girls* astride him, pulling the wire tighter and tighter. He wonders if they will sever his head, and, if so, will they pick it up, kiss his mouth like Oscar Wilde's Salomé:

*I have kissed thy mouth, Jokanaan, I have kissed thy mouth. There was a bitter taste on thy lips. Was it the taste of blood?*

Josh's second realization is that it was a Pink Floyd record that Hell referenced when she walked in, a spoken bit from *The Wall*, a groupie's shallow conversation in a hotel room just before Pink goes apeshit. He thinks she might have been played in the movie by that chick from *Rocky Horror*, the one in the sequins and hot pants, but maybe not. He wants to kick himself for missing this, but *dying*.

Josh's third realization is that time is a strange and fluid thing, and

217

that his time upon the earth, twenty-seven years (shades of Jimi, Jim, and Kurt), has been less than an infinitesimal eye blink on a cosmic scale, a mere speck of dust in an hourglass built for massive alien gods. In a few seconds, Josh knows that he will cum, and die, at once. That soon, Cass and Hell will shudder and stop, get up, wrap the sheets around his lifeless shell, shower off the blood, dress, and walk out to his library. There, they will take precisely one book, wrapped in silk, and light the candles situated around Josh's altar space. They will step into the kitchen, light each burner on the stove, blowing out each flame so that the apartment will fill with flammable gas. Soon, all will be flames, and the girls and book will be on their way back to Todd, and there is nothing Josh can do about it.

This saddens Josh somewhat. He's spent much of the last few years accumulating and curating his library, collecting weird old books from all corners of the earth, a pursuit that had become more serious over the last year as his band broke out, ascending from playing shitty dive bars where only the sound guy's girlfriend showed up. This month, Josh and his band returned from playing a series of sold-out arena shows, each one filled with forty thousand damp-pantied teenage girls that sang along and cried when the show was over. Thanks to the arcane secrets found in his collection of strange old tomes, Josh's life of late has been pretty damn good.

Also good, despite the ebbing and slipping of Josh's conscious mind, is the feeling of the twin girls astride him, pinioned to him, rocking back and forth, their bare torsos joined at the navel to a single pair of hips, two slender, shapely legs, and one seriously hungry snatch, devouring his sex as his blood spatters onto their arms, their faces, their breasts. Josh is in ecstasy, but wonders if it is genuine, or merely the effect of the drug the girls gave him. Regardless, at this moment, considering vast oceans of time and space, the inevitable fall of the human race, the rise of long-considered-dead gods and monsters that would, ultimately, be succeeded by a blind, coleopterous hivemind as the sun blackened to cold ash, Josh really doesn't care.

It is 2:34 A.M.

This is the best birthday ever.


### III


"So, THIS IS where the magick happens." Josh laughs at his own joke as the girls look around his library and ritual space, examining statuary and large leather-bound volumes. Josh points out a few of his treasures. "*The Clavicule of Solomon*, *The Little Albert*, Agrippa's *Book Four*, Honorius of Thebes, *The*

*Magus.* This one, though . . . this is the real prize." He picks up a silk-wrapped bundle that sat on a low table surrounded by unlit white candles. *"Al-Azif.* Dee's translation. *The Book of Dead Names.* Some spend lifetimes looking for this book. I bought it on eBay. Cost a pretty penny. Our mutual friend Todd even placed a bid, though he was outclassed and in over his head pretty much at the word go. Todd would love to get his hands on this. It's the great granddaddy of occult books, written a thousand years ago by a crazy Arab who claimed to have deciphered the secret languages of angels and insects. Rumor has it he was torn to pieces by invisible demons in a crowded public market." Josh sets the bundled book back onto the table amid the candles.

"Can we maybe talk about something more pleasant?" asks Cass, running her hand along Josh's shoulder.

"Sure. Wanna go get high?"

"Pot makes me sleepy," says Hell, reaching out and touching the silk-covered book. "You should try one of these." She held up a tiny, purple tablet, then placed it onto her sister's tongue.

"What's that, X?"

"Y."

"Why?"

"Letter Y. Short for Yithian Dreamtime. It's new. Todd's got connections in Asia. C'mere." Hell beckons with a finger. Josh leans in. Cass kisses him, slipping the tablet from her tongue onto his. They push it back and forth with their tongues as it melts, leaving a chalky, but not unpleasant texture in Josh's mouth. Cass and Josh linger awhile, kissing, then break apart. A scant breath later, Hell is kissing him. He feels their hands explore his torso, caress his hair, unbutton his shirt, his jeans. He runs his hands along their sides, their hips, aroused and, even though he's seen the videos, perplexed by the point at which the two became one.

"I'm going to fuck you so hard," whispers Cass in one ear.

"I'm going to fucking tear you apart," whispers Hell in the other, biting down on his earlobe for punctuation.

II

THE KNOCK COMES at 11:45. Josh sets down the joint he's been rolling, stands up, smooths out the tails of the black, button-up shirt he is wearing, sweeps back his hair, and answers the door.

They stand there in a little black dress, two knockout redheads from the waist up, plump lips, coy eyes, lots of cleavage. From the waist down, one pair of long legs emerges from the so-short skirt, terminating in a pair of red stiletto heels. Josh takes in the sight, amazed even after seeing numerous video clips (courtesy of Todd) to meet them in the flesh. He has been half convinced that Cass and Hell were CGI, special effects dreamed up in Silicon Valley, not flesh-and-blood girls from Porn Valley. "Wow," says Josh after a few moments. "You must be Cass and Hell."

"Yeah," purrs one of the girls. "Todd says it's your birthday."

Josh smiles. "In fifteen minutes."

The girl on the left chuckles. (Cass or Hell? Josh wonders.) "Can we come in?" she says. "I really liked your last record."

"Sure. Thanks. My manners. Come on in."

The two girls walks through the door, look around. "Are all these your guitars?" asks one, affecting a nasal, urban accent. Hell, Josh decides. The other chuckles at this line. There are only two guitars in the room.

Josh wonders if he is missing some sort of pop culture reference, but decides to play along. "Yeah, that's my '56 Les Paul, and that one—"

One of the girls presses a finger to Josh's lips. "I really liked your last record. And I wanna give you a birthday to remember."

"I prefer hip-hop," says the other.

"I like hip-hop," says Josh. "I just got the new Bishop Takes Queen. Want me to put it on?"


I


"YEAH, HEY, TODD. It's Josh. How you doin'? You're not still sore about that book, are you? Shit, if I hadn't won it, any of a dozen people other than you would have. You didn't even have a chance. And unlike them, I'll at least let you play with it when I'm done reading it. More than I can say for those wanna-be black magicians out there. It's like I always say, buddy . . . What's mine is yours.

"Say, speaking of which, wanna get in my good graces? Maybe even encourage me to take up speed reading? Look, it's my birthday tomorrow. Yeah, happy birthday to me. So the guys are throwing me a party tomorrow night, but since this one's special, the big two-seven, I was hoping you might hook me up with one or two of your special little friends. Oh? You know just the girls? From the vide—oh! Oh, shit, the Siamese twins? Sorry, yeah, I mean conjoined twins. I know they're not Siamese. Sure, I'd be all over that. Send 'em by, say, around midnight?

"Thanks, Todd. I owe you one. Big time."

# CHAPTER TWENTY

# THE PERSUADER

## JEFFREY THOMAS

ER MOTHER HAD named her Nikita after the Elton John song by that name, which had been popular in Vietnam, but when the child went to school and classmates began calling her Niki, thereafter that was the name the girl insisted her parents call her.

Though odd to his ears, Minh hadn't objected to either name. From the start he had wanted his daughter to be as Western as possible, at the same time without disavowing her Vietnamese heritage and identity. He maintained that the only way to be successful in a new country was not merely to adapt to it, but to enthusiastically embrace it. In 1980, at the age of sixteen, Minh had come to the United States from a refugee camp in the Philippines, where he had arrived as a boat person the year before. His parents had paid a good sum for his passage on that boat, they themselves having remained behind. They had been Catholics, and when he arrived in the United States it was through the relocation efforts of the Roman Catholic Church that Minh was taken in by an American family of Catholics, the Parkers. It was the Parkers, kind and generous, who had taught Minh the importance of fitting in, of being a member of his new society and not some awkward, helpless or resentful outsider.

Since then, living in the States and having befriended other Vietnamese, mainly from the Massachusetts communities in Worcester and Dorchester, he'd met plenty of people who had never got used to American food and hence pretty much avoided it. He'd once seen a friend order spaghetti in a restaurant, for want of noodles, and put vinegar on it in an attempt to make it more palatable to him. The friend had asked the waiter if they had soy sauce he might put on it, but they didn't. Accustomed to the strong coffee back home, this friend found American fast food coffee weak and milky. For his part, and largely due to having lived with the Parkers, Minh could eat cheeseburgers, pizza, and drink Dunkin' Donuts with the best of them.

Where some of his friends spoke broken English even after having lived in the United States for years, Minh read novels by John Grisham and James Patterson. He followed football and baseball, whereas these certain friends of his stuck to soccer. Minh had his citizenship and he had voted for Barack Obama and in front of his little house in Worcester he displayed an American flag. In the summer, he grilled in his neat little backyard, occasionally inviting white coworkers to cookouts on Memorial Day or the Fourth of July. Every Sunday he attended the 8:00 A.M. Mass at the Blessed Sacrament Parish on Pleasant Street.

But lately he attended Mass alone, because his wife, Kim-Ly, ten years younger than him and still beautiful at forty-one, had divorced him two years ago and married a white man with more money than he, a pit manager she had met at one of the casinos in Connecticut. Niki had continued to live with her father, because she had always been closer to him, and because her mother claimed than her new husband Don didn't care for Niki, though Minh knew it was Kim-Ly who didn't want a teenage daughter around her neck as she embarked on her new life.

Niki was now sixteen, and increasingly she had found excuses not to attend Sunday Mass (feeling ill, feeling tired, some outing with friends), until finally, despite Minh's loud berating, she had stopped going to church altogether.

From the rearview mirror of Minh's car hung a laminated picture of Father Francis-Xavier Truong Buu Diep, a Catholic priest who had been martyred in Vietnam in 1946 when he sacrificed his own life in exchange for the freedom of sixty arrested parishioners. He was soon to be canonized. Nowadays, when Minh drove to church alone, the future saint's serious, mustached face dangled on its string of beads as if he wagged his head in grim disapproval.

MINH CAME HOME from work at a quarter past midnight to find his house silent. These days his daughter often stayed up late, and though he liked being able to see her for a little bit before he retired, he would still chastise her about shutting off the computer or getting off her phone and going to bed. She'd missed school sometimes as a result of being too tired to get up in the morning, but tonight was Friday, so this deep stillness struck him as somewhat odd.

He hated working second shift: three to eleven-thirty. He had accepted it because the money was better due to shift differential, and as fewer people preferred a night shift there had been less competition in winning the job. His former place of employment, also a biotech company, had laid off a great deal of its workforce and so the local job market had suddenly been flooded with people like himself, anxious for something else in that field. Since he had started the new job four months ago, he and Niki had only briefly crossed paths except on the weekends (and sometimes he worked four hours on Saturday morning, too).

Kim-Ly had never expressed concern that Niki spent her evenings alone—to do so might be to invite taking some responsibility for her daughter, herself—but it made Minh profoundly uncomfortable. He had warned Niki from the onset, "I'm going to call you every night at first break and at lunch, and you'd better answer me . . . got that?"

"Yes, Ba," she had sighed, turning her face away in profile. She was as beautiful as her mother, but in a fresher, more innocent way. Her delicate face, her huge white smile—a smile he had bought at great expense—made his heart ache with pride, as if he had brought her into this world all on this own.

"And I don't work so far from home. I can drive here to check on you and drive back to work in half an hour. I'm going to do that sometimes on my lunch break, but I'll never tell you before. You won't know I'm coming. Got that?"

"Yes, Ba."

And he had done that several times since he'd started the new job, but it had taken forty-five minutes instead of a half hour and so he had had to stop lest his tardiness catch his supervisor's eye. But he had never stopped calling her at every break, and every lunch period. Lunch was at 8:00 P.M. Tonight when he'd called, he'd asked, "What's up? Hey, I hear voices behind you."

"I'm with Olivia."

Olivia was a Vietnamese schoolmate, a good girl by Minh's estimation, with a part-time job at a sandwich shop. "Are Olivia's parents home?"

"Sure, sure. Don't worry," she groused.

"Did you do your homework?"

"Ba, you always ask me the same stuff. I could just play a recording."

223

"What did you eat tonight?"

"*See?*"

Having left his shoes with a jumbled mix of both their shoes by the back door, he padded through his quiet house and to her closed bedroom door, off the same little hallway as his own bedroom. The door locked from only the inside, and he meant to jiggle the knob gently to assure himself it was indeed locked. But the knob turned freely in his hand and, almost without willing it, he cracked the door inward. He hesitated, considering that Niki may have simply forgotten to push the button in the knob, but then he swung the door wide. He saw by a lamp left on, atop her computer desk, that her room was empty.

He swore under his breath. Alone this way, in a moment of intense private feeling, it was in Vietnamese that he swore. Anger and fear surged up, but anger seemed the more appropriate response. He was sure she was unharmed, but only pushing the boundaries she ever seemed to be widening. He instantly had his phone out and punched her number, as he turned in a little circle casting his gaze about her room.

He felt uneasy being in her room without her. It seemed a violation of her privacy, which he liked to respect. More than that, it was embarrassing, as if he'd blundered in here and accidentally found her naked. Her clothing was draped around in empty effigies of her. He averted his eyes quickly from a pair of black pantyhose that lay on the floor like a shed skin. Atop her vanity, her perfumes and lotions and cosmetics were mustered like toy soldiers. Over the past year she'd been wearing heavier and darker makeup, painting her lips shades encroaching on blackness, an all-the-more dramatic effect for her lips' fullness. Thickly outlining her already striking black eyes in more black. And favoring black clothes, complementing the long spill of her hair.

Her phone was going unanswered. His anger ratcheted higher with each ring. He had stopped breathing, as if he were holding back his resources for an explosive release.

A month ago she had said to him, in a strong tone, "Ba, I want to get a tattoo." She had not stated *I'm going to get a tattoo*, but neither had she asked *can I get a tattoo?* She had been testing his response. Yet could she really have been surprised when he'd barked at her that it was out of the question? "In Vietnam, if a girl has tattoos it means she's a hooker!"

"Hel-*lo* . . . we're not in Vietnam, remember? God, some of my teachers have tattoos. It's my body, you know."

"Until you're eighteen, that's *my* body." He'd jabbed a finger at her. "When you're a woman you can make yourself ugly all you want."

Her phone went to voicemail. Minh let go the air he'd been holding back. "Where are you? It's almost twelve-thirty! You answer me now! You hear me?

If I find out you're with a boy I'll cut his throat in front of you! I'll go to jail and you can live with your whore mother!"

Just as he was lowering the phone, it rang. He jerked it back up to his jaw. Niki was there, and said laconically, "I'm on my way home."

"Where were you?" he snapped.

"*Friends.*" Then she was gone again.

Friends. This time she wouldn't even give him any names, afraid he'd complain to these friends' parents. Or, afraid he'd find out she hadn't been with the people she claimed to be with. He suspected it hadn't really been Olivia. A boy. He swore, she was out with a boy. Kim-Ly had said she was only seeing friends at the casino, too. Yeah . . . and she'd ended up leaving him for one of those *friends*. After all they'd been through together to make a good life for themselves in a country they had not been born in, abandoning him for some tall, beefy white guy with his five o'clock shadow and oily obnoxious grin that Minh had fantasized about putting a load of buckshot through.

When he'd found out Kim-Ly meant to leave him for another man, Minh had applied for a firearms license. He'd bought a Mossberg 500 Tactical Persuader with a pistol grip. During one argument with Kim-Ly he had almost gone to bring the shotgun out and use it on her. At least, he had felt the fleeting impulse. Ultimately, he had never threatened her with it, nor Don. It remained hidden in his closet, a cold black core of pain and hatred in the darkness.

Now, how could he sleep until Niki came home, and until he'd let her know just how unacceptable this was? He thought to go open a Heineken to smooth out some of the vibration rattling through him and wait in the kitchen, but he found himself looking more closely around him at this room he seldom spent any time in. Was there evidence here of a boyfriend? Or even of drug use?

Some of the items atop her bookcase were unsettling to him. Morbid toy figurines, and odd decorations he couldn't recall having seen before, and could hardly identify. Flanking these objects were two thick white candles, burned low and deformed in their holders.

When she'd been a few years younger—back when she'd been less involved with friends and still made time for him—she had convinced him to watch movies with her, either rented or on cable. She delighted in horror movies and seemed to take pleasure in how uncomfortable they made him, laughing when he was startled. He'd chided her that in Vietnam ghosts and evil spirits were no laughing matter, because it was known they were real and to be feared. Over the years he'd taken her, along with Kim-Ly, to Vietnam a number of times to visit his family, and he'd reminded Niki of his old family home in Biên Hòa.

"You know the middle room, where they bring the motorbikes in at night? There's a window on the left wall. Do you remember it? The glass is all painted over, and my mom hung a big calendar over it, too. You don't remember it? Anyway, you know why they covered that window up a long time ago? On the other side of the wall is a little space between my family's house and another house. At night, a woman used to stand out there looking through the window at my family. She was a ghost, Niki."

Niki had widened her eyes at this story and said, "*Cool*. Did you ever see her yourself?"

"No, but one time, right before I left Vietnam, I was alone in that room at night and I'm sure I heard a voice outside the covered-up window."

"*No*. What did it say?"

"It said, '*Đốt cháy mọi thứ đi.*'"

Niki understood Vietnamese, though she rarely spoke it. "Why did she say that?"

"I don't know."

"Oh man . . . I wish I'd heard that."

All of this had not been the reaction he was hoping for.

Lately his daughter reminded him of the young girls in some of the horror movies he'd watched with her. Girls who slowly changed in personality, began speaking horribly and acting in alien, frightening ways as demons took possession of them.

He tilted his head to read some of the spines of her books. Definitely not John Grisham and James Patterson. Straightening, he began turning away from the bookcase, debating whether to go so far as opening the drawers of her vanity and bureau, when a lone book caught his eye. It was too large to fit in her bookcase among mostly paperbacks and manga. It lay on her bedside table, occupying all of the space aside from her alarm clock.

The book reminded him of the Bible the Parkers, both now deceased, had gifted him with decades ago and which he still treasured. Physically, only superficially: it was thick with pages, bound in black covers, and obviously old. He would guess, much older than his Bible. But also, like his Bible, he had the sense of immense potency contained, barely contained, behind its closed cover. That cover was like confronting a closed door in the front of some rotting old cottage discovered unexpectedly in a forest . . . maybe abandoned and unoccupied, or maybe not. He couldn't say, though, why he had this feeling about the book without even having touched it, what it had triggered in him to send a shiver spreading across his back, transforming into sleeves of gooseflesh down his arms as it passed. It was as though he had met the eyes of a frightening face hovering outside his daughter's bedroom window.

He stepped nearer to the bedside table, leaned lower, hesitated. For several beats he couldn't bring himself to move his hand to the book. In a faceless, invisible way, it seemed to leer at him malignantly, triumphantly. He thought of the smug grin Don always wore, Don whom he'd never had the courage to express his fury to, Don who had stolen his woman. But of course, he was superimposing this sentience onto the book. It was a long-dead thing, just a carcass of the living matter from which it had originated.

He reached out and opened it.

He was having that Heineken. It was almost an hour since her call and she still wasn't here.

He paced agitated in his kitchen, waiting for whoever was driving her home to pull into the driveway behind his car. He wanted to be close to the back door, which opened onto the driveway, so he could see who it was behind the wheel. As he paced, his thoughts lurched sickeningly, again and again, back to that book resting obscenely beside her bed.

He had opened it to its title page. This had read:

*Necronomicon.*

*Complete John Dee edition.*

*1564.*

He had then flipped at random through more of the pages, only pausing to read a few fragments here and there, but he thought he could tell as much from its aura as those excerpts what this book was about. One of the passages he had lingered to read had said, "*And while there are those who have dared to seek glimpses beyond the Veil, and to accept HIM as a Guide, they would have been more prudent had they avoided commerce with HIM; for it is written in the Book of Thoth how terrific is the price of a single glimpse. Nor may those who pass ever return, for in the Vastnesses transcending our world are Shapes of darkness that seize and bind. The Affair that shambleth about in the night, the Evil that defieth the Elder Sign, the Herd that stand watch at the secret portal each tomb is known to have, and that thrive on that which groweth out of the tenants within—all these Blacknesses are lesser than HE Who guardeth the Gateway; HE Who will guide the rash one beyond all the worlds into the Abyss of unnamable Devourers. For HE is 'UMR AT-TAWIL, the Most Ancient One, which the scribe rendereth as THE PROLONGED OF LIFE.*"

Oh, the general meaning here was only too clear to Minh. He was not familiar with "Thoth," the "Elder Sign," and so on, but the HE, the HIM, the Most Ancient One referred to in these lines could only be Satan. Who else would lead the rash—the sinful, the unfaithful, the fallen—into the Abyss?

He had known his daughter harbored rebellious impulses; he'd been prepared for that since before she'd even begun exhibiting them. It was natural. But in his wildest fears, which had generally involved sexual activity and drug use, he had never expected her to turn to something as poisonous as this. It was, and probably consciously so, the very antithesis of everything he had tried to instill in her. Had he really repressed her so badly that she would react in such an extreme manner? He didn't see himself that way. He'd never tried to control or bully his wife, either. The unfairness of it, the disproportion of their response to him, doubled the pain he already carried and split him through his core.

He had slammed the book shut and jerked his hand away as if from a dead body he had touched by accident in a darkened room. He felt tainted by the contact.

Now, he set down his beer as he came to a decision of great importance. He strode to his bedroom and retrieved the Parkers' Bible from atop his bureau. He carried this to Niki's room, moved the blasphemous book and rested the Bible in its place. When she came home, he would tell her the Bible belonged to her now.

Despite the waves of corruption he believed radiated from the book—though he had to admit the possibility that the blackness pulsing in the air was actually his own anger—he carried it in both hands back to the kitchen, slammed it down on the table, and finished off his beer.

That was it; he'd given her enough time. How far away could she be that it was taking this long? He dug out his phone and was just about to call her again when another idea came to him. In the phone's list of contacts he found Niki's friend Olivia, whom he had always liked.

He hesitated before entering her number. If it turned out that Olivia was home, he feared angering her parents. Still, if she was home, she must be alone in her room at this hour, and unless she told them later they wouldn't know. He sent the call, and immediately wished he could take it back, but it was too late. He hoped it would go to voicemail, and then he cursed at himself for that thought. Always polite to a fault, was Nguyen Van Minh. Where had it ever gotten him? Too polite even to confront Don. Politeness was weakness. His daughter was of supreme importance; why should he be reluctant to briefly inconvenience her friend?

A groggy voice came on the line. "Hello? Niki?"

She must have seen from the Caller ID that it was his phone, and thought Niki was using it. That told him much, right there: that Niki wasn't with her. "No, Olivia, it's her father. I'm sorry to call you so late but my daughter isn't home. I was hoping she was with you."

"No, Mr. Nguyen, I'm sorry. She isn't."

"Do you know who she's out with?"

A few seconds of silence, as if the girl had drifted back to sleep. The silence told him a lot, too. "I'm not sure, Mr. Nguyen," she said at last.

"You're not sure, but I think you have some idea. Could it be a boy?"

"I . . . I don't know. I haven't really seen Niki a lot recently, to be honest. She's been hanging out with other friends for a while."

"I see. And does she have a boyfriend?"

"Well . . . she did tell me there was a guy she liked. I guess he likes her a lot, too."

"What's his name?"

"Todd. That's all I know. Except she said he's out here from L.A."

"L.A.? Is he a boy in school?"

Another long pause. "I don't think he's a boy, Mr. Nguyen."

Now it was his turn to lapse into silence.

As his silence dragged on, because Minh couldn't fill his lungs to speak, Olivia grew nervous and babbled, "I'm sorry, Mr. Nguyen—I know I should have called you about stuff myself. I've been worried about her, I really have. She's just been so different lately."

More different than he had thought. "It's not your fault," he managed to get out, meanwhile staring hatefully at that book, as incongruous on his kitchen table as a severed head. "I should have been paying more attention to her. I should never have taken the night job. This is my fault." He closed his eyes tightly, as if he might shut out this new reality. "Thank you for telling me, Olivia. You go back to sleep now. I'm sorry I woke you up."

He lowered the phone, but didn't open his eyes for a while longer.

HE HAD FAILED, utterly—he saw it now. He had tried to build a home, a life, for Niki that would help her grow up as a true American, as fully integrated into society as anyone born here. And now he was confronted with how she had contemptuously turned away from that very life. He felt as though all his efforts had been a farce. He reflected bitterly that his white coworkers, even those who had been to cookouts at his house, probably still saw him as a foreigner. A fake American. An eternal outsider except to his own, whom he had half turned his back on.

It had been fifteen minutes since he'd let Olivia go. Niki had yet to arrive home. He lifted his phone to his ear again and listened to his rings seeking her blindly in a seeming void, signals beamed futilely into space.

But she picked up. "Almost there," she hissed impatiently, before he could speak.

"What is that book in your room?"

Niki hesitated. Her manner grew wary. "What book?"

He went to the table, opened to that title page again, and struggled with the words, "The *Necronomicon.*"

"Jesus Christ, you went in my *room?*" she screeched.

"It's a black magic book, huh? For devil worshippers?"

"Oh God . . . 'devil worshippers,'" she scoffed. "Listen, don't you touch that book, okay? It's very expensive . . . you have no idea. My friend trusted me to borrow that."

"Your friend Todd?"

Again, she hesitated before replying, but in the background—above the hum of driving—Minh was certain he heard the murmur of a deep voice. Finally, Niki replied. "What, are you looking in my computer or following me around or what? Todd is just my friend's brother, and he's giving me a ride home."

"What friend's brother—Olivia? I've had enough of you lying to me! That book is satanic. What do you want to do, destroy your soul?"

Niki laughed, and said, "It isn't satanic. You don't have a clue. Satan is a Christian concept . . . a *human* concept. That book holds truths older than the human race . . . older than our planet." Her words came more rapidly, with the fervor of a convert. "We're not any God's favorite pets, Ba. The things that are really out there beyond all of this insignificant stuff around us and the insignificant stuff that we are—they don't love us. In our egotistic human way we put a name on every beetle and worm, because that's how we think we can control the universe. But these things, the things that are more godlike than any God we could dream up, we're so beneath them they don't even have a name for us! We don't control *anything* in this universe, and knowing that is to know freedom."

"You're talking crazy," Minh blurted. "What has this man done to you?"

"Opened my eyes, Ba! To the only greatness that's really out there!"

"Enough, babe," Minh heard a male voice caution or command, in the low, smooth tone of a seducer.

His daughter's voice came more under control, and she spoke to Minh as if he were the child. "I'll be there soon. I'll give Todd his book and he'll go. He's only my friend's brother, all right? And never mind what I said . . . everything is okay. Why don't you just go to bed now?"

Either Niki disconnected then, or the driver had reached over and disconnected for her. The phone was now just a meaningless piece of compressed matter Minh held against his face. It might as well have been a bone.

As he was lowering the phone, trembling outside and in, tears rising to the surface of his eyes, Minh heard a voice begin speaking just outside his closed kitchen door. It was as though someone stood at the window in the door, which was covered by a venetian blind, peeking in at him. For only a second did he believe it was Niki, having forgotten her key, asking to be let in.

Just at the edge of hearing, this soft, muffled voice muttered, "*Đốt cháy mọi thứ đi.*"

Minh's body went rigid. The gears in his brain locked up. He just stared at the door, afraid to venture near it. Afraid of lifting the blind even more so than of opening the door. But he knew he must, and suddenly he was flying at his back door, jerking it open and laying bare the empty night.

He stood gazing into the blackness.

HE HAD REMOVED the cooking grate from his barbecue grill, filled the bottom with a cairn of charcoal, and laid the heavy black book atop it. Just as he had been prepared to squirt the book with lighter fluid, however, a desperate fear flooded through him. Looking down into his grill, he had realized it was the Parkers' Bible resting there on those charcoal briquettes. Either he had mixed the two books up in Niki's bedroom, or the evil book—made all the more vile and powerful by the cumulative energies of every lost soul, every "rash one," who had handled it in its long history—had exerted its will over him, tricking him into switching the books around again so he would destroy the wrong one, and restore the grimoire to Niki and her friend.

He set the lighter fluid aside, reached in to rescue the Bible, and the moment he touched it his head cleared and he knew the truth. This *was* the monstrous book. It hadn't tricked him earlier tonight, but he believed completely that it had just attempted to trick him now.

He picked up the lighter fluid again, doused the *Necronomicon* thoroughly, and dropped in a wooden match. Nguyen Van Minh stepped back quickly as a ball of fire puffed up into the air in front of his face, like an escaping spirit.

Now, he sat in a white plastic chair, in his neatly mowed little back yard surrounded by its white-painted fence, holding on his left knee an open bottle of Heineken that for all he knew might be his last. He watched sparks rising from his charcoal grill, like phosphorescent insects rising aloft only to become extinguished, their lives ephemeral and inconsequential.

Across his thighs rested the Mossberg 500 Tactical Persuader.

He didn't know what he was going to do when Niki's friend arrived with her. He supposed that depended on how Todd reacted to the news that his "very expensive" book had been destroyed. He supposed it depended on whether, standing beside his beautiful daughter—now the same age that Minh had been when he'd come to this country—Todd gave Minh a smug grin at having come into possession of her.

Minh wondered if, under dire circumstances, Kim-Ly were capable of rising to the occasion and looking after Niki henceforth. But he wondered, too, if Niki were too far lost now for anyone to look after. For anyone to save her from the Abyss.

He wished someone would give him guidance, before they arrived. Specifically, he wished that voice from his youth—the ghostly voice behind the window—would return a final time, to advise him as she had all those years ago, when she had exhorted him in Vietnamese to *"Burn everything."*

# OVER THE MOON
## JOSEPH S. PULVER, SR.
## IN HIS OWN WORDS

## ANNA TAMBOUR

*i'm a sucker for love stories!!!!!!!!!!!!!!!!!!!!!!!! ! they keep saying pulver's brutal, pulver's gory, pulver's a coldhearted monster. can't they see the romantic in there???????????????????*

This, therefore, other than a few italicised intros and one question posed by me (AT), is a *they*-free glimpse at this most lovable, quotable, infuriatingly modest, comically shy to communicate with those he admired most (Ligotti and Barron top of his list), punctuation-and-grammar-and spelling recrafter and ignorer, generous, original, learned "bumpkin" as he called himself, inspiring and self-sacrificingly helpful bEast, every snippet quoted from our years of correspondence.

.๑෨.

Give an angel an inch and they want a mile. Then theyll seek freedom.

.๑෨.

AT: Maybe you're influenced, but you sure aren't derivative. *Sin and Ashes* is unique, and it's so unusually honest emotionally. It's the opposite of pose.

233

I'm so glad that you have managed to keep true to your own visions, not to mention I'm awed that they haven't destroyed you, but that you have taken them in hand. You wield words in ways that exercise them more than they've been used to. They don't get to put on makeup and primp either. You have also a most unmodern beauty of standing back in what you are writing too. There's a veracity there without the ego first, if that makes any sense. That you have lived, are living, and know pain in every declension of it, but you don't revel in victimhood, or cruelty and snideness for its own sake. I do hate the linking of other writers with you, as you are more much more than the ones who are said to have influenced you. Your eyes have seen, your heart has experienced, and you're still very much alive and experiencing; these elements make the very poetry of a simple act, beautifully expressed and meaningful. *She took off her limits. One at a time.*

JP: Shucks. Thanks. [Hard to blush w/ a full beard, but I am.]

*She took off her limits. One at a time.* -- Is that something of mine? I'm too much like Miles [Davis] I play them and then move on. I can barely remember the titles. In fact, the text Ellen took for *BEST* I thought was something else :) I had to go look in up in *SIN* to see what she wanted ............... . For the life of me I can't SEE why she took it!!!!!!!!!!!!!!!!!!!!!!!!!!!!!!!!!!!!!!!!!!!

As I see it, all I do is respond to what I see or feel -- I go where FELT takes me. I try to bend and mold it, as I can............... I do not want to be someone else. I want to be better, but will not lose whatever ME I put in the work. If you don't bleed on the page you cheat the work [and yourself!] and down the line you've cheated the reader. I will not commit that sin! !!

No ego in it as they won't let me buy one. Hell, I've begged and offered up my soul!!!!!!!!!!!!!! I would love to see what others see in my stuff. I spend hellish amounts of time looking at these things and almost NEVER am happy w/ the end result.

.9e.

Writers are, to me, great liars and thieves as well as great dreamers, shapeshifting is what we do.

.๛.

I never wanted to write. Didn't started until I was 40, and that was an accident, then I quit for a few years after the critics rained. I do not see myself as a writer, but as a 16-year-kid up in his bedroom with a guitar he's trying to learn to play. They are not words to me, *they are notes*. I adore writers, the book junkie in me always did, but I'm not a storyteller - wasn't given that muse. Lot of days I wish I were! !!!!!!!!!!!!!

.๛.

Having been tied to the whipping post, the gallows' pole, and the STAKE, a few times ++++++[just keep adding them!], I'm delighted to "help" another creator in any way I can. The one Lovecraftain "thing" I hold dearest, is the community among the writers. They shared, cared, and helped each along as they could. They made room at the table for others they felt worthy.

.๛.

Really wanted/hoped a woman to get into Cassildas head I do, but thats a male going where he really cant, perhaps close, but NOT there. Im also sick of the old boy school when it comes to HPL, Chambers, Bierce, etc, and after over 40 years of reading this stuff, I want to see, HEAR!, more womens voices in the fictional realms of this stripe.

.๛.

I have a love/hate thing when to comes to HPL.

.๛.

I've been reading WEIRD fiction of various stripes and mixtures for 50+ years, my tastes ain't too bad [grin] and I like WHAT I LIKE. Don't give a rat's ass what most others think. When I sit in my easy chair w/ a book or a tale, that tango is between the writer and me.

.๛.

I NEVER read in bath or bathroom!!!!!!!!!!!!!!!!!!!!!!!!!!!!! NEVER!

᳒

One critic, who years ago called my 1st novel "toilet paper", has since said. "Pulver can take his place alongside Campbell, Lovecraft, and the masters of weird fiction." And he now BEGS me to submit to him and is happy to say he's edited me several times. My dear lady, this writer did NOT change a thing/WORD. *He's come to me.* You are an original, look at how many of the greats were not accepted or recognized in their time. Do what you do and screw the naysayers.

᳒

I do not think much of my own work. I'm NEVER happy w/ it!!!!!!!!!!!!!!!!!!!!! But I love the work and NEED to write, so whatever it is, win, lose, or draw, I keep doing it.

᳒

Don't let the assbags get you down.

᳒

Depressed!!!!, in pain, feeling boring and supremely uninteresting. Please remember, few people can stack stupid as high as I can when I'm down in the Blackness. Add nothing seemed to be going right--boy, do I understand "minusly creative"! !!

᳒

I take a pain pill here and there *as I HAVE TO* - don't like 'em. But for the most part, I lie down, on my side or on the floor on my back w/ my legs up until things calm - be it one day or 5. I've lived w/ it for 4+ decades. I fell 62 feet through a roof of a construction site and wound up hitting the cement in a sitting position. Made a "mess" of 5 vertebrae. Traction [back then], then home to recover in bed. Laid in bed for a year! !! I was lucky.

᳒

Don't like the face I see in the mirror, so it's important(! !!) to me what lies beneath I can stand, or at least, live w/! Those that know me, know I like what I like and a loaded .8 gauge in my face won't sway me.

.90.

Writing or editing, I "never!!!!!!!!!!" consider the reader or critics until a book's coming out. Then it's sheer TERROR!!!!!!!!!!!!

.90.

*On living in Germany:*
I do enjoy, when I don't ache for the sometimes beautiful monster America is.

.90.

*On physical books:*
To take WORDS in my arms, to have and to hold, the tango, my armchair upgraded to NOT CLOSED~ ~~ YES! YES! YEsssssssssssssssssssssss ss!!!!!!!!!! Generations to come forgive me! Love REAL books! !!

.90.

When I walk by my bookcases, those spines speak to me. Postcards and love letters from old DEAR friends. You do not get that from "E"! !! I read on computer when I have to, subs research, etc... I have read a couple of things [I fell for] that were set aside and bitched [like a madass drunk w his jones cranked] to the writers about finishing them.

.90.

I hate when I see "[X] horror writer", or "Author [Y]". Want to spit nails! Author is great, but can be a pain in the ass. Couple of my friends insisted I use "I write horror" for a time to promote myself. Did. Then dropped it. I think I dropped all those tags, hope I didn't miss any.

.90.

I have a huge thing for names -- long story. To me, if a name is wrong blows the whole text.

.୨୧.

I take up the work when the muse takes me....[that's lot, but--]........... If I sit here and say, "GO!" nothing happens. I need to spend time breathing, bitchin', and trying to laugh! !! I need to talk to people -- the ones I care about!, to cook, to read, to sit at the kitchen table for 4 hours lost in conversation over a pot of tea w/ friends!!! ! *I need to sit outside w/ tea and listen to the magpies!!!!!!!!!!!!!!!!!!!* As I said, I never wanted this or planned on it. Just happened one day and I can't turn it off....... There's many a day I wish to hell I could!

.୨୧.

How our tales are presented is Important!!!!!!!!!!!!!!!!! *Our names are on them and our blood is in them!*

.୨୧.

Most of my editing/revision happen as I go. Sometimes will spend 2 or 3 hours on a paragraph at war w/ word choices............ . I once spent an entire afternoon rewriting a transitional sentence as I wasn't happy with 2 f'in' words and refused to give up the fire. But don't ask me what the hell text it was, I forget shit like that [laughSSSS] ........ .

.୨୧.

So I'm sitting here, dancing to some oldies in my chair really, smoking what a Steppenwolf smokes, looking at, sweating over the master file for the new collection

.୨୧.

I'm a stone cold word [water] & music [AIR] junkie!!! I LOVE discovering a new writer that steals my heart!!!!!!!!!!!!!!!!!! What a damn rush! I see a new one by the writer, get it, it's in my paws, I'm sure gonna read it soon as they let me!!!!!!!!!!!!!!!!!!!!!!!!!!

*This most generous and anti-egotistic man said this in so many variations,*
*always having to do with collaborations with others, or about others, that*
*there could be a collection of variations:*
I'm over the moon

ഇ

This is the current draft, starting to FEEL done?
????????????????????????????????? I can feel the "done" as I start to fret so
over it!!!!!!!!!!!!! The terror rises!!!!!!!!!!!!!!!!

ഇ

You learn to write by breathing, falling down, singing, laughing, gettin' yer
heart busted and pissed on, and by doing it. Not in a class!

ഇ

Me, learn German? Its on my getitdone list, but I spent so much time editing,
and in Pulverland w/ these WEIRD words, I never seem to get around to it,
or get out to hear it. And every time I start to look at it, 7 things come up . . .
Sorry, I thought I told you. Short version: I felt like a ghost, useless, and
needed to SEE if I really could write, so before I find found myself on my
death bed wondering what if and having fallen in love w/ someone mad
enough to dare dream the writers dream, I came here.

# CONTRIBUTOR NOTES

A two-time finalist for the World Fantasy Award and the Shirley Jackson Award, MIKE ALLEN edits and publishes Mythic Delirium Books. His short stories have been gathered in three collections: *Unseaming*; *The Spider Tapestries*; and *Aftermath of an Industrial Accident*. His dark fantasy novel *Trail of Shadows* is forthcoming from Broken Eye Books. Mike has also been a Nebula Award nominee and a three-time Rhysling Award winner. He's deeply grateful to the late Joe Pulver for choosing to include him in *Leaves*, and deeply saddened that Joe left all of us too soon. You can follow Mike's exploits as a writer at descentintolight.com, as an editor at mythicdelirium.com, and all at once on Twitter at @mythicdelirium.

ALLYSON BIRD used to be a housing manager for Moss Side and Hulme in Manchester and then lived in Yorkshire. Her collection of short stories, *Bull Running for Girls*, won best collection in the British Fantasy Society Awards 2009. *Isis Unbound* won the Bram Stoker Award for superior achievement in first novel in 2011. She now farms and writes in New Zealand.

MICHAEL CISCO is an American writer, academic, teacher, and translator currently living in New York City. He is best known for his first novel, *The Divinity Student,* winner of the International Horror Guild Award for Best First Novel of 1999. His novel *The Great Lover* was nominated for the 2011 Shirley Jackson Award for Best Novel of the Year, and declared the Best Weird Novel of 2011 by the *Weird Fiction Review*. He has described his work as "de-genred" fiction.

CODY GOODFELLOW has written nine novels and five collections of short stories, and edits the hyperpulp zine *Forbidden Futures*. His writing has been favored with three Wonderland Book Awards for excellence in bizarro fiction. His comics work has been featured in *Mystery Meat, Creepy, Slow Death Zero,* and *Skin Crawl*. As an actor, he has appeared in numerous TV shows, videos by Anthrax and Beck, and a Days Inn commercial. He also wrote, co-produced, and scored the Lovecraftian hygiene films *Baby Got Bass* and *Stay At Home Dad*, which can be viewed on YouTube. He "lives" in San Diego, California.

MICHAEL GRIFFIN has released a novel, *Hieroglyphs of Blood and Bone* (Journalstone, 2017), and a short fiction collection, *The Lure of Devouring Light* (Word Horde, 2016), and the novella "An Ideal Retreat" (Dim Shores, 2016). His short stories have appeared in magazines such as *Apex, Black Static, Lovecraft eZine,* and *Strange Aeons,* and the anthologies *The Madness of Dr. Caligari, Autumn Cthulhu,* the Shirley Jackson Award winner *The Grimscribe's Puppets, The Children of Old Leech,* and *Eternal Frankenstein.* He's an ambient musician and founder of Hypnos Recordings, an ambient record label he operates with his wife in Portland, Oregon. Michael blogs at griffinwords.com. On Twitter, he posts as @mgsoundvisions.

NIKKI GUERLAIN writes all sorts of strange doodads. Her work appears both in print and online. She lives in the Pacific Northwest, dabbles in alternate realities, and works for the government. Nikki keeps to herself but if you walk through the forest at ungodly hours you might cross paths. Favorite Thing to Talk About: weird flexes. Least Favorite Thing to Talk About: her writing.

ROSS E. LOCKHART is an author, anthologist, editor, and publisher. A lifelong fan of supernatural, fantastic, speculative, and weird fiction, Lockhart is a veteran of small-press publishing, having edited scores of well-regarded novels of horror, fantasy, and science fiction. Lockhart edited the anthologies *The Book of Cthulhu I* and *II, Tales of Jack the Ripper, The Children of Old Leech* (with Justin Steele), *Giallo Fantastique, Cthulhu Fhtagn!, Eternal Frankenstein,* and *Tales from a Talking Board.* He is the author of *Chick Bassist.* Lockhart lives in Petaluma, California, with his wife Jennifer, hundreds of books, and Elinor Phantom, a Shih Tzu moonlighting as his editorial assistant.

NICK MAMATAS is the author of several novels, including *I Am Providence* and *Sabbath.* His short fiction has appeared in *Best American Mystery Stories, Year's Best Science Fiction and Fantasy, Weird Tales, Asimov's Science Fiction,* and was collected in *The Nickronomicon* and *The People's Republic of Everything.* Nick is also an anthologist; he won a Bram Stoker Award for

*Haunted Legends* (with Ellen Datlow), and was twice nominated for the Locus Award for *The Future is Japanese* and *Hanzai Japan* (both with Masumi Washington). His more recent collections include *Mixed Up*, co-edited with Molly Tanzer. His most recent novel is *The Second Shooter*, from Solaris.

DANIEL MILLS is the author of the novels *Revenants* (2011) and *Moriah* (2017). His short fiction is collected in *The Lord Came at Twilight* (2014) and *Among the Lilies* (2021) and his nonfiction work has appeared in *The Los Angeles Review of Books*. In 2019 he created the historical crime podcast *These Dark Mountains*, which concluded its first season in 2020. He lives in Vermont.

S. P. MISKOWSKI has received two National Endowment for the Arts Fellowships. Her second novel, *I Wish I Was Like You*, was named This Is Horror Novel of the Year 2017 and received a Charles Dexter Award from *Strange Aeons*. Four of her books have been nominated for a Shirley Jackson Award, and two have been finalists for a Bram Stoker Award. Her stories have been published in *Supernatural Tales*, *Black Static*, *Identity Theory*, and *Nightmare Magazine*, and in numerous anthologies including *The Best Horror of the Year Volume Ten*, *Haunted Nights*, *The Madness of Dr. Caligari*, *There Is No Death There Are No Dead*, and *Darker Companions: Celebrating 50 Years of Ramsey Campbell*. Author site: spmiskowski.wordpress.com.

SUNNY MORAINE is a writer of science fiction, fantasy, horror, and generally weird stuff, with stories published in outlets such as Tor.com, *Clarkesworld*, *Lightspeed*, and *Shimmer*, along with the story collection *Singing with All My Skin and Bone*. A PhD in Sociology, whose doctoral dissertation was on extermination camps, Sunny also writes, narrates, and produces a serial horror drama podcast called *Gone*. They live near Washington, D.C. with their husband and two cats.

NATE PEDERSEN is a librarian, historian, and writer in Savannah, Georgia. He edited the Lovecraftian anthologies *The Starry Wisdom Library* (PS, 2014) and its upcoming sequel *The Dagon Collection* (PS, 2022), as well as *Sisterhood: Dark Tales and Secret Histories* (Chaosium, 2021), an anthology featuring horror stories set in female religious communities. His nonfiction works include *Quackery: A Brief History of the Worst Ways to Cure Everything* (Workman, 2017) and *Patient Zero: A Curious History of the World's Worst Diseases* (Workman, 2021), both written with Dr. Lydia Kang. His website is natepedersen.com.

As editor of the journal *Crypt of Cthulhu* and of a series of Cthulhu Mythos anthologies, ROBERT M. PRICE has been a major figure in H. P. Lovecraft scholarship and fandom for many years. In essays that introduce his anthologies and their individual stories, Price traces the origins of Lovecraft's entities, motifs, and literary style. Price's theological background often informs his Mythos criticism, detecting gnostic themes in Lovecraft's fictional god Azathoth and interpreting "The Shadow over Innsmouth" as depicting a kind of Cargo Cult. His annotated five-volume collection of Lovecraft's fiction, juvenilia, and revisions awaits publication. In 2015 Price received the Robert Bloch Award for his contributions to Lovecraft scholarship.

JOSEPH S. PULVER, SR. released four acclaimed mixed-genre collections (*Blood Will Have Its Season, SIN & ashes, Portraits of Ruin,* and *A House of Hollow Wounds*); a collection of King in Yellow stories (*King in Yellow Tales, Vol. 1*); and two weird fiction novels (*Nightmare's Disciple, The Orphan Palace*). His editorial projects included *A Season in Carcosa, The Grimscribe's Puppets* (Shirley Jackson Award winner), *Cassilda's Song* (2016 World Fantasy Award nominee), *The Madness of Dr. Caligari,* and *The Doom That Came to Providence* (the 2015 NecronomiCon Providence round-robin). His fiction and poetry received over two dozen Honorable Mentions from Ellen Datlow, and appeared in many notable anthologies, including *Autumn Cthulhu, The Children of Old Leech,* Ellen Datlow's *The Year's Best Horror, The Book of Cthulhu, A Mountain Walked,* and *Best Weird Fiction of the Year.* His work has been praised by Thomas Ligotti, Laird Barron, Michael Cisco, Livia Llewellyn, Jeffery Thomas, and many other writers and editors. He received the Robert Bloch Award from NecronomiCon Providence in 2017 (in absentia) for significant contributions to the weird fiction field. Before his death in 2020, Joe was also a regular contributor to the *Lovecraft eZine.* More information about Joe and his creations can be found online at thisyellowmadness.wordpress.com, the memorial and estate information site maintained by his wife, Kat.

JOHN CLAUDE SMITH has published three collections, four chapbooks, and two novels. His debut novel, *Riding the Centipede,* was published by Omnium Gatherum in 2015, and was a Bram Stoker Award finalist. He is presently shopping around one novel, while putting the finishing touches on another. Busy is good. He splits his time between the East Bay of northern California, across from San Francisco, and Rome, Italy, where his heart resides always.

SIMON STRANTZAS is the author of five collections of short fiction, including *Nothing is Everything* (Undertow Publications, 2018), and editor of several anthologies, including *Year's Best Weird Fiction, Vol. 3.* He is also co-founder and associate editor of the irregular nonfiction journal, *Thinking Horror*, and columnist for *Weird Horror.* Combined, he has been a finalist for four Shirley Jackson Awards, two British Fantasy Awards, and the World Fantasy Award. His short stories have appeared in over a dozen best-of anthologies, and in venues such as *Nightmare, The Dark,* and *Cemetery Dance.* In 2014, the anthology he edited, *Aickman's Heirs,* won the Shirley Jackson Award. He lives with his wife in Toronto, Canada.

Shortlisted for the World Fantasy and Crawford awards, ANNA TAMBOUR has written three novels and four collections. Her stories have appeared in publications such as Tor.com, *Forbidden Futures, Asimov's;* and a number of anthologies, though if you read any of her books—say, her latest novel *Smoke Paper Mirrors* and/or her last collection *The Road to Neozon*—you can rightly consider yourself a rarity. Her next collection is *Death Goes to the Dogs.* Tambour also takes photographs of the unnoticed.

JEFFREY THOMAS is the author of such novels as *The American* (JournalStone), *Deadstock* (Solaris Books), and *Blue War* (Solaris Books), and his short story collections include *Punktown* (Prime Books), *The Unnamed Country* (Word Horde), and *Haunted Worlds* (Hippocampus Press). His stories have been reprinted in *The Year's Best Horror Stories XXII* (editor, Karl Edward Wagner), *The Year's Best Fantasy and Horror, Vol. 14* (editors, Ellen Datlow and Terri Windling), and *Year's Best Weird Fiction, Vol. 1* (editors, Laird Barron and Michael Kelly). Thomas lives in Massachusetts.

Since 2000, E. CATHERINE TOBLER has sold more than 120 science fiction and fantasy short stories to markets such as *Apex, Lightspeed, Fantasy,* and *Interzone.* Her *Clarkesworld* story, "To See the Other (Whole Against the Sky)" was a finalist for the Theodore Sturgeon Memorial Award. She has published seven novels with small press markets, and co-edited the fantasy anthology *Sword & Sonnet,* which was on the Ditmar, Aurealis, and World Fantasy award ballots. In 2019, her thirteen-year run as editor at *Shimmer Magazine* made her a Hugo and World Fantasy finalist. In June 2020, her first short fiction collection, *The Grand Tour,* was published with Apex Book Company. She currently edits *The Deadlands.*

DONALD TYSON is a Canadian presently living in Cape Breton, Nova Scotia. A fascination with horror fiction drew him into the field of the occult. He writes both occult fiction and occult fact. His 2006 novel *Alhazred* details the early adventures of the mad author of the *Necronomicon*, and in 2010 he produced a biography of Lovecraft's life titled *The Dream World of H. P. Lovecraft*. Further adventures of the mad Arab appear in Tyson's 2015 *Tales of Alhazred* and in his 2020 Alhazred novel, the *Red Stone of Jubbah*. A second volume of Alhazred stories will come forth in 2022 with the title *Return to Isle of the Dead and other Tales of Alhazred*. Stories by Tyson not dealing with Alhazred, some of which appeared in the *Black Wings* series of anthologies edited by S. T. Joshi, were gathered and brought forth in 2020 under the title *The Skinless Face and Other Horrors*.

DAMIEN ANGELICA WALTERS is the author of *The Dead Girls Club, Cry Your Way Home, Paper Tigers,* and *Sing Me Your Scars.* Her short fiction has been nominated twice for a Bram Stoker Award, reprinted in *Best Horror of the Year, The Year's Best Dark Fantasy & Horror,* and *The Year's Best Weird Fiction,* and published in various anthologies and magazines, including the Shirley Jackson Award finalists *Autumn Cthulhu* and *The Madness of Dr. Caligari,* World Fantasy Award finalist *Cassilda's Song, Nightmare Magazine,* and *Black Static.* She lives in Maryland with her husband and a rescued pit bull named Ripley.

DON WEBB, winner of the Death Equinox Award and Fiction Collective Award, has been writing Lovecraftian fiction for thirty-four years—not to brag but Lovecraft only did so for twenty. He has worked as a Christmas tree salesman, fireworks operator, and an educator—teaching speculative writing for UCLA Extension since 2002. He served as High Priest of the Temple of Set for six years, which is kind of damn spooky. Don's recent books are *Building Strange Temples*, a Lovecraftian collection, and *Energy Magick of the Vampyre*, a how-to book for vampires.

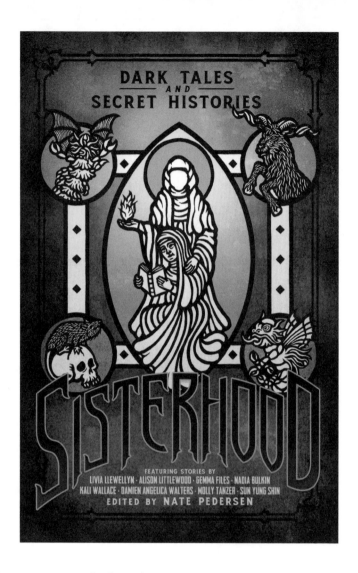

In churches, convents, and other religious communities, sisterhood takes many form
forged and tested by such mundane threats as disease and despair, but also by terro
both spiritual and cosmic—Satan's subtle minions and the cosmic nightmare of the Out
Gods. *Sisterhood: Dark Tales and Secret Histories* presents sixteen stories by some of t
leading women in horror. Their settings range around the globe and across the centurie
from 14th century Spain to 17th century Virginia to England in the present day.

Contributors include award-winning and critically acclaimed authors Nadia Bulkin, Liv
Llewellyn, Molly Tanzer, Sun Yung Shin, Gemma Files, Kaaron Warren, Damien Angeli
Walters, and Selena Chambers. Original cover art by Liv Rainey-Smith.

ISBN 978-1-56882-408-6 – available now – trade paperback